Outward BLONDE

TRISH COOK

ADAPTIVE BOOKS

AN IMPRINT OF ADAPTIVE STUDIOS
CULVER CITY, CA

Copyright © 2016 Adaptive Studios

Visit us on the web at www.adaptivestudios.com

Library of Congress Cataloging-in-Publication Number: 2016943462

Outward Blonde (B&N Edition) ISBN 978-1-945293-04-7

Printed in the United States of America.

Interior design by Neuwirth & Associates.

Adaptive Books
3578 Hayden Avenue, Suite 6
Culver City, CA 90232

10 9 8 7 6 5 4 3 2 1

To all my late-blooming, tough-talking, artistically inclined, super-sensitive sisters: Keep doing you. Your day will come. Maybe not in high school, but who wants to peak there anyway?

Outward
BLONDE

CHIEF COMPLAINT:
Insect bite, excessive sweating, fatigue

FAMILY/SOCIAL HISTORY:
Patient is in fourth grade. Originally from NYC but recently made a move to Africa, which was aborted due to illness. *(Thank God,* the patient adds. *I HATED it there. When's Daddy coming home?)* Her favorite pastimes are watching TV and flipping through her mother's fashion magazines in her pajamas, eating Oreos in bed, feeding Oreos to her dog while reading fashion magazines and watching TV in bed in her pajamas, and singing Beatles songs with her dad while he accompanies them on the guitar.

HISTORY OF PRESENT ILLNESS:
This ten-year-old female received an insect bite while on her family's philanthropic mission in Africa. Patient reports it was "probably humongous gross disgusting scary hairy nasty bug." She does not know exactly what type of bug it was, or if it was a flying or walking creature. Says the bite/ sting hurt "a really, really lot" and she cried "a really, really lot." When child began sweating profusely and sleeping excessively soon thereafter, suspected bite was from a tsetse fly, an insect known to live in the region visited. Mother determined a probable diagnosis of sleeping sickness and immediately flew child home and brought her to the ER.

ALLERGIES:
Mother reports that child has no known allergies. Child reports she is allergic to Africa, sleeping in a tent, and bugs. *("It's true. I mean, just look at my butt.")*

(continued on next page)

NEW YORK HOSPITAL REPORT
EMERGENCY DEPARTMENT RECORD

CURRENT MEDICATIONS:
1. Benadryl (to alleviate itching from bite)
2. Gummy vitamins (child calls them "Go away Ursula pills" and says she takes them before bed. She is afraid of the dark and has a difficult time sleeping alone in own room.)

PHYSICAL EXAMINATION:
Patient is alert and energetic. A small insect bite is noted on patient's right buttock, which she admits to picking at it because "it itched worse than my school uniform." No sweating is noted. When mother is questioned as to extent of perspiration during episode and how it compares to normal rate, she replied that the patient does not enjoy sports or being physically active and therefore she has no comparison. Patient clarified, "It was hot as you-know-what there, Mom. A zillion degrees. I was worried I was going to fry like an egg." Bloodwork negative for Trypanosomiasis (Sleeping Sickness).

DIAGNOSIS:
Insect bite, subsequently scratched, resulting in mild skin infection (patient)
Anxiety (mother)

ASSESSMENT AND PLAN:
Apply a small amount of Neosporin to bite three times daily until healed. Cover with bandage to ensure child no longer scratches it. Informed mother both Benadryl and jet lag can contribute to excess fatigue, so not to become alarmed if patient sleeps more than usual for the next week or so. Also gently suggested the heat of the country visited was most likely main factor in child's worrisome perspiration. Recommended mother follow up with a mental health professional to address anxiety.

chapter

1

"You're not going to believe this, Jem!" I say when my best friend finally picks up FaceTime. Her cheeks, nose, chin, and forehead are slathered in one of those masks she uses whenever she thinks she might be getting a zit. Which never actually happens. That girl is flawless.

"Try me." Her lips are barely moving, which means the mask must be almost dry, which means she's probably more interested in peeling than talking right now. That will change once she hears my news.

"Guess who I just matched with on Tinder?"

Jem's mouth moves the tiniest bit downward, her attempt at a frown. She looks just like my mom after a fresh Botoxing: incapable of any facial expression. "Using an app to find a boy is kind of pathetic, don't you think?" she asks.

"Jem, Jem, Jem. You didn't say the magic word. A girl like me deserves a real *man*, not some immature boy."

"Well, what you're going to get on Tinder is a real creeper, Lizzie," she warns. "And I like partying with you too much to let you be found all over the city in a bunch of different garbage bags. Not to mention, I'd be such shit at giving you a eulogy. One, because I hate public speaking, and two, I wouldn't be able to bring up any of our best times together without giving the adults at your funeral a coronary. So no."

"You haven't even seen who it is yet. Pretty sure you'll think he's worth the risk."

Jem closes her eyes and puts a hand over her heart, adopting a sweet little voice that's nothing like her loud normal one. "What I'll miss most about my BFF Lizzie Finklestein is sneaking out with her on school nights, using our never-fail fakes to get into all the best bars, doing body shots until we puke, and making out with random college guys who have no idea we're still in high school. I'll never forget the time we 'borrowed' her mother's Benz and almost ran over a group of Japanese tourists in Times Square. . . ."

I hold my hand up in front of the computer screen. And in my hand is my phone, which still has the picture of Hot Tinder Man on it.

"What . . . the . . . FUCK?" Jem is impossible to impress and I'm pretty sure I've finally done it.

"I know, right?" The only thing standing between me and this guy at the moment is my mom, who doesn't take her Ambien until right before she goes to bed. When she zonks out, I'm sneaking out.

"It's not really him," Jem says. "You do know that, don't you?"

"Everyone knows he's on Tinder," I tell her. "And that he likes his girls younger. We're perfect for each other. It's, like, fate."

"Oh, please." Jem peels off an inch-wide strip of mask starting at her chin and ending at her hairline and shakes it at the screen. "It's an old, bald, smelly, fat creeper pretending to be him so he can rape and dismember you."

"Dismember. Good SAT word, Jem. Mrs. Lemelson would be so proud," I say, invoking our prudish, perma-single English teacher. "But I guarantee you it's really him. If you don't believe it, come to the Standard with me and see for yourself."

Jem's peeling like crazy now. "It's not him, and that fat smelly old creeper is going to throw you into the Hudson once he dismembers you. Do you really want to be shark bait?"

"I thought you said he was going to leave me in garbage bags all over the city?" I tease. "Besides, I'm pretty sure there are no sharks in the Hudson. And if you were really that worried, you'd be my wingman."

Jem strips off the final bit of mask. Her face is a gorgeous deep caramel again, except for the smallest pink dot you've ever seen on the side of her nose. It's probably from the colored pens we used in art class today. She points to the supposed "zit."

"I can't be seen in public like this. Activate your Find My Friends app so I'll at least be able to tell the cops where some of your body parts are."

I shrug. "Okay, but you're missing out. Because I'm pretty sure James Franco would be up for a threesome. Just think of the pictures we'd get pretending we were going to go through with it—"

"Fake Franco, you mean," Jem interrupts me.

"He's the real deal," I tell my friend, and click the Face-Time screen down before she can try to convince me some more he's not who he says he is. Or worse, decide to come along and initiate a threesome for real (which she knows I'd never participate in, leaving her with James Franco all to herself, and she's smoking hot so who could blame him, so, like, no way).

There's a knock at my door. My mom peeks her head inside my cavernous room. She peers first at my king-sized canopy bed, which is currently covered in pillows of every shape and size but not me. Then she glances over to my dog's bed where Poochie—my adorable googly eyed Shih Tzu with a crooked underbite—is fast asleep. She's twitching and smiling and probably dreaming about bully sticks, her favorite treat. Whoever decided dried bull dick might be a good dog snack is a certified psycho, but Poochie is obsessed with it so I guess I'll have to keep buying it.

Finally, Mom realizes I'm sitting on my white leather chaise by the window, like always. My laptop is on my lap, like always. And I'm not doing my homework, like always. Mom has on a silky nightgown and robe. That must mean it's Ambien time.

"You almost ready for bed?" Her eyes are glassy and she's a bit wobbly—both sure signs the medicine is already taking effect.

"Yeah! Don't you like my pajamas?" I gesture at my crop top and miniskirt. I hide my high heels under a throw so she's less likely to realize the outfit screams "going out" and not "going nighty-night."

Mom ignores my clothing and stares straight at my forehead, where a subtle, stubborn swath of acne has been camped out since sixth grade. If Jem had my skin issues, she'd never go out again. Luckily there's such a thing as cover-up or neither would I. "Did you remember to put on your prescription face lotion?"

Figures that even when she can barely focus, all she can see is my flaws. I don't reply. She won't remember my answer in the morning or that she ever asked anyhow.

Mom mumbles goodnight and shuffles down the long hall of our penthouse apartment. It takes her forever to get there. As a little kid, I used to hate the yawning distance between us. Instead of staying tucked in, I'd make a break for it every night, jumping as far from the mattress as possible and sprinting away to be with her and my dad. Warm and safe between them was the only place I could ever get a decent night's sleep. After all, Ursula the Sea Witch didn't live under THEIR bed.

So good thing I'm not a little kid who's scared of an evil fictional octopus anymore (mostly), since that kind of comfort isn't even an option now that my parents are divorced, Dad went to live out his save-the-world dreams in Africa, and Mom decided she prefers being in a medicated coma to snuggling. Even better is that I actually like how far away they are from me these days. Especially at night. Because you do the math: divorced dad living in another country + mom's room being down an endless hall + her having an anxiety disorder that requires daily doses of Klonopin x Ambien = me being able to do whatever and whoever I want to, whenever I want to.

Which, tonight, is none other than James Franco.

Elizabeth, 21

1 mile away   active now

About Elizabeth

Coco Chanel says a girl should be two
things—classy and fabulous—but I say
why stop there? Add beauty, brains,
sophistication, and social standing and
you've got me, the girl of your dreams. Men
of distinction, style, and flair, hmu. Let's
stay up late in the city that never sleeps.

chapter
2

I wait five more minutes after my mom retreats to her room, then creep my way past the gym we never work out in, formal dining room we never eat in, and family room that never has any family in it. I tiptoe, just in case my mom's not completely out of it yet. Once I get to the dome-ceilinged foyer, I know I'm home free. Make that, free of my home. I slide out the thick, ornate door.

In the elevator, a familiar wave of excitement hits me. It's a mixture of butterflies, that feeling you get when you're on a roller coaster hurtling downhill and you can't quite figure out if you love it or you're going to die or both, and the heady warmth generated by a few shots of vodka. I feel super badass. Nothing can bring me down tonight.

I walk through the lobby and Grover, our evening doorman, raises an eyebrow at me. His are of the typical bushy old-man variety. Long white hairs curl over the top of his gold wire-rimmed glasses. He needs to do some serious manscaping.

"Another late-night study session, Miss Elizabeth?"

"Yup! AP bio is a killer!" I chirp. Not that I'm actually taking AP bio, or AP anything. Or that he can actually do anything to stop me from going out—no ringing doorbell or phone will wake my mother now, and my dad certainly can't do crap from Africa. Still, I'd rather have Grover think I'm out studying than sluttying.

"This is the fourth time this month you've visited the library so late," he says, beaming with grandfatherly pride. "You must have your heart set on Harvard."

"Harvard would be great, of course," I tell him. "But I've actually got my heart set on Bowdoin."

The truth is, my grades aren't exactly Ivy League at this point—my version of studying usually involves a quick flip through SparkNotes followed by a major Netflix binge. And so I am eternally grateful to my absent father, who is both a distinguished alumnus and major donor at Bowdoin. His prominence at the "Little Ivy" is going to be my ticket in, minus the sweat and all-nighters normally required to gain admission to such a prestigious institution. I love being a legacy.

My Uber pulls up in front of the building. Grover's overgrown eyebrows wave goodbye as I slide in the backseat. I get dropped off at the Standard, High Line, a trendy hotel in the Meatpacking District. I'm meeting James at the Top of the Standard, known for its killer views, creative cocktails, and upscale clientele. It's the perfect spot for our first date.

I take the elevator up to the eighteenth floor, flash the bouncer my ID, gain easy entry like I'm actually the age it says on it. I head to the bar, give the guy who's sitting where I want to sit on a flirty look, and order: vodka club, short glass, lemon not lime. The guy—who would actually be semi-cute if he wasn't what Jem and I call football fat, our preference being broody and moody art school guys who are universally skinny—responds just the way I hoped. I thank him for vacating his post, sit down, forget he ever existed.

There's no sign of James yet, but I'm sure he'll find me soon. Before I left, I sent him a sexy pic so that he'd be able to spot me in the crowd, but it was mostly just a way to show off my cleavage. I like to keep things spicy.

I start rehearsing in my mind all the things I'm going to say when he gets here. How I'll charm him with witty repartee and laugh at all his jokes in return. How I'll pretend I have to think about my answer when he suggests we hit his place after a few drinks. How we'll become a full-blown item after that, and people won't even care that I'm not quite seventeen yet and he's whatever, because I'm me and he's him and together we are perfect.

We'll probably even get our own super-couple nickname. I've always wanted one of those. FinkFranc, maybe. No, that sounds too ridiculous for even the gossip rags. I'll leave it to them to come up with something better.

My phone interrupts my mental review. It's a Tinder message from him.

I just realized why you look so familiar!

I squint around, trying to find him in the ever-expanding crowd. I can't for the life of me see anyone remotely resembling James Franco.

Same! I type back, smiling to myself. Better for him to believe I had no idea who he was until now. Don't want him to think I'm after his fame when it's actually his sexy self I'm hot for. As for him, he probably assumes I'm Dakota Fanning—I get that one all the time—and only put the name Elizabeth on my Tinder profile to keep stalker fans at bay. A message buzzes right back in.

You're even more gorgeous in person. The little upcurving of my lips bursts into a huge grin. It dies a quick death when I see his next words. *But sorry, this is not going to happen.*

Don't worry, I'm not who you think I am, I type back. *And I promise no paparazzi followed me here.*

Football Fat Guy asks if I'd like another drink. I look down and realize I've already drained the first one. I nod distractedly. Once James stops fretting over nothing and whisks me away, any mistaken impression I might be giving about my level of interest in FFG won't matter.

My phone goes off again. *Not worried, and I actually do know who you are.*

I type right back, *Pretty sure it's a case of mistaken identity.*

What comes next floors me. *Lizzie, I volunteered with your Dad's charity recently. He talked about you a lot and showed me pictures. You're even wearing the monogrammed necklace he said he gave you when he last visited New York. I knew I recognized it in that shot you sent me earlier.*

The cleavage-highlighting one. Shit. My heart races and I reach for the necklace. Dad presented it to me the last time he was in the States, which was around the holidays. We were at the Plaza hotel, me in this overstuffed green velvet chair and him staring at me over a steaming silver teapot, awkwardly making conversation like it was a bad job interview or even worse first date. The fact that all around us were thrilled little girls dressed like Eloise and their adoring parents made our lack of connection even sadder.

I wonder how our relationship went from super tight to virtually nonexistent, and realize: easy. Mom has a panic attack just *thinking* there might be another tsetse fly incident. And hanging out in a buggy tent somewhere so off the grid there aren't even hot showers or a reliable WiFi signal always sounded fairly terrifying to me as well. So right after Dad left, Mom got my therapist to appeal to the court that spending school vacations and summers in Africa with him would be too stressful on account of my (nonexistent) PTSD from our first trip there. The judge bought it, Dad just kind of accepted it, and that part of the divorce agreement was put on indefinite hold. I'm sure we never would've gotten to the point where we don't even know each other anymore if the judge made a different decision or my dad had spent more time here, but that's not what happened. And so it is what it is.

And yes. I guess we could work on our relationship through modern technology during the intermittent times he has access to it. But whenever he tries to call or FaceTime me, all I want to say is *Are we really that disposable?* Or *Wasn't I at least worth fighting for?* So most of the time I figure it's better not to answer at all.

While my dad is busy messing up my life from a distance, James—or fake James like Jem assumes he is, who really knows at this point—isn't done messing it up IRL yet. *So anyway, I know you're not really 21. And as beguiling as you are, tonight can't go down. I got crucified in the press last time I didn't realize a girl was underage, you know? Say hi to your dad for me.*

I throw back the drink FFG bought me a minute ago. The anticipatory butterfly-roller-coaster-badassery morphs into meh and bleh. I have no clue how I'm going to spin this one in a positive way. I made such a big deal about the date to Jem and the rest of my friends.

He says hi back, I lie and put away my phone.

The turn of events is disappointing but not altogether surprising. The day my dad left me and Mom was the day my charmed life stopped being quite so charmed. His putting the kibosh on my impending relationship with a hot famous guy in absentia, all the way from Africa, is just more salt in an old wound.

I hate myself for being such a cliche: *Daddy issues.* I decide I should put the phrase on T-shirts and socks and underwear and sell them. Other people must have fathers who abandoned them too. My new crappy father clothing line would probably be an overnight sensation. Maybe I'd even get a show in Fashion Week.

My next thought is: *Dad didn't think I was worth the effort. So using him as an inspiration for my fabulous new venture isn't either.* Fine. Forget Fashion Week. I'll just drink some more instead.

"Are you okay?" FFG asks. His eyes are nice—sort of a cornflower blue, just like my dad's—even if they're ensconced in a less sharply angled face than I normally find attractive.

I give him a noncommittal shrug. He hands me yet another vodka club, perfectly ordered.

"If someone stood you up—and I'm not saying anyone did, but if they did? That must be the dumbest guy alive, because you're really beautiful," he tells me.

Beads of perspiration pop out of FFG's forehead at an alarming rate. I'm kind of touched by the fact he's so impressed by my physical presence I'm actually making him sweat. It's really sweet and sort of funny.

Another few drinks and *everything's* funny. Not to mention fuzzy. And fun. FFG starts looking cuter than he did at first glance. His suit is well-cut and expensive. Eyebrows neatly groomed, unlike Grover's. Cuticles trimmed, nails buffed. And he smells good, like sweet clover and fresh mint. FFG tells me he went to Columbia on an athletic scholarship. Football, like I suspected. Bonus points for being real Ivy League.

Wait . . . "went"? He's already out of college? This one is older than the guys Jem and I normally go for when we're at the bars. It doesn't count that I came here to meet James and he is way older than me or FFG, because James is famous and that negates the age differential.

"Want to get out of here?" FFG asks, his eyes darting away like he's scared of rejection. I consider my options. On the one hand, even though FFG seems nice enough, he's ancient and not even close to my type. On the other, I have nothing better to do and nothing stopping me since my mom won't be conscious for hours and hours. I can't decide so I distract.

"Let's dance first," I say, and drag him up to Le Bain, the rooftop dance club.

I learn more about FFG in the new venue. Starting with his actual name, which is Brad. He's originally from Somewhere-orother, New Jersey, played defense and captained his college football team, majored in business, and currently works on Wall Street. He is even older than old. Twenty-five.

He actually has moves. I'm impressed. I turn around, grab his cheeks, and kiss him. He's not half bad.

"You're wild, Dakota," Brad says. Of course I gave him a fake name. My mom would have a fit if she knew I was hanging out with a twenty-five-year-old. Besides, I might be buzzed, but I'm definitely sober enough to know there's no relationship potential here.

"You have no idea," I tell him. And it's true. Jem and I have done some insane things together, like the joyride in my mom's Benz around Times Square. It was fun until it was almost a disaster. Story of my life.

"I'd love to find out," Brad says, staring down at my cleavage instead of into my eyes. "You want to hit the hot tub?"

There are three here—one on the dance floor, two in more secluded spots. I'm pretty sure even in the one visible to everyone, people are doing the nasty. No way I want to risk STDs or some weird, jetted immaculate conception in it. Plus, I don't have a bathing suit with me and the ones in the vending machine skeev me out. I can't help wondering if they're used.

"I don't think so," I tell him, wrinkling my nose.

"Maybe we could go somewhere quieter then, where we can talk?" he suggests. "My place?"

I nod, even though I know this doesn't fall under the category of what adults like to call "making good decisions." But then I think to ask a key question first. "Where's your place?"

I'm hoping somewhere close to mine, so I can maximize the fun-having potential before I head home. Grover should be off duty by that time, and the graveyard shift guy tends to nap on the job. So I'll be able to sneak back into my room just in time to fake sick and get out of school. What my mother doesn't know won't hurt her, and it's not like missing class is going to impact my already mediocre grades. Besides, the school year is almost over. Do teachers actually expect us to still be paying attention this late in the semester?

"Hoboken," Brad replies.

Disappointment sets in. "As in, you don't live in the city?"

He shakes his head and smiles. "No. But I have an unob-structed view of the Manhattan skyline from my place, and it's beautiful just like you."

"I don't think that's such a good idea," I say, proud I'm being so responsible. Usually after this much vodka, I'm all like YOLO regardless of how misguided the suggestion is.

I'm all set on heading home. But then I think about my huge bed in my huge room and how lonely it is in there, even with Poochie by my side. I know I'm not eight anymore, and no longer believe Ursula is waiting to grab me with her hid-eous tentacles at least most of the time, but snuggling with a living, breathing human remains my preferred method of falling asleep. I hesitate.

"Let me drive you home at least," he says. "I have my car here, and I haven't been drinking."

He holds up his Coke, which I assumed was rum and Coke or vodka and Coke or anything alcoholic and Coke this whole time. I take a sip and it's just plain Coke. So I guess he really is sober.

I think about it some more. It's a huge red flag that Brad drove into Manhattan from New Jersey instead of taking the PATH or ferry like a normal person. On the other hand, some-times you just have to say what the heck.

"What the heck," I say, grabbing his hand and dragging him outside.

The valet pulls up in a shiny red sports car and holds the door open for me. I slide inside. Brad gets in and revs the engine. We start barreling down the deserted West Side Highway. Watching Brad's perfectly manicured hand work the gears gets me thinking.

"I've never tried a stick shift before." I'm all of a sudden dying to get my hands on that thing. It's like a complete anachronism. Who drives stick anymore except for old guys like Brad?

He glances at me, then back at the road, and clears his throat. "I'll show you how this weekend. Maybe we can get together on Saturday?"

"I kind of was hoping for tonight," I tell him, grabbing it and attempting to shift gears while we roar down the fast lane. Brad swerves to the right. A horn blares.

"Dakota, that's not safe. Can't it wait until Saturday?"

"Live fast, die young!" I giggle and lean over to take an up-close-and-personal selfie of me and Brad.

He swerves left this time and sirens blare behind us. I sit back, unconcerned, and check out the pic. I'm giving duck lips. He's serious as a heart attack. The contrast is hilarious. I snap the photo to my friends.

"Shit," Brad mutters under his breath, and pulls over. He's sweating more than ever as he stares in the rearview, watching the cop come toward us. I wonder if now might be a good time to mention that Botox stops embarrassing hyperhidrosis.

"Chill out," I tell him. "You're sober, right? No big."

He sweats some more and rolls down his window. Before Brad or the cop can say a word, I decide to save the day.

"Sorry, officer, my cousin was just driving me home after a big study sesh. I'm trying to get into Harvard and Brad here got a perfect score on the SAT. So I figured, who better to tutor me?"

Brad is giving me a look that screams stop. I ignore him. I know what I'm doing. "Well anyway, wouldn't you know it, a bee stung Brad while he was driving and he was so startled, he swerved. But we're fine now. Thanks for your concern, though."

The cop shines his flashlight around the car. I squint and put a hand to my forehead to block the glare. Droplets drizzle down Brad's brow. I decide he *has* to get Botox for his problem or he'll never have another date ever again.

"Have you been drinking?" the cop asks Brad.

"No, sir."

He holds out a Breathalyzer. "Care to prove it?"

Brad nods and blows. It registers a zero. The policeman looks surprised and maybe a little disappointed. He turns to me. "How about you, young lady? Any funny business going on here tonight?"

"Of course not," I say in the same suck-up tone I used on Grover earlier. "The SATs are serious business. All I did tonight was study, study, study."

The sentence has one too many "s's." They come out like "sh's."

"Is that so?" he says, eyeing me suspiciously. "Well, I'll just have a look at both your IDs. Registration and insurance too."

Brad hands the officer his license and car info while I rummage around for mine. I finally come up with my school ID. I figure it will make my Harvard aspirations seem more legit. Plus the cop will probably recognize my last name from all the donations my family has made to the Fallen Officer Fund over the years, and send me on my merry way.

Those contributions of course happened before Dad decided to aim his philanthropic boner on West Africa. According to a recent *Upworthy* article, his latest effort is developing cooperative community farms in the Congo so people can eat and earn a living through their own crops and livestock rather than subsisting on bats and rats and some weird animal that looks like an artichoke, because undercooked bushmeat can spread Ebola. Or something like that.

"Here you go, sir," I say, flashing Mr. Officer a huge smile. "Thanks for keeping our city streets safe!"

The cop heads back to his cruiser and I turn to Brad. "You have to learn to relax or you're going to drop dead from stress before you turn thirty."

He sighs. "Listen, Dakota, I like you. But I have to be at work in a few hours, and I really wish you hadn't pulled that stunt back there. I don't have time for trouble like this."

I make flirty, pouty lips. "I'm sorry. Forgive me?"

But Brad seems immune to my charms by this point. He grips the wheel so hard I can't believe it doesn't shatter. "Please tell me you're not *really* still in high school."

I give him a cute little shrug. He sweats some more buckets.

The cop comes back and hands Brad his paperwork. "Mr. Cavanaugh, you're free to go. Please drive more safely in the future," he says. "As for you, get out. You're coming with us."

I point to my chest. "Who, me?"

"Yes, you," he replies, his older partner opening my door and escorting me out of the car. He tells Brad, "Don't worry, we'll take good care of your cousin. You're welcome to follow us to the station if you want to keep tabs on her."

Brad looks at me standing next to the cops and shakes his head. "Thanks, but I'm sure my aunt will be happy to pick her up."

Then he gives me a death stare and takes off.

chapter
3

"So how old are you really?" the younger cop says, shining a super-potent flashlight at my ID and frowning. We're standing on the shoulder of the West Side Highway.

"In school? I'm a junior," I reply, confused. "Please, I really need to get home now. My mom will be so worried."

To prove I'm sober—which I'm not in the least—I start walking heel to toe on the lane line. I wobble around in my stilettos, my path more of an s-curve than straight. Younger Cop grabs me by the arm and pulls me back to the curb.

"You're gonna get yourself killed like that, Miss Beaver," he says.

I can't even be appalled at how badly he's butchering my mom's maiden name—it's pronounced BOW-VEE-AY, and it's French and classy, not an animal that chews on logs with its buck teeth—because I'm so appalled at my extreme-level dumb-assery.

I must have handed the police my fake ID instead of my school one.

The fake has my mom's maiden name on it, a birthdate five years earlier than mine, and if you look closely enough, a signature that is an obvious handwriting font. The real one showcases my enrollment in a well-known private school and recognizable last name.

Shoot.

Me.

Now.

"My cousin Harry is NYPD," I lie, plastering a huge smile to my face. "He said maybe once I graduate college—hopefully Harvard!—I should take the test too."

"Harry Beaver? Never heard of him." The cop's thick New York accent makes it sound like he's saying "Hairy Beaver." Which is so not true. I'm bald as a Barbie doll down there thanks to my bi-monthly trips to the waxing salon. "You sure have a lot of cousins, Miss Beaver."

"Harry is always talking about how New York cops take care of their own. The brotherhood and all," I ramble on, aiming for sweet and friendly and oh-so-let-go-able. "So I'm sure we can all agree this was just an unfortunate mix-up. I'll just take my ID back and call a cab now. Thanks so much for your service."

"Did you know misrepresenting your identity is a felony?" Younger Cop asks.

"Since I've never actually used that ID and was planning on cutting it up when I got home, no felony was committed, right?" My voice and legs are shaking now, but I still have a shred of hope I can talk myself out of this situation.

"Wrong. Possession is still a felony. Any guess what the bar code on your I.D. came up as when I scanned it?"

"Elizabeth Beaver, of course," I say, mispronouncing my own fake last name on purpose.

"Try canned peaches," he tells me. "Let's go."

"For a misunderstanding? Please," I beg them. "I haven't hurt anyone."

Younger Cop grabs my elbow. "You're coming with us."

I shake him off. "I don't think my parents would like hearing that the NYPD manhandled me."

He puts a firm but gentle hand on my back, directing me toward the squad car. "I'll be extra careful with you then, sweetheart."

This is SO unfair. If only James had held up his part of the bargain . . .

. . . if my dad hadn't messed that up too . . .

. . . if Brad wasn't such a nervous Nellie driver . . .

. . . if I'd remembered my motto *all guys suck* before going out tonight . . .

"DON'T TOUCH ME!" I screech, flailing at the cop. "DO YOU HAVE ANY IDEA WHO I AM?"

In an instant, I totally snap. It's like all that vodka obliterated my filter. The exact words elude me now but it's not pretty. Which does not get me let go. It gets me thrown in the back of the cop car.

"It smells like armpits and onions back here," I observe, filter still MIA. "Can you please open a window?"

"Suck it up, Princess," Older Cop scoffs.

But the odor proves a deadly combo for someone who has consumed far too many vodka and clubs with lemon, and sucking it up is not even a remote possibility. Because I am too busy puking it up.

NYPD INCIDENT REPORT

OFFENSE/INCIDENT TYPE:
Felony possession of false identification, false impersonation, intoxication, threatening an officer with bodily harm, resisting detention.

LOCATION OF OFFENSE:
West Side Highway approaching the Holland Tunnel

TIME OF OFFENSE: 4:07 a.m.

NARRATIVE:
On the morning of 06/07, I Deputy Gonzalez along with Deputy O'Connor observed a Lamborghini swerving dangerously. Suspecting possible inebriation, we pulled vehicle over. The driver, a polite 25-year-old Caucasian male, was apologetic and denied drinking. He submitted voluntarily to breathalyzer and was found to be unimpaired. His driver's license was checked and cleared for any crimes or unpaid tickets. Driver was dismissed. Passenger was held for further examination. She presented officers with identification containing a falsified name and birthdate. When questioned, she further misled officers, and eventual detainment was resisted. Suspect subsequently vomited in squad car, the odor of which was overwhelmingly vodka and confirmed inebriation. Later established suspect is a Manhattan minor who has been cited on two previous occasions, once for reckless driving without a license (in Times Square district) and once for open container/ underage drinking (Tribeca district).

chapter

4

Instead of my mom, I opt for calling the cool young associate who helped me out of a similar jam last year. Thankfully she gave me her emergency cell number and told me to use it if I ever ran into trouble again. Which is now. She's fresh out of law school and aiming for partner at the firm my family keeps on retainer, so she's more than happy to make the late-night/early morning run.

Once she gets to the police station, she fills out the appropriate paperwork and promises the cops I'll show up for my assigned peer jury hearing. I feed her all kinds of lines about how I need to grow up and start taking responsibility for my actions, so after much begging she agrees to let me be the one to tell my mother about my arrest. I know it's probably the right thing to do and maybe would even go through with it, except I don't want to put my summer service trip with Jem in jeopardy. It's basically a two-month party in the Greek isles, with like a day of ushering baby sea turtles into the ocean while we tan so we can get our school-required service hours. Best to just wait until I am safely out of the country, and only spill the beans if my mom happens to notice the extra charges on the monthly accounting the law firm sends her.

Back home, freedom never tasted so sweet. I sneak past the napping overnight doorman, take the elevator up to our apartment, and tiptoe to my room. Mom is nowhere to be seen. I am golden. I throw my going-out clothes on the floor in a ball, pull on an oversized T-shirt and yoga pants, tuck Poochie under my arm, and climb under the covers. No chance I'm going to school today. Too tired. Too hung over.

I'm already half asleep when my mom flicks the light on in my darkened room. "Get out of bed, Lizzie. You're going to be late again."

I chatter my teeth dramatically. "I think I have a fever. I'm so cold, and I have a humongous headache."

Mom walks over and lays a hand on my forehead. "You don't feel very hot," she says, eyeing me with suspicion.

"I know, I don't feel so hot at all. I feel really crappy."

Mom crosses her arms and sighs. I hold my breath. This could still go either way. She might tell me to give school a shot and to go to the nurse if I can't make it through. Or she might just cave. She usually caves, if she even notices I haven't gone in the first place.

"Do you have any tests today?" she finally asks.

I honestly don't know. "No."

She caves. "Fine. Take some Advil and get some sleep. I'm sure you'll be better by tomorrow."

But of course I'm not better by tomorrow. I'm still shivery and my "headache" is now a "migraine." Only when my mom comes to check on me, that is. Otherwise, I watch Netflix and relax. If I'm going to fake sick, I might as well get more than twenty-four hours out of it.

On day three, I have my peer jury hearing. I tell Mom I'm going to the doctor for a strep test because now my throat hurts too. I head to the police station.

I give my name to the lady working the desk and she leads me down a long hallway. "So you're one of the lucky ones, huh?" she says while we walk.

"I guess I am," I reply, though I'm thinking lucky would've been not getting arrested in the first place.

"You better know you are, honey. If not, you'd be in real court, getting a real conviction on your record. You should really thank the police officer that brought you in for not pressing charges."

I suppose she has a point. "I'll be sure to do that."

She deposits me in a dark wood-paneled room. Three kids stare at me from behind a long table. They are wearing light blue polo shirts embroidered with a *Peer Jury* logo on the chest. It is like a really sad uniform for the saddest extracurricular ever. What some kids will suffer through to get into college. I am more grateful than ever for my dad's connections at Bowdoin.

"You can have a seat, Elizabeth," the girl in the middle says. She looks just like the class president at my school, down to her clear-framed glasses and thick bangs. "I want you to know we're not here to judge you or what you did, but to help you make reparations for the harm your actions have caused. We practice restorative justice here, not punitive justice."

I nod. If I learned anything from the other night, it's to not say every thought that crosses my mind out loud. So I don't mention the fact that bangs are strictly for the five-and-under set, and that she'd get way more respect—not to mention guys—if she grew them out.

"Why don't we start by you telling us what happened the night in question?"

"Okay, sure," I say, mainly sticking to the story I told the cops that night. "I was invited out by an actor I admire. But it turns out he'd worked with my dad's charity, and decided he couldn't date me because it would be a conflict of interest. So I got a ride home from a friend instead, but he accidentally swerved when a bee stung him and we got pulled over. The police officers let him go but kept me over a small misunderstanding. I regretfully lost my temper, and that's why I'm here."

I fold my hands in my lap and stare down at them. I hope this signals repentance. I glance back up, expecting I'll get maybe a few hours of community service and be on my way. Because how long could my mom possibly think a rapid strep test takes?

"Where was this date supposed to happen?" the nerdy, awkward guy on the jury asks. He looks like he builds fully functional robots in his spare time.

"At a restaurant," I say, leaving out the "and bar" portion of the truth.

"But the police report says the incident occurred at 4:07 a.m. On a school night," he continues, perplexed lines creasing his forehead.

"Yes. That's true."

"So how do you account for your time between the cancelled dinner date and the ride home from . . . did you say a friend before? Because this says the driver of the car was your cousin," the first girl jumps back in.

"I decided to do some SAT prep instead. With my cousin tutoring me. He got a perfect score. I'm aiming for Harvard. I study all the time, sometimes really late. That's not unusual for me."

"Me too!" Robot Guy exclaims. "Except my mom makes me go to bed by midnight on school nights. You're lucky your parents let you stay up as late as you need to."

Head Girl eye rolls him to the next century, then turns back to me. "Even though you are not under oath, may I remind you that dishonesty during this process means we have the right to refer you back to the detaining officer, who can then assign you to a real court of law."

I nod. My heart is racing, but I know I need to act cool and confident if I want them to believe my half-truths. "Understood."

"So why did you provide officers with a falsified ID if you were only out studying?" the gorgeous plus-sized girl who has been silent up until now asks.

"Honestly, it was a mistake. I grabbed the wrong one," I say, hanging my head and mustering up some misty eyes.

"Why do you have false identification in the first place?" Gorgeous Girl asks.

I search my brain for a plausible explanation that does not include getting into bars. I finally stumble across one. "This is going to sound really stupid, but I was desperate to vote in the next presidential election. Except after I got the ID, I found out having one is a felony. I got scared, hid it in my wallet, and meant to cut it up but forgot to. The only time I've ever pulled it out was that night, and I completely, totally regret all the trouble it caused."

Robot Guy pipes back in. "How did you even know how to obtain an ID like that?"

He has no clue how easy it is. Everyone I know has a fake. And everyone I know who has gotten caught with one got off with a warning. Or by taking a quick alcohol education class online. No one but me ended up at peer jury. An ironic sense of injustice washes over me.

"Not to gossip, but there are some kids at my school who use false identification to buy alcohol. So I just approached a student known for that kind of behavior and he said for the right price, he would get me one."

"So you're telling us you never used your identification for the purposes of underage drinking?" Robot Guy asks.

I shake my head.

"Then how do you explain this?" Head Girl asks. She points a clicker at the screen on the wall and up comes a video of me with the cops. I'm tottering around on my high heels, slurring, sloppy as Lindsay Lohan on a bad night. When my "charm" doesn't get me what I want, I go completely ham.

Head Girl clicks off the video and stares at me. I don't even have to fake the weepy eyes and hanging head this time. I'm so mortified. I don't even remember saying half those vile things. Seeing myself like that makes me consider never drinking vodka again, and I love vodka. Or at least I thought I did before watching this.

"I'm so sorry," I whisper. "I'm appalled at how I acted. Honestly, I am."

"You can wait out in the hall while we deliberate," Head Girl says.

I plunk myself down on an uncomfortable bench and reach for my phone. Jem will cheer me up. I'm sure she can make this whole thing funny and not as terribly sad as it seems right now.

I have about a zillion messages. All of them are some variation of OMG YOU BROKE THE INTERNET! I'm pretty sure I don't want to know why.

I click on to my friend group chat. The first message is from Jem. *So hilarious! Can't believe you tried to walk the line in Louboutins. Fail!*

Wait, what? Did I text her that part before I barfed in the back of the cop car?

Haha. Embarrassing, I type back. *How did you know about that?*

The replies come in rapid-fire. *Dashcam video went viral*
You're famous
It's everywhere
Entertainment Tonight
Betches
Fuckjerrytv
Page Six even gave you your own celebrity nickname. The RBB!

The lava pit that's been brewing in my stomach all morning is about ready to blow. Apparently the humiliating video I was just forced to sit through privately in the peer jury room is somehow out there in public now—all over the newspapers, TV, *and* Internet. The thought of everyone in the world seeing my gross rant makes me want to curl up and die.

If my mother catches a glimpse of that thing, I'll never hear the end of it. She'll probably make me take the remedial version of the Miss Manners classes I hated back in third grade. Crap! What if she doesn't let me go on the service trip over it?

I gnaw a manicured fingernail. I wonder how I'll get out of trouble this time. If it's even possible at this point. What does RBB even stand for? Before I can come up with any answers, I am called back into the Peer Jury room.

"We deliberated long and hard whether we should just send your case back to the detaining officer," Head Girl begins.

"I mean, you didn't exactly tell the truth until we forced you to," Gorgeous Girl interjects.

"But in the end, we felt your remorse was real and that you seem willing to make honest reparations for the offensive things you did and said to the police," Robot Guy concludes.

I nod and pray they'll cut to the chase quickly. I'm panicking now. I need to get home and do some damage control. Maybe cut off all the electrical supply to my house for a few days until this whole thing blows over.

"So what we've decided is to help you get some well-needed perspective into how fortunate you are," Head Girl says. "And to gain some compassion for others who are less fortunate than you. We hereby require you to do thirty hours of community service at a homeless shelter, as well as take a privilege seminar. We expect proof of completion within ninety days or a date in regular court will be scheduled."

The punishment seems pretty over-the-top for the crime, especially since I already apologized to them and honestly do feel bad about what I did. But I'm in no position to argue. I guess I'll just have to figure out a way to finish my service hours and the class before Jem and I head off to Athens later this month. "Thank you," I say, standing up and shaking everyone's hand. "You won't regret this."

I bolt home. There, I find my mother alert, clear-eyed, and

waiting for me in the family room. Definitely not normal. Going straight to my bedroom as planned isn't an option.

"So, do you have strep?" she asks.

"No. My head still hurts, though." This is no longer a lie. I have a dull throb at the base of my skull that won't quit.

"I have quite a headache myself. Care to venture a guess why?"

"Your latte had too much foam and not enough espresso in it this morning?" I joke.

She doesn't even crack a smile. In fact, my mom's mouth is pulled into a tight little frown. Normally, her fillers don't allow for such a wide range of motion. She must be really, really mad if she's putting so much effort into making that face. "Did you really think I wouldn't find out?"

"I have no idea what you're talking about," I say, even though I'm pretty sure I do.

My mom tries to hand me her iPad, dashcam video already playing on it. I hold my hands up and shake my head. I can't stomach seeing it a second time.

"What do you have to say for yourself?" she demands.

I shrug and try not to cry.

"I'd sue every media outlet showing that horrid video for talking about what a spoiled brat you are, but how can I when it's obviously the truth?" Her words are a punch in my already painful gut.

"Mom, I know I said some really embarrassing things. I'm really, really sorry. No punishment you can think of can make me feel worse than I already do."

"Seriously, Elizabeth, how could you besmirch our family name like that?" she yells.

Besmirch is a funny word and I'd totally laugh, but I don't because I've never seen her so angry. She's scaring me. I'm used to zombie Mom, not zombie apocalypse Mom. "Please calm down. Someone else will do something even more embarrassing tomorrow and it will be like this never happened."

But she's not done freaking out yet. "I can't believe I'm even saying this, Lizzie, but I think you need to spend the summer with your father in Africa. I didn't raise you to be rude and ungrateful."

I let that last one sink in, my mouth hanging open. She can't be serious. "I know I lost my cool. And I completely regret it. But that's beyond harsh, don't you think?"

Mom doesn't answer. I try a different tactic.

"A peer jury is already making me do thirty hours of service at a homeless shelter and take a class to remind me just how privileged I am. And if it's good enough for the NYPD, I think it should be good enough for you."

Mom stares at me like I'm the biggest disappointment on Earth. I head for my room, hoping a little time and distance will chill her out. I throw myself on the bed and think about reading the *Page Six* article. I decide against it for now. I don't think I can handle it at the moment.

Poochie tucks herself under my arm and licks my face. At least my dog still loves me. I close my eyes and take a long nap.

I wake up feeling pretty good until I remember my mom's Africa threat. I NEED to find a new angle to convince her it's a terrible idea. I fire up my computer, thinking I'll do some research on what other gross diseases I can get in the Congo. But before I can start, Jem sends an attachment in the group chat.

We thought your dashcam video could use a little spicing up, her message says.

I click the link. It takes me to YouTube. A title shot comes up. *RBB: The Prequel.* Jem walks into the frame and says, "Hi! I'm the RBB . . . you know, the Rich Bitch Billionairess made famous on that dashcam video?"

At least now I know what RBB stands for. A parody of an old rap song called *O.P.P.* starts up, its re-worked chorus running in a never-ending loop. *I'm the RBB, Yeah you know me!* Even I have to admit, it's pretty catchy.

What follows is a full-fledged acting out of what happened *before* I got in trouble with the cops—as if people hadn't already gotten enough of a show with what happened after—starring none other than my BFF Jem as me. Her video starts with fake me petting fake Poochie. Then fake me sneaks out of my fake apartment. Fake me stares at pictures of real James Franco in a real Uber, and then fake me gets stood up by a fake James. Next, fake me gets hammered with a football fat guy who looks like Zach Galifianakis— the slovenly *Hangover*-era Zach, not the svelte *Birdman* one. Fake me acts stupid and drunk in fake Zach's car, and we get pulled over by the fake cops as a result. Fake me then freaks out on the fake cops and then fake pukes in the back of their fake car. The video already has hundreds of views and it's only a few hours old.

My other friends start chiming in.

Genius!

That must've cheered you right up, Lizzie!

What an EPIC night! Can't believe I missed it!

I type and untype, trying to think of the right way to say what I need to say. I know my friends think the video is cool. And that Jem just made it to be funny. But what they don't realize is that I'm already in a crapload of trouble. And that another video—one that further incriminates me—is only going to make things worse.

I finally settle on *Haha, yeah. But you guys have to take it down now.*

Jem fires back immediately. *No way! Do you see how many likes it's getting? People love it (and you!)*

She just doesn't get it. I try again. *No seriously. My mom is threatening to send me to Africa for the summer.*

But Jem's stubborn. *She'd never go through with it. Besides, this will probs get you your own reality show. You can't leave when you're filming!*

Please????

Dude, I'm only trying to extend your brand. You're welcome.

The only brand I've ever wanted to have is my own clothing label. Instead I got a personal label—the RBB—and I hate the way it fits. It's so unflattering. I can only hope what I told my mom before is true: this will all blow over soon. Let Jem have fun with the video she made until it does. I guess I would think it was funny too, if it wasn't about me.

Mom stops by my room just before bedtime. "I honestly can't go to the Congo," I tell her before she can say anything. "Because of my PTSD and all. You know."

Mom still seems un-medicated, or at least way less medicated than usual. Miracle. Another miracle, though not for me: she's not falling for it.

"Dad and I are pretty sure you'll survive," she says. "And that this visit is exactly what you need. It will do you some good to see how the rest of the world lives."

"Since when do you talk to Dad?" I'm completely caught off guard by this latest news.

"Since you started going down the wrong path. Since you became the RBB."

I pet Poochie harder. She thumps her tail and stares up at me adoringly. "Mom, seriously. I'd rather die than go to Africa for the summer."

"Do you really mean that?" Ever-so-slight—almost unde-tectable—worry lines crease my mom's forehead. That means she must have an appointment with Dr. Freezeface and his bag full of line fillers soon.

"That I'm not going to the Congo? Yes. One hundred percent."

"Why not?"

I have a list of reasons, none of which she'll want to hear, including:

1. I don't want to.
2. Like, really, really don't want to.
3. Extreme heat = extreme perspiration = extreme discomfort
4. Jet lag x sleeping in a sleeping bag = chronic under-eye bags
5. Tsetse flies flying around = potential death
6. No Internet = potential death (of my social life)
7. Living in a tent = pain worse than tsetse fly bite and dead social life
8. Living in a tent with my dad after so many years apart? Beyond awkward
9. Animals that should be in a zoo roaming free, and sometimes being served for dinner
10. The darkest dark at night, even darker than the black evening gown worn by Ursula the Sea Witch

(who may or may not still be using the space
underneath my bed as her pied-à-terre in NYC)

So I just answer, "Because."

"That's not even a reason. You will, and you are," she says,
and shuts my door.

To which I say, no. What're they going to do, forcibly make
me get on a plane? I don't think so. That's kidnapping.

Sightings

By the *Page Six* Team

A leaked dashcam video of the wild child everyone's referring to as the Rich Bitch Billionairess (Hint: she's the daughter of Manhattan socialite Margot Beauvier and third-world philanthropist Benjamin Finklestein) shows the sixteen-year-old throwing a tantrum of epic proportions after the car she was a passenger in was stopped for erratic driving at 4:07 a.m. last week. When questioned, the allegedly impaired and definitely underage heiress screamed, "Do you have any idea who I am? Well you're about to find out! Welcome to the national news. My parents will sue your ass so hard you'll be living in a tent. I hope the bugs that live in there with you bite your poor ass off!" No word yet on what the long-term repercussions will be. May we suggest a stint at Brat Camp for the RBB?

chapter
5

I wake from a horrible dream about a huge tsetse fly trying to carry me off me to Africa. I sit straight up in bed, heart and thoughts racing just like they did when I was little. I open my mouth to yell for my mom but nothing, not even a strangled yelp, comes out.

I inhale the powdery-soft scent of the baby blanket I named Buddy when I was two. Despite reassurances otherwise from my old therapist Ellyn at the Womyn's Centre, the breathing exercise does not relax me. In fact, I am freaking out more than ever because now I'm convinced I hear voices whispering outside my door. Even worse, I'm afraid to get out of bed to confirm no one is actually there because Ursula might grab me.

Ridiculous. I'm clearly still deep in the nightmare.

My door creaks open. I'm disappointed my dream self doesn't ninja out of bed and fight with every molecule in her body like a superhero. Turns out Dream Me is just like real me, lounging around like a potato hoping the intruder will think I look so cute and comfortable he just turns around and leaves.

The light flicks on. I open one eye a squinch and see an unattractive older couple surveying me. The woman grabs my arm and shakes me awake even though it turns out I really am already awake. So much for the *of course I'm still dreaming* theory.

I open my eye a tad more and see she has on a baseball cap with a frizzy ponytail coming out of it and a big tattoo on the back of her neck that says *bird by bird.* Whatever that means. Her frizzy ponytail looks like it could hold a whole nest of birds in it, so maybe that's it.

I'm shaking and praying—to who or what I don't know—that it won't hurt too much when they kill me. Also hopefully that all that stuff about the white light and the dearly departed escorting people into heaven is true. And me declaring myself an atheist in fourth grade so I didn't have to go to synagogue *or* church anymore—my parents were giving me the choice between both of their religions—won't be held against me by whatever deity might exist. Because I'd love to see Scootchie, the dog we had before Poochie, again. If I have to die, at least that would be kind of cool.

"Get up, honey," she says in a much sweeter voice than I expected a killer to have. "We're not going to hurt you."

So maybe they're just SVU types? That's almost worse. I pull my arm away and curl up into a ball, the human equivalent of a roly poly bug. "I can write you a check for any amount of money you want. Just please don't touch me. I'm a virgin," I whimper.

The guy, who looks like he should be named Clem, laughs. "Lying is a sin."

I want to tell him his face is a sin. And that I'm not lying. But I keep my mouth shut.

Bird's Nest pulls me upright, then plunks herself down on the bed next to me without being invited. She has terrible manners to go along with that deplorable pompom ponytail. "Here's what's going to happen, honey. You're going to put on some sweats—"

"Please don't make me do that." Sweats are so unflattering. They make me look fat. No way am I down with this plan.

Her grip tightens on my upper arm. It doesn't hurt now. But I'm pretty sure it would if I tried to make a break for it like I've been thinking about doing.

"Like I said, you're going to put on some sweats. Then you are going to choose no more than five personal items—no clothes and nothing pointy or illegal, please—and place them in the backpack I'm about to give you. We are getting on a red eye. From there, you'll be driven to your final destination."

"I'd rather you just go without me. Please and thank you."

I flop back down on my bed and close my eyes. I figure if I refuse to be kidnapped, maybe they can just steal a bunch of stuff and get out of here. If not, that they'll just kill me as quickly and painlessly as possible. I have no intention of going to my "final destination" willingly.

Gray sweatpants and a gray sweatshirt land on my bed. Then the lady plunks a military-looking, multi-pocketed backpack that's khaki-greenish-brown—a color Jem and I like to call "guh-brown"—next to the groutfit. The clothes and bag clash hideously.

"Please put these on, gather up any personal items you feel you can't live without—though believe me, you can—and meet us outside your room. You have three minutes."

They leave and I scramble for my phone. It's not where I left it. It's nowhere I look. And of course there's no landline in my room; no one has those anymore. I have no way to call 911 or text my mom to come save me.

I decide I'll *pretend* I'm going along with the kidnappers and then make a break for it once I get into the hall. I sprinted the length of this apartment so many times as a kid I know the path by heart and could do it blindfolded. Even though I am normally opposed to any sort of exercise, I'm positive I can get to my mom's room, lock the door behind me, and call for backup before those two know what happened.

I put the sweats on. The pants are from a bat mitzvah the year everyone turned thirteen and there were two and some- times three or four parties to attend every weekend, and the sweatshirt is from a resort in Lake Como we went to on our last family vacation before my parents got divorced. I hope I don't trip on the pants when I make a run for it. I can't even believe I just used the word *run* in reference to myself, even if it was just in my head. I almost laugh until I realize this is dead serious and I am running for my life. At the last minute I put on socks and some brand-new Mizunos my mom bought me that time I almost went out for cross country—before I remembered how much I hate sweating/running/any form of cardio—because the new uniforms looked like Stella McCartney designed them.

I start throwing everything I think I'd want with me into the backpack just in case I'm so out of shape I can't even outrun old fatasses like Clem and Bird's Nest. What would get me through whatever torture they've got planned? Make all the reporters amazed at my ingenuity and resourcefulness once I escape and find my way back to safety? I settle on the most important stuff and slide out my bedroom door.

I am just about to start sprinting when I completely freeze. All the lights in the apartment are on.

My mom is not only awake, but she seems more relaxed and coherent than she has in years.

What's worse, guess who's sitting next to her on the couch? MY LONG-LOST FATHER. Wearing an even less attractive outfit than mine. He's got on a knee-length white linen tunic, matching manpris, mandals, and a hemp headband. More strands of silver have invaded his shoulder-length copper hair since the last time I saw him.

"You look like ginger Jewish Jesus," I blurt out. Now I'd really have to laugh, if only I didn't feel so much like crying.

"Lizzie." He's standing there, holding his arms out like I'll throw myself into them like I used to when he came home from work every night.

I ignore the overture. "If you hadn't noticed, the apartment has been broken into. This doesn't concern either of you?"

My dad clears his throat. "Darling, Elsa and Eddie are here to escort you to Camp Smiley."

I shake my head and point to my butt. "I got bitten by a tsetse fly last time we went camping, remember? I had to be medivaced home or I would've died."

My dad gives my mom a *WTF?* look. "She still thinks that's what happened?"

I stare from my mom to my dad and then back again. "What?"

My dad shakes his head and sighs. "That you were medivaced home is true. The tsetse fly bite and the potential death part are untrue. It was a complete overreaction on your mother's part."

"Overreaction? We couldn't be sure what had bitten her at the time, Benjamin, and better safe than sorry," my mother jumps in. "I can't believe you still expected I'd be willing to move my child to a place that was far more remote and dangerous than you ever let on after a scare like that. It could have just as easily been sleeping sickness!"

"I still can't believe you acted so enthusiastic about my philanthropic plans when we were first married, and then abandoned them—and me—over a mosquito bite," he shoots back at her.

"Oh, I abandoned you? Ha! You took off and left us here without a second glance, even though you could have easily picked a safer place to fulfill your save-the-world fantasies, one where we could all be together—"

"Lizzie is far more resilient than you've ever given her credit for, she would've been just fine living in Africa, but no, you went back on the plan—"

"Excuse me." I interrupt what's turning into one of their famous fights. "You're fixing cleft palates all over the Ivory Coast now, Dad? That's really nice of you, but I'm unfortunately not available to join you this summer at this Camp Smiley, especially escorted by strangers. I have other things to do with Jem, who is always there for me, unlike *some* people I know."

I start walking back to my bedroom. Elsa and Eddie hover too close for comfort. I stop in my tracks.

"Camp Smiley is a wilderness and exploration educational experience that's saved a lot of teens' lives," my dad says. "Kids who are struggling with the same kind of issues you are."

"My only issue is I'm running out of treats for Poochie," I say with a little laugh. It comes out hollow and bitter.

"Substance abuse, disregard for the law, suicidal ideation," my dad says, ticking random problems off on his fingers like he's reciting the ABCs. "I'd say you're dealing with some pretty big issues right now, Lizzie. And rather than allowing you to fall into the depths of despair, we're sending you to a place where you can reconnect with the light inside you and find greater meaning in life."

"Mom," I say through gritted teeth. "You can't be buying all this New Age crap, can you?"

She plays with the antique sapphire-and-diamond ring that took the place of her wedding band. "Better to fix things now, Lizzie, than have a scandal even worse than police tapes on our hands."

"I said I was sorry," I hiss. I'm beyond pissed. "What more do you want out of me? Do I have to sign something in blood? Fine! Where's a knife?"

"That's exactly the kind of talk that has us so worried," Mom says. "We need to keep you safe."

I know I said I'd rather die than go to the Congo, but it's an expression. As in, not meant to be taken literally. "I'm not suicidal," I say, my voice rising steadily to a yell. "But if I was, I'm glad your only concern is what a scandal it would be."

"Time to go now," Eddie says, taking my elbow. I try to shake him off but that only makes his grip tighter.

"Daddy loves you, Sunshine," my father says. "I always have and always will."

"Stay strong, Lizzie," my mom adds. "I'm sure Camp Smiley will be better than Africa in any case."

My dad shoots her a look. She makes a face back at him. "I just meant it will be safer, Benjamin. Cleaner. More sanitary."

"Tell your parents you love them," Elsa whispers to me.

Instead, I stick both my arms in the air and give them the finger.

TEN ITEMS EVERYONE SHOULD PACK WHEN THEY'RE BEING KIDNAPPED

1. Poochie (I tell her to play dead until further notice)
2. A half-eaten bully stick for Poochie (she's already gnawing on it and I can't bear to take it away)
3. Buddy, my baby blanket (don't judge)
4. Reading glasses (even if you hate reading, because who knows when you might need to see up close)
5. Prescription zit cream, Clairsonic facial brush, and Tanda Zap zit zapper (I use them together every night so technically they count as one thing)
6. Hair products, boar bristle brushes (round and paddle), shampoo, regular conditioner, leave-in conditioner, hair clips for blow drying purposes, blow dryer, thermal protection spray, flat iron, conditioning oil (these I also count as one item since they are in the same category and my straight, shiny, beautiful hair is only kept that way through the magic of quarterly Keratin treatments which require careful upkeep or I'll end up with split ends or, worse, hair so damaged I can't get Keratins anymore, in which case I'll have to make do with professional blow-outs or, worse yet, my hair in its natural fuzzy/curly state)
7. Jo Malone perfume, Blue Agava & Cacao and Earl Grey & Cucumber scents (in case they don't let me shower as often as I like to, at least I can still smell consistently delicious)
8. Travel makeup bag (which contains six thousand mascaras, eye pencils, eye shadows, lip glosses, bronzers, etc)
9. Nail polish, cuticle scissors, clippers, pedicure flip-flops
10. Various hair removal devices (gotta keep things clean and smooth)

Yeah, I know that's ten-ish million items. Elsa and Eddie can bite me.

chapter

6

Elsa rummages in the backpack while we're waiting for the elevator. "Look, I'm going to let you get away with having too many personal items for now. Most of what's in here will get confiscated when you check in to camp, but don't you worry. You'll get everything back when you graduate."

I shrug, too numb from what just happened to worry about it. WTF kind of parents ask creepers to come steal their kids out of bed in the middle of the night and take them away?

"Also, I just love how all you kids talk tough but always bring your blankie and wubby to camp," she says.

The weird word distracts me from my silent pity party. "What's a wubby?"

"Your little stuffed animal lovey toy."

Good Poochie, I think. *Way to play dead!* She's the only family I have left.

Elsa wants me to carry that beast of a backpack myself. It weighs about fifty pounds after everything I put in it. I try to sling the ginormous bag over my shoulder but it drops to the floor with a thud instead. Poochie gives a little yelp.

"What was that?" Eddie asks.

I clear my throat and cough, hoping I sound like my dog. "Allergies."

Eddie stuffs an enormous hand into the backpack and pulls out a shaking Poochie. "It'll be better if your parents watch her while you're at camp," he says, petting her gently. "Too dangerous for a cute little pup out there. Wouldn't want her to get eaten, now would you?"

I watch as he delivers Poochie back through the front door and into my mom's waiting arms. Mom hands the guy my phone in return. He tries to shove it back at her but she's having none of it. *Please, I just want her to text me she's gotten there safe. Air travel is dangerous, you know. Of course I'll take care of the return shipping.* Eddie mumbles and grumbles but Mom won't give it up. Finally he takes the phone, but puts it in his pocket rather than giving it to me. *Sorry, against the rules,* he tells her.

Mom closes the door without meeting my eyes. Something inside me dies. At least it's not Poochie. I love her too much and would never put her life at risk. The same clearly does not hold true for how my parents feel about me.

I sling the lightened load over my shoulders and let myself be nudged into the waiting elevator. Grover watches me being taken away from his usual post. He looks almost as sad as I feel.

"You take care of yourself now, Miss Elizabeth. Work hard and you'll be back in no time." His long eyebrow hairs do a mournful, slow dance over his glasses.

I try to wave back but my hands have fallen asleep under the weight of my over-stuffed pack. I worry my tingly arms mean I'm having a stroke. I worry I'm losing my mind because I'd actually choose a stroke right now over being taken away by these two creeps. I wonder if this is the kind of anxious internal chatter that drives my mom to take pills all the time.

The cab to the airport smells worse than the cop car I barfed in. Elsa and Eddie make me sit in between them in the backseat. I'm hot and nauseous and scared. I refuse to admit it.

My shaking leg outs the fear part. Elsa puts her hand firmly on my knee. "Could you please stop that? It's making the whole car rock like a sinking cruise ship."

"It helps me relax," I tell her.

"Maybe we could say a little prayer together instead?" she suggests. "That always calms me."

"I'm not really the praying type."

Eddie harrumphs. "Might do you some good."

"No thanks."

I shake my leg harder, but pretty soon it's making even me feel seasick. I stop. My escorts seem to relax. I don't mind them thinking I'm giving in, because I have a plan for when we get to the airport. The cab pulls up to the terminal.

"Now get your backpack on and follow us," Eddie orders.

I do what I'm told until we get to the TSA guy. When he asks my name, I answer louder than necessary. I figure anyone who watches TV or surfs the net or reads the *Daily News* will recognize me, know I'm being kidnapped, and call the cops.

No one even glances in my direction.

TSA Guy yawns. "How old are you?"

"Sixteen. These aren't my mom and dad, by the way."

He peruses the papers Elsa hands him.

"And I'm here against my will," I add.

"I see." He reaches for his walkie-talkie. I assume he is

calling for backup, someone to come escort Elsa and Eddie away and me back home. But he only clicks a button so there's no more static. "This paper says they have legal custody of you right now."

He holds up a court order, which both of my parents have signed. "Oh," I whisper.

"I'm sure everything will be okay," he says.

Elsa nudges me. "Let's get moving."

Seeing no other option, I trudge through the terminal. Wait in a hard plastic seat instead of an airline club for the flight. Board in Group 4, and stuff myself into the middle seat of the last row, which doesn't recline. I have never travelled so uncomfortably in my entire life.

The flight is headed to Utah. Ski season is long over for the year. Is there anything else to do there? I scour my brain but fail to come up with anything else the state is known for, other than polygamy. If they're planning to sell me into a cult where I'm some guy's fifteenth wife, no thanks.

The only bright spot is my phone falls out of Eddie's pocket when he gets up to go to the bathroom. It's dead but at least Elsa doesn't notice because she's too busy snoring. I stash it in the billowy pockets of my sweatpants.

We land with a bump hours later, shuffle off the plane, and retrieve the guh-brown backpack from baggage claim. The airport is deserted. I slip my phone into one of the pack's innumerable zipped compartments while Eddie and Elsa flag down a van emblazoned with a Camp Smiley logo.

The driver pulls over to the curb and rolls down his window. He's about my dad's age and has a brushy crew cut and bulging muscles. Even in his neck. He looks like a real-life G.I. Joe.

"Get a move on," he says, opening the door.

"Bless your soul!" Elsa calls after me as I climb into the van. "I hope you find peace and serenity!"

There are four other kids my age sitting inside. I plunk down in the middle row next to a guy who looks like he could be Brad's younger brother: tall, muscle-y, sandy brown hair, blue eyes, looks like he walked out of a J. Crew catalog except for the scowl. He's wearing a name tag that says Jack.

"Hey," I say to him.

He grunts and gives me a little half wave, like it's too much effort to actually lift his hand all the way up and move it around. He doesn't say anything. He looks salty AF.

"Kindly refrain from speaking until I've had the opportunity to explain the rules and expectations of Camp Smiley to the group," the driver says. "Now put this on and listen up."

I peel the paper from the back of the sticker and put it over my heart. It reads *Elizabeth*.

"I go by Liz—"

"I said, no talking!"

I shut my mouth.

The two girls in the front seat turn around to stare at me. One is super androgynous. She's sporting a platinum faux-hawk—which looks even cooler given the contrast of her delicate Asian features—and an IDGAF attitude. She looks like she gets lots of chicks, even ones who always thought they were 100 percent straight. She's Sam. The other has the kind of long, straight, glossy hair I wish I had and pay dearly to try and achieve. She's exotically pretty, with olive-colored skin and a perfectly straight nose that my guess is didn't require surgery to repair a "deviated septum" to get, like some people I know. Ahem, me. She's Chandra.

There's only one other kid in the van, and he's taking up the entire third row with his spindly body and inability to sit still. He's Ari, and he's totally my type: shaggy shoulder-length dark hair that keeps falling over his eyes, so artsy-skinny we could share jeans, big brown eyes highlighted by eyelashes that go on for-e-ver, unmistakable bad-boy vibe. I reward him with a smile. He gives me a cool nod of his head.

The driver puts the van in park, stands up, and turns around to face us. He leans his elbows on the back of his seat. I can practically see the blood rushing through the veins in his temples. The dude is intense.

"I'm Director Willis," he says, pointing to his name tag. It reads: *Dr. Willis*. I feel sorry for his patients. He has zero bedside manner, a hard stare, and probably cold hands too. "And what I say from here on out, you do, no questions asked. When I tell you to jump, you ask how high. Understood?"

Jack and Chandra nod. I sneak a peek at Ari and he rolls his beautiful eyes at me. He's a kindred spirit, just like I thought.

"Now, I'm sure you're all wondering what you can expect from your time at Camp Smiley, a proven program that allows teens headed down a dark path to rediscover the light within," Director Willis continues. "And I would hope you're also contemplating the poor choices that led you here, and how you'll remedy those during your time with us."

Ari snorts. Director Willis glares at him.

"I can assure you, there is nothing funny about why any of you are here," he says. "And nothing funny about that ten-mile hike you'll be taking every day from here on out, either. You'll be sore, tired, and begging to stop. This is exactly what you're supposed to feel. It's what hard work feels like, which is something I hear none of you have been doing very much of lately. Now, once you reach your daily destination, you'll make camp, practice survival skills, prepare and eat communal meals, journal, meditate. At the nightly Truth Circle, you'll share the ways in which you are working to become whole again. Wash, rinse, repeat. Got it?"

Ari taps my shoulder, nods toward Chandra, and whispers, "I'd like to work her hole."

I crack up. It's confirmed: he's a bad boy. I like bad boys.

Director Willis points a finger at me. "You. Don't think you're going to get away with disrespecting me or the rules at Camp Smiley, Elizabeth. I can't wait to see your spoiled candy ass trying to make it through the solo overnight trip you'll have to complete to graduate. Being alone without any material comforts in the wilderness will break you, my dear, if you're not careful. I've seen it happen before. Are we clear?"

I nod. He's right. There's not a chance I'd survive in the woods by myself, nor do I have any interest in trying. Which is why I'll just have to convince my mom to get me out of here before it becomes an issue. She'll understand it's way too dangerous an assignment.

Director Willis starts lecturing again. "Every few days you will return to Outpost, which is where your journey begins in a few short hours. There you'll do individual therapy sessions, launder your uniforms, and resupply before heading back out on the trail."

Chandra's hand shoots in the air.

"Yes, Chandra?"

"I just want to say, I'm excited to get started," she tells him. "I really screwed up and I want to prove I'm better than that. Thanks."

"You're welcome," Director Willis says, his smile softening. "Helping kids like you is why I came to work at Camp Smiley after leaving the military."

"What did you screw up?" Ari calls from the backseat.

"No speaking without being called upon," Director Willis tells him.

I turn around to catch another glimpse of Ari. He raises his hand. He's still lying across the back row, so all you can see is his elbow up. Director Willis ignores him. "Any other questions before we head to Camp Smiley?"

Sam clears her throat and sticks a finger in the air.

"Yes, Samantha?"

"How long is this bullshit going to last?" she asks.

I clap a hand over my mouth to stop myself from LOLing. Ari doesn't bother and cracks up.

Jack whirls around. "Cut it out! Do you want to get us all in trouble?"

Ari flips him off and points at Sam. "She's the one who said it, not me. I can't help it if she's funny."

"Seriously, both of you," Chandra chimes in. "Stop being so disrespectful."

"You will all quickly learn that using foul language and speaking out of turn earns the entire group demerits," Dr. Willis tells us. "You just earned a warning, Samantha. Next time, the real consequences begin and I can guarantee you won't like them."

Sam shrugs. "Okay. It's Sam, by the way."

"And to answer your question, you will stay at Camp Smiley for the duration of the program. Yes, Ari?"

"How long exactly is a 'duration'?" he asks, making air quotes.

"Don't be a smartass," Director Willis snaps.

"I'd kind of like to know that too," I say in an almost-whisper. Like, am I going to make it to Greece? Jem will never forgive me if I don't. She thinks she needs me there on account of her resting bitch face, which makes it hard for her to meet new friends.

"It's as long as I say it is, Elizabeth," he whispers back sarcastically.

The guy's a total dick. "It's Lizzie," I tell him.

"Again, my call, Entitled Elizabeth."

Sam raises her hand. "So we don't get out of here until you say so?"

He nods. "Affirmative. The staff determines when the group as a whole has fulfilled the requirements of the program. They present the case for my approval. I get the final yay or nay."

"So even if I had done everything asked of me, but, say, Lizzie fucked something up—" Sam pushes on.

"I warned you about using foul language, Samantha," he says. "You just bought your group zero bathroom privileges at Outpost today."

"So we can't even take a dump now if we have to?" Ari jumps in. "Not letting people crap as a punishment. That's the stupidest thing I ever heard."

"Mouth shut, mister," Director Willis says. "And I think you'll find it's a very effective consequence you'd prefer not to repeat."

I stick my hand in the air and wait until Willis acknowledges me. "Excuse me, sir, but I have a medical issue that requires me to use the bathroom more frequently than most people." I hope Ari thinks I mean pee and not poop. Even though I do mean poop. Not having a bathroom in close proximity is one of my biggest fears. "I need access to facilities. I can get a note from my doctor if necessary."

"No note needed," Dr. Willis tells me. "And no bathroom needed either. One last thing: there is no inappropriate physical contact amongst anyone, whether of the opposite sex or same sex."

"Can you define inappropriate?" Ari asks. "And also if there are certain acts that are still considered appropriate? Like, maybe, blow jobs are out but hand jobs are okay?"

I clap a hand over my mouth to keep from laughing. Ari is absolutely terrible, in the very best way.

"Zip it!" Director Willis says. "What I mean is, no one touches anyone. Period. I'm done talking now, and so are you all until further notice."

He gets back in the driver's seat and heads out into the night. Ari flops back down, taking up the entire back row. In front, Sam curls up in a ball, hoodie obscuring half her face. Chandra inches away from her until she's practically hanging off the edge of the seat. Jack stares out the window, sullen and sour.

And then there's silence, except for Sam's soft snoring.

Darkness, except for the light of the moon.

Nothing but the unknown lies ahead.

Everything we know lies behind.

Ari is right: this is the stupidest thing ever.

chapter

7

Director Willis whips open the sliding side door of the van, waking us all up. Fresh, pine-scented air mixed with campfire smells fills my lungs. I blink and try to focus.

"Everyone grab your pack and get out," he commands.

At first glance, Camp Smiley looks a lot like Camp Greenlake, where I was supposed to spend the entire summer one year. I lasted approximately forty-eight hours before I got too homesick to even get out of my sleeping bag. I couldn't toast a marshmallow to save my life—it always caught on fire instead of achieving that crunchy on the outside, gooey on the inside golden brown I craved. The sun and stars were too bright. The woods were too quiet. The kids were too loud and sporty. My concerned counselor finally called my parents, who I treated to a litany of complaints. They came and picked me up.

I'm sure Camp Smiley will be just as bad a fit for me as Camp Greenlake turned out to be. Too bright and too quiet and too loud and sporty for my tastes, uncomfortable surroundings,

socially mismatched. My mom probably didn't realize Camp
Smiley was an actual *camping* kind of camp when my dad talked
her into sending me here. She's sure to give him an earful once I
tell her, and then spring me.

"Girls, please join Counselor Scarlet for patting down and
gearing up," Director Willis commands. "Boys, you go with
Counselor Jed for the same. I look forward to seeing you all
frequently until you prove you're ready to rejoin civilized
society. "

The guys' counselor looks exactly like what you'd think a
Jed would: scruffy beard, gangly bod, wavy brown hair, man
bun. The weird part is, he's still kind of dirty-sexy. Ari and
Jack head off with him.

Counselor Scarlet is a total hippie chick with blonde dreads
and a nose ring. She's wearing the exact same thing Jed is:
knee-length khaki shorts, a black fleece pullover with white
collared polo shirt peeking out from under it, high white
socks, and hiking boots that are trying to pass as real Timberlands but failing miserably.

"She's kind of hot," Sam whispers to me.

I nod. "They both are, in a total jam band kind of way."

"Are you two lesbians or something?" Chandra asks, wrinkling her perfect nose.

Sam rolls her eyes. I laugh.

"Well, I'm not," Chandra says. "Just so we're clear."

Scarlet waves us over to where she's standing. She's got a
friendly smile. "Welcome to Camp Smiley, Chandra, Sam, and
Lizzie," she says. "You can give me those name tags. We're
family now."

She holds out her hand and we peel the stickers from our
clothes.

"Welcome," she says, crumpling up the tags and tucking them into her khakis. "I know you are all going through a tough time, and you'd probably rather be anywhere but here. But tough times are the ones that teach us the most, so dig in and work hard at Camp Smiley. Don't let the circumstances that led you here define you here. Be the person you're meant to become. I believe in you."

I mutter to Sam, "I feel like maybe Director Willis doesn't share her optimism or enthusiasm about us."

Scarlet laughs. "I heard that. And he may seem tough, but Director Willis is also fair. Just do your best and he'll be your biggest advocate. You'll see."

She leads us through some overgrown bushes and brush, away from the cabins. We come to a tarp hanging over a tree branch. Scarlet takes our backpacks and hands each of us a journal with a tan leather cover and a pencil that appears to be made out of an actual stick in return. We also get an energy bar. I guess it's our breakfast. One glance at the nutrition label is enough to give me a heart attack.

"I think *energy* here is defined as *make us really freaking fat*," I say to Sam.

"We'll burn all those calories hiking," she reassures me, tapping the band around her wrist. "I'll track it on my Fitbit to prove it, okay?"

"I'm going to get everyone ready privately now," Scarlet tells us. "At tonight's campfire—we call it Truth Circle here at Camp Smiley—you'll be expected to give a short introduction. It would probably help if you jot down a few sentences in your journal about how you ended up here and what you hope to get out of the experience. Think carefully about what you want to say. First impressions matter, right?"

"Absolutely," Chandra chimes in. "My parents always said *you can't take back a first impression.*"

My first impression of Chandra is she loves being the teacher's pet. I hope Scarlet doesn't fall for it.

Scarlet takes me by the arm and leads me behind the tarp first. "You can take off your sweats now," she says, staring at the sky while she waits.

"Okay." I strip off the groutfit and stand there in my lacy bralette and thong. "Now what?"

"Oh sorry, I didn't realize you'd kept your underwear on," she says when she glances back at me. "You'll have to take that off too."

"What? Why?"

Scarlet pats the clothing in her arms, which appear to be an exact replica of what she and Jed are wearing. "Your uniform comes with its own undergarments."

I stare at the pile, then down at my pretty lingerie, then back at Scarlet. "Could I have those now? I'm pretty cold."

"Sure, just let me do a quick strip search first."

"Where exactly would I be hiding anything?"

She laughs. "You'd be surprised the creative hiding places some kids use."

Just like everything else that's happened over the past twelve hours, I can't figure a way out of doing what she says. I get naked. Scarlet pokes around inside my mouth and under my tongue. Armpits, the back of my neck, thighs. Last and worst of all, she makes me squat and cough—TO SEE IF ANYTHING SHOOTS OUT MY BUTT OR VAG. When nothing does, I get to put on my uniform.

It's not exactly flattering. The cotton granny panties ride up in a perma-wedgie. The sports bra gives me uniboob. The socks have thick toe seams that won't stay straight. None of the clothing has ever even heard of fabric softener. The boots are stiff and uncomfortable.

I walk out from behind the tarp as Chandra is walking in. "You better hope you don't have any drugs stashed in your hoo-ha," I joke as we pass each other.

"What makes you think I do drugs?" she demands.

"Nothing. JK. Sorry." A nervous little giggle flies out of my mouth.

"Addiction of any kind is not a laughing matter," she huffs, and disappears with Scarlet.

I walk over to where Sam is sitting, writing in her journal. She looks up at me and makes a face.

"Nice outfit," she says.

"Just wait, you're next," I tell her. "BTDubs, if you have anything in any orifice you'd rather not let Camp Smiley confiscate, you should probably take it out now."

"Does a Diva Cup count?"

"Depends on how attached you are to it. Literally." It would be pretty funny if it came flying out during the squat and cough session. They'd probably be like "A-HA!" until they saw what it actually was, and then go "OH NO!"

I'm starving, so I nibble on a few small bites of the energy bar. It tastes like a mixture of sawdust and stale prunes. I chuck it at a squirrel that's staring at us. He stares at it disdainfully and walks away. I don't blame him.

My stick-pencil has no eraser, and my journal is soon a mess of lines and scribbles but no actual words. I finally settle on: *I snuck out, had too much Tito's, and was unfortunately disrespectful to a police officer. Also unfortunately, the dashcam recorded my rude behavior and the video went viral. And then my*

*friends made another video of me that portrayed me in a not-so-
great light, which hundreds of people saw too. If this had happened
to anyone else, they might've gotten a few hours of community service. Instead, I ended up here. I think we can all agree the punishment does not match the crime. I hope to enjoy my short time here
getting to know everyone, helping my parents see this is all a huge
misunderstanding, and then leaving to attend my two-month service
trip to the Mediterranean.*

Scarlet returns with Chandra and takes Sam away. Chandra
sits down and gets back to work without even a glance in my
direction.

"So if it's not drugs, what are you addicted to?"

"Excuse me?"

"I mean, like, what's your problem?"

"That's kind of a personal question," she says, and goes back
to journaling. "Plus, I never said I was addicted to anything. I
just said addiction isn't funny. Which it isn't."

"Willis and Scarlet both said we'll be baring our souls every
night at Truth Circle. I'm going to find out sooner or later."

"I guess it'll have to be later, then."

I'm sure Chandra thinks this is the end of the conversation.
But she has no idea how much I hate journaling. Or awkward
silences. I change the subject. "Well then, what kind of doctor
do you think Willis is?"

Chandra throws her pencil down and glares at me. "It's Director Willis, not Doctor Willis."

"Well, his name tag said D-R-period Willis," I say. "Where
I come from, that means doctor, not director."

"Will you just be quiet and let me work on the assignment?"
Chandra bites on the end of her stick pencil. I hope some wood-
land creature crapped on it in its former life as a tree.

"I bet he's a proctologist," I say. "Because he's such a pain in the ass."

Sam returns carrying her geared-up backpack. Scarlet is lugging the other two meant for Chandra and me. They are stuffed to the gills. Even the outside is taken up. There's a rolled-up sleeping bag attached by stretchy cords on the bottom, plus a water bottle, shovel, and compass hanging from carabiners off the side.

"Ready to go," Scarlet says, dropping bags at our feet. "Sorry, but I had to take a lot of your stuff out to fit everything else in, Lizzie."

Though I want to immediately start digging around inside to see what's left—please, please let it be my hair and face stuff—I'm distracted by a familiar rumbling in my gut. Though it shouldn't really be a surprise after getting kidnapped in the middle of the night and eating a stale sawdust/prune power bar, I can't believe my IBS chose now to act up.

IBS = Irritable Bowel Syndrome. No girl wants to even admit she poops at all, and IBS makes you poop A LOT, at the most inconvenient times. It's the worst. There's no cure because doctors don't consider it a big deal, but it IS a big deal because it's humiliating. Especially if the bathroom I need to use has people in it when I need to use it, since I refuse to poop in front of anyone. In which case I might explode and die. But death is preferable to public pooping I guess. It's a terrible cycle.

"Scarlet," I say, clenching my glutes and doing massive Kegels. "I need to use the bathroom."

"Okay, sure," she says. "Follow me."

I stand up and hobble after her. She takes me only as far as the other side of the tarp.

"We'll just be over on the other side waiting for you," she says, walking away.

I follow her back to where Sam and Chandra are still sitting. "Wait, what?"

"We'll wait here while you relieve yourself," she repeats.

"Aren't you going to show me where the bathroom is? I mean, outhouse?" I try to remember what we called it at Camp Greenlake for the two days I was there. I finally latch onto the right word. "Kybo?"

Short for *Keep Your Bowels Open*, the counselors told us. Gross.

Scarlet shrugs apologetically. "Sorry. I have to enforce the bathroom ban while we're at Outpost today," she says. "Director Willis let me know it's a group consequence for Sam's swearing earlier. Besides, you have to get used to nature peeing anyhow."

"It's not pee," I whisper.

"Sorry, dude. My bad. That sucks," Sam laughs.

Scarlet unclips the shovel from my backpack. Then she digs around inside and pulls out a small roll of single-ply toilet paper. It is definitely going to chafe. She tries to pass off both the shovel and itchy toilet paper to me.

I stare at her, my mouth hanging open. What am I supposed to do? Dig a hole behind the tarp and poop in it?

She answers my unspoken question before I can even formulate the ridiculous words. "All solid waste and toilet paper has to be buried in a hole at least six inches deep. So dig first, then squat and do your business, then throw the toilet paper in, then fill the hole back up with dirt."

She says this all like it's normal. This is so not normal. Who poops (a) out in the open and (b) in a hole (c) that is self-dug and (d) then fills it in again?

"I . . . don't think I can do that," I say. Like, how could I do that? Is she crazy?

Scarlet looks at her watch again. "Well, if you don't really need to go right now you can always step off the trail later. But just an FYI, there's not always as much privacy there. Not that anyone cares, believe me. Bodily functions are natural and normal and you'll all realize that very quickly."

I am more horrified than ever. If I try to hold it in—which would be near impossible—that means I'll be stuck doing it later with everyone watching? Even hot Ari and dirty-sexy Jed and crabby Jack? I take the shovel and toilet paper from Scarlet and head behind the tarp.

And I dig.

And I squat. There are noises. Angry tears drip down my face as violence exits my butt.

And it's insanely mortifying, not to mention really tough on the quads. In fact, it's probably the most exercise I've gotten in years. I am going to be sore later, both my quads and my poor badonk from using the generic, completely not-soft toilet paper.

I wipe and realize I have an even bigger problem than the lack of a private bathroom. Make that any bathroom at all. Or toilet. I never realized before what a luxury it is to have one with a heated seat, bidet, and butt blow dryer like I do. I vow to make sure my fabulous Japanese Toto knows how much I appreciate it when I get home.

"Uh, Scarlet?" I call to her, my voice small and shaky. "Do you have a tampon by any chance?"

She tosses one over the tarp. It's also generic as well as unbleached, according to the biodegradable wrapper. There is no applicator so my finger gets treated to a wave of crimson tide.

I pull my pants back up.

I fill my hole back in.

When I come back over to her side, Scarlet squirts a huge glob of hand sanitizer in my palm. It does the job. My hands are squeaky clean, stinging, and smell faintly like my beloved vodka when I'm done rubbing it in. "You survived?"

"I guess so," I tell her, though honestly, just barely. My legs are still shaking from squatting. The super-plus tampon Scarlet gave me feels like a surfboard stuffed up my ladyparts. I guess didn't push it in far enough; a cough or sneeze will surely send it shooting down my leg. Not to mention, I have killer cramps.

I don't know how much more of this I can take, or what I'm going to do to get out of it. The only thing I know without a doubt is: I will. I always do.

CAMP SMILEY
WILDERNESS EXPLORATION AND EDUCATION EXPERIENCE

Transforming your child, renewing their smile!

Confiscated Article Itemization
(To Be Returned Upon Graduation)

Camper: Elizabeth B. Finklestein

1. Clarisonic facial brush
2. Mason Pearson round brush
3. Philip B. Russian Amber Imperial Shampoo
4. Molton Brown Indian Cress Conditioner
5. GLOSS Moderne High-Gloss Serum
6. Oribe Gold Lust Nourishing Hair Oil
7. Kiehl's Heat-Protective Silk-Straightening Cream
8. Jo Malone London Lime Basil & Mandarin Conditioner
9. Sedu Icon Privé Flat Iron
10. Sedu Icon Privé Hair Dryer
11. Jo Malone London Earl Grey & Cucumber Cologne, 100ml
12. Jo Malone London Blue Agava & Cacao Cologne, 100 ml
13. Prada Vela Large Cosmetics Bag, Black
14. La Prairie Cellular Eye Cream Platinum Rare, 20 ml
15. Fresh Black Tea Instant Perfecting Mask
16. Bliss Fabulips Kit
17. Sisley-Paris Sun Glow Duo Honey Cinnamon
18. Guerlain Lingerie de Peau BB Cream Multi-Perfecting Makeup

19. Dior Beauty Rosy Glow Blush
20. Le Métier de Beauté Lueur Stylo Brightening and Highlighting Pen (2)
21. Tom Ford Beauty Extreme Mascara (3)
22. Bobbi Brown Hot Nudes Eye Palette
23. Edward Bess Fully Defined Brow Duo (2)
24. Clé de Peau Beauté Eye Liner Pencil (5)
25. Chantecaille Waterproof Brow Definer
26. Artis Fluenta 5-Brush Set
27. Dior Beauty Diorshow Mascara (3)
28. Dior Beauty Diorshow Kohl Pen (2)
29. Yves Saint Laurent Beauté Rebel Nudes, Coral Reformer
30. Chantecaille Galactic Lip Shine
31. Guerlain KissKiss Lipstick, Fancy Kiss
32. Sisley-Paris Confort Crème Lip Balm
33. Tanda Zap Pink Zap Acne Eliminator
34. Tweezerman Smooth Finish Facial Hair Remover
35. Laura Mercier Tweezers
36. Iluminage Touch Epilator
37. Tria Beauty Fuschia Hair Removal Laser
38. Bliss Trim and Bare It
39. Deborah Lippman Billionaire and Good Girl Gone Bad Nail Lacquer
40. Sephora Collection Travel Tips Mini Mani Kit
41. Nike Flyknit iD, Multi-color, size 6
42. Gray sweatpants, size large, "Peace, Love, Jordan's Bat Mitzvah" on the rear
43. Gray sweatshirt, size XL, "Eat, Play, Celebrate David!" on front

chapter

8

Jed and the boys reappear. Ari is actively scowling.

"What's wrong?" I whisper.

"Dude threatened to stick a finger in my ass if I didn't squat and cough," Ari whispers back. "I want my ass to stay a virgin forever, thanks."

"Worse happened over here," I say, not that I'd actually tell him my poop-in-a-hole story. "You don't even want to know."

Ari gives me another round of awesome eye contact. Make that eye *crack*. It's more addicting than binge-watching the latest reality TV shit show.

"We gotta bust out of this place," he says.

I grin at him. "Great minds think alike."

Jed walks over and inserts himself between us, slinging one arm around me and one over Ari. I'm bummed we're separated. We were totally bonding. Practically almost a thing.

"Everyone, gather round. Let's set our intentions before we hike," Jed says. Everyone forms a circle and leans in. "I'll start with a lyric from the Grateful Dead, the best band there ever was and ever will be: *When I had no wings to fly, you flew to me.* Let's all be each other's wings today, shall we?"

Scarlet compliments his choice of inspiration. "Beautiful message. And let me just add that *the future belongs to those who believe in the beauty of their dreams,*" she says. "Eleanor Roosevelt. Be sure to always dream big, okay guys?"

"Great quote, Scarlet," Jed says, smiling at her. I get the feeling they are hooking up or at the very least flirting with the idea of it. Maybe Ari and I can double with them before we PTFO.

"Okay then, everyone put one hand in the circle," Scarlet says. We unwrap our arms from around one another. Seven hands pile into the middle of our huddle. "On three, yell *Dream Big*! One, two—"

"Wait," Chandra interrupts. "I have an inspirational quote I'd like to share too."

Scarlet and Jed exchange a look. I like to think they want to roll their eyes and complain about what a big pain in the ass she is. And then jump each other's bones. "Go ahead, Chandra," Jed tells her.

"*The way to get started is to quit talking and start doing.* Walt Disney said that."

She nods like we're supposed to be thrilled about taking life pointers from a guy that supposedly froze himself when he died. I mean, who wants to come back as a wrinkled old man with a mouse fetish and zero clue how to use social media? Not even him is my guess.

"One, two, THREE!" Scarlet yells.

"Dream big!" four of us mumble, one of us screeches. Guess who the screecher is.

We take off on a "hike" that is at more of a trot than walk kind of pace. And for someone like me who actively avoids physical activity, it seems like a sprint. I am heaving and panting after a minute in. Only Chandra is slower than me. Scarlet is forced to fall back so she's just ahead of us turtles.

"Come on, girls!' she coaches, jogging backward as she watches the pathetic state of our physical fitness. "Pick up the pace!"

Pretty soon Sam and Ari are tiny little dots, they're so far ahead of us. Scampering through the woods alongside Jed, they look like three beautiful deer. Even Jack—who's so tall and buff he resembles an actual lumberjack, which made me think he'd be slow—is just about keeping up with them.

Meanwhile, Chandra and I trip over roots and rocks as we try to stay with slowed-down Scarlet. Sweat stings my eyes until I can't even see what I'm tripping over anymore. I eventually fall flat on my face, which is just one of the many reasons I hate sports/exercise: far too much potential for injury.

"You okay?" Scarlet calls over her shoulder, still jogging ahead.

I don't move. She circles back around. Grabbing me by the armpits, she sets me back on my feet and brushes some dirt from my cheek.

"Just a little tumble. You're fine."

"Yeah, I know," I say. My throat burns not only from being winded, but from the awful lumpy feeling you get right before you cry. I am not normally a crier and I've already broken down once today, though thankfully alone and behind the tarp. I refuse to bawl like a baby in front of Scarlet and Chandra.

"The first day is always toughest, Lizzie," Scarlet says, patting my back. I take a deep breath and will the crappy crying feeling to go away. "You'll be okay."

"Do you think I could call my mom?" My voice catches at the end of my request, on the word mom. Almost crying because I miss my mommy is so embarrassing. I'm glad the rest of the group didn't just witness that.

"Everyone gets a quick phone call home tonight," Scarlet assures me. "We always let parents know their campers are safe and adjusting well to life at Camp Smiley after the first full day."

"Thanks." I have so many things to report that will totally freak my mom out. I'm positive I can convince her to get me out of here. Now if I can only stay alive until then.

"Okay, let's get back to it, ladies," Scarlet says.

Chandra is leaning over, hands on her knees. "My asthma," she pants.

Scarlet walks over and puts an ear to Chandra's back. "It doesn't sound like an asthma attack," Scarlet says after a minute. "I don't hear any wheezing or whistles. I think your body is just acclimating to the new demands you're putting on it. You two aren't used to doing much cardio, are you?"

"None, TBH." I feel sorry for Chandra despite how annoying she's been so far. All that gorgeous color has run out of her face. She genuinely looks like she's dying. Maybe she needs a medivac? "Should we call Director Willis just to be sure she's okay?"

"He doesn't normally come out on the trail," Scarlet says. "And don't worry, if there are any true medical emergencies, Jed and I are both certified first responders."

"Oh. Okay. I just thought, since he's a doctor . . ."

Scarlet laughs. "What made you think he's a doctor?"

"His name tag. It said D-R-period Willis," I tell her.

"D-R is the abbreviation for director in the military, " Scarlet explains.

"Told you," Chandra pants.

I feel kind of dumb. But also dumb is using military lingo in the real world, where people might confuse a director for a doctor. "Oh."

"Let's take a quick water and snack break before we head back out, shall we, girls?" Scarlet says.

I drop my pack and start rummaging around in it. There's almost nothing left of my personal items. Just my hairbrush, toothbrush, glasses, Buddy, and some temporary flip-flops from a long-ago pedicure I don't even remember packing. The rest of the bag is crammed with camping gear, most of which I have no idea what it does.

I check the outer compartments in search of snack foods. I finally find the treat pocket—but not before I make an amazing discovery: Scarlet has totally missed the fact that I stuffed my phone into the most remote, hidden pouch. I might not have a charger right now, but just knowing a means of modern communication is waiting for me to bring it back to life makes me feel hopeful I'll be able to get out of here. Like, if I can't convince my mom to get me released, my phone and feet will do the trick.

I contemplate the beef jerky I find in the snack pack. I thought I was hungry until I smelled it. It's rank like Poochie's bully sticks, and I have to wonder why she loves the stinky stuff so much. I get misty again thinking about Poochie. I pinch myself hard as a distraction. I have *got* to pull myself together.

Chandra is taking huge drags off her inhaler. I decide maybe she's addicted to Albuterol. "It's definitely asthma," she says between puffs. "In fact, it's probably the worst attack I've ever had."

"Have you ever heard of an anxiety attack, Chandra?" Scarlet asks quietly.

Chandra's breathing and coloring are almost back to normal now. She puts her inhaler away and scowls. "That's NOT what this is."

"Okay. Just a thought," Scarlet says. "Now both of you chug your water before we push ahead so you don't get dehydrated. We still have four and a half more miles to go."

I take a sip from my water bottle and immediately spit what goes into my mouth right back out. "It tastes like egg farts!"

"Water from wells is an acquired taste," Scarlet says, sipping hers like egg-fart water is the most delicious thing on Earth. "Like coffee. Or caviar, or escargot."

"I don't eat any of those either," I say. My phone call cannot come soon enough.

"Let's get back to it, girls," Scarlet says. "We have a lot of catching up to do."

I check the trail ahead of us and see that's she's right. Ari, Jack, Sam, and Jed aren't even specks in the distance anymore. They've completely vanished.

"What if we don't?" I ask, worried that maybe we've gotten separated from them forever. I want to see Ari one more time before I get my mom to pull me tonight. "Or can't?"

"We can and we will," Scarlet says, giving each of us a hand and pulling us to our feet. "You girls are much more capable than you give yourself credit for. Now come on."

CAMP SMILEY

WILDERNESS EXPLORATION AND EDUCATION EXPERIENCE

Transforming your child, renewing their smile!

Counselor: *Scarlet Godchaux/Jed Hart*

TEAM SEVEN:

Name	Age	Reason for Admittance	Hometown
Samantha (Sam)	16	Vandalism	Berkeley, CA
Ariel (Ari)	16	Defacing public property, running away	Skokie, IL
Jack	17	Bullying	Short Hills, NJ
Chandra	17	Gambling	San Diego, CA
Lizzie	16	Drunk and Disorderly Conduct	New York, NY

chapter

9

Scarlet's assessment turns out to be overly optimistic.
Correct: we do eventually catch up to the rest of the group.
Incorrect: this does not happen during the actual hike. By
the time we trudge into camp, Ari, Jack, and Sam are spread
out along the waterfront, lounging against their backpacks
in complete chill mode. Chandra and I, on the other hand,
have sweated through our shorts, practically coughed up a
lung, and had zero more conversation because it's hard to
talk when you can barely breathe. Not that I particularly
wanted to talk to her, but silence except for anaerobic gasping
is even worse.

"Go. Relax," Scarlet tells us, then saunters over to Jed.
They're lost in deep conversation a second later. I wish I had a
Jed in my life.

"Hey!" Sam says when I collapse down beside her. "What
took you so long?"

I stare over at Ari. Maybe he can be my Jed. "I'm not exactly a gym rat."

"No? I love moving my body. Best drug there is. A total natural high."

"I don't think mine has ever produced an endorphin." I know everyone loves to say *oh blah blah I feel so great after I work out* but like, no. "Speaking of drugs—"

"Is that what you're in for?" Sam interrupts.

I shake my head and look around to make sure no one else is listening. Chandra is having some intense debate with Ari, and Jack appears to be napping. I'm in the clear. "No, but I think it might be why Chandra is here," I tell her.

"Come on now," Sam says. "My guess is a scarf and barf issue for her."

I shrug. "Maybe, but I made a joke about hoping she didn't have anything stashed up her cooch and she yelled at me *addiction isn't a laughing matter.* So I was thinking maybe she was snorting Adderall. You know, for studying and getting her GPA up to, like, a 5.0."

Sam grabs a handful of fine, reddish sand and lets it trickle through her fingers. "IDK, man. I doubt it. But here's what I know for sure: Ari is into graffiti. His tag is a huge jizzing dong, which he spray-painted all over town until the cops busted him. Jack claims he almost killed someone. And Jed is obsessed with the Grateful Dead."

Ari's story confirms why I'm attracted to him, beyond just his physical hotness—he's a total artiste. A street artiste. Swoon. As for Jack? I can't see it.

"Jack doesn't strike me as a failed murderer," I muse. "He seems too depressed and boring to work up that much feeling for anyone, you know?"

"Well, Chandra doesn't seem like the kind of person who would do anything bad enough to land her here either. Life is strange."

"What about you?" I ask.

Sam doesn't meet my eyes and draws patterns in the sand with her finger instead. "Fell in love with a fuckboy," she finally says.

"Wait, what?" This is so not what I expected to hear. One, because I assumed Sam was into girls. But two, because how does that warrant getting sent to East Bumbutt, Utah?

Before I can get more details, Jed and Scarlet tell us to wash up. There are no facilities as far as the eye can see, so I'm guessing they aren't referring to actual showers. Which I would pay any amount of money for right now.

Our leaders take off their boots, socks, fleeces, and shirts. This leaves Scarlet in the uniform sports bra and khaki shorts, Jed khaki-shorted and shirtless. Mmmmmmmm, shirtless Jed. They wade into the reservoir.

We follow their lead, stripping down to the same amount of clothes. Guys bare-chested and girls in sports bras, all of us in our shorts, we look like a campaign for a Dove Real Beauty ad. We run the gamut of skin shades and body types, from curvy Chandra to straight up-and-down athletic Sam to ripped-abs Jack to rib-juttingly skinny Ari to completely average me. Jed hands us each a travel-sized bar of soap. It's the kind that floats. I am so grateful the water is cool and non-eggy, I go in as far as I can without actually submerging myself. It feels almost as good as a vodka club with lemon tastes. Which I could also totally go for right now, even though I know I said I was giving them up forever.

"This is considered getting clean?" Chandra mutters as she lathers up whatever skin is showing.

For once, I agree with her. "I know, right?"

We try to rinse off all the sweat and dirt without getting our clothes too soggy. We only have a single uniform and one extra pair of underwear to last us until we get back to Outpost. I guess we'll be double and sometimes triple-wearing stuff. Disgusting.

Worse, the body parts that need the most washing are covered up. There's no reaching them. And I am at a distinct disadvantage, getting my period and having an IBS attack all in one day. I feel like I should get a dispensation on reusing my underwear after that. Actually, I feel like I should burn them.

Our fake half-bath ends way too quickly and it's time to set up camp. Jed demonstrates how to pitch our single-person tents. They look more like those preschool fabric tunnels kids love to crawl through than the gorgeous, spacious, hotel-like one Jem's family glamped in when they went on safari.

"Out here on the trail, we'll set our tents up in the shape of an H," Jed says, walking to each spot and using his arms to explain the formation. "Guys, you'll be the top two vertical prongs over here. Scarlet and I will form the center line, with me in front of the boys' tents and Scarlet closest to the girls. Ladies, you'll make up the bottom prongs. With one extra, of course." He chuckles at his own joke.

Scarlet laughs along with him. "Now everyone grab your gear and give it a shot."

I fish my tent out of my backpack. Jed made it look so easy, but I totally don't know where to start now that I'm on my own. I poke a few poles where I think they should go but they get stuck. I am drowning under swaths of fabric.

"This is impossible!" I mutter.

Jack lets out a whoop. I free myself from the pile of gear and see his tent is already up. He crawls inside, pops his head back out, and semi-smiles. He looks like a different person when he's not being salty. His face lights up so he's almost halfway cute.

I scowl and grab another pole. It doesn't fit. And another. It's still not the right one. I throw everything down in frustration. I close my eyes and try deep breathing. Nope.

I open my eyes again. Now Sam's tent is fully assembled too. My fists clench into tight little balls. I want to hit something. Someone. My parents, mostly, for sending me here. I glare at Sam instead.

"What? It's easy. Here, let me help you," she says.

Whiz. Boom. Bam. I have a fully functioning tent.

"How'd you do that?" I ask, mouth hanging open. Left to my own devices, I would still be staring at a pile of polyester and poles weeks from now.

"Watch closely this time," she says, walking over to where Chandra is failing as epically as I was a minute ago.

I concentrate as Sam works her magic. Chandra stares at the ground, not even paying attention.

"You're welcome," Sam says when she's done.

"Huh?" Chandra looks up. She swipes away some tears and says, "Oh. Wow. Thanks."

Scarlet walks over and gives Sam a high five. "You're very handy, Sam. And a great teammate."

She glows under the compliment. "Thanks."

"Don't you *dare* start liking it here," I whisper after Scarlet goes over to see how Ari's doing. "You're the only thing keeping me sane at the moment."

"Don't worry," Sam whispers back. "I'm not falling for any of this bullshit."

Once Ari manages to get his tent set up—he doesn't look like he's trying very hard, or even trying very hard to move very fast—Scarlet demonstrates how to make fire using only sticks and a clump of dried grass.

"Pay attention, because after the first few days, this will be your responsibility," she tells us. "And no fire means cold meals and very limited light after dark, so you'll want to pick up this skill quickly."

She takes a long stick and fits it into a knot in a flatter stick. Then she rubs them together until a puff of smoke appears. That smoke turns into a spark, which Scarlet blows onto the pile of dried grass, which creates a flame. She patiently feeds the flame kindling, starting with tiny twigs and moving up to actual logs. After a while, it all adds up to an actual fire.

"So that's how it's done," she says, wiping her hands on her shorts. "You guys can give it a try in the morning before we start hiking again."

Jed tells Chandra to get a can opener, cooking pot, and ladle from his gear. She comes back with it all. He hands me the can opener and an industrial-sized can of beans to open, and gives Jack some limp, watery hot dogs and says to cut them with the ladle. Scarlet asks Ari and Sam to gather more branches.

I pour the opened can of beans into the pot and Jack deposits the wiener pieces. We put the pot over the fire. Ari and Sam add more sticks as needed.

And then we sit and stare. Contrary to the old saying, a watched pot does eventually boil. It just doesn't do it quickly enough. Especially when you've hiked forever and you're starving.

"Dig in!" Jed says when dinner is finally ready, scooping a heaping portion of franks and beans into the tin cup we all got in our gear packs. He shovels the food into his face with a crude wooden spoon. The guy has terrible manners: not waiting for everyone to be served and seated before starting, chewing with his mouth open, talking with food in there, gobbling instead of nibbling.

My fledgling crush on him dies. That's how it always is with me; I notice something I can't handle and buh-bye go my feelings. I can never tell what's going to be a deal breaker and what I can let slide until I see it. It always freaks me out how I can go from desperately digging someone one day to desperately trying to get away from them the next, but I guess that's why so many people get divorced, right?

I ladle some unhealthy slop into my cup, wondering how I'll ever be able to avoid what happened to my parents in my own life if my feelings are that fickle. Will I ever be able to accept someone, flaws and all? So far, no. Which is why I've broken up with every single boyfriend I've ever had. Before we ever do the do, I might add.

By the time the rest of us sit down by the fire to eat, Jed's done. He starts serenading us with Dead tunes on the ukulele. He's not half bad, even though the songs are.

"Hey, can I use your spoon, Jed?" Ari asks during a break in the music. "I didn't get one with my gear."

Jed smiles and shakes his head. "Nope. You're just going to have to make your own, man."

Ari frowns. "So what am I supposed to do until then?"

Jed shrugs and launches into another song. "This is called 'Scarlet Begonias,' and I dedicated it to our other awesome trail guide."

Scarlet blushes the same color as her name.

"This is such bullshit!" Ari growls. "Don't you guys think?"

I nod in agreement. Sam and Jack shrug like, *whatever who cares*. Chandra stares down at her food. The counselors ignore our mini-protest, harmonizing to the terrible song instead.

Ari eventually gives in and uses his fingers. Jack basically drinks dinner from his cup. The lightness and kind-of cute are gone from his face now, the sad storm brewing all over again. Sam watches, then follows suit. I think for a bit, then fish my stick pencil from my pack and use it to spear beans and dog pieces one by one. It's a painstakingly slow way to eat, but it'll have to do for the moment. Chandra doesn't take a single bite. She looks as miserable as I feel.

We finish eating—or not, in Chandra's case—rinse our cups out in the reservoir, and put them back in our packs. Scarlet announces it's time for Truth Circle. We gather around the fire.

"Mother Earth, today another group of beautiful young people with unlimited potential joined us on our journey," she says, eyes toward the dusky sky. "They've temporarily lost their way in the world, but come to us with open hearts, curious minds, and unbroken spirits. Allow us to light their way back to happiness, to anoint them with love and laughter, to help them manifest their true and perfect selves."

"Welcome!" Jed says, putting his hands in prayer position and bowing slightly at the waist from where he's sitting. "We honor you and are here for you."

"It's time for formal introductions," Scarlet says, still standing in front of us. "I'll start. I'm Scarlet and I've been working at Camp Smiley for the past three years. I'm a graduate of the University of Utah with a major in social work. But before that, I was a teenage girl who felt cruddy about herself, misunderstood and unappreciated by every adult in her life. I only felt better when I was doing drugs. I was failing at school, friendships, relationships. At life. My parents got so worried about me, they sent me here. And that's when everything totally turned around. So believe me when I say I feel you guys. I know you're probably all scared and angry and sad right now. But trust me, it's all going to work out. In fact, it's going to be great. I know from firsthand experience."

Scarlet walks over and sits down next to Jed. He wraps his arm around her. She rests her head on his shoulder. They are like total relationship goals. Even with his poor table manners, she still loves him and he clearly adores her back.

"Me next," Jed says. "My teen years sucked too. I was raised by a single mom who dated one loser after another. We moved constantly and I was always having to find new friends. It was an exhausting and lonely way to live. I envied kids with nice clothes and houses and two normal parents. So when my mom's latest boyfriend went after her physically, all the anger I'd been holding in came out. I beat the guy unconscious, and it scared the crap out of me. Luckily, the judge sent me to Camp Smiley instead of juvie. Best thing that ever happened to me. I made lifelong friends. Became confident in my abilities. Gave up stuffing my feelings and fighting. Learned how to forgive. I know it's hard, but try to be open to the fact that this might be the best thing that ever happens to you too."

Ari fake sneezes. "Fuckthat!"

"Truth, man. I even met my soul mate here," Jed says, and squeezes Scarlet a little tighter. She grins up at him. I can't believe it's possible to meet "The One"—if there even is such a thing—at a place like this, but seeing is believing. "Now it's time for you guys to tell your stories. Who wants to start?"

Chandra's hand shoots in the air. Of course. She's such a freaking try-hard. Jed gives her a nod.

"I'm Chandra and I'm here because I completely disrespected and dishonored my family by using my God-given talents for bad instead of good," she says. "I just want to prove that I'm worthy of their forgiveness and make them proud again."

Scarlet reaches over and pats Chandra's knee. "Everyone is worthy of forgiveness, and I'm sure whatever mistakes you made, you can make up for them now. Care to add anything more?"

Chandra shakes her head. "It would take winning the lottery to make up for what I did. Or a miracle."

"Believe in miracles," Scarlet tells her. "I do."

"Everyone, I want to introduce you to a Camp Smiley tradition," Jed says. "We snap when we want to show our support for someone, or that we agree with them."

He snaps enthusiastically. Jack and Sam join in. Ari just sits there staring at the fire. Snapping always hurts my fingers, so I don't.

Jack stands up. "I'll go next," he says. "I'm Jack and I used to be a totally normal, happy guy until I did something that almost killed someone. I came here to figure out how to be a good person again. That's pretty much it."

"You're a good person who made a poor choice," Jed tells him. "We all do sometimes. We're all human."

"Truth," Scarlet agrees.

"Whatever." Jack sits back down and nudges Sam with an elbow. "Your turn."

Sam's holding a pine bough, stripping the needles off of it and throwing them into the fire. They sizzle and smell nice. Like Christmas. "Uh, I'm Sam and I'm here because I fell for someone really wrong for me, and it turned into a total shit show."

"Care to elaborate?" Jed probes.

"I guess the only other thing I have to say is, be who you say you are or you'll end up friendless, arrested, and in Utah."

Everyone snaps even though Sam hasn't really told us anything. Neither have Chandra or Jack, really. I want the dirty deets. The counselors let it slide.

"Ari?" Jed prompts.

"I'm here because my parents can't handle that I want to be an artist," he says, and adopts a total mother voice. "*Ooooh, Ari. You should be a doctor and mohel like your dad. Now that's a good career path!* Like no. I'm not cutting off the tips of baby dicks for anything."

"Do you think maybe getting arrested on multiple occasions might also have something to do with their concern?" Scarlet asks.

Ari shrugs and spits into the fire. "I mean, yeah, I guess so. It was either here or juvie. But still, they can't tell me who or what to be.'"

He has bad manners too. But my crush doesn't poof away like it did when Jed was stuffing his face. So I guess it's not a deal breaker this time.

"You have to obey the law, Ari, if you want your parents to take your ambitions seriously," Jed agrees. "They're not going to support a future that puts you in and out of jail, you know?"

"Art shouldn't be a crime," Ari says, patting my thigh. It sizzles beneath his palm. "Your turn, Lizzie."

I stand up, plant a huge smile on my face, and prepare to turn on the charm. "Hi, I'm Lizzie. I'm sixteen and from Manhattan. Go Yankees!"

No one snaps. I clear my throat and start over. "I just want to say, if this was the Hunger Games, I would totally volunteer as tribute for any of you."

Still nothing.

"Anyhow, I can't wait to get to know you all a bit better before heading off on my summer service trip to Greece, where I'll be working to save the turtles. Always remember, *if you can dream it, you can do it*!"

I wait for the snaps again. Nope.

After a long silence, Jed finally says, "Maybe you could share just a little about what brought you here and what you hope to get out of Camp Smiley?"

"Right." I regroup. What *did* I do to deserve to be in this dump? Nothing, really. I'm not even sure how to explain the ridiculous chain of events. "Okay, see, I had a date with James Franco but he bailed because he knows my father and it was like a conflict of interest—"

"Wait," Sam interrupts. "What?"

"How does James Franco know your dad, but you didn't *know* he knew him?" Ari asks.

"I know, right?" I laugh. "It's like a tongue twister. And a brain twister. Oh, the tangled web I weave."

"Yeah, but really, why?" Chandra pipes in.

"My father has a charity in Africa," I tell her. "I guess James Franco worked with him there."

"Oh, wow! Cool! You must be so proud of your dad," Chandra says.

The big lump creeps back up my windpipe. I avoid eye contact and look down, trying to get ahold of myself. And that's when I notice an ugly raised rash on my shins and calves. It's enough of a distraction to make the crying feeling go away.

"I guess," I say, scratching my increasingly itchy legs.

"Anything else you'd like to add?" Scarlet asks.

"Yes. I seem to have an issue here. See?"

"Yeah, you have a little rash," Scarlet says. "I'll get you some cream after the welcome ceremony is over."

"I don't think I can wait that long," I tell her, raking lines up and down my legs. "It's making me crazy. Can you get it for me now instead?"

Jed stands up, grabs my arm, and pulls me aside for a private pep talk. "Don't you want everyone to see how strong and capable you are? How you can handle a little discomfort like a mature adult?"

"I'd rather just have my legs feel better."

"Show me you can hang a little longer and we'll let you have a little extra time on your call home. Deal?"

It's just the opening I've been waiting for all day. "I've got a better deal for you, Jed. Get me discharged from Camp Smiley because of this rash, and I'll get you VIP tickets and a meeting with Jerry Whatshisface the next time the Dead are on tour."

Jed bursts out laughing. "Jerry *Garcia* has been gone since 1995. God rest his soul. Besides, Director Willis would never agree to let you leave over a harmless parasite."

"P-p-parasite?"

"Yes. Cercarial dermatitis. Caused by microscopic parasites. Only about seven percent of people are susceptible to it like you."

"ARE YOU KIDDING ME?" I scream.

"Shhhhhhhh. It's no worse than a mosquito bite," Jed says, completely unconcerned about my medical emergency. "No need for drama."

I force myself to calm down. Now is not the time to freak out about bugs living in my legs. I have to give bribery another shot while I still have the chance. "You know, you're a really good musician yourself. Maybe even better than Jerry Garcia. I can put your music in the hands of the biggest producers in the world. If you get me out of here, you'll totally get a record deal."

"Nice try," he says, and walks back to the campfire.

I follow him, itching and scratching the whole way. I have had it up to my vag—which thankfully I never immersed in the water or else I'd have bugs crawling up my chachie too—with Camp Smiley. I cannot think of a place that sucks worse than this. Not even Africa.

Scarlet and Jed each light a bundle of what looks like hay. They walk in a circle, waving smoke at us. It smells like smoke shop incense. Desperate and sad.

"Welcome to Camp Smiley," Scarlet intones. "May you use your time here to shed light on who you are, why you've acted in ways that are harmful to yourself and others in the past, and how to become the person you were born to be."

"May this sage cleanse your mind, body, and soul so that tomorrow you may start anew," Jed chants.

But you know what? They can both kiss my parasitic ass. Because my only starting a-new is going happen in a-nother place a-ltogether. Now I just have to figure out how to make a-break for it.

CERCARIAL DERMATITIS: *also known as swimmer's itch, lake itch, duck itch*

Cause: Short-term allergic reaction from flatworm parasites of the schistosomatidae family. Ducks and snails most often serve as their invertebrate hosts. Cercariae cannot infect humans, but do cause an inflammatory immune response in them.

Symptoms: Burning, itching, tingling of affected area. Raised red pimples appear within hours of infection. These may turn into blisters before disappearing a few weeks later.

Treatment: Generally goes away without intervention. Antihistamines and anti-itch creams such as calamine lotion help alleviate symptoms until then. Home remedies include Epsom salt baths or applying baking soda paste to affected areas.

chapter
10

Scarlet pats baking soda and water mixed into white slop on my squirmy legs. "You feeling better now, Lizzie?"

Though the home remedy calms the rash, I still can't get over the fact I could be on *Monsters Inside Me* right now. "Honestly? I'm horrified something's eating me alive."

"Oh, the parasites aren't living anymore," she tells me like it's no BFD. "They die as soon as they burrow under your skin."

This is even worse news than when I found out I had to poop in a hole. "So you're telling me this mess of blisters is a graveyard of DEAD bugs?"

Scarlet laughs. "Yeah, I guess when you put it that way. You're funny, Lizzie."

"Hosting zombie parasites in my legs is not funny."

Scarlet takes Sam to have her phone call and Jed takes Ari. They split into single-sex pairs at the edge of the reservoir.

"So do you get to do a lot of volunteer work with your dad's charity too?" Chandra asks. "What a great experience that must be."

"Nope," I tell her. "The first time I've seen my father in six months was last night, when he showed up at my apartment and had me ripped out of bed and sent here."

"Oh. I'm so sorry," Chandra says, giving me a pitying look. "So no killer college essay then either, huh?"

"Don't look so sad. It's fine." I say, and try to change the subject. "What kind of a disgusting place has parasites in the water anyway?"

"Any lake can have them," Jack says, baby blues glowering at me like I'm the dumbest person on Earth. "Anywhere in the world, according to my AP bio teacher." Figures he actually takes AP bio.

"Lake Como didn't," I tell him.

"If Lake Como is actually a lake, then it did," Jack retorts, and heads off.

Ari plunks himself back down with us. "Well that was completely useless," he says. "The entire conversation consisted of me saying *get me out of here* and him saying *only if you agree to stop tagging* and then we both basically hung up."

"Isn't Lake Como that place in Italy where George Clooney has a mansion?" Chandra interrupts. "You've actually gone there?"

"George Clooney? I don't know." I try to recall the finer details of that trip. Mostly I remember loving the pizza and pasta and hating the funicular—this gondola thing that takes you up a big hill—because I'm scared of heights and also because we had to climb up another hill to see a lighthouse after we got off. "But I mean, like, maybe he does. It's pretty nice there—"

"So your family is like the Kardashians or something?" Ari asks.

"Do you see us plastered all over magazine covers and the TV?" Sarcasm: my lame attempt at flirting.

"No."

"Well, there's your answer. We're just a typical normal family."

"You vacation in rich places and famous people go to work at your dad's far-flung charity," Chandra says, getting up and dusting sand off her butt when she sees Sam walking back to us. "It all equals boatloads of cash. None of which is actually normal or typical."

"Wrong," I yell at Chandra as she walks away. "Not even."

Sam and Jack come back and sit down.

"Well that was brutal," Jack says.

"Your parents hung up on you too?" Ari asks.

"No. My little sister started crying so hard about how much she misses me, she couldn't even talk," Jack answers, stone-faced as ever. "So I just told her it was going to be okay, I'd be home soon, said a quick hi to my mom and dad, and that was that."

Ari turns back to me and smiles. "So, Lake Como. Playground of the wealthy. That always the way you roll?"

I like the attention. I smile back at him. "I mean, it was a nice vacation."

"Sounds fun."

"Hey Lizzie, can you cover my tuition?" Sam jokes, breaking the connection between me and Ari yet again. "My parents told me I have to pay for the property damage I caused before they'll even *consider* letting me go away to college. In other words, *you want fries with that?* is pretty much my future. I can't believe I'll never get to be a turfgrass science major."

"That's a major?" I thought turf was made of recycled tires. So it doesn't make sense that people would go to college to learn how to shred rubber and put fake grass on top of it. "All the kids I know seem to major in business or, like, pre-med or pre-law."

Chandra is back with the group two seconds after she left, looking even more depressed than Jack already is. "My parents weren't home," she says, sniffling back more tears. "Scarlet says I can try again tomorrow."

Ari ignores the Chandra drama. "There are tons more interesting things to study than business, medicine, and law, Lizzie. And there are also better ways to spend two hundred grand than wasting it on a useless piece of paper."

I know it's my turn to make a call, but I want to keep the conversation going with Ari. He's so cute, I'm basically magnetized to the sand. Besides, Jed and Scarlet are too busy chatting right now to care.

"Like?"

"Well, if you really want that piece of paper, then film-making. Glass blowing. Fashion design. Website development. Creative stuff. If you're a renegade like me, you could use the cash to travel the world and have experiences instead of wasting your best years sitting in a classroom."

Chandra jumps all over him. "College is for expanding your intellect, Ari. Not making craft projects. And a college degree is required for any sort of respectable job, so how does that make it useless?"

"Anything you could ever want to learn about is online for free, or out there in the real world if you look hard enough." He glares at her. "Besides, what's wrong with the arts?"

She glares back at him. "Why would you waste your time at an institute of higher learning making bongs?"

Ari looks like his head is about to explode. But then a smile creeps up his cheeks instead. "I'd tell you to calm your tits, but I just realized maybe glass blowing reminded you of why you ended up here," he says, wagging his eyebrows at her. "You know, using your God-given talents for evil instead of good. Blowing people."

She rolls her eyes at him. "Gross. My God-given talent is with numbers, you jackass. I'm here because I gambled away my entire college fund online. Satisfied?"

Ari winces and says, "Oooh. Ugly. There's always Khan Academy, I guess."

We all sit there uncomfortably. Awkward silence.

Jack's the first one to crack. "I'm going pre-law in college," he announces. "Unlike Ari here, I think college is really worthwhile and so is the law."

"I agree with Jack," Chandra says. "There will always be a need for smart lawyers fighting for our rights."

"Plus, you'll make total bank," I add. Our lawyer certainly does off of my family, whether it's by setting up the terms and conditions of my massive trust, helping my dad found charities, figuring out who gets what in the divorce, or getting me out of trouble.

"You probably wouldn't understand this, Lizzie, but I'm not in it for the money," Jack says, giving me an extra-salty look. "I want to be a public prosecutor. Working for the government. Helping society."

Great. Another dig at "rich people," a.k.a. me. Who knew it was an offensive thing? It's not my fault who my parents are and what their financial status is.

"Sorry, I didn't realize felons were allowed to be lawyers or work for the government," I shoot back at him.

"Not sure where you got the idea I was a felon, but you're wrong."

"You'll be a great lawyer, Jack," Chandra says.

"I'm still undecided," I announce. "I don't really know yet what I'm interested in for, like, a career."

"Gah, I knew it," Chandra mutters under her breath.

I give her a cold stare. She flinches but doesn't break eye contact. "What?"

She presses her lips together.

"Go on," I tell her.

"You won't like it."

"I want to hear whatever completely incorrect assumption you're making about me now."

"Okay," she says, taking a deep breath and then letting it out really slowly. I wonder if maybe she has her own Ellyn at the Womyn's Centre teaching her useless breathing exercises. "I just think it's sad you don't have any actual goals or aspirations. With all your family's money, you could really make an impact on the world. Instead, you're probably never going to add anything substantive to it."

I'm so offended. "I have goals and aspirations!" I yell. So what if I'm not sure what they are right now? I'm friggin' sixteen years old. I'm not *supposed* to know yet. I start listing things that sound interesting, but I've never actually considered doing until this very second. "I want to intern at fashion week in London, Milan, AND Paris! Be a brand ambassador for *Vogue España*! Sail every ocean and stop at every beach where baby turtles need help getting to the water!"

"What is it with you and turtles, man?" Ari asks.

"They're cute." I wonder if he knows I think he's cute too. I try to get everyone off my ass by throwing the attention onto him. "What about you, Ari? What's up after high school?"

"Definitely not college. Right now I'm thinking marrying you would be my best bet. We'd make a decent couple. You can fund my art and it won't matter if I never make a living off it. And there's always divorce and alimony if we don't work out, right?"

"Ever hear of a prenup, Ari? You wouldn't get a cent. Nice try, though."

I'm more disappointed than I care to admit that he only seems interested in my money. His judgment of me sucks just as bad as Chandra's, only in a different way. It's like they can't see how cool I actually am because they're too busy imagining how cool my life must be, and how much better they could live it than I am currently.

"JK," he yells as I stalk away.

I wish I didn't still think he was hot but I do. I also wish I wasn't a victim of classism here at Camp Smiley. Who knew I was a member of a minority group that gets discriminated against for no reason? Now I guess I know how Jem feels when she walks into a boutique and the salespeople follow her around but not me, even though her family has as much money as mine, just because she's a Caramel in Laura Mercier tinted moisturizer and I'm a Nude.

"Would you rather talk to your mother or father tonight?" Scarlet asks when I get to her. "When we're dealing with divorced families, we have students alternate calls between parents."

"My mom," I say, zero hesitation. I know she'll be just as appalled as I am at the conditions here.

Scarlet dials the number. I take the phone from her and walk a few paces away. I need some privacy. My mom answers on the first ring.

"Mommy!" I say, my voice cracking.

"Thank goodness you're safe!" my mom yells. "I told Eddie to let you text when you landed and I never heard from you! I was worried sick!"

"He wouldn't let me have my phone," I tell her. I neglect to mention the part about stealing it back after it fell out of his pocket. "They take absolutely *everything* from you here! Even my prescription face lotion!"

"Well, that's not right," my mom says. "Your lotion is a medical necessity. You wouldn't want that acne on your forehead to get any worse than it already is."

My hand flies up to my face. "It's fine," I mumble.

"How's everything else going, honey?"

"It's AWFUL! I had an IBS attack and they made me poop in a hole I had to dig myself because this girl swore so we weren't allowed to use the bathrooms even though they were RIGHT THERE."

"What? That's barbaric!"

"I know! And then I got my period, and had to walk seven miles with massive cramps, and they made us take a bath in a LAKE in our CLOTHES! So, like, the most important parts didn't even get CLEAN!"

"That's so unsanitary! I just don't know what that camp is trying to prove by not allowing you proper toilet and shower facilities."

"I know, it's so gross! And you know what else is gross? My legs! They have dead parasites in them from that disgusting lake. So now I have a terrible itchy rash from my knees down to my ankles!"

"What? No! There is no way I'm letting you stay at a place like that. I don't even know what your father was thinking, convincing me it was a good idea to send you there!"

Finally. My bad luck streak is ending. Mom's going to pull me from the program.

A wave of relief washes over me. My PTSD from being kidnapped and stress over all the Camp Smiley suckiness surges out of my body. I imagine myself falling down in a pile of skin and bones and grateful tears. I might be really, really mad at my mother for a lot of things. Like letting my dad just walk out on us without a fight. And taking pills instead of facing reality. And sending me here. But if she lets me come home now, I might just have to give her a pass.

"He always chooses what he wants over our needs," I agree.

"Now that's not true and you know it," she says. "He loves you and only wants the best for you."

"I'm not so sure about that."

"Wait. What's that? Hold on, your father wants to talk to you."

"Why are you guys still in the same place?" I yell into the phone but she's already gone. I don't get how my parents could go from not talking for years to, like, hanging out all the time.

The next thing I hear is my dad's voice. "Now listen to me, Lizzie. You are at a wilderness camp. Which means you are in the wilderness. Camping. There are no bathrooms in the wilderness. Or showers. You camp. In tents. You bathe. In lakes. You make do. Just like millions of people all over the world have to every single day of their lives."

Relief is replaced with regret. That he was ever in my life, if this is how he chooses to treat me. That I ever actually thought he loved me. That my mom ever met him, even though that means my very existence would be obliterated.

"Just because you like to live like a hobo doesn't mean I should have to." Tears are streaming down my face. I can't hold them in anymore. "I didn't even do anything that bad. I apologized for what happened. I was going to do my community service like the peer jury told me to. I don't deserve this!"

Dad sighs. "Honey, you *do* deserve this. Everyone deserves a second chance at greatness. You weren't born for mediocrity. Camp Smiley is your opportunity to find out how strong and resilient and creative you are. To figure out where you want to be and who you want to become. You'll thank me someday, I promise."

My mom yells in the background, *Benjamin! She is not staying at that camp!* He yells back *She's staying! It's good for her!* Lovely to know that even when my life does a total 180 in a day, everything is the same as ever with them.

My tears turn into full-on sobs. "I promise I won't ever thank you. You have no idea how bad it is here!"

"Sometimes, the things that seem like the worst actually turn out to be the best," he says, quiet and firm. And then he's gone. And I can't fight with dead air, so I hand the phone back to Scarlet and bawl like a baby.

CAMP SMILEY

WILDERNESS EXPLORATION AND EDUCATION EXPERIENCE

Transforming your child, renewing their smile!

JACK

ARI

JED

SCARLET

LIZZIE

CHANDRA

SAM

chapter

11

Scarlet pats my shoulder and waits for me to pull myself together. I sniffle and wipe my face with the back of my hand. I'm sure I look like hell, which certainly isn't going to help me convince Ari I'm more than just dollar signs in a bank account.

"Everything's going to turn out just the way it's supposed to. You'll see," she says.

I nod, but there's not a chance I'm sticking around to find out what's supposedly supposed to happen. I'm ditching out the first chance I get. And if something eats me before I find the nearest town, I hope my dad spends the rest of his life regretting he ever sent me here. Regretting leaving us. Regretting being such an awful father.

Once I regain my composure, Scarlet deposits me in my tent and zips the mesh door shut. Everyone else is already all tucked in. "Lights out," she says.

This is Camp Smiley's idea of a joke. Of course there's no electricity in the wilderness. The only illumination comes from the embers of the dying fire and our assigned headlamps, and those things are basically useless. A firefly could shine brighter.

I toss and turn, clutching Buddy and scratching my legs. I try to come up with an escape plan. Specifics elude me once again. My final strategy is this: whatever. Just get me out of here. I'll wing it.

I sit up, sling my backpack over my shoulders, and start moving the zipper ever so slowly. Tooth by tooth. It doesn't make a noise. Score.

I inch my body out in the cool night air and tiptoe past Scarlet's tent. The mesh is unzipped and flapping in the wind. I'm pretty sure she's shacking up with Jed. Whispers and giggles are coming from where he's supposed to be sleeping alone. Double score.

I realize I don't have the first idea which direction to head in. I need a co-pilot. And even though he was being rude before, I decide my best bet is Ari. I silently slide the zipper to his tent open and climb inside. He's asleep, his adorable lips parted ever-so-slightly. I snuggle up and whisper in his ear.

"Hey."

He lets out a shriek. It's enough to pierce an eardrum. I clamp my hand over his mouth. He thrashes next to me.

"Shhhhhhhh. It's just me, Lizzie."

"What was that?" Jed yells from his tent. "Everyone okay?"

"Fine," Ari yells back. "I had a bad dream. Sorry."

Rustling noises. Leaves crunching. Footsteps coming our way. Panicked, I stuff myself into Ari's sleeping bag and curl into a ball at the bottom half of it. It smells like mushrooms and Axe down there.

"Hey, you okay?" Jed asks. It sounds like he's right on top of us.

"Just a nightmare. It's cool," Ari tells him.

"Well, I feel you, man. I used to have this recurring one about the Penguin. You know, from Batman?"

"Uh-huh," Ari says.

"Well, in the dream, the Penguin was always trying to sneak in my bedroom window and it seemed so real. I could, like, see him floating there. Freaked me out something fierce."

While Jed TMIs about his childhood, Ari reaches down, grabs my hand, and puts it on his bulge. I snatch it back and punch him in the balls. He grunts.

"AW MAN!"

"Yeah, I know, Ari. Nightmares are scary stuff," Jed says. "But nothing to be ashamed of. You sure you're good now?"

"Definitely," Ari croaks.

"Night, then."

"Night."

Once I'm sure Jed is gone, I pop back out of the sleeping bag, gasping for air. "You're such a jerk," I hiss.

"I thought you liked me," Ari whispers.

"Not anymore."

I want to leave but know I have to wait until everyone's back asleep. So I just lie there. Pretty soon Ari's hand finds its way into mine.

"I was just joking around. I joke around a lot. Sorry."

I shrug even though I know he can't see me in the darkness. I hate that he automatically assumed I wanted the D. I wonder why all guys seem to think that, when it's so not true.

Ari rolls over toward me. Our faces are so close his nose is practically touching mine. I'm still seething. But there's just something about him. I wish chemistry wasn't so complicated and unpredictable.

"I shouldn't have done that," he whispers, hands getting lost in my hair. It's romantic, like a Taylor Swift song. "I didn't mean to make you mad."

I don't move. I can barely breathe. Being someplace you're not supposed to be with someone you're not supposed to be with is such an aphrodisiac. Ari's lips graze mine. I'm still mad but I can't resist; it's an expert-level kiss. Just enough tongue. A nibble here and there.

He licks my earlobe. I nuzzle his neck. He presses himself closer.

"You wanna do it, Lizzie?" he whispers.

The magic moment comes to a screeching halt. I'm pissed all over again. "Not even a little," I tell him, sitting up.

"Why not?"

"Are you crazy?" It's such a ludicrous question I don't even have an answer for it. Like, just no. "I came here to tell you I'm busting out tonight, and to ask if you wanted to come. But never mind after that crap you just pulled."

"Is that you I hear, Lizzie?" Scarlet calls out.

"Um, yeah," I yell back.

"Are you out of your tent?"

"Sorry. It's my IBS again." It's the only legit excuse I can think of.

"Hurry up then," Scarlet says. "I'm coming to check on you in a minute."

"What's IBS?" Ari asks.

I don't care if he knows about my poop attacks now that I

found out what a repulsive horndog he is. "It's like Montezuma's revenge. Only for life."

"Is that something you bring back from your fancy vacations?"

"Yeah. I mean, it's basically the runs."

"Gross."

"Whatever."

"Ari, are you and Lizzie talking now?" Jed yells. "You know that's not allowed after lights out."

"No," Ari yells back, then whispers to me. "Go ahead. I got you covered. I owe you one for taking things too far, too fast before. Sorry again."

I have no choice but to trust him. I grab my headlamp, sling my pack back over my shoulders, and set off running. Ari makes a big deal of opening and closing his zipper as loud as he can. Crashing out of his tent. Making the loudest fake fart noises ever. His Oscar-worthy performance almost makes me want to forgive his rude transgressions.

"Jed! Scarlet! Help! I think I caught Lizzie's IBS!" he moans. "My stomach is killing me!"

I keep laughing and running, faster than I ever have before. I'm so happy to be free, I might even be producing endorphins.

I have no idea where I am or where I'm going. I can't see two feet in front of me, and I don't even care. Everything's going to be fine. Anywhere is better than Camp Smiley. I keep moving.

And then I hear a noise.

An animal noise.

Bear? Coyote? Mountain lion?

My heart starts racing. *I'm too young to die. I don't want to die a virgin. Please don't let this be happening now.*

"Don't come any closer!" I yell at whatever is stalking me.

More creepy noises. I whirl around. My crappy headlamp finally fixates on the killer animal. It's a baby raccoon.

I stare at him. He stares back. His expression is a mix of *don't mess with me, GTFO*, and *how YOU doin'*. He's the Joey from *Friends* of raccoons. Like he might go back to his little raccoon house, shrug off his little leather jacket, light a cigarette, and start bragging. *You shoulda seen the hot chick I met in the forest tonight.*

"What's your issue? Get out of here! Shoo!"

He doesn't move. If he could laugh, I bet he'd be busting a gut. *Yeah, and she thought she could be the boss of ME. Ha!*

I rifle through my backpack and throw a beef jerky at him. He picks it up with his cute little paws—the guy might be a dick but his hands are adorable and his masked face is pretty dope too—sniffs it, then tosses it back on the ground.

"You have good taste," I tell him. "My dog Poochie has a less discerning palate. I mean, she eats bull penis all the time. She probably would've gobbled that jerky right down by now."

Just thinking about Poochie makes me homesick. I have no idea where I am. The initial rush of excitement over running away has worn off. The problem with being so impulsive is that it makes all my half-baked ideas seem so solid until they inevitably go bad. I remember another quote: *The trouble with trouble is, it starts out as fun.*

Now I'm scared. I feel so alone. I hate being alone.

I dig in my pack some more, hoping something sparks a brainstorm about what to do next. I keep a running conversation with my raccoon friend to calm my nerves in the meantime.

"What am I going to do now? How can this toilet paper help me get out of here?" I muse, holding up the roll of singleply. "You might as well rub sand on your butthole, it's so rough. I'm guessing raccoons have like a self-cleaning butt, or anuses of steel that pinch everything off perfectly so there's no residue. Or that maybe you don't mind residue, because you're a wild creature and you're more concerned with finding food and not getting eaten than worrying about an itchy ass. Right?"

He cocks his head and I swear he nods.

"Got it," I say, holding up the roll and giving it a shake. "You don't mind having an itchy ass because you're too busy trying to stay alive. Which means this toilet paper is of no use to you or me right now."

I toss it back in the pack and grab a handful of power bars and my water bottle. It's only half full. I probably won't starve out here, but I will have to find water soon or I'll dehydrate and turn into jerky myself.

"See these energy bars? BTDubs, they taste like dirt. Good luck swallowing them without tons of water. You'd probably choke. My water tastes like egg farts. I guess maybe you have a nice fresh stream somewhere around here? Well good for you, because egg fart water makes me dry heave."

Mr. Raccoon hangs on my every word. He's growing on me. I show him my glasses. They haven't helped me spy the nearest town yet, but at least he seems to like them.

"These? Are for reading. The only good thing about being at Camp Smiley is no school and no reading. You're lucky you're a raccoon and don't ever have to do either."

My raccoon makes a little purring sound.

"You know what, Bandit? You're pretty cool," I tell him. "I hope you don't mind if I call you Bandit. . . ."

I'm pretty sure my new BFF Bandit smiles.

"Is there *anything* in here that's going to help me find civilization? Let's see . . . I have purple pedicure flip-flops. A pedicure is when you paint your toenails so your feet don't look gross."

I pull off my fake Tims and knee socks that used to be white but are currently mud brown. "Look how badly I need a pedi, Bandit! I have blisters. Pruned-up skin. And check out these parasite bites."

Whirrr-purr-purr, says Bandit, a concerned look crossing his masked face.

"Oh thanks, you're sweet," I tell him. "I know they're still probably the prettiest feet you've ever seen out here. But believe me, they normally look so much better than this."

Bandit picks up the beef jerky and gnaws on it thoughtfully.

"Glad you're enjoying that now. I personally cannot stand the smell, but I guess with a crusty butt and eating roadkill and whatever you do out here in the woods, you're used to rank odors."

Bandit polishes it off and gets to work on washing his cutie little face with his cutie little paws. I want to hug him and pet him. I wonder if he might let me. I decide he probably would.

"Bandit, you're making me so homesick for my puppy Poochie."

I reach back into my pack and my hand lands on Buddy. I get another one of my great ideas: what if I throw Buddy over Bandit, scoop him up, and then tie it around me with him in it like a Babybjörn? We'll share protein bars and secrets. He'll fight all the bears and coyotes and mountain lions and Ursula and anything else that wants to hurt me out here in the dark.

He'll be my furry friend until I find a town, and then make my way home.

I creep closer to Bandit. He smiles wider, so I figure he's into it as much as I am. Closer. Closer. I fluff Buddy into a mini-parachute, holding the corners and letting the middle bubble up in the wind. Buddy flutters down on top of Bandit. He looks surprised, then pleased.

I'm just about to wrap up my little bundle of awesomeness when Bandit starts hissing and spitting and blowing a fit. He kind of almost scratches my arm. It doesn't break the skin or anything, but it maybe leaves a mark. Who knew such cute hands had such big claws?

I scream and jump back, letting go of the corners of the blanket as I do. "Chill out! I was just being friendly! You could have just said no thank you!"

Bandit scowls at me and runs off.

DRAGGING BUDDY BEHIND HIM.

I do not take kindly to having my baby blanket stolen by some two-faced baby raccoon that made me believe we were friends. I sprint after him.

"GET BACK HERE WITH MY BABY BLANKET!"

"LIZZIE, GET BACK HERE RIGHT NOW!" Scarlet screams at me from somewhere far away. I keep running. Screw Scarlet.

Sticks and rocks and thistles bite into my bare soles—why did I have to try and bond with Bandit by showing him my beat-up feet?—but Buddy is worth any pain the woods can dish out. I need to get him back. I've never a spent a night without him before and I don't want to start now.

I've almost caught up to Bandit when something grabs hold of my ankle.

"AHHHHHHHHH! LET GO OF ME!"

A branch snaps. I fly up in the air. And then I'm hanging upside down. Swinging by one leg.

I'm completely stuck.

Bandit stares at me thoughtfully. Then he basically laughs his raccoon ass off and runs away.

"ELIZABETH FINKLESTEIN, TELL ME WHERE YOU ARE RIGHT NOW!"

I try to loosen the noose from around my ankle, but it's impossible to wrestle myself upright. It's not like I have abs of steel. And any time I get even slightly close to reaching the rope, it tightens around my leg.

My ankle is being suffocated. I think it's broken. Going to be cut off? I have zero coordination with two feet. I would be the world's worst foot amputee.

"LIZZIE!"

It's either let Scarlet know where I am or wait until whoever set this trap comes back to check on it. I'll probably have dehydrated into jerky and starved to death by then. And even if I'm found before that happens, I still might wish I'd dehydrated and starved. Because the person who set this trap might want to, like, sell me into slavery or roast me alive over a spit and eat me for dinner. F my luck.

I have no choice. "I'm right here!"

"Come here this instant!" Scarlet bellows.

"I would, but I'm kind of up a tree," I yell back.

"Then come down!"

"No. Like, hanging from a tree," I explain. "By one leg. In some sort of trap."

Scarlet has me keep talking until she locates me. Then she climbs the tree better than any monkey, shimmies out onto a branch, and pulls me up there with her. Then she cuts the rope and climbs back down before helping me do the same.

The lecturing starts when I'm safely on the ground. "You may not realize this, but we don't own these woods. We share the wilderness with hunters, trappers, wildlife, and insects, all of which can be extremely dangerous to a lone camper," she says, shaking her head angrily. "Director Willis is *not* going to be happy when he hears about this."

"I'm sorry. Do we really have to tell him?"

"What did you think you were doing, Lizzie?" she yells, ignoring my question. "You could've gotten killed out here! You're lucky that was just a rope and not a steel trap. Your foot could've been chopped off! Not to mention there are all kinds of wild animals out here—"

"I know. I made friends with one!"

"Stop trying to make everything a joke," Scarlet says. "We'll discuss the consequences to your actions tomorrow. Tonight we just need to get some sleep. Now let's go."

I try to follow her but my ankle won't cooperate. "I think it's broken."

Scarlet sighs and drops to her knees. She massages my foot, probes different bones, makes me twist and turn it into all sorts of painful positions. "It's not broken," she concludes. "Just sprained. It'll be good as new in a few days. Lean on me and let's get you back to camp. I have first aid supplies there."

I put my arm around Scarlet and limp/hop alongside her. "Do you think we could go find my baby blanket first? The raccoon I met earlier stole it."

She stops short. "What?"

"A raccoon took my blanket."

"Lizzie, I've just about had it with your stories."

We start walking again. Back toward camp. Not the way Bandit headed.

"Wait," I say, remembering the almost-scratch. "Could I get rabies from him?"

She sighs. "Rabies. From a nonexistent raccoon. I don't think so."

I imagine what my funeral will be like after I die from rabies. Scarlet will feel terrible she didn't believe me about Bandit. Jem will try to give a eulogy but fail because like she said, all our escapades would scandalize the grown-ups so she has nothing to talk about up there. Ari will shake a fist to the sky and yell, *Why did I try to get in her pants instead of finding out what a great person she is while I still had the chance?* Mom will wail, *I wasted all these years on prescription drugs when I could've spent them working on my marriage and hanging out with my daughter.* And my dad will finally admit, *Hey, I was a selfish jerk and it's my fault she's dead. If I hadn't left during her formative years, she would never have gotten in trouble with the police and I would've loved her enough not to send her to that horrible camp.*

"Lizzie! Did you hear me?" Scarlet's voice brings me back to reality, where I am not dead yet but would rather be than go back to Camp Smiley.

"Huh? No, sorry."

There's a howl off in the distance. Odd chirps that are probably huge bugs and like, spiders and bats. And I cannot. Even. Handle. This.

"I said, do you have anything to say for yourself?"

I stare into the darkness and do a quick inventory. I used to have everything I wanted, except maybe an intact, fully functioning family. And now all I have is a rabid scratch on my arm. A sprained ankle. A missing baby blanket. A hole to poop in. A shovel to dig it with. Single-ply toilet paper. A roughed-up butt from it. Unbleached, ginormous tampons. Parasites in my legs. Parents who don't care about me. Friends who have no idea where I am and no way of saving me.

"Nope. I've got nothing," I tell her.

Scarlet makes me wait in front of her tent. She comes out carrying a white plastic splint. She puts it on me and gently tightens the gray Velcro straps around it.

My ankle has its own heartbeat. Ka-thunk. Ka-thunk. The boot makes me look like Bigfoot. My escape plan sucked. I hobble back to my own tent.

"No more stunts, Lizzie. I don't want your attitude and behavior negatively affecting our group dynamics. Let me tell you, getting the silent treatment tomorrow until your peers can assign you a consequence for your actions is going to suck," she says, zipping me back in.

I try to relax through the noise of unseen forest critters, the pounding of my heart, the deep, black, never-ending darkness. I wish I was snuggled up with someone cute, and he only wanted to spoon and talk instead of getting all handsy. But I'd settle for any human contact, really. Even a sleepover with Chandra would be preferable to being all by myself in this tent.

I crave Buddy. His soft, tattered silk edges. His fluffy, cottony middle. The stitching that says how much I was loved and adored when I was brought home from the hospital. I start to cry again. I wonder if I'll never stop.

WANTED

FOR BLANKET STEALING

BANDIT THE RACCOON

$1,000,000 REWARD

chapter

12

At some point I guess I finally fall asleep. But it's not like I get the recommended eight hours or anything. Light filters through the fabric walls of my tent at dawn, waking me way earlier than any normal human should be up. I limp outside. The sun is just rising.

Scarlet and Jed glance up at me from where they're sitting. They go right back to talking over coffee. Chandra is busy playing with a stick in the fire. No one says anything. Whatever. They're mad. Fine. Who cares.

Jack appears from behind some trees, carrying his toilet paper and shovel. He looks like he swallowed a bitter pill. I look away. How embarrassing. Sam is crouched near the reservoir, so I clomp over to her.

"Hey."

She gives me a little wave. I give her the hairy eyeball. She shrugs and shakes her head like *what can I do?* I guess this is the silent treatment Scarlet was talking about. As advertised, it sucks.

Sam is trying to make a fire with some sticks. She's sweating. Nothing is happening despite all her effort. I feel sorry for her.

But then a little plume of smoke appears in the nest of dried leaves and grass. Sam chucks the sticks, drops to her knees, and starts blowing. Out of the smoke comes a spark.

"Yes!" Sam crows.

The spark fizzles out. No fire. Sam still grins. She likes failure?

"I'm so almost there, Scarlet!" she yells triumphantly.

Scarlet walks over and surveys the faintly charred nest. "You absolutely are!"

I don't get it. They are celebrating nothing. And then Chandra walks over carrying a burnt stick. It's nothing to celebrate either.

"Look!"

She gives it to Scarlet like a preschooler proudly presenting her mommy a misshapen lump of clay. Scarlet ooohs and ahhhs over it. WTF.

"That's the best one I've seen in a really long time, Chandra. Great work!"

"I found a sharp rock that looked like an arrowhead this morning," Chandra says. She's so excited, her words come tumbling out on top of one another. "And then I stumbled across the perfect stick. I got a hot coal from the fire onto the end of it like you told me to, let it burn for a while, and scooped out the burnt part with the rock. Ta-da!"

"That's really awesome," Scarlet tells her. "Come on. Let's go put it to good use. Jed and Jack are probably done making the oatmeal by now."

This place is even more insane than I realized, I think. *I NEED to get out of here.*

Leaves rustle overhead as we walk the wooded path back to where the fire is. I look up, hoping maybe it's Bandit and Buddy. But it's Ari. He's crouched on a branch above us, a finger over his pursed lips. *Shhhhh.* He pounces down to the ground. "Rawr!" he growls.

Scarlet throws a hand over her chest. "Are you trying to give me a coronary?"

"I was just trying to show off my superior tree-scaling skills." He laughs. "Not to mention my surprise attack ones."

Her hand falls back to her side. "Kudos on that."

He grins. "Kudos accepted."

He smirks at me. I try not to but I can't help but smirk back. The guy has alarming amounts of charisma. And he DID apologize for being an ass and then helped me escape last night, even if I ended up getting caught. Have to give him credit for that.

Back at camp, Jack and Jed are stoking the fire shirtless. While Jed's stomach is undefined, just smooth taut skin, Jack has an impressive six-pack. It's a waste of a perfectly killer body, seeing as he has such an unappealing—make that virtually nonexistent—personality.

"I made breakfast," Jack announces, holding up a spoon that looks like Michelangelo carved it. "Plus something to eat it with."

Jed gives him a fist bump. "See? You're still the same competent, accomplished, hard-working person you always were."

A flush burns up Jack's cheeks. That flash of a different person—maybe the one he was before he tried to kill someone—reappears, if only for a second. Even his abs seem momentarily happier.

"Awwwww, you're blushing!" Ari heckles. "Fag!"

Sam punches Ari's shoulder. "It's not cool to use gay slurs to mean 'uncool.' Geez."

Chandra, Jed, and Scarlet snap their agreement. Even I try to. Ari definitely picked the wrong word to bust Jack's chops with. But I also know what it's like to say the wrong thing at the wrong time—hello, dashcam video?—and to have everyone get on your ass about it. I guess it's something we both have to work on.

Ari kicks the ground with his un-Timberlands. "You losers are really getting on my nerves."

He storms off. Jed goes after him.

"I'm starving," Sam says, ignoring the drama. She fills her cup to the top with oatmeal. "I worked up a huge appetite hand-jobbing those sticks."

Chandra crinkles her regal nose. It seems to be her favorite facial expression. "Hand-jobbing?"

"Creds to Lizzie," Sam says with a nod in my direction. "She says making fire with sticks looks like a double-fisted hand job on fast forward."

Jack's mouth drops open. No doubt he's judging me, making the same incorrect assumptions about how easy I am as Ari did last night. I would set him straight but why bother. No one's allowed to talk to me anyhow.

"We need to have a serious discussion this morning once everyone is here," Scarlet says before Jack or Chandra can start slut-shaming me. "About last night, and what the appropriate consequences for what happened might be. Lizzie, the silence aimed at you will be over once we do that."

Oh joy. Can't wait. I sit. I stew.

The smell of the fire reminds me of a long-ago family vacation in Laguna Beach. Every night we'd make s'mores at the big fire pit overlooking the Pacific. *We'll never be that happy again*, I think. I realize we'll also never take vacation as a family again, happy or not. I stare at my oatmeal, a gaping hole forming in my stomach and my heart.

Jed and Ari reappear just as everyone is finishing up breakfast. Sam takes a finger and runs it around the inside of her cup to get every last oat. Chandra and Jack lick their unsanitary stick spoons clean. I empty my cup on the dirt. The pile of oatmeal sits there steaming. I sit there steaming.

"Go ahead," Jed says to Ari. "Tell them what you just told me."

Ari shuffles his feet. Dust settles on his socks and boots. "Sorry," he mumbles.

"Can you elaborate, please?" Jed prompts.

Ari stares directly at Sam. "Sorry I used a word that's offensive to the LGBTQ community."

"Are you apologizing only to me, or everyone?" she asks, giving him a death stare.

Ari shrugs. "Uh. IDK. You know . . ."

She stands up and sticks her hands on her hips. "I'll have you know I'm at Camp Smiley because the GUY I banged couldn't stop bragging about it to the entire school. So I scratched *fuckboy* into his car and took a bat to his taillights. And I would have gotten away with it, if it wasn't for the security cameras."

"Just like that Carrie Underwood song!" Chandra exclaims. Figures she listens to country.

"Huh," Ari says. "Sorry again. I had you pegged for a dyke."

Sam's eyes get all watery and I think she's about to mad-cry. But then she actually starts laughing. "You, me, and everyone else," she says, shaking her head. "And FYI, Ari? Dyke isn't PC either. It's lesbian, got it?"

"Let's discuss consequences for Lizzie's actions now that everyone is back," Scarlet says, then turns to me and adds, "You should be glad we weren't at Outpost when you decided to run away. I think you'll find your peers much less strict than Director Willis."

Chandra raises her hand.

"You don't have to raise your hand to speak here, Chandra," Jed tells her. "Just say whatever you're thinking."

She puts her hand down. "I think Director Willis should be the one to punish Lizzie, not us. And he actually *does* require us to raise our hands before speaking."

"I guess we're more informal on the trail. And here at Camp Smiley, we don't give punishments," Scarlet explains. "We assign natural consequences for poor choices. So let's talk about who was negatively impacted by Lizzie's decisions last night."

"We all were," Jack says, running a hand through his hair. His abs ripple. It's obscene. He needs to put a shirt on. "Because, like, we could already be packed up and heading out now. Instead, we have to spend extra time talking about this, which means we'll be hiking during a much hotter part of the day and it will be harder than it has to be."

"Good point, Jack. Anyone else?"

"Well, Lizzie obviously hurt herself too," Sam says, pointing at my splint. "Maybe that's consequence enough?"

Jed and Scarlet make eye contact. Jed's eyebrows shoot up in an unspoken question. Scarlet shakes her head.

"How about an apology like I just had to give?" Ari adds when he sees they're not convinced. He's really trying to suck up to me after last night. I'm touched by his remorse. I'm trying not to like him but I kind of still do.

"Maybe Lizzie should have to do something to actually help the group today, instead of holding us back," Jack suggests. I'm fine with being helpful as a consequence but offended by his implication that I'm normally a lame-ass. Even though I am.

Jed and Scarlet share another look. Jed nods. Scarlet smiles.

"That sounds reasonable. Let's put it to a vote," Jed says. "All in favor, raise your hand."

Sam, Ari, and Jack stick their arms in the air.

Chandra says, "I still think Director Willis would be more qualified to make this decision. Saying sorry and a vague," here she makes air quotes with her fingers, "*doing something to help the group* doesn't sound like it matches the severity of what Lizzie did."

"We appreciate your concerns," Jed says. "But Camp Smiley is a democracy, and here the majority rules. Lizzie, go ahead."

"Me?" I point to my chest. I'm hoarse from not enough sleep. I clear my throat. "What?"

"Your apology," Scarlet says.

"Oh. That. Okay." Normally I tell teachers and parents exactly what I think they want to hear, but so far, that hasn't worked for me in the wilderness. I go with brutal honesty instead. "I mean, I really miss my friends. And my bed. And my dog. And bathrooms. And showers. To be honest, I miss everything about my life. So when I talked to my parents last night and they didn't pull me from Camp Smiley like I thought they would, I ran away. Sorry for that, and for making us late this morning. I still don't want to be here, but I guess I have to make the best of it." *Until I can find another way out*, I silently add in my head.

I expect to get yelled at for telling the truth. Instead, this. "Thanks for articulating how hard it is to be out here," Jed says. "And how brave you have to be to accept the challenge. I'm sure you've just described how most of the group feels."

Ari, Sam, and Jack nod. Chandra shakes her head.

"Not me," she declares. "I'm happy to be here."

Of course she is.

We pack up camp and hike away from the reservoir. While we trudge through the forest, I ponder why I haven't been able to talk my way out of this situation yet. I've spent a lifetime talking my way out of *everything*. How are things any different now than when the judge said I didn't have to live in Africa or I got out of staying at Camp Greenlake for more than two days or even going to school when I'm not in the mood (which is, like, at least one day a week)? I don't come up with any answers.

I gimp along. Instead of breaking into two groups and letting the faster people run ahead like yesterday, Scarlet and Jed make everyone go at my pace. Even turtle-y Chandra has to wait for me to catch up.

"Sorry," I say. My ankle throbs some more. I'm getting a migraine from the hot sun beating down on my scalp. I'm starving.

"Can't you just *try* to go a little faster?" Chandra asks impatiently. Like she's not slow as molasses. She should be glad I'm hurt or everyone would be annoyed with *her* for being the slowest one.

I scowl at her but I attempt picking up the pace. It doesn't help much. Everyone hates on me silently. Today's hike sucks even worse than yesterday's.

Once we're deep in the middle of nowhere, Scarlet says, "I've got the best surprise for you today, guys. You're going to love this."

Sam points at something I'm not seeing. "Cool."

"What?" I squint off into the distance, hand on my forehead to block the blaring sun. It's just the view as always. Mountains and trees and birds and nature.

She nods at a stripped tree with little nubs coming out the sides and what looks like a dinner plate bolted to the top of it. "It's one of those Outward Bound things, I bet."

"Finally! Something rad to do!" Ari says. His whole body is vibrating with excitement.

The group stops directly below the tall-ass pole. "I'm going to grab the harness and carabiners. You guys decide the order you're going in," Jed says.

"We're climbing that thing?" There is not a chance I'm climbing that thing. No way. I hate heights.

Chandra stares up, eyes enormous. She looks like a deer in headlights. I hate sharing anything in common with her—especially after she wanted to rat me out to D-R-period Willis—but there's no denying we both want nothing to do with this latest activity.

"I'm going first!" Sam crows.

"I call second!" Ari yells.

"Third," Jack says.

I don't bother saying anything, because fear has stolen my spit. It feels like there's a wool sock on my tongue. And I AM NOT. GOING UP. THAT POLE.

"I guess you're fourth and last then, Chandra and Lizzie." Sam cranes her neck to see our ultimate destination. "Sorry. You snooze, you lose!"

I don't bother telling her I'm not unhappy with this turn of events. By the time they get to me, I'll just explain I can't do it on account of my migraine and ankle and stomach ache. Besides, I couldn't haul my ass up that pole if I tried. I have zero upper body strength.

Scarlet pulls out two different-sized vest thingies and metal clips from her pack. "Okay, what order did you come up with?"

"Me, Ari, Jack, Chandra, then Lizzie," Sam announces.

"I'm going to turn that around, then. I want you to go in reverse order today," she says like it's some sort of gift. "Those of you who always feel the need to be first, consider why you're compelled to do that. For those of you who prefer to wait until later, notice what it feels like to lead."

Sam lets out a little *awwww man* and Ari punches a fist in his palm. Jack shrugs, resigned as ever to his fate. Which leaves me, heart in my throat, intestines in an uproar, arms crossed. Scarlet still somehow manages to strap me into the harness and connects me to a long cable that's in turn connected to a series of other cables above the pole of hellishness.

"Scarlet, I can't. My ankle."

"You'll be fine."

"I have a headache. My stomach is killing me."

"Stop making excuses and climb," she tells me.

"But I'm deathly afraid of heights."

"Challenge yourself, Lizzie," she says. "If you fall, the cables will catch you. Nothing bad can happen."

"Yeah, but nothing *good* can happen either."

"You'd be surprised," Scarlet says.

"But . . ."

"No buts. Go."

I stare at the beast in front of me. The pole has to be a good thirty feet up in the air. And the climbing pegs stop before you even get to the top. So what am I supposed to do, heave myself up onto that dinner plate? Like, no. This is beyond stupid.

"Come on, Lizzie," Sam urges. "You can do it."

Ari nods. "You totally can. It's easy."

I roll my eyes at him. Easy for a monkey like him. Hard for a sloth like me.

"One step at a time, Lizzie," Scarlet tells me.

"Bird by bird." This from Jack. I whirl around.

"Did Elsa and Eddie kidnap you too?"

He looks at me like I'm insane. "What? *Bird by Bird* is my favorite book. It's about writing, but mostly just about life. See, the author's brother had a huge project on birds for school, and he waited until the night before it was due to even start. He was sitting at the kitchen table crying with a pile of books in front of him, and his dad told him the only way to get through it was to go bird by bird. You get it? When something feels too big to handle, you break it down into smaller pieces so it's not so overwhelming."

At least that explains what otherwise seemed like a really dumb tattoo. Scarlet is thrilled at our little bonding moment. "Jack, that was so kind of you to share your wisdom and knowledge with Lizzie," she tells him. "Lizzie, please thank Jack for his contribution and coaching."

I look up again at the pole and my stomach goes ham. "I'll be right back," I say, unclipping the carabiners, grabbing my shovel and toilet paper roll, and limping toward a bush that's far enough away to be noise cancelling and big enough to cover my butt. "Feel free to start without me!"

I dig. I squat. Wave after wave wrenches my guts. I figure everyone knows by now I've got stomach issues so whatever. I wonder again how my parents could think anything good could ever come out of this experience.

"Almost done?" Scarlet is standing right in front of me, frowning.

I let out a little yelp. "Didn't anyone ever tell you not to sneak up on people? Especially when they're in the middle of an embarrassing IBS attack?"

"Lizzie, we're waiting for you. No one can do the assignment until you do." She's calm but firm. "It's your turn."

I fill in my poop hole. She squirts sanitizer into my hands. I rub it in. We head back to the group.

"We're all in this together, Lizzie," Sam tells me when we get there. "We're here for you, so that means you need to be here for us too."

"Ugh," I groan, putting my hands on the first pegs and surveying the platform high above my head. It makes me dizzy just looking at it. I reach up with my left hand, then my right. Right foot, then left. I'm shaking and I'm only two feet off the ground.

"Come on, Lizzie," Jack urges. "Climb!"

Right hand, left foot. Right foot, left hand. I'm four feet up now. I can still jump back down and not get hurt, if I'm careful to only land on my good foot. I gave it a solid effort, right?

"Remember that you're not supposed to hold us back today." This gem from Chandra.

Hand, foot. Foot, hand. I'm higher on the pole than I am tall. The top is still miles away.

"Keep going! Just like that!" Sam says. "You're killing it."

I climb up a few more rungs. Then a few more. I'm at the halfway point. I make the mistake of looking down. I panic.

"I . . . I can't go any farther," I say, my voice quivering. This time I really mean it. It's like I'm stuck and I can't move an inch up *or* down. I am one with the pole. Forever.

Everyone yells encouraging things. But it soon becomes apparent no coaxing or complaining or coaching is going to move me.

Scarlet says, "You can let go now, Lizzie. Jack and I will lower you to the ground."

Even this is nearly impossible for me. How can I trust they'll catch me and I won't come crashing down? I peel my fingers from the metal pegs one clammy appendage at a time. I lean back. The cables hold me. I float to the ground like a dandelion puff.

"Good try," Jed says, patting my shoulder.

I want to cry. I don't. This seems to be par for the course for me at Camp Smiley. The counselors make us do things I don't want to do. I get upset and try not to fall apart in front of everyone. It's all such a waste of time and energy. I'm not learning anything.

"Next," Scarlet says, clipping Chandra into the climbing vest. "You are strong and in control. You can do this."

Chandra takes a deep breath, closes her eyes, and starts to climb. She has a running conversation with herself as she goes. Though I can't hear the exact words, it sounds like an argument. She's like a crazy homeless lady up there.

Chandra makes it a little farther than I did. Then she suddenly loses the fight with herself. She lets go of the pegs. Ari, who's the belayer this time, practically flies into the air. He recovers in time to get her safely back down.

"I tried," she says, grabbing her inhaler from her backpack and taking puff after puff. "I just couldn't do it."

"You'll get it next time," Jed tells her.

She shakes her head miserably. "I doubt it. I'm more the academic type. Athletics aren't exactly my forte."

No shit.

Jack clips into the harness without a word and starts up the pole methodically. He does great with the climbing, but once he gets to the tippy top, he's stumped. He's a big, muscular guy, and the platform he needs to hoist himself onto is tiny in comparison to his gigambo feet.

"Jed," he calls down. "What's the best way to get up here?"

"Whatever way works best for you," he replies.

Jack hesitates, reaching one hand up to the platform, testing it for stability, then bringing it back down to the pegs again. "It feels super shaky up there," he says. "How do people usually do this?"

"There is no usual," Scarlet tells him, then looks at us. "Why don't you guys give him some coaching?"

Sam puts a hand over her eyes to block the sun and goes into Captain Obvious mode. "Just get both hands up on the platform, put one foot at a time on it, and stand up."

Jack gives a few halfhearted tries but always ends up back in the same place. "It just seems impossible," he calls back down. "Are you sure it can be done?"

"Positive," Scarlet says. "What's the worst that can happen, Jack?"

"I don't know," he says. "I could make a bad decision?"

"And what if you made a bad decision? Would you—or anyone else—die?"

"I mean, no. I guess nothing terrible would happen," Jack says, moving again. Hands up. He slowly creeps one foot onto the platform. Eventually heaves the other foot up there and slowly, slowly stands up. When he's fully upright, he scans the horizon.

"Yeah. Cool."

"You just have to trust yourself, Jack," Jed tells him. "Trust that you know what the right thing to do is, and that you'll do it."

He nods and gazes out over the treetops. "That's not going to be easy after what happened."

"Have faith. Now time for the best part," Scarlet says. "Jump. We'll catch you. Think about what you want to leave behind when you leap, and what you hope to leap into."

Jack thinks for a minute, then steps off the platform into thin air. "I have to admit, that was pretty awesome," he says after landing, a small smile forming around the corners of his mouth.

Jack is a totally different person when he's not busy being depressed. His eyes have this soft glow that makes them look like they're dancing. And his smile. It's sweet in a lopsided, goofy way. Right now he looks more like a happy little boy than the broody-moody guy he normally is.

"My turn!" Ari says, and scampers up the pole once he's clipped into the safety gear. He's swinging and grabbing and scrambling like it's the most natural thing in the world. He practically cartwheels up to the platform, screams, "I'm the king of the world!" and then throws himself off with the same enthusiasm.

"What did you leap away from and into?" Scarlet asks.

"Sorry, I wasn't really thinking about any of that stuff. ADHD. What can I say." He shrugs and bounces around on the balls of his feet.

Next Sam makes her way up the pole, not going as fast as Ari but not as slow as Jack (or me or Chandra, for sure). She gets herself onto the little dinner plate okay too. But even though she looks cool as a cuke up there, the pole is shaking like a junkie needing a fix. "Stop moving the pole!" she yells down at us.

"That's you," Scarlet calls back up to her. "It's your body's natural reaction to perceived danger. Don't worry, we've got you."

"What? That's crazy. I'm totally calm."

Sam's words say one thing and the pole says otherwise. And when it comes time to jump, her body agrees with the pole. She just can't make herself do it. Minutes pass. Still nothing. No matter what we say, she won't go.

"Hey Sam, guess what? You have to come down now," I finally yell up to her. "Because I decided I really want to try again. I need to redeem myself or I'll be, like, regretful forever."

It's a lie. I have zero regrets about not finishing the assignment. I just feel sorry for Sam, all stuck up there.

"Really? Okay. I guess I can do that for you, Lizzie," Sam says. She crosses her arms over her chest and leans back. After landing, she walks over to me with the safety vest. "It wasn't nearly as scary as I thought it would be. Your turn."

Everyone stares at me and waits. But I only said that stuff to get Sam out of a tough situation. I thought that was obvious.

"I, uh . . . changed my mind," I finally say.

"Conceive it, believe it, achieve it," Scarlet says, clipping me back into the safety vest. "Let's go."

"Do I have a choice?"

"We always have choices in life," Scarlet says, nudging me back toward the pole. "I'm here to help you make the right ones."

I start climbing. Slowly, slowly. I get to the same point where I was stuck last time. And I'm about to quit again when Scarlet tells me something rather disconcerting.

"Not to worry you, Lizzie, but the belaying line is stuck at the moment. It won't catch you right now."

"WHAT?" I look down to see if she's kidding, but she's busy tugging on the cable. It doesn't look like anything is happening. Maybe she's serious?

"See if you can go a little farther up, that might get it loose."

Looking up makes me even dizzier than looking down. I'm nauseous. I can't do it.

Then I remember that dumb *bird by bird* story Jack told me before. *Rung by rung*, I tell myself. *Just take it rung by rung.* I start climbing. Pretty soon, I'm at the top. Not on the plate thingy, but close to it.

"Can I come down yet?" I ask Scarlet. My voice is shaking but I'm surprisingly okay otherwise.

"Not quite," she says. "But I almost have it. If you can just go a little higher . . ."

I'm almost positive she's bluffing now. She's smiling, and I kind of doubt she would be if I was about to maybe die. But do I actually want to test whether I'm right? Not betting my life on it.

So I grip onto the platform and put my good foot on it. Next I haul my hurt foot up there. The boot provides a surprising amount of stability. I feel totally balanced.

"That's it!" Sam yells. "You did it!"

Ari has two fingers jammed into the sides of his mouth and is whistling so loud my ears hurt. Jack gives one of his whoops. Even Chandra gives a *woo-hoo*.

Scarlet tells me the line is clear. I guess I'll never know for sure if it was ever actually a problem. I jump. I'm dandelion fluff again.

Jed announces that I've completed my consequences for running away. He says I allowed us to move forward instead of holding us back by getting Sam to come down off the pole. He also compliments me for having the balls to get back up on it myself.

I can't stop smiling. I'm actually embarrassed by how proud I am of myself at the moment. This doesn't mean I hate Camp Smiley any less. But it does kind of mean I like myself a little more.

chapter

13

The residual good feelings from making it all the way up the pole don't even last an hour. It starts drizzling during the second half of our hike. Which turns into a downpour when we get to camp. By the time we're done setting up our gear, everyone and everything is sopping wet. The white plastic splint around my ankle is crusted in mud. My foot is filthy.

Our tents get soggy. All the sticks and grass are too soaked to make a fire. Dinner is cold and so are we. Jed tells us to hunker down in our sleeping bags right after we eat. Scarlet says we should use our time to journal and meditate but I don't bother. I'm bored and lonely.

Frustrated and pissed off.

Sad and tired.

Every time I think Camp Smiley can't get any worse, it does. I want to get out of here more than ever. I NEED to get out. It might have to wait a few days, until my foot is feeling a little better, but after that—watch out. I toss and turn and itch and miss Buddy and listen to the raindrops on my tent all night.

In the morning, the sky is clear again. Steam is rising off the puddles left behind by the storm. Mosquitoes dive bomb everyone. Scarlet and Jed sit a little ways off in the distance, far enough to get the point across that we're on our own when it comes to breakfast but still close enough to keep an eye on everybody.

We try unsuccessfully to get a fire started. Jack comes the closest, getting a spark but no actual flame. We give up and eat our sawdusty, prune-y energy bars.

Sam pulls at the bottom of her shorts. Her inner thighs each have a wide, red stripe on them. "Shit, this hurts."

"Chub rub is the worst," I agree. Just another reason to avoid hiking and jogging and working out in general.

"You think that's bad?" Ari says. "My balls are so chafed, I'm going to be walking like I fucked a horse today."

My unwanted crush on him remains despite the disturbing news about his nuts. There's just no predicting why one thing instantly curbs my attraction to someone and another doesn't. Like why are chafed balls fine, but when my last boyfriend got a bad haircut I had to break up with him immediately?

I idly examine my legs. The parasite bites seem to be getting better from what I can see. They're kind of fading into little pale pink blotches and don't itch as much anymore.

Except the ones covered by my Bigfoot boot, that is. Those itch like hell. And when I scratch them, they hurt like hell. I undo the Velcro and take the splint off to see what the deal is under there.

"Nasty," Ari says when I set my swollen ankle free. "It looks like you poured a bag of Flamin' Hot Cheetos on it."

He's right. Between the deep purple bruising and the irritated rash, it's turned a color not found in nature. I rake a nail over the itchiest part. It starts to bleed. It must look enticing to the mosquito that lands there. I smack it away. More pain. "OW!"

Chandra's hands have been stuck in her pockets ever since she finished her breakfast. Even though her fingers are hidden, I can see she's wiggling them around in there. "What in heck are you doing?" I ask her.

She shrugs and looks pained. "Nothing."

"Is that some kind of relaxation exercise?"

Sam snaps. "That's it! I just figured out what you're obsessed with—masturbating!"

"That's not it at all!" Chandra yells. "I would never . . . you know."

"Why not?" I ask. "I mean, who knows better than you what you like and how you like it?"

"Shut up!" she says, even as her hands continue moving.

"So if you're not playing the girl version of pocket pool, then what are you doing?" Ari asks.

Chandra tears up and presses her lips together. "Nothing."

"It's obviously not nothing," he says.

Jack emerges from the woods, single-ply in hand. His poop schedule is just as predictable as he is. He tucks the roll back in his backpack and sits down next to Ari.

"What's going on?" he asks.

"I can't talk about it in mixed company," Chandra says, a flush creeping up her cheeks.

She gets up and walks over to her tent. Sam and I follow. My ankle hurts more than I expected it to without the splint on it. I basically hop over on my good foot.

Chandra scowls when she sees us. "What do you two want?"

"We want to help," Sam says. "Right, Lizzie?"

I nod. I'm actually not convinced I care. But okay.

Chandra shifts from one foot to the other. She looks like a little kid who has to pee. Finally she throws her head back, screams, shoves her hand down the front of her khakis, and scratches violently.

"I can't stand it one more second!" she yells. "I wish I could stick my entire hand up there!"

I start giggling. Sam tries not to, but pretty soon she's laughing along with me. Tears start rolling down my face again, but at least this time it's because the situation is so hilarious.

"It's not funny!" Chandra protests. "Do you think I could have parasites in it?"

"I mean, maybe," Sam says. "You should probably ask Scarlet to take a look."

Chandra's eyes get deer-in-headlights huge again. "At my . . . you know? Are you crazy?"

I shrug. "She's trained to handle medical problems. I'm sure she'd do it in the privacy of your tent. No big."

"Yeah, it'd be just like going to the gyno," Sam says.

"I've never gone to a gynecologist," Chandra replies, more horrified than ever.

"Not to state the obvious, but like, it's a good idea to get checked once you're sexually active—"

Chandra gives Sam a withering look. "Which is why I don't need one yet."

"Oh. Wow." Sam's mouth falls open and she turns to me. "She's a virgin. I thought those were a myth by junior year. Like unicorns."

Like me, I want to add, but don't. Everyone always assumes I've done more than I have. I'm used to it.

"Kindly shut up about the status of my hymen and help me," Chandra says. "Something that doesn't require Scarlet looking at my privates, please."

"Honestly? You probably just have a yeast infection from sitting around in wet underwear all day," I tell her. "You just have to take a pill and put some cream up there and you'll be fine."

"Okay, fine. But where am I going to get pills and creams?"

"Hey Scarlet, can you come here a second?" I yell, waving her over.

"What's up?" she asks when she gets to where we're standing.

"What's up is my ankle really hurts and I think the rash is getting worse from being in the soft cast," I begin.

"If this is an attempt to get out of our hike today, it's not going to work," she tells me.

I lift up my foot so she can see the Flamin' Hot Cheetos tinge.

"That looks like it might be getting infected," she admits.

"Yeah, and it's not just me," I tell her. "Show her, Sam."

Sam lifts the hem of her shorts. Blazing chub rub is on full display.

"Ouch," Scarlet says.

Chandra sticks her hands in her pockets and winces.

"Chandra has a raging yeast infection, and Ari says his balls are so chafed it feels like he had sex with a hedgehog," I finish.

Scarlet sighs. "It doesn't normally rain out here this time of year," she says. "Especially that much. We were kind of unprepared for it. Let me go have a chat with Jed so we can figure out what to do."

We head back to the fire and sit down with the boys. Scarlet walks over to Jed. I can see her gesturing to her thighs, crotch, and ankle. He says something. She nods. Scarlet returns holding a medical kit.

She hands a tube of Vagisil to Chandra. "Believe me, you're not the first to have this problem on trail," she says. "Put this on the affected area as often as you need to. We'll add an oral antifungal to that when we get to Outpost tomorrow."

Chandra disappears into her tent with it. The next thing we hear is *ahhhhhhh!*

Sam gets Gold Bond powder for her legs. Scarlet tells her to share it with the boys. Ari seems delighted by the prospect of giving himself what he calls "ghost balls."

"Greatest feeling around," he says.

I get antibiotic cream for my infected bites. It does nothing to stem the itch. It does everything to attract mosquitos. I kill four before I even finish rubbing it in.

"Jed and I decided we should stay put today," Scarlet announces. "We want to give everyone a chance to heal a bit before we head to Outpost tomorrow, so we won't hike. You'll practice skills instead."

If you had told me a few days ago I'd be practically wetting my rain-soaked granny panties over being allowed to sit around the woods all day, especially without my phone or Netflix, I never would have believed it. Back then, I had no idea what roughing it really meant.

"Wooohooooo!" I yell, swatting away another bug.

"The assignment for those of you who haven't made spoons yet is to work on those," Jed tells us. "Everyone else, try to get a fire going. Find your inner spark by creating an outer spark."

I hobble off with Ari and Sam in search of a fat yet flat-ish stick that might have potential for becoming a spoon. Chandra and Jack look for sticks and leaves that are dry enough to burn. We search under logs, pilfer low-hanging branches, gather twigs. None of what I find looks quite spoon-worthy to me.

"You think this would be good?" Sam asks.

I take the stick she's holding out to me and turn it over in my palm. "I'm pretty sure Jack and Chandra are going to give unsuccessful hand jobs to branches all day, so it won't really matter. I mean, we can't burn in the spoon indentation without fire."

She cracks up. I like that she gets my sense of humor.

"But yeah, it's perfect," I tell her.

Sam bends down and picks up another stick. "Ah-ha. Got you, sucker! Look, I found its twin. You can have it."

It's like she's giving me the last Birkin bag on Earth. I was never going to find a good one myself. Mostly because I wasn't looking very hard, but also because I'm not, like, the stick whisperer. "For me? Really?"

"Really."

"Thanks."

"No prob. It's nice to have a friend out here."

"It would be even better to have a friend to get *out* of here with," I reply.

"Maybe we can dig a tunnel out of here with our spoons once we make them." She laughs.

"You better make a huge fire today," I yell over to Chandra and Jack.

"You got it," Jack says, surprising me with one of his infrequent smiles.

I watch. I wait. I wonder how long it would actually take for me and Sam to dig an escape tunnel.

How to Make a Survival Spoon

1. Find a stick that's not too long, short, fat, skinny, hard, soft, moldy, slippery, wet, or curved. These exist only in fairy tales.
2. Settle for the least ish of the above. Wait for someone to make fire.
3. Wonder how you will ever procure a hot ember from fire, place it in the center of the stick, blow steadily until it burns a spoonish-shaped depression, and then get it out of there without scorching the crap out of yourself.
4. Hold breath when a single spark is produced. Exhale when spark is extinguished by the wind a second later. Roll your eyes as producer of said spark (Chandra) bursts into tears.
5. Give up. Eat with fingers.

14

No one ends up making fire. Or a spoon. We just get sweaty. And blistered. And frustrated. And annoyed. We eat two more cold meals. Wilderness just never stops sucking.

After dinner, Jed says, "For tonight's small group discussion, I want you to think about who or what you are missing most and why. Share what you'd say to that person or object if it was here with you right now."

Oh lord, more talking. I've had it up to here with all the over-sharing and feelings and TMI blah blah blah. Truth Circle makes me want to rip my hair out.

My hand flies up to my head the minute my brain brings up the word *hair*. I pat around, trying to figure out how my Keratin is surviving all the sweat that poured through it the past few days. Salt is the worst thing for chemically-straightened hair, and sweat = salt city. My curls/frizz will be back in no time. I can already feel a perma-bump forming where my ponytail was today; that's always the first kink to return. Not a good look.

"I'll get us rolling," Scarlet says. "I miss hanging out with my dad most, because he's always been my biggest fan. I have this vivid memory of when I was five or so. I was sitting on his lap in his Karmann Ghia convertible—he loved that car—and he was letting me steer. He leaned down and said, 'You can do anything you put your mind to, Pumpkin. Don't let anyone ever tell you otherwise.' So if he were here right now, I'd thank him for instilling such confidence in me. And if I ever win the lottery, I'm buying him that car again. He regrets ever selling it. Next, Jack."

Jack shifts uncomfortably. "Yeah, uh . . . I'd say I miss my little sister Chelsea the most, because she looks up to me so much. After all the stuff that went down, I pretty much don't feel like I deserve her admiration anymore. So I guess I'd tell her I hope that someday I can be half as good a person as she thinks I am."

"That's an awesome sentiment, Jack," Jed says. "But I'm sure you're every bit as good as Chelsea thinks you are."

He shakes his head. "I'm not. I won't ever be again. But thanks anyhow."

Ari goes next. "I miss doing art the most. I love the adrenalin buzz that comes from not knowing if I'm going to get busted, and having to finish fast and still make the whole thing look tight. I'd say, 'Hey, graffiti, I miss you, man. Let's go tag something.'"

"Art is a great creative outlet, Ari," Scarlet tells him. "And I'm glad you found your passion. In the future, though, you should probably spray paint canvases instead of walls that don't belong to you."

He gives her an eye roll to the next century. "That, like, misses the whole point."

"Just think about it," Jed tells him. "Your goal is to keep making art. Which they probably won't allow you to do from jail when you get arrested for defacing even more public property."

Ari shrugs. Jed sees it's a losing battle and moves on. "You know what I miss most when I'm out here on the trail? My mom," he says. "The way she smells like blueberry pie in the summer. How she always has my best interest at heart. That she believes in me even when I don't. I'd tell her, 'Mom, thanks for giving birth to me. Now come give me one those awesome hugs.' Sam?"

She gives him a look. "I guess I miss my friends most."

Scarlet tilts her head. "Care to elaborate?"

Sam shrugs. "I screwed everything up with them. Over a guy, which they could not believe and maybe I still don't either. Ugh."

"Was there something about this guy that your friends didn't like? Rightfully so or not?" Jed asks.

"You have to understand: I came out in seventh grade," Sam says. "I've been to every pride parade since then. I'm the president of the Gay-Straight Alliance at school. My mom is the president of the local PFLAG chapter. And I cheated on my long-term girlfriend with him. So I'm basically an asshole and I deserve them not talking to me."

"Have you tried apologizing to your girlfriend?" Scarlet prods gently. "Or explaining to your friends what happened?"

"Ex-girlfriend, and no. What's there to explain? It happened. I *wanted* it to happen. Which makes me as fake and phony as they say I am," she says, crossing her arms over her chest. I can see she's done talking about it.

"I miss Poochie because she's such an awesome dog," I jump in before anyone can bug Sam with another question. "I'd say, 'Poochie scootching moochie, you're my wittle scoopums.'"

Everyone stares at me like I'm going to say more. I am not. That's *exactly* what I'd say to her.

Chandra pipes in. "I miss being comfortable."

Scarlet nods. "Totally understandable. You give up a lot of comforts when you come to Camp Smiley. Tangible ones, like sleeping in a bed and showering whenever you want. But also more intangible things, like having your parents there to help you whenever you need them."

Jed says, "You have anything to add to that, Chandra?"

Chandra shrugs. "I kind of meant comfortable in my skin. I guess I'd say, 'I hope someday I'm the person I always thought I was again.'"

"Shit, me too," Sam says.

"Me three," Jack adds.

"I am who I am," Ari says. "But apparently who I am sucks according to my parents. Which is just as bad as not knowing who you are."

"I'm not who everyone else thinks I am," I say out of the blue. And it's true. I'm not a rich bitch like that video dubbed me. Not a slut, like every guy always assumes. Not an unmotivated, selfish jerk like Chandra implied during our conversation about college. Not, not, not.

"Interesting observations, everyone," Scarlet says. "Great job. Thanks for sharing. We'll delve further into the theme of identity tomorrow. It's the most important issue you'll tackle in your teen years and young adulthood. Time for bed now."

I lag behind when everyone else is busy zipping into their tents. I'm feeling desperately homesick. I want to stop THINKING so much all the time. I want Netflix and music and shopping and Jem back in my life again so I can turn my brain OFF. Even though I know it's a long shot—and will only serve to reinforce the annoying misconceptions everyone has about me—I decide to go for it.

"You know how you said if you ever won the lottery, you'd buy your dad a Karmann Ghia?" I ask Scarlet once we're the only two left outside.

"Yup. I totally would." She nods.

"What color?"

"Hunter green, just like the one he used to have."

"What if I told you I could totally make that happen?"

She raises an eyebrow at me.

"Seriously. I can be your lottery ticket. Just say the word, and I'll have it delivered to his house tomorrow. A hunter green one. All you have to do is let me go home, and it's a done deal."

Scarlet crosses her arms over her chest. She hasn't said anything—especially not no—yet. I try to close the deal.

"It'll make both our dreams come true. Right?"

I hold my breath. I think I might have her. Scarlet finally breaks her silence.

"Honestly, Elizabeth, I'm disappointed in you. I really thought you were starting to see the value in what Camp Smiley has to offer. But I guess we're just going to have to work harder until you truly know how all of this is in your best interest."

"Sorry," I mumble. "I was just trying to help. You, that is. Make your dad's day. But if you don't care about his happiness . . ."

"I don't want to hear another word from you," she says. "Now go to sleep."

chapter

15

But sleep eludes me, like the finer details of how to put all my great ideas into action. Without Buddy or Ari to keep me company, I have total insomnia. The sun blares me out of my sleeping bag at an obscene hour of the morning.

I'm already exhausted and in a horrible mood, but then I see that my ankle's an entirely new shade of angry. Doritos 3rd Degree Burn, maybe. It hurts like hell.

I hobble outside my tent. I'm the last one up, per usual. Chandra is sitting by where the fire should be if we could only make one, dark circles under her eyes. She looks like she's been crying again. Sam grunts hello, pats powder on her inner thighs, winces. Ari walks back from a "bathroom" break in the woods completely bowlegged.

"We can't get to Outpost fast enough," he says when he finally gets back to the nonexistent fire. "I need to get these damn clothes off. My balls are killing me."

"Tell me about it," Sam says, pointing to her chub rub.

I lift up my ankle so everyone can see it in all its Cheetos/Doritos-colored glory.

Chandra shudders. "That is disgusting."

I let loose with a tirade that's been building up in my head all night. "Like, how is anything going to be different even after we wash these uniforms? We'll just have to wear them for another three straight days without showering. And then what? Sam's chub rub will keep getting worse. Ari's balls will chafe some more. My leg will get more infected. And how is Chandra's yeast infection ever supposed to clear up if she's wearing the same pair of underwear all the time?"

"HEY!" Chandra yells. "Not in mixed company!"

Jack makes a face. "What's a yeast infection? Or don't I want to know?"

I shake my head. "You definitely don't want to know."

"Huh. The uniform doesn't bother me," Jack muses, smoothing his barely wrinkled shorts. His mood seems a little better now than when we first got to Camp Smiley. I wonder how it's possible that he's inching toward happier and more relaxed instead of crabbier and more pissed off like the rest of us.

"Yeah, but you're the only one," Sam tells him.

Everyone in the group halfheartedly attempts to make fire. No luck again. We choke down more sawdust energy bars with egg-fart water. I don't think anyone should be forced to live in such deplorable conditions.

Jed and Scarlet come to check on how we're making out. They've been having their usual morning coffee together. Over their very own fire. That we're not allowed to cook or dry our clothes over. Because we need to learn how to make one ourselves. It makes me angry AF.

"Come on, guys. Time to pack up your gear," Jed says.

"Be sure to hydrate," Scarlet adds. "It's an eight-mile hike back to Outpost."

Everyone scatters. Except me. I CANNOT take one more second of this.

"Get moving, Lizzie," Scarlet says.

I cross my arms. Shake my head. No way. I've had it.

"What's gotten into you?" she asks, taking a seat next to me. "You seemed to be doing so much better the past few days. You were caring and thoughtful of the rest of the group. Except for your pathetic bribery attempt last night, I was really starting to believe you were getting it."

I show her my infected leg. Choke back tears that are probably more mad than sad this time. Thanks, Mom and Dad. If what you wanted me to learn at Camp Smiley was how to be really unhappy, you succeeded.

"A nice hot shower and some antibiotics will fix that right up, I promise," she tells me. "I know being in the wilderness has been a struggle so far for you, Lizzie. But I want you to know I saw something really special in you when you helped Sam overcome her fears on that pole, and then you overcame yours. And when you fought for your friends' comfort and health when you knew they were hurting. You're a born leader. You'll do great things in life if you can just harness that power for good. Trust me."

I sniffle. Wipe my nose on my sleeve. A hot shower sounds nice. "Do we get to sleep in actual beds at Outpost?"

Scarlet nods. "And there's a mess hall where we eat communal meals. Made by our very own cook. She griddles a mean pancake. Whips up some great burgers and fries too. There's even actual silverware. And Willis stokes the campfire himself after dinner so everyone can make s'mores."

She's making Outpost sound pretty good. Not anywhere near as good as going home, but a nice interim stop until I can figure out how to get back to the Upper West Side. I'll go. It's better than staying here in wet clothes with no fire.

Now the only thing standing between me and a hot shower, real bed, decent food, and s'mores is an eight-mile hike on my infected, swollen foot. Wearing soggy socks, ill-fitting underwear, droopy khakis, and a mildew-y shirt and fleece.

"This uniform is the absolute worst," I tell her. "I can't believe someone ever thought this was a good idea. Hiking and camping clearly calls for stretchy, breathable fabric. Tech material that wicks away sweat and rain and then dries quickly. Pants and shirts and underwear and socks that cover all the right parts instead of chafing them."

If I'm an expert at anything, it's what to wear in any given situation.

Scarlet shrugs. "Totally agree. But Director Willis is a traditionalist, and these are the traditional Camp Smiley uniforms. Plus, I'm sure most parents wouldn't be pleased with the extra expense for those kinds of clothes when they're already spending enough to send their kids here."

"Wait. So our parents actually have to *pay* for these ugly things?"

"Yup."

I get a great idea. It's more well-thought-out than most. And it's completely possible if I can only get Scarlet on board. I make my pitch.

"What if some new uniforms got donated to camp? From Lululemon? Enough for everyone? Even you and Jed?"

Scarlet tilts her head like she's thinking about it. More convincing looks like it's in order. I keep talking.

"Think about it. Having comfortable clothes means fewer issues like Sam's chub rub and Ari's nut chafe and Chandra's yeaster. Fewer issues mean we can concentrate better and learn stuff faster. Learning stuff faster means we graduate sooner. Graduating sooner means parents pay less. Paying less is good because you said it's expensive here."

I'm on a roll. I love my idea. Camp Smiley wouldn't be nearly as bad in Lulu Wunder Under pants and Swiftly tech tops.

"That all sounds reasonable," Scarlet says. "But I unfortunately don't have any contacts at Lululemon, or have any idea how to solicit donations. So I just don't see it happening, especially in the time you'll all be here. Sorry, Lizzie. It was a nice thought."

I raise my eyebrows and stare at her. She's being so thick. "*I'm* your contact at Lululemon, Scarlet. *I'm* the donor. I'll order everything online, have it FedExed to Outpost, and we can be comfortable by tomorrow. It's an awesome idea, right??"

Scarlet thinks some more. "I'll tell you what—I'll mention it to Director Willis when we get back to Outpost."

"Do you think he'll say yes?" I squeal, throwing my arms around her and giving her a huge hug.

She returns it, but says, "I wouldn't get your hopes up, but I'll ask."

"When we have Lululemon uniforms, I'm banning khaki," I ramble. "Khak is wack. I can say with all confidence no one has ever looked good in khaki."

Scarlet laughs. "I don't disagree with you."

"Neither does Lululemon," I tell her. "Which is why they don't make stuff in guh-brown. I'm going with simple black and white for our new uniforms. It's classic, classy, and flattering on everyone."

"I love your enthusiasm and your giving spirit," Scarlet says. "But I have to warn you, Lizzie, it's a total long shot. Now let's go."

Scarlet helps me disassemble my tent and pack up. We rejoin the group. Everyone is waiting for us, cranky and tired.

"You wouldn't be so annoyed if you knew what awesomeness awaits us," I announce as we head off on our hike, Scarlet and Jed leading the way.

"Huh," Sam grunts. She's looking more chapped than even her thighs.

"If Director Willis says it's okay, I'm going to order Lululemon uniforms for all of us." I get that butterflies on a rollercoaster feeling just thinking about how much better everyone is going to look. I'm almost as fired up now as when I was sneaking out to meet James Franco.

"He'll never okay that," Chandra says.

"Why not?" I ask. "It won't cost anybody anything, and then we'll be comfortable on the trail. So we'll learn faster and stuff."

"For real?" Jack asks.

I nod, grinning.

"Yes!" Ari says, bow-legging along painfully. "Whoever said money can't buy happiness was wrong."

"He'll never say yes but I wish he would. I've never had anything from Lululemon before," Chandra muses. "I've always wanted those leggings the popular girls wear to school. My parents don't think they're appropriate, or worth the money."

"Well, now you'll have a pair of your own," I tell her. "And who knows? Maybe you'll turn into a popular girl too. Anything's possible, you know?" I can practically feel the full-on Luon fabric that's going to be covering my bod pretty soon. I can't wait. I'm so excited.

"Thanks, Lizzie," Jack tells me. "That's nice of you."

"I thought you didn't mind your uniform," I tease.

"I said I didn't mind it. I didn't say I actually liked it. New gear would be totally dope."

I can't wipe the silly smile off my face. Giving stuff to people in need feels awesome. Maybe I need to give my dad more credit. Maybe he left for Africa so he could feel this great every day, and not just because he hated me and Mom.

chapter

16

We trudge into Outpost that afternoon. I'm so excited to see actual buildings and bathrooms, you'd think it was a Waldorf or Ritz-Carlton. Funny how low my formerly high expectations for guest accommodations have fallen. Now as long as there's a roof over my head and a toilet in the near vicinity, apparently I'm thrilled.

Maybe this was what my dad wanted me to learn? If so— check. I can graduate now. Maybe I can convince D-R-period Willis to let me call him? And then I can head to Greece? Where I promise not to complain if my seat isn't in first class or the room on the ship is too small?

"Here's where us girls will be staying tonight," Scarlet says, opening the door to a cabin and ushering me, Sam, and Chandra inside. The guys keep walking to the cabin next door.

There are bunks with actual mattresses and actual pillows in here. Woohoo! The mattresses are two inches thick and covered in vinyl that will definitely crinkle every time someone rolls over, but who cares. And so what if the pillow is flat and dingy and has definitely had a date or two with some lice? It is my official new BFF. After crashing on the ground these past few nights, I'm sure sleeping here will feel like heaven.

"Pick a bunk, drop your packs, and let's get going," Scarlet says. "Time for some good old-fashioned talk therapy."

I hope my therapist at Camp Smiley is cooler than Ellyn at the Womyn's Centre who taught me the breathing exercises. She wore long skirts, no bra, and tall men's socks with felt Birkenstock clogs. I hated her.

I imagine I'll be meeting with an old guy who has a big nose and crazy wispy, all-over-the-place gray hair. I realize I am actually picturing Einstein and not even Freud in my head. I start to giggle.

Scarlet leads us to a row of teepees set up on the outskirts of Outpost. They are tan and tall and of course triangular. Or would that be cone-shaped? A pyramid? I didn't pay a lot of attention in Geometry.

Scarlet tells Sam and Chandra to wait outside for a minute. Then she reaches for the fabric opening, pulls it aside, and we walk in together. Light streams into the otherwise dusky room. Sitting in one of those barstool-height canvas and wood director chairs is I guess the therapist, who looks nothing like Einstein and everything like Blake Lively.

Her fashionable clothes, jewelry, and perfectly highlighted hair are not at all what I was expecting. She gestures to an identical director's chair set up next to hers. I feel like I'm a guest on a fabulous talk show during *Roughing It!* week instead of getting my head shrunken by a head shrinker.

"Hey, I'm Lake," she says, patting the seat of the open chair. "Come. Sit."

Lake = Blake? Maybe this is my parents' way of apologizing after they really thought about the terrible things I told them I'm being forced to endure out here? Maybe they felt so bad they got an actual star to bail me out of Camp Smiley? Maybe they finagled me a part in her next movie too? If so, I'm all in.

"Hey . . . B . . . Lake," I say, extending my hand. I'm grinning because I've survived the worst four days of my life and now I'm finally getting the hell out of here. And I have to give my parents credit—I appreciate much more how good I have it after my short-lived stint at Camp Smiley. Well played, Mom and Dad. Well played.

"You seem pretty happy for a girl who got sent to the wilderness a few days ago," Lake says, smiling back at me. "You're adapting well to Camp Smiley, I take it?"

A beam of sunlight peeks through where the three poles come together to form the top of the teepee. I notice something disconcerting: Blake is missing her famous mole. Crap.

Unless there was some presto change-o plastic surgery-ing since I've been gone, Blake is really and truly Lake. My assigned therapist. Not a celebrity. Which must mean none of this is a glorious set-up to get me out of here.

"Oh no," I tell her, my smile disappearing into a scowl. "I can honestly say I hate Camp Smiley. And I hate my parents even more for making me come here."

Lake doesn't bat an eye over my harsh words. "Yeah, I get that. I'd be pretty pissed if my parents had somebody grab me out of my bed in the middle of the night and sent me away without warning."

She stares at me. I stare back. I mean, we both already agreed this place sucks. Haven't we covered it all already?

"So, are you more angry with your mom or your dad at this point?" she asks once it's apparent I'm not offering up anything more.

So many thoughts race through my head, I don't know where to start. "They both suck equally, but for really different reasons. Too many to list, actually."

"We should start small then," Lake tells me. "One reason for your mom, one for your dad."

I stare up at the light filtering through the teepee top. I guess I could refuse to answer her, but it doesn't seem worth the fight.

"Fine. My dad sucks because he ditched me and my mom when I was twelve to go save the world. Who cares about your own family when there are poor people and weird animals halfway around the globe to take care of instead?"

"That must have been really difficult," she says.

I nod. I like that she's agreeing with me. I've never had a cool therapist before. Telling Lake the truth is a nice change from the lies I used to tell Ellyn. She kept a straight face no matter what outrageous thing I said. I told her one time my future career goal was to be a cam girl—I was all of thirteen—and that I'd already started "modeling" part-time on a fetish site, farting into the camera for any old pervert that asked. She seemed impressed and encouraged me to keep on "exploiting the patriarchy."

"I can imagine your dad leaving must have been very hurtful to you. How did your mom react?" Lake asks.

"She just went, like, boneless and helpless."

"Helpless parents are scary, right?"

"Yeah," I say, leaning forward in my chair. It feels like I've been holding these thoughts in FOREVER and they're all tumbling out now regardless of whether I want them to or not. I would never burden my friends with this kind of heavy emotional stuff. I like Jem and the rest to think I'm fun and freewheeling, not feel sorry for me. "My mom gave up without a fight. She just let him go like, *okay, whatever, you do you, don't worry about us.* And then her awful anxiety took over and, well, look at her. She's like permanently turnt with all her prescription meds. She might as well have left along with him."

"That's an interesting way to think about it," Lake notes. "Like they're both gone even though your mom is physically still there."

"Exactly."

"If I were you I'd feel pretty disappointed in the people you looked up to most," Lake says. "And really, really mad about it."

"Yup. And now what? My parents totally got rid of me by sending me here. I'm a homeless nomad living in the woods. FML, you know?"

"Yeah. I get it. So what do you think you can do with all that anger and hurt?"

I shrug. I can't do anything more than what I've been doing: Trying to ignore it. Trying not to think about it. Trying to figure out a way to escape. Muddling through until then. What other option is there?

"Have you told your parents how you feel?" she asks.

"There's no point," I tell her. And there isn't. I hardly ever speak to my dad and talking to my mom is a waste of breath. She doesn't remember our conversations the next day, seeing as they mostly happen at night before she goes to bed but after she's taken her Ambien. "It wouldn't change a thing."

"We can't change other people, that's true," Lake says. "But we *can* change ourselves."

"Yeah, but I'm not the one who needs to change," I say. "My parents do."

"Maybe you all need to change a few things," she suggests. "And then meet somewhere in the middle."

"I don't think so," I say, realizing she's not really on my side. I should have known. My parents are paying for this gig, so she's basically their employee. "I mean, shouldn't my parents accept me for who I am? And shouldn't they realize all the things they're doing wrong?"

"Shouldn't you all do that for each other?" Lake asks.

"No," I say, realizing what a mistake it was to open up to her. "That's not how it works. You can't just do terrible things and expect your kid to be okay with it."

"I think that's enough heavy stuff for today, Lizzie," Lake says. "I appreciate your honesty. Is there anything you'd like to ask me before we wrap it up here?"

Curiosity gets the best of me. I can't *not* ask. "Yeah. How do you manage to look so awesome out here in the woods?"

Lake flips her perfect hair over her perfect shoulders and laughs her perfect laugh. "Ha, thanks. There's a super-cute little ski town a few miles down the road, so it's pretty easy to keep a good look together. That's actually where I live, not here at camp. I just come a couple times a week to do therapy. These heels would not be a smart choice if I was hiking all the time, right?"

She crosses her legs, dangling the most adorable mule from her petite foot, all buttery Italian leather. She probably thinks I'm fawning over her amazing shoes. Okay, fine, I am. But I'm also thinking: so a cute little ski town is only a few miles down the road with designer clothes just waiting to be bought, and I'm stuck here at camp for teenage screw-ups wearing no-name fleece and khakis.

"So . . . same time, a few days from now?" Lake asks.

"Okay." Why not. I'd rather sit here than hike. I just won't tell her anything anymore. I'll talk about fashion and ish instead.

"I can tell I'm really going to enjoy working with you, Lizzie," Lake tells me. "I see that there's a really deep, well-meaning, sensitive person behind those walls you've built around your heart because of your family situation. And I can't wait to hang out with her."

Jack walks in as I walk out. He holds the tent flap open for me.

"Gallant," I say.

"My mother taught me to treat ladies with respect," he tells me.

"It's a dying art, and greatly appreciated."

"My pleasure."

I head outside. Funny how much more like myself I already feel now that I'm back in semi-civilization and about to be ensconced in Lululemon again. I just turned on my flirt as easy as if James Franco had actually shown up at the Standard that night. And for Jack of all people, who's cute-ish but not my type at all.

Scarlet is waiting for me outside the tent. "Isn't Lake great?"

"Sure," I tell her.

"You know what else is great?" she says. "A real shower."

I cannot explain how welcome this thought is. Under normal circumstances I wouldn't get excited about what is undoubtedly a tiny, slimy stall. But after days of only swiping at my face and arms and legs with parasite water, I am positively desperate to get in it. Mold and spiders and foot fungus be damned.

"Yes! Can I finally get rid of my tube of used tampons now too?"

"In the trash and not the compost though," Scarlet says, as if I'd put my bloody rags into the bin that gets spread on the vegetable garden.

We grab Sam and Chandra from their respective therapy sessions. Sam has an old lady who looks nothing like anyone on Gossip Girl. Chandra has a dude who actually does resemble Einstein. Freud's nowhere to be seen.

"Time to finally get clean!" I whoop.

"Thank God, I smell like pepperoni," Sam says, sniffing her armpits.

I point to my netherlands. "At least you don't smell like tuna." Hiking and sweating, bathing in parasite lakes, and unbleached organic tampons do not the best fragrance make.

Sam cracks up. Chandra winces. I don't imagine her yeast smells any better so what's she getting all grossed out about?

Scarlet drops us off at the bathroom and hands us each a pail with holes in it that contain some soap, baby shampoo, and a skimpy wash cloth and towel. They are rougher than even the toilet paper. I am going to have to be careful or my vajayjay will be sobbing by the time I finish cleaning her up.

We step inside the shower/bathroom cabin. I was right. The facilities are basically what you'd get in prison: three shower-heads sticking out of the wall. No stalls. No privacy. Nothing but open space.

AND I DON'T CARE I'M SO HAPPY TO BE GET-TING CLEAN. I start stripping off my clothes.

"Not to be weird, but like, is this going to be weird?" Chandra is standing in the corner holding her pail and looking terrified.

"Everything about this place is weird, who cares," I answer. I turn on the shower and get under the water. Heaven.

"I mean, like, getting naked together and showering right next to each other," Chandra clarifies. She still hasn't taken off one stitch of clothing. Sam is down to her sports bra and underwear.

"It will only be weird if you keep making it weird," Sam says.

"But, like, we'll all be able to see each other naked and . . ." Chandra trails off.

Sam makes a face at her. "And what?"

"Just that maybe we should take turns," Chandra says. "One person go at a time, so we can have some privacy."

Sam whips off the rest of her clothes and plants her hands on her hips. "Why? Because I'm a lesbian? I mean, a lapsed lesbian? Or whatever the fuck I am now? And the sight of you naked might make me go crazy with desire? Get over yourself." Sam whirls around, turns on her shower, and waits for it to get hot.

"No! I was just brought up to be modest," Chandra huffs, still fully clothed and not making any move to change that fact. "I'm not comfortable being naked in front of other people. Sorry, not sorry."

"Just get under the shower, Chandra," I tell her. "It feels so good."

But she's still staring at Sam. "But while we're on the subject, does this mean you're, like, bisexual now?"

"No, because that would mean I'm equally attracted to both genders, which is definitely not the case," Sam says, rolling her eyes. "So let's just say I'm somewhere on the very high end of the Kinsey scale, just not exactly where I always thought I was."

"No one is going to stare at you or lust after you or whatever it is you're afraid of, Chandra," I tell her. "Just get yourself clean. Especially your yeasty cha-cha."

Chandra still doesn't move from the corner. "So do you think you'll date another guy? Or go back to girls? Or what?"

"I don't know! What do you care? Just because I've dated a lot of girls doesn't mean I see every single person on Earth with a vagina as a potential partner, so it's not your concern." Sam squirts shampoo in her palm and starts sudsing her fauxhawk. "But since you're so worried about it, let me set your mind at ease. You are not even *close* to being my type. For one, I dig blondes. Two, your butt. Too big. Three, your tits. Not big enough. Four—"

"You don't have to be mean," Chandra says. "I'm already self-conscious enough about my body as is it."

"Well, you don't have to be stupid and self-absorbed," Sam tells her, soaping up her body. "News flash: the whole world doesn't revolve around pretty, perfect, juicy you."

"Sam, chill," I say. I don't think Chandra means to be any of those things; she's clearly just sheltered and has zero clue. "Think of this as an educational opportunity. Maybe Chandra's never met a gay . . . I mean formerly gay . . . you know what I mean . . . girl before. Be cool. She's just curious. Right, Chandra?"

Chandra nods. She takes off her shorts, shirt, and socks but keeps her underwear on. She creeps over to the unused showerhead, turns the faucet on, and waits. Then she gets under the water, still in her underwear, and screams.

"AHHHHHHHHH! IT'S SO COLD!"

"Reason five, because you're a dumbass," Sam says. "Turn the handle the other way."

"I already did that," Chandra protests.

"Try again," I tell her.

She does, and the water gets hot immediately.

"See?" I tell her. "Even though you're standing here not quite naked in front of two girls you barely know, on a slimy floor, using an off-brand shampoo, it's the best shower you've ever had, right?"

Scarlet opens the door a crack and yells, "Five-minute warning, girls!"

"Ugh," I groan.

"Seriously, why?" Sam groans along with me. "And sorry I jumped down your throat, Chandra. Truce?"

CAMP SMILEY
RULES OF THE TRAIL
(To be signed by all campers)

➺ **Teamwork makes the dream work.** I will lead when I am called to, follow when it's called for, and engage all my teammates in the search for solutions, resolutions, and meaningful experiences. I will give of myself generously and accept assistance graciously.

➺ **Conceive it, believe it, achieve it.** I will think carefully about who and what I want to be, have faith in my abilities, invest myself fully in all my pursuits, and keep striving until I reach my goals.

➺ **Today's struggles build tomorrow's strength.** I acknowledge that no matter what has happened in my past, I alone have the power to change my future. I see now that my problems do not define me. I am capable of great things in life.

➺ **I *wish* is a dead end; I *will* is an open road.** Wishing things were different won't change anything—I must commit to taking action on my own behalf. Going forward, I pledge to gain control of my emotions, stand up for what is right, and live my life authentically. I recognize that I am responsible for my successes and failures; I know I will not be awarded what has not been earned. I understand my flaws and strengths and am actively working on both. Starting today, I promise I *will*: change, grow, and flourish.

Signed: *Elizabeth B. Finklestein* **(under duress, bitches)**

chapter

17

Later, when we're putting on our freshly laundered uniforms in the cabin—even right out of the dryer they're still stiff and uncomfortable—I catch a glimpse of myself. The mirror over the sink is not actually made of glass, but of some other kind of warped, fuzzy, semi-reflective metal. It's like one you'd find in a funhouse that makes you look way fatter or way skinnier than in real life, or shorter or taller. So I can see myself, but not as clearly as normal.

Maybe that's why the girl staring back at me looks nothing like the person who was forced into the wilderness a few days ago. My hair falls in beachy waves past my shoulders and there's not even a hint of the hideous frizz that usually overtakes my head when I forgo my potions, lotions, and heat-styling tools. My face is tan, without the hassle of all that contouring and mascara-ing and bronzing. And the spray of acne that has never left my forehead all these years has mysteriously vanished. I have to think the janky mirror makes people look hotter than normal; it would just be too weird if misery somehow suits me.

"Are you in love?" Sam asks, breaking into my deep thoughts.

"God no," I tell her, still checking myself out. "But sadly, still crushing despite concrete evidence that I shouldn't be."

Sam snorts. "So you want to get with yourself? Remind me to fall asleep fast tonight, before you start rubbing one out on the top bunk and making me seasick from all that rocking."

"Gross!" Chandra says. She's sitting on the bunk across from ours.

I look at Sam and laugh. "I wasn't referring to me. Even though I must say, I do look pretty damn good for someone who's been living out in the woods."

"Who then?" she asks.

I give her an embarrassed little shrug.

"Don't tell me. It's Jack,"she guesses.

"Wrong."

"Come on, I see the way he looks at you."

"Yeah, like I'm a total idiot."

"He likes you," Sam insists. "I can tell."

I sit down next to her on the bottom bunk. "If you must know, it's Ari."

"Why? He's so rude," Chandra interjects.

I shrug. I can't explain why I catch feelings for one particular person and not another.

"Jack's way nicer," she adds.

"I don't know what to tell you," I tell her.

"Ari's not worth pissing off Director Willis by having inappropriate contact with him," Sam says. "Don't even think about it."

"Ugh," I tell Sam. "I already did, a little. Which is probably why I can't stop thinking about him."

"You have some serious issues, girl," she says.

"Well, our parents definitely think we do." I grin back at her. "Or we wouldn't be here."

Dinner is delicious as advertised. I gobble down two burgers, a plate of fries, and three ears of corn. I avoid the beans. I'll probably never be able to look at a can of Bush's again after having them for dinner—usually cold—every single night out on the trail.

I'm practically in a food coma, but I refuse to go back to the cabin before I get my s'mores. D-R-period Willis makes a big deal of lighting the campfire. He doesn't have to search for dried grass or twigs or logs, of course. He uses crumpled-up newspaper and fire starter logs. And he doesn't sweat it out with sticks to get a spark like we have to, either. He just takes out a long-ass BIC and voila.

Flames crackle in the newspaper and spread to the logs. The fire is roaring a minute later. It seems pretty unfair to make us put in such a huge effort to get the same result when it's really this easy.

Willis raises two hands to the sky like a cut-rate late night televangelist. "Give us a sign that this group is growing stronger every day, making better decisions, and becoming whole again."

He lowers his arms and basically makes jazz hands at the fire. It lights up in all the colors of the rainbow.

"Ooooooooooh, pretty," Chandra murmurs.

"Please," I whisper to Ari. "I saw the empty packets of Mystical Fire when I threw away my tam—" thankfully I stop myself before I complete the word tampon, no need for him to be thinking about my cycle, "—trash earlier today."

Back in the day, my dad was chief of the Adventure Girls troop. Usually our "campouts" were at hotels with indoor waterparks, but one time we went upstate and stayed at an actual Girl Scout camp for a weekend. It was kind of like Outpost, but better, because we wanted to be there and we were with our dads. No one could've been prouder when my father gave a speech that ended in the same kind of fireworks Willis just put on. I honestly believed he had real magical powers until I Googled it one day. Like everything else about my happy family, the magic turned out to be a lie.

"Those spectacular colors in the fire signify the wonderful progress this group is making for the most part," Willis says, passing out Hershey bars, graham crackers, marshmallows, and really long forks with wooden handles to roast them with to everyone but me. I give him a questioning look but he shakes his head no.

I want a marshmallow. Why can't I have a marshmallow? I consider stealing what's left of the bag and stuffing them all in my mouth before Willis has a chance to do anything about it.

"Now did anyone notice the log over here that still hasn't caught fire?" he continues, pointing to a sad stump swollen with moss and lichen. That thing will never burn. Too moist. He should know that by now. Even I know it after four days in the woods. "Don't be this log. Share your light with the group. Be a beacon of hope and achievement, not the damper that thwarts everyone from giving their best effort."

He's looking right at me. Is he implying *I'm* the swollen wet lichen log?

Everyone else turns and stares too. Anyone who hadn't noticed I wasn't roasting a marshmallow along with them before knows now.

"There are no participation medals at Camp Smiley," Willis goes on. "What you get is what you've earned. Nothing more and nothing less. Hard work is rewarded. Bending and breaking of rules is not. It's as simple as that. And so, Elizabeth, because you ran away, staged a rebellion that resulted in not completing one day's hike, and attempted to buy your way out of Camp Smiley through bribery, you will not get to enjoy s'mores with the rest of the group tonight."

"What?" I yelp.

"You also won't have the pleasure of speaking to anyone starting now and extending until the next time you're back at Outpost again."

So no one's supposed to talk to me for the next four days either? I already completed my consequence for trying to run away. I got everyone medicine for their aches and pains, so that "rebellion" was actually a nice thing. And even Scarlet said my efforts were pretty good recently, minus the bribery part. "That's not fair—" I begin.

"It's very fair. I also hope you'll use the quiet time to consider how you might make friends without trying to buy them with expensive clothing from Lululemon."

"What? We're not getting our new uniforms now?" Ari complains. "What about my balls?"

I am fuming. Everyone else looks really bummed too. Even Chandra. How's she ever going to get in with the popular girls without her Wunder Under leggings?

chapter

18

Scarlet drops us girls off at our cabin. She pretends I don't exist and talks directly to Sam and Chandra instead. "I have to go to a staff meeting now, but I'll be back to check on you all later. Be good and don't get into any trouble."

"I'll make sure Sam and Lizzie don't speak to each other," Chandra tells her. "And that everyone stays put."

"I appreciate that," Scarlet says, picking up my boots on her way out. "I'm taking these, by the way. Director Willis thinks Lizzie is a flight risk. He wants to make sure she's at the Skype meeting he's scheduled with her father first thing in the morning."

Sam rolls her eyes at me in solidarity. I roll mine back at her. Sam turns back to Scarlet. "Lizzie says, *this sucks.*"

Scarlet sighs. "Lizzie needs to realize that playing by the rules doesn't always equal giving up or giving in. Sometimes, the best thing we can do for ourselves is accept the wisdom other people are trying to pass on to us."

She walks out the cabin door carrying my boots, hooking the rickety old latch from the outside as she goes. Like that would ever keep someone in who really wanted to get out. It looks like it's hanging on by one rusty nail.

I hop up onto the top bunk, totally dejected. Play by the rules and accept others' wisdom my ass. Even when I *try* around here, it's not enough. Everything I did—well, with the exception of my first run into the woods—was to help other people. Chandra would have her entire arm stuck up her chacha right now if it wasn't for me. Sam's chub rub might have festered into flesh-eating bacteria. Maybe Ari's entire ball sack would've fallen off. Who knows? Even me offering to buy Scarlet's dad his dream car or get Jed a record contract would've made their lives better. But instead of thanking me, D-R-period is acting like I'm the second coming of Hitler, leading everyone into evil.

Screw them all. I didn't even do anything to deserve to be here in the first place. If only I could figure out how to get to that ski town Lake mentioned earlier. I'm sure I could find a way to the nearest international airport from there and hop a flight to Greece before anyone ever figured out what happened.

Once the thought forms in my head, it sticks. It's a plan. I'm out of here. Tonight.

It's not hard for me to stay awake while everyone else passes out from exhaustion. Settling in is always tough for me. And without Buddy, it's been harder than ever. I watch and wait as a soft, dusky glow fills the cabin. Having that many stars light up the sky out there would be totally romantic if only I had someone to get romantic with in here.

Instead, I have Chandra. Her mouth is wide open, an arm thrown over her head, legs askew. She looks like a big old rag doll. I'm pretty sure Armageddon couldn't wake her.

And then there's Sam in the bunk underneath me. She snoring, and the noise she's making sounds like it belongs to a delicate little bird. I stifle a laugh at her high-pitched *wheep-a-wahnah*.

The good thing is, they're both asleep. Even better: Scarlet still hasn't returned from her "staff meeting." My guess is there never was any meeting at all and she's doing it in a teepee with Jed right now.

This is my chance, I think. I sit up slowly. The vinyl covering the mattress crinkles and Sam's snoring stops. I freeze in place. It starts back up again. And for my next move. . . .

I can't figure out for the life of me what my next move should be. I lie back down and turn over onto my stomach. The vinyl crinkles more. "Shhhhh," Sam says.

When I hear her breathing slow and feel confident she's sleeping again, I peek my toes over the mattress. Then I start inching the rest of my body in that direction. Shins, knees, thighs, until I'm folded at a right angle and everything from the waist down is hanging off the top bunk.

I'm almost there—about to let myself drop quietly to the floor—when something takes hold of my splint and I come crashing down on my good foot. It's like the ankle noose, only worse this time, because it's a person and not a rope. Arms and legs are all over me. A hand claps over my mouth.

"Ursula! Let me go!" I whisper.

"Who the fuck is Ursula?" Sam whispers back.

"The octopus from *The Little Mermaid*?" I answer through her fingers.

"You're nuts, Lizzie," Sam says. "And you scared the shit out of me."

I peel her hand away from my lips. "I didn't want to wake you."

"So you weren't going to say goodbye this time either?"

I shake my head. "Sorry. This place is the worst. I figured if you didn't see me, it would save you from getting in trouble for not trying to stop me."

Sam nods over at Chandra. "Yeah, okay. I get that. But I can't believe you're leaving me alone with only her to talk to."

"Well, there IS another option," I say, another one of my great ideas forming in my head.

"Which is?" Sam asks.

"You could come with me! Then you'd have ME to talk to instead of her. I'm way more fun and you know it."

Sam laughs. "Yeah, but, like . . . what would we do even if we got away with it?"

"Who knows. Who even cares?" I tell her, really warming up to having a partner in crime. "Let's just go on an adventure. Figure it out as we go."

"This place sucks and I'm in no hurry to get home after how badly I screwed everything up," she finally says, lacing up her boots. "So why not? We'll be two badass bitches on the run. Thelma and Louise. I like that."

I have no boots since Scarlet took them. So I stuff my feet into the temporary flip-flops I found in my backpack. They're about as durable as a Kleenex but better than nothing.

"Come on, let's roll," I whisper, pushing my body against the screen. It doesn't budge. Apparently the latch is much more durable than I expected. I throw my weight against it harder. Still nothing.

"Here, let me," Sam says, giving the door a karate-style kick. It flies open with a huge creak. Chandra sits bolt upright.

"I'm telling!" she bellows.

Sam bolts over to Chandra and clamps a hand over her lips. "You're not telling anyone anything, you got that? You were fast asleep and you never saw us leave."

Chandra peels Sam's hand away. And then bites her.

"OW!" Sam growls.

"Chandra—" I jump in.

She shakes her head and sticks her fingers in her ears. "Tell Lizzie I'm not allowed to talk to her."

I try to reason with her. I go with phrases ranging from *What do you care* to *You'll like it even better here without me putting a "damper on your best efforts."* But even after I pull her fingers out of her ears, she won't listen to me.

"Let me go," she whispers fiercely. "I need to find Scarlet."

Desperate times call for desperate measures. I reach into my backpack and grab my phone out of the dark recesses of the most hidden pocket. I hold it up. Chandra gasps.

"Where did you . . . how did you . . . ?"

"If you dare peep a word to anyone about us leaving, I'll call your parents pretending to be the gyno and tell them your yeast infection is actually gonorrhea you got from banging all the guys at camp. Right now. I'm serious."

The truth is, my phone is dead. And I couldn't go through with my threat even if it wasn't; I don't even know Chandra's last name. But she can't be sure of any of that.

"They'd never believe you," she says, looking horrified.

"Well, they probably didn't think you'd ever gamble away your college fund either. But you did that, didn't you?" I say, going for the really hurtful stuff. "I'm a pretty good actress. But whatever, take your chances. What do I care?"

Sam and I head for the door. Chandra is bending over, her

hands on her knees. She's probably having another "asthma attack" that's actually an anxiety attack.

"What is your problem?" Sam asks, scowling back at Chandra.

"Just slow your breathing down," I tell her, channeling Ellyn from the Womyn's Centre. "Imagine a happy place. You'll be fine."

Chandra stands back up and sticks her hands on her hips. "No," she says. "No I won't. Nothing about my life is fine right now. It's a huge mess."

"What? Why? Keep your mouth shut and your parents still think you're a virgin. Promise," I tell her.

She runs a hand through her glossy mane. "Well, maybe I don't want to be a virgin anymore."

"Come on now," I say. "You don't actually mean that."

"And maybe I don't want to be here anymore, either."

"You don't mean that either," Sam says. "Of course you want to be here. You're happy to be here. You said so yourself."

"Maybe I changed my mind," Chandra says.

"You did not!" I say. "Honestly, you're the biggest try-hard I've ever met."

"What's worse than a try-hard who sucks no matter how hard they try?" Chandra asks.

"Is this a hypothetical question?" Sam says. "Because we don't have time for it. We've got to get out of here before Scarlet comes back."

"The answer is, nothing," Chandra announces. "I'm a total fail at Camp Smiley. I can't keep up on the hikes, my spoon is crooked and it dribbles, I'm too scared of heights to win at the pole climb or any of those stupid Outward Bound challenges, and I can't make fire. All this after I tried and failed to quadruple the money my parents worked so hard to save up for my future. Just because I was such a snob I wanted to go to a name-brand school instead of the crappy state one they could afford. Failure is stuck to me and I hate how it feels."

For the first time since I met her, Chandra is acting like an actual human. It definitely makes me hate her less. "I don't think it's snobby to want to go to a good school," I say. "Especially if you have the grades and the test scores."

"It doesn't matter now. I won't be going anywhere," Chandra says.

"That's a total bummer," Sam says, grabbing my hand and pulling me out the cabin door. "You should talk to your therapist about it."

But Chandra gloms on to us worse than that wad of chewing gum Jem accidentally spit into the back of my hair from laughing so hard at Mrs. Lemelson's regrettable new dye job in English class. "I mean, I've already crossed over to the bad side," she says hopefully. "There's no way to redeem myself. So why stop now?"

Sam and I give each other a look. "What are you trying to say?" I ask.

"I'm coming with you," she announces.

I ponder. Sam gives me a palms up and a shrug. I shrug back. I cave. "Fine. Just don't slow us down, okay?"

The three of us creep past the boys' cabin hunched over like old ladies. My splint and flip-flops make it rather hard to be inconspicuous. I think we've made it undetected when Ari shines his wimpy headlamp through the window.

"Busted," he snickers. "Where do you guys think you're going without me?"

"Anywhere is better than here," I whisper. "First stop, the ski town that's just a few miles away. After that, who knows. Wanna come?"

"Hell yeah," he says. "Let me out of here."

I unlock the latch and out pops Ari, followed by Jack.

"What the—" I say when I see him.

"I'll come along as protection," Jack says. "It's not safe for you to be walking alone in the middle of the night. I'll make sure I'm back before they ever know I left."

"I'm never coming back," Ari says, running ahead of us. "Not ever."

"We can take care of ourselves," I tell Jack.

"I was raised right, remember, Lizzie?" he replies. "I *want* to."

"Have it your way." I sigh, but I'm only pretending to be annoyed. I love that I'm not alone in this. I love that I pretty much rallied the entire camp against D-R-period. Wait until Chandra finds out how good being bad feels. She might even get addicted to it.

We tiptoe our way along the same driveway I watched Lake's car disappear down after our session today. There must be a road at the bottom of the hill. We can follow it to town, provided we can figure out what way town is.

This turns out to not be much of a problem: there's a little cluster of lights off in the distance to the right and absolute pitch-blackness to the left. To the right we go. Pebbles jab into the bottom of my foam flip-flops as we trudge along. Ari is now behind everyone instead of up front.

"What are you doing back there?" I ask him.

"You'll see," he says, sticking a thumb out and walking backward.

A pickup comes rumbling to the side of the road and stops. The driver rolls down his window and says, "You need a lift?"

"No," Chandra says, a hand flying over her heart.

I'm inclined to agree. I've seen enough *I Can't Believe I Survived* shows to know what kind of torture awaits hitchhikers who take rides from strangers.

"Sure, thanks," Ari says, zero hesitation. He tosses his pack in the front seat and hops in. "I'm Ari. You?"

"Shane."

"Thanks for the offer, Shane." I decline for the rest of us, even though he doesn't look like a serial killer. He looks more like Jed's clean, clean-shaven cousin. "I don't think we can all fit."

"There's plenty of room in the cab," he says, gesturing with his thumb at the back of the truck. There's a kayak paddle and a tire from a mountain bike rattling around back there, but nothing else.

"But there are no seat belts," Chandra says.

Ari rolls down the window. "You'll be fine. Town's only a few miles away, right, Shane?"

Shane nods. "Yup. I'm always happy to give counselors from Camp Smiley a lift to town when I see them. You aren't usually heading out this late, though."

"We were hoping to grab a drink before the bars close," I explain. "It's Chandra's birthday and we need to do some shots."

"I've never done that, either," she says as we climb in the back of the truck.

"Well, maybe you should," I tell her.

"Who knows," she says. "Maybe I will."

Chandra and I sit on either side of Jack. His arms are draped over our shoulders. I feel . . . something. Safe, I finally conclude. Like he's not one of those guys who's going to try something funny two seconds from now. I relax into him. Sam sits between his legs, leaning back against him, so I guess she feels the same way too. He steadies us all as we bounce around, unencumbered by seat belts.

The wind whips my hair in my face and I don't even care if it's getting curlier or messier or knottier. I'm oddly content, staring up at the stars, breathing in the warm night air. I feel the exact opposite of how I felt at Camp Smiley: happy, wild, free.

Shane heads down the main street of town. It is positively darling. There are a bunch of shops and restaurants, plus several boutique hotels and an old-fashioned movie theater with only three screens instead of twenty. The twinkling lights of civilization make me nostalgic. I had no idea the magnitude of my feelings for New York—and my real life—until I saw them.

But even though my hopping hometown is the city that never sleeps, apparently chic little ski towns in Utah do. They go to bed way EARLY. No restaurant or bar is open and it's barely past midnight. Shane pulls into a parking lot and gets out of the truck.

"I kind of figured nothing would be happening this late on a Monday night, but you guys seemed so excited I wanted to at least give it a shot for you," he says. "What can I say. That's Utah, man."

Ari pops out of the cab of the truck. "What the hell are we going to do now?"

"Geez, I'm even a failure at being bad," Chandra says.

"Don't worry, you guys. We'll figure something out," I say, even though I have no idea what that might be at the moment.

"I just have to do a few things inside and then I'll be happy to drop you back at Camp Smiley," Shane says, grabbing the kayak paddle and bike parts out of the truck. "Maybe one of you has some hidden hooch there?"

Shane disappears through the front door of what is clearly a ski shop during the winter. The window displays right now are more about biking, kayaking, fly fishing, and other outdoorsy activities I have zero interest in.

I pace, trying to think of what to do next. And that's when I see a flash of familiarity on one of the mannequins, that skinny upside-down reflective horseshoe.

She's wearing Lululemon! I just want to run my hands over some decent fabric and remember what it feels like to be comfortable.

"I'm heading inside for a sec," I tell the gang. "Wait here."

I push through the door. The jingling of bells announces my arrival. Shane is rigging the wheel that was in the back of the truck on a fat tire bike frame.

"I just have to finish setting this up for a customer who's coming to get it in the morning and then I'll give you a lift back," he says. "Sorry your friend's birthday got ruined. Director Willis probably kept you guys forever at one of his legendary late-night staff meetings, huh?"

"Right. You guessed it." I notice Shane's phone plugged in on the counter. "Do you mind if I use your charger for a few minutes? My phone just died on the way here."

Shane glances up at me from the bike again. "Sure, no problem."

I retrieve it from my backpack and plug it in. There's just a picture of an empty battery with the tiniest sliver of red on the end. It's going to be a while. "Thanks. Hey, do you take Apple Pay?"

"Yup."

I have another brilliant idea. I am full of them tonight. "I know it's after hours, but would it be cool if I bought some stuff? You know, as a birthday present to make up for not being able to celebrate with my friend."

"Go for it," he tells me. "Sale stuff is over in the corner."

I ignore the sale rack and head straight for the Lululemon one. Everything I was dreaming of buying online is here, in all the right sizes. I gather up something for everyone. Make that, a lot of things for everyone, including me, of course. I plunk the huge pile of clothes on the counter.

"You're getting all that?" Shane chuckles.

"Oh, I'm not done yet," I tell him. "Do you have any shoes that aren't, like, clip-ins for bikes?"

"I mean, not really," he says. "We're really more a gear than shoe store. But we might still have some Crocs in the sale bucket over there. . . ."

It's not the answer I want to hear, but okay. I already wore holes in the temporary pedicure flip-flops. "Great," I tell him, and start digging through the bin.

The only pair I can find that aren't, like, giant water skis are camouflage with fake fur on the inside. They'll have to do. I deposit those on top of the pile of clothes. At the last minute I grab a pack of neon Sharpies from a counter display for Ari, so he can do full-color graffiti in his journal.

Shane starts ringing things up, starting with the pens. "These are on sale too. Thought people would want to label their gear with them, but turns out most of our customers prefer good old-fashioned black ink."

"I like to live colorfully," I tell him.

My phone returns from the dead. I grab it. I have a bunch of texts. Twenty are from my mom the night I left, apologizing for having me hauled away but insisting it's for my own good. One is from my dad, telling me how much he loves me and how he wants to re-establish our relationship once I'm "in a better place."

And then there's Jem.

Where the fuck are you? You can't just disappear on me like that.

So what? You're just never going to talk to me again?

If I were you, I'd be PROUD AF. What you did was ballsy and hilarious. Be happy. Don't be a hater.

Ok, I probably should've taken the video down when you first asked me to. But everyone loved it. And you too, of course. So why?

Plus, I'd think you'd be happy for me. Now I have something big to put on my college apps: produced and starred in viral video. Received over ten-thousand views. Featured on TMZ.

Fine! I'm sorry. Satisfied? Not everyone has an in at Bowdoin, you know.

So her video of me went viral too? On TMZ, no less? Ugh. I don't even want to know how my mom and dad took that one.

Normally, I'd rush to assure Jem that I'm not mad and never was. I'm the always fun, always cool, always chill friend. Everything's a joke; nothing is serious.

But the truth is, I AM kind of mad. Even still. Most of the finer details of what happened that night I only shared with my BFF. They weren't meant for public consumption. And she shared them with the entire world.

"Where's the nearest international airport?" I ask Shane.

"Vegas," he says. "I'm actually headed there tomorrow for a bachelor party."

I'm willing to forgive and forget if you figure out how to get my passport to Vegas ASAP I type to Jem. *I'm coming to Greece. Get ready.*

Two seconds later, she's typing back. *So should I just go to your place and ask Marge for it or what?*

NO, I reply. *DO NOT TELL HER ANYTHING. Especially not that you talked to me. The 'rents want me to stay in the woods forever. Get creative and maybe a little criminal.*

I watch the three little dots dance on screen and expect a huge reply from the amount of time it's taking, but in the end, all I get is this: *On it. Talk later.*

"Uh, that'll be eight hundred and sixty-two dollars," Shane tells me, looking apologetic. "Don't worry if you want to put something back. I know being a Camp Smiley counselor probably doesn't make you the big bucks."

I smile. "Nah, it's okay. I just got a big birthday check from my rich grandma."

The transaction goes through. While Shane bags the stuff, I poke at my phone until I find the next available seat to Athens. The earliest flight I can get is a red-eye tomorrow. I buy it using one of my mom's credit cards, which I of course have memorized from using it so often. She'll never notice the charge until I'm long gone.

"Is there, like, a bus or a train from here to Vegas?" I ask Shane. "Or is an Uber or limo a better option?"

"Wait. So now you're buying a ton of presents AND taking her to Vegas for her birthday?" Shane asks. "She must be a great friend."

"She's kind of going through a rough time," I tell him. It's not even a lie. "And we all have the next few days off, so what the heck, right?"

He hands me four stuffed-to-the-gills shopping bags. "After that transaction, I have a lot more cash to gamble with," he says, staring at my huge haul. "If you want, I could drive you guys there tonight instead of waiting until tomorrow to leave. It would be nice to have some company."

"Yes!" I say before he has a chance to his mind. "Thank you!"

I forward the flight info to Jem, along with a text telling her I'll be in Vegas by the morning and she needs to somehow get the goods to me at least two hours before my flight. And to keep her mouth shut in the meantime. That last part worries me most, considering what happened last time I told her something on the down low.

"I'll be out in a few minutes," Shane says. "Just need to close up the store and grab a few things from my apartment upstairs."

"Great. One last favor—can I use the facilities?"

"Of course. It's over in the corner," he says, nodding in the general direction.

In the bathroom, I fling off my terrible, uncomfortable uniform and put on the wonderful, magical clothes. I look like myself again, except for the curly hair. Full-on Luon has never felt so good.

I stuff the crappy uniform in the trash and walk outside carrying my new loot. I go into my best Santa impression. "Ho ho ho! Have you been good little boys and girls this year?"

"Fuck yeah!" Sam says, running over to me.

"Come here, dearies, and see what Santa has for you!"

Everyone crowds around and I distribute the leggings and shorts and shirts and socks and underwear. Camp Smiley uniforms start flying into the garbage can as my friends ditch their terrible clothes for awesome new ones, right out there in the parking lot. Even Chandra forgoes modesty this time.

"This is the nicest thing anyone's ever done for me," she says, enveloping me in an awkward hug once she has the Wunder Unders on. I wriggle away, blushing.

Ari grabs his package and bows. "My nuts and I thank you."

"No, seriously," Chandra tells me. She's got tears in her eyes, but I actually think they're from happiness this time. "Thank you."

"I forgot what it felt like to be comfortable," Jack says. "I take it back. That uniform sucks."

He gives me an awkward side hug. I accept it. His heart beats slow and steady in my ear.

Sam starts jumping around in the parking lot. "You're the bomb, Thelma! Or am I Thelma and you're Louise? Whatever, woot woot to you!"

I get more than ever now why my dad likes helping people. It feels GOOD. Better than even buying things just for myself.

"It was nothing," I mumble, but I can't stop smiling. "And guess what else? Shane's gonna give us a ride to Vegas! We can have a whole day of fun there before my flight leaves for Greece. Who's in?"

"Me," Sam whoops.

"Me too!" Ari yells.

"Me three," Chandra practically whispers.

I give her a high five. "That's the spirit!"

Jack hesitates. "Sounds great, but I think I'll just head back. Thanks for the offer."

"You sure you wouldn't rather come with?" I ask, running my hands over the new leggings-and-tank-top combo. I'm so happy. So *comfortable.*

"I don't think I should. But I won't say a word to Willis or the counselors, promise," he says, pretending to turn a key at his lips and throw it away.

"You sure? It's gonna be lit."

He shrugs. "I kind of feel like I deserve to be at Camp Smiley. You know, for what I did. "

"What did you actually do?" I ask. I really can't believe he *meant* to almost kill someone. The more I see him in action, the more he seems like a gentle giant than the Incredible Hulk.

"I'll never tell," he says, and starts walking back toward camp.

"Here comes Shane," I say, rallying what's left of the troops. "It's time to PAR-TAY!"

"Ready?" Shane asks.

"Ready!"

I'm about to hop into the back of the truck when we hear the pounding of footsteps coming toward us in the darkness.

"Oh shit," Sam says.

"Busted again," Ari says, throwing up his hands in disgust.

I'm sure we all expect to see Willis bursting back into our lives, pissed as hell and spitting fire. But instead it's Jack. He's breathing hard.

"Sometimes, you have to say what the heck," he pants. "Isn't that your motto, Lizzie?"

I nod. "Yup."

"I don't know what it is about you," he says, shaking his head and smiling at me. A real smile for once.

"I do. It's that I'm FUN," I tell him. "And I get the feeling you haven't had fun in a really long time. "

He jumps in the back of the truck and pats the spot next to him. Is he flirting with me? Do I even kind of WANT him to?

I'm about to get in back with Jack and the girls when Ari says, "Ride in front with me? I want to show you something."

I hesitate. "Uh . . . okay?"

I'm not so sure I want to see whatever it is, given how he acted the last time we were alone. Still, I slide in first and he follows. It's a snug fit. I'm hyper-aware of him next to me and on guard. Just in case.

"You know how everyone is always, like, baring their souls at Camp Smiley?" Ari says once Shane hits the highway.

I look over at him. This is so not what I expected. "Yeah?"

He's staring straight ahead. "You probably thought I was just being a dick, never telling my own sob story, right?"

"I didn't think that." Not really, at least.

He turns to me. "Well the truth is, I honestly love what I do. I don't feel bad about it—I'm *good* at it. I don't feel like it's anything to apologize for. I want to make it my life. And yeah, I know technically there might be legal problems here and there but . . . do you know anything about street art?"

"Only the basics. Banksy or whatever."

"See, there's so much more to it than that," he says, sounding super excited instead of his normal sarcastic self. "Street art is, like, a global movement. It really says something, you know? And it's creative as shit, man. There's this one guy who makes his stuff out of chewed-up gum and it's beautiful, if you can believe that. Another uses mosaic tiles to make his pieces. This one girl—Swoon? She's my favorite. She does these hand-cut wheat-paste murals that are all about social justice and stuff. It's all so unique and inspiring, you know?"

"I can't imagine Director Willis likes your graffiti guy alter ego," Shane interjects. "He probably thinks that would be a bad influence on the campers, right?"

"Ha, yeah, that's why I pretty much keep it quiet when I'm at Camp Smiley," Ari tells him, nudging me with his leg like *Can you believe this guy actually believes we're counselors.* "I wish I could show you some of the stuff in my online portfolio so I could explain it better."

I reach into my backpack and take out my phone. There are no more messages from anyone, including Jem. I guess no news is good news.

"Wait, what?" he says when I hand it to him, a huge grin taking over his face. "You're the dopest chick I know."

I blush. I'm flattered. Maybe he's not a complete ass after all. Maybe he's crush-worthy still.

Ari signs into his Cargo Collective and hands me back the phone. "Here. Check it out."

I scroll through the photos he's uploaded. His bold, wild graphic designs are each punctuated with a huge schlong spurting out a rainbow of sperm. They're crude, rude, cool, and oh so Ari.

"You're really talented." I hand him the pack of neon Sharpies. "Look, I bought you these so you can do some full-color graffiti in your journal."

"Like I said, you're the dopest." He grins, stuffing them in his backpack. "It's so rad you get what I'm trying to say with my art, Lizzie. Most people don't."

I'm not sure what there is to get. He makes pretty designs. Featuring dicks. Jizzing. It's not that deep. "Really?"

"Yeah. Usually when I try to explain it's not really about a guy's junk, it's about spreading love wherever you go and the awesome possibilities in life, they're all like *what?*"

"Some people have no imagination," I tell him.

chapter

19

Ari passes out almost instantly after our big conversation, slumping into me. He's sharp and bony and there's no way I'm going to get any rest next to him. His pointy elbows keep poking me as he thrashes around in his sleep. There will definitely be bruises.

I stay awake and stare out the window instead. The scenery goes from mountainous and I guess pretty—now that I'm not being forced to live directly in it—to scrubby and brown to ugly and nothing. Just when I start to think we'll never see civilization again, bright lights appear up ahead. It's the Strip, in all its gaudy glory. I get the butterflies on a roller-coaster feeling. This is the best adventure yet.

I get even more excited when I get this text from Jem: *Proceed directly to the concierge at the Bellagio. Got a couple of surprises up my sleeve.*

"Hey, Shane, can you drop us at the Bellagio?"

I take it as a good sign that Jem has me heading to the poshest hotel in town. I take it as an even better sign that (a) she hasn't said she can't figure out a way to get me my passport, (b) no one seems to be tailing us, and (c) I haven't gotten any texts or calls from my parents or anyone from Camp Smiley. I can't imagine they'd think to track my phone, not after clumsy Eddie "lost" it on the plane.

"Sure thing," Shane says.

He drops us off there and the whole groggy crew stumbles into the lobby. From the opulent dancing fountains to the intricate glass art, everything about the Bellagio is rich and over-the-top. I realize now why Jem picked this particular hotel for our rendezvous: it's built to look like Lake Como. She knows how much I loved my family trip there. Mainly because we were still a family then.

Chandra turns in circles, trying to take it all in. "It's like heaven!"

"Whoa," Jack says, his eyes wide.

"No shit," Sam says, gaping around.

Ari gives high fives all around. "Me likey."

I tell them to have a seat, then walk over to the concierge desk. I wonder what I'm supposed to say when I get there. Everything I think of sounds too suspicious. I worry that wearing fake camouflage Crocs and a grubby white plastic splint in such a classy place will tip him off that I'm an escapee from Camp Smiley and I'll get sent right back there.

"Regina George, I presume?" The concierge greets me before I have to say anything.

Mean Girls is my favorite. Jem and I can quote every line. We must've watched it together a hundred times. I love that she picked a fake name from the movie for me to check in under. "Uh, yes?"

"Gretchen Wieners has reserved the Chairman Suite for your exclusive use today, complete with an early check-in," he says, sliding a little folder with key cards in it across the counter to me. "She said to tell you *I'm such a good friend.*"

I smile so wide I feel like my face might split in two. Leave it to Jem to apologize with *Mean Girls* jokes and by throwing money at the problem. The Chairman Suite is clearly the best of the best. Maybe, just maybe, I'll think about forgiving her.

"May I send your bags up to your personal butler?"

"I'm actually travelling light today. No bags."

"In that case, you'll find we have some lovely shops here," he says, handing me a brochure. "If you have the time and inclination, I'm sure you'll find something to your liking."

"Thanks." My heart rate speeds up as I read the names of the stores. Chanel. Armani. Hermès. Prada. Tiffany. All my favorites.

"Please do not hesitate to contact me should you need anything beyond what your butler Henri offers, Regina."

I gather everyone and we take the elevator to the top floor. I slide the key card in the door. We head inside the luxurious suite.

It's bigger than most apartments in New York. There's a fancy marble foyer, living room, dining room, two bedrooms, two baths, a fully stocked bar, and best of all—an automatic toilet complete with a heated seat and butt blow dryer. Just like the one I have at home.

"Holy shit!" Ari says, throwing himself onto the plush king-sized bed. "This place is bigger than my house!"

"It's twice the size of mine!" Chandra says.

I go to admire the view from the living room. It's stunning. Sam and Jack wander in with Henri not far behind them. He's carrying a silver tray with champagne flutes on it, along with a full bottle of Veuve Clicquot and a carafe of fresh-squeezed orange juice. A slim crystal vase holding a single red rose completes the picture. "A mimosa for you and your friends to start your day, Ms. George?"

"Why yes. How lovely. Thank you."

Henri pops the cork, pours champagne and OJ in equal measure, and hands us each a flute. We raise our glasses to toast.

"To Lizzie," Jack says.

"To ditching Camp Smiley!" Sam says. "Hey, do you mind if I borrow your phone, Lizzie?"

I hand it to her.

Chandra joins us in the living room. "Ari says he's going to blow dry away the chafing on that special toilet," she says. "I don't know if he's ever going to come out of the bathroom."

"So what's the plan now?" Sam asks.

Everyone stares at me. I honestly have no idea. Don't they know I'm a big picture person and I need someone else to figure out the details? "I think we need to wait to do anything until I hear from Jem again." I wing it. "Just make yourselves comfortable for now, okay?"

"Fine by me," Jack says, heading for a bedroom. "I'm exhausted. I'm going to catch some shut-eye."

This leaves me with just Sam and Chandra. Ari is still AWOL in the bathroom. I hear water running in there now. I don't blame him at all for jumping in the shower. The rainhead and steam combo here certainly beats the weak stream of the Outpost prison ones.

I plop down onto the couch and get snuggly under a throw. I can't believe how comfortable it is. "Let's see what's on Netflix."

The girls sit on either side of me. I click onto the latest season of *Orange Is the New Black*. The jail those women are in reminds me of Camp Smiley. Which reminds me that everything about this hotel is a jillion times better than being there. Camp Smiley can suck it.

Sam hands me back my phone. She does not look happy.

"What's wrong?" I ask her.

"I'm just annoyed that I actually let all that Camp Smiley bullshit get to me."

"Like, how?" Chandra asks.

"I was just thinking about how Jed and Scarlet thought I should apologize to my ex, and try to explain what happened to my friends. So I just did."

"And?" I ask.

"I texted them. Only my ex texted back. *k period*. I feel stupider than ever."

"Maybe your ex just needs more time," I point out. "And maybe everyone else isn't awake yet, and they'll surprise you with their reaction when they see your apology."

"And maybe they still hate my fucking guts," Sam says. "I should have just left it alone. Let things cool down some more."

I try texting Jem. No reply from her either. I have no idea what to expect.

We're on our fifth episode when I hear the door open. And then a very familiar bark. I fly off the couch and into the foyer.

"POOCHIE!" I scream, scooping her into my arms and giving her a giant hug.

She goes insane, giving me kisses all over my face, which by now has tears streaming down it.

"What are you crying about?" Jem demands. "You should be happy! Did you completely lose it out there in the woods?"

I barely register the roasting because MY PUPPY. IS. HERE. I don't think I've ever loved anyone as much as Poochie, or ever will. She's the absolute best.

"Poochie," I whisper over and over, covering her soft little head in kisses.

Jem points at my Crocs, which I am still wearing. They might be fugly, but the truth is they're really comfortable. "What are thoooooooooooooooose?" she yells.

I laugh, throwing one arm around her and holding Poochie in the other. "Hey guys! My best friend, Jem, and my puppy are here!"

"Hey," Sam says, waving at us from the couch.

Jem peeks around the corner at her. "Who's the lesbasian?" she whispers to me.

"What?"

"You know. The lesbian Asian girl? On the couch?"

"Oh, that's my friend Sam," I tell Jem. "And she's actually more homoflexible these days—"

"TMI," Jem says, holding up a hand.

Chandra walks over. "Nice to meet you, Jem. Can I hold your puppy, Lizzie?"

"I mean, you can try. But Poochie's not a big fan of people who are not me."

And she's not, usually. But Poochie snuggles right into Chandra's arms. Chandra heads back to the couch and the two of them start cuddling like they've known each other forever.

"Lesbasian, check. Brainy Indian girl, check. You befriended a whole rainbow of winners out there in the woods, didn't you,

Lizzie?" Jem says, laughing at her own "joke." "Looks like I got here just in time."

I'm about to tell her how my new friends are way cooler than she realizes, but I let the snarky comment slide. I have a lot to thank Jem for at the moment. No need to piss her off after everything she just did for me. I change the subject instead.

"How did you get Poochie and my passport and all my stuff without my mom getting suspicious?"

The tips of Jem's tiny shell-like ears turn magenta. It's my only clue that she has any feelings at all about our latest caper—in this case, pride in her ability to steal stuff without my parents figuring it out. "It was no biggie," she says, ears glowing.

"Come on, I doubt that," I say. "Anyhow, a zillion thanks."

"Dude, none of this was as hard as you think. I just snuck past the nighttime security guy who always sleeps on the job, used the keypad code to get in, went to your room, packed up everything, and left. Your mom never even knew I was there."

I grin at my crafty BFF. "Brilliant. But that still doesn't explain how you got here so fast."

"Oh, whatever." She waves a hand in front of her face. "No one was using the corporate jet, so I asked our pilot and he said yes. Zero skin off anyone's ass."

I walk over and start rummaging through the bag she's packed for me. A quick perusal confirms she's gotten EVERY-THING right, from underwear to swimwear to resort wear to evening wear. The collection she curated for me couldn't be more perfect.

I know I shouldn't belabor the point, but I can't stop thinking about the Camp Smiley edict *when you see something awesome, say something awesome.* "Seriously, I can't tell you how much I appreciate everything you've done for me. It was so incredibly generous of you—"

"Zip it, Polly Sunshine, I owed you for getting you in trouble over that video," Jem says. "Now let's hit the pool."

"Hey everyone!" I yell. "Pool time! Drinks are on me!"

"I don't have a bathing suit," Chandra says from the couch where she's still snuggling with my puppy.

"Follow me, you two," I say and wheel my luggage into the ginormous hall bathroom. I shimmy Chandra into a bright bikini that looks great with her coloring, and hand Sam a halter top and boy shorts. They're cute on her. Jem piles Chandra's hair into a messy, chic bun and does her makeup with an exaggerated cat eye and pink lip stain. Sam won't let Jem near her, even with just mascara. Instead, she puts on some lip balm and refreshes her fauxhawk with some water from the tap.

"Ready," Sam announces.

Chandra gapes at herself in the mirror. "I look like a prostitute."

"Yeah, but a classy, over-twenty-one one," Jem says. "And we need to be able to darty at the pool."

I toss Chandra a pretty white embroidered dress to wear over the bikini, along with wedge sandals. "Here. No more prostitute, right?"

She nods. "I know this was supposed to be, like, this big fun outing, but now that we're here, I'm kind of scared. I feel like it's just another bad decision on my part. Like, what's the point? I can't go home. If I go back to Camp Smiley, I'm in bigger trouble than ever. My parents are going to find out and be even more disappointed in me than they already were—"

"Slow down, sister," Jem says, rolling her eyes at me. "Is she always this much of a buzzkill?"

I sling an arm around Chandra, feeling protective of her. "She just has bad anxiety," I tell Jem, who rolls her eyes and heads off to get her luggage.

"Ugh, this is exactly how I felt before I took the ACTs," Chandra says. "Completely unhinged. I couldn't think of anything except how hard my heart was beating, and how fast my thoughts were racing, and how I was never going to remember anything, until I was pretty convinced I was actually dying. . . ."

"It's all going to be fine, I promise," I tell her. "Just try to have fun, okay? We'll worry about all the other details later."

"Did anyone text me back yet?" Sam asks. She looks worried too. We need shots to loosen up this crowd. Everyone's too on edge.

I glance at my phone. Nothing. "Not yet, but I'm sure someone will soon."

Jem comes back wearing a fabulous black bikini and an open-front embroidered silk cover-up. "Who's the total hottie in the bedroom?"

Figures she'd dig Ari. We generally have the same taste in guys. "He's taken."

She makes a face. "By whom? Not one of these chicks?"

I raise my eyebrows and give her a pointed look.

"Oh. Okay. Fine. Be greedy," she says. "Don't share with your best friend who just went through all the trouble of coming out here and saving your ass. . . ."

"Let's get the boys up," I say, ignoring her guilt trip. "I'll even let you wake up the hottie. You can look, you just can't touch, okay?"

Jem goes directly to Jack's bedroom. Huh. I wouldn't have thought he was her type. I feel oddly protective of him. I've seen Jem gobble up and spit out nice guys before. It's not pretty. I'll have to warn him.

I walk into the room where Ari is snuggled in bed and give him a gentle nudge.

"Mom, no. I'm sleeping."

"It's Lizzie, not your mom. We're going to the pool."

He rubs his eyes and pulls me down on the bed with him. Our faces are *this close* to each other. He could just lean in the teensiest bit and we'd be kissing. "Sure you wouldn't rather stay here with me?"

I have to admit, there's definitely a part of me that would love to stay here with him. But as the one who basically convinced everyone to come here, I also feel a big responsibility for making sure everyone else has fun today. "Tell you what," I propose. "Let's go to the pool now, and revisit that idea later."

"Fine with me," he says, and rolls out from under the covers. Totally naked. I cover my eyes and dash out of the room. When is Ari going to figure out he needs to slow down around me? That boy can seriously be dense.

I buzz Henri and ask him to watch Poochie while we're out. The six of us head down to the pool. Jem has a private cabana reserved, complete with our own private cabana boy.

He brings Miami Vices without us even asking for them, or having to show ID. The frozen drink has massive calories in it—not to mention about four shots of alcohol each—but this is a celebration of freedom. Totally worth it. Cabana Boy spritzes us with Evian whenever we look the slightest bit warm.

"This drink," Chandra says, sucking it up through a big pink straw. "It's so good. Why didn't anyone ever tell me alcohol could taste this good? I've only taken sips of beer before, and it was gross. I thought it was all like that."

"Stick with me, Chandra," I tell her. "I'll turn you on to all kinds of great bad stuff."

"BTDubs, happy day before your birthday, Lizzie!" Jem toasts me.

We all clink our glasses and slurp down our drinks. And drink some more. We tan and take selfies and people-watch. And chug more drinks.

Chandra heads off to the bathroom, weaving slightly but with a humongous smile on her face. I've never seen her so happy or loose. She's almost likeable. Sam, on the other hand, has turned into Chandra: uptight and unhappy.

"Can I borrow your phone again?" she asks.

"Sure."

She punches a number into it and heads to a quiet corner. A second later, she's talking fast and furious. And she still doesn't look happy.

Chandra comes back and takes another huge chug of her drink. "Guess what?' she says, a big smile on her normally oh-so-serious face. "There's a poker tournament going on in the casino. They didn't even ask me for ID when I went in to check it out. I guess your whore-ish makeup job was effective, Jem."

"That's because I'm the bomb at makeovers," she says, smiling and taking a huge gulp of her drink. "I'm so good at them, I should probably have my own YouTube channel. Maybe I'll start one after our trip, Lizzie, and use you as my model. I mean, you ARE pretty famous after that video I made, that should get me lots of attention, making over the RBB into a good girl or something, I'll do like a reverse Sandy at the end of *Grease* on you—"

"Do you think that's such a good idea?" Jack interrupts Jem's buzzed rambling, his brow furrowed.

"Yeah, why not?" Jem says, looking offended.

"I was talking to Chandra," he clarifies. "I mean, because of how you ended up at Camp Smiley and all?"

"I was just watching," Chandra says, waving off his concern with a giggle. "For now, at least. But if any of you guys felt like giving me some seed money, I'm pretty sure I could turn it into a lot more."

"I don't have any cash with me," I tell her. I don't mention the part about how I would never give it to her even if I did. No way do I want to add to her gambling problem. "Come sit down and hang out with us."

But Jem's already rummaging around in her bag. She peels five hundred-dollar bills from her wallet and hands them to Chandra. "Think you can double this?"

"I'll quadruple it," Chandra promises.

"I split any earnings you make 50/50," Jem tells her. "If you go bust, no big deal."

"For real?" Chandra asks. Her eyes are practically glowing at the cash in her hand.

"Yeah. Sure. Why not?" Jem replies. "I'm feeling lucky."

"Me too!"

And with that, Chandra's running back toward the casino. Jack and I go after her but she slides by the security guard before we can catch up.

"Can I see your ID?" he says, stopping us in our tracks.

"No pockets," I tell him, pointing at my bathing suit.

"No wallet," Jack says.

"No pockets, no wallets, no shirts, no shoes, no service," the guard says, crossing his arms over his chest.

Jack and I stare at each other, then the guard, then back at each other again. There's no getting in.

"At least we tried," I tell him.

"Ugh," he replies. "It's not good enough. She's going to get herself in trouble in there."

I shrug. "I mean, maybe she'll actually win. I feel like all she wants is a do-over. Like if she somehow hits it big today, it'll make up for losing so much the last time."

Jack shakes his head. "You can't solve a problem with the problem that started your problems."

"You sound like Confucius," I say. "Wise but confusing."

His worried frown is replaced with a smile. "You're funny, Lizzie."

"And fun," I remind him.

Unable to go save Chandra from herself, we head back out to the pool.

I head over to where Sam's sitting. Her head is in her hands. "You okay?"

"Yeah, I guess so." She sighs. "I mean, not that it's surprising, but my ex says she can never trust me again. And that she thinks it's better that we don't talk at all, at least for now."

"I'm sorry," I tell her.

"And I mean, I get it," Sam continues. "She has every right to be hurt. And my friends have every right to be, like, confused. But I just wish at least ONE of them would forgive me. Is what I did really that unforgivable? Am I unforgiveable? And if yes, how do I move on with no one and nothing in my life?"

I don't have an answer to that, so I say, "I think your friends need a Camp Smiley lesson in forgive, forget, and move on."

"What about the other part of that one?" Sam says, looking more miserable than ever. "*When you've wronged someone, rescind, repair, and then relax*. Like Jed told us the other night, you can't *make* someone accept your apology. You can't force someone to forgive you. The best you can do is admit you were wrong, do whatever you can to fix the harm you've caused, and then hope for the best."

We sit in silence for a minute.

"I guess all that stuff they told us actually sank in," I say, surprised that the kind Camp Smiley messages I wanted to roll my eyes at on the trail actually seem to have real-life applications.

"Ugh, I know," she replies. "I'm starting to feel like I should just go back."

The sad fact is, it's probably the right thing to do. While I'm running TO something, everyone else ran away for nothing—basically, for me—and in a few short hours, I'm abandoning them all. And then they'll have nowhere to go and nothing to do. "I'm sorry. It's all my fault."

"No," she says. "I wanted to come. It's just another one of my desperate, dumbass decisions. No wonder my parents were so worried about me."

I wonder if my parents were truly worried about me too, and not just being over-the-top hard-asses by sending me to Camp Smiley. Because of MY sometimes dumbass impulsive decisions. Like sneaking out to meet James Franco. And getting into Brad's car. And grabbing his stick shift while he was driving down the West Side Highway. And yelling at the cops. And trying to run away from Camp Smiley not once but twice. It's starting to sink in that I'm kind of a handful.

The live DJ announces there's going to be a contest on the stage set up at the far end of the pool. A Mr. Hunk contest. The winner of which gets $500 cash and a bottle of nice champagne.

"I'm entering!" Ari says, heading toward where the DJ is signing people up. His cocktail sloshes on the pool deck, he slips on it, and his legs go right out from under him. He falls hard on his butt. When he gets back up, he's covered in pink slush.

Jem and I start laughing so hard we can't stop. Ari glares at us and walks away. "Ooh, a tough guy," Jem says. "I like that. We both like that, right, Lizzie?"

I laugh and nod. "You know me too well."

Jem puts a hand on Jack's arm. "You should do it too."

She's been not-so-subtly hitting on him ever since they met back in the suite. So far he's not falling for it. I'm surprised. Most guys would jump at the chance to get with her.

"Yeah, you should," I agree.

Jack blushes. "No way. Not a chance."

"I'm not taking no for an answer," Jem says, grabbing Jack's hand.

He pulls it back from her. He's not budging. "I said, no thanks."

"Fine, let's go watch hot Ari take his clothes off instead," Jem says, giving Jack a dirty look. "So is he totally hung, Lizzie? I want to know if it's going to be worth the trouble to push through the crowd to get in the front row."

I give her the evil eye. "How would I know?"

She gives me an even eviler eye. "You would *know* because you told me before he was naked when you were in the bedroom together today. Did the woods give you Alzheimer's or something?"

Jack's eyes get huge, but he doesn't say anything. I really don't want him—or any of my other Camp Smiley friends for that matter—thinking I did anything today with Ari back at the room. Especially something that big. I am so not a "quickie" kind of girl.

More silence. Then, this. "You know what? Sometimes you have to say what the heck," Jack says, standing up. "Right, Lizzie?"

"I think the phrase is, *sometimes you have to say what the fuck*," Jem corrects him with an eye roll.

"I don't like to swear, especially in mixed company," he replies, and heads over to where Ari and a bunch of other guys are lining up. He still looks embarrassed but stands his ground.

I go back to the corner where Sam is still sulking. "Come on, let's get you out of your depression."

"How?"

"By watching Ari and Jack make asses out of themselves in the Mr. Hunk contest."

She sighs and stands up. "Fine. I have nothing better to do. It's not like anyone's texting me back."

Jem, Sam, and I push our way to the front of the stage and start screaming for the cute guys. Some shake their butts. Some strip to their underwear. Some strip to nothing. The more I drink, the funnier it is.

When it's Ari's turn, he does a combo platter of the Macarena, Electric Slide, and the Whip/Nae Nae. It's more of a comedy routine than a sexy one. But he's clearly having a good time up there, and everyone watching is too. He ends to rousing applause.

And then it's Jack's turn. He stands there frozen, like he has no idea what to do. I'm sure he's regretting his spur-of-the-moment decision to join in. But when the beat drops, he finally starts moving. It's kind of awkward at first, but then he seems to forget there's an audience and loosens up. His moves are decent. I figure he's a solid 5/10—until he whips off his Lululemon shorts, right down to his form-fitting Lulu underwear. It's like his chiseled six-pack abs and muscular arms and buff legs are staring right at me. Jack breaks into a huge grin.

The crowd goes wild. We stomp our feet and clap. Jem puts a hand over her heart and says, "Well, if I can't get with him, you should. Someone has to experience that bod."

"He's a great guy, but I just don't think of him like that," I tell her.

She sticks out her lower lip. "I'm telling you, one of us HAS to. It would be a crime not to. How about I'll take Ari and you take Jack? That way we can both have fun."

I look over at her, hoping she's kidding. It's hard to tell. "Ha ha, no. I'm telling you, Jack's not my type."

The DJ declares Jack the winner and hands him the money and champagne. Jem and I try to go congratulate him, but he's swarmed by women. I'm feeling a little tipsy. Maybe a lot tipsy. That last Miami Vice is kicking in. I let out a hiccup.

"I might need to go sit down."

"Me too," Jem giggles. "We are going to have the best time in Greece!"

I put my hands on her shoulders and she puts her hands on mine and we start jumping up and down.

"We totally are!" I scream.

Sam puts her hands on both our shoulders and jumps with us. "I wish I was going too! But I'm not! So I have no clue what to do now!"

We all go back to the cabana and curl up on our lounge chairs. Ari is already there. He's sulking.

"I should've won that! The crowd loved me, especially that chick with the fake boobs and leopard-print dress," he says. "She even slipped me her number."

I scan the crowd. She is trashy and SUPER hot. So now I guess I have to worry about Jem AND leopard-dress girl.

Jack shows up with his prize-winning bottle of Perrier-Jouët champagne before I can worry any more about it. Ari grabs it from him, puts it between his legs, and puts pressure on the cork with his thumbs. A second later, the cork comes flying across the cabana and thwacks me right between the eyes. Everything goes black.

"I'M BLIND!" I howl.

I can't see. But I can still hear. And the sounds are of Ari and Jem cracking up.

"You almost killed her!" Jem howls, barely able to get the words out she's laughing so hard.

"Epic," Ari says, laughing along with her.

"Are you okay, Lizzie?" Jack is suddenly next to me. He puts an arm over my shoulder and pulls me close. I nestle into him.

"I can't see!" I moan. "I'm going to suck at being blind. The only upside is at least I'll never have to read another book."

"Poochie will be a great guide dog," Ari says, still yucking it up. "And there is a thing called Braille, you know."

How will I help the poor little baby turtles if I can't see where they are? How will I know if the latest Paris Fashion Week collection makes my butt look cute? How can I help set up photo shoots for *Vogue España* when I can't see if the lighting's any good? Blindness does not fit well with my future goals. "I hate reading with my eyes. What makes you think I'd do it with my fingers?"

"Your eyes are closed, dumbass," Jem says. She's right. I open them slowly.

At first I can only see blurs of color, but eventually everything comes into focus. Jem is holding out a glass of champagne to me.

"Don't mind if I do," I say. I down it. The bottle is soon empty. Everything starts looking fuzzy again. I'm not sure if I'm still suffering the effects of a cork in the head or if I'm just turnt.

"They'll never let us on the plane this wasted," Jem says. "We need to take a nap and sober up."

The five of us head back up to the Chairman's Suite. Jack announces he needs a shower and closes the bedroom door behind him before Jem can join him. I hear her try the knob but it's locked. I head into the other bedroom, Ari and Poochie following close behind me. Both jump on the bed.

"Now about that private time we rescheduled before . . ." Ari says with a wink.

My heart speeds up. "I'll be right back."

I slip into the bathroom. I brush my teeth, fix my hair, spritz on some Jo Malone, freshen my makeup, and put on deodorant. I'm trying to do this all at the speed of light—the last thing I want Ari to think is I'm having another IBS attack in here, that's so not sexy—but when I go back out into the bedroom, it seems I haven't been quick enough.

BECAUSE JEM IS ON THE BED. WITH ARI. THEY ARE INTERTWINED. A TANGLE OF TONGUES AND HANDS AND BODY PARTS.

I pick up Poochie and bury my head in her fur, trying to shield myself from the scene unfolding in front of me.

I mean, I know Jem's just being Jem as usual. Doing what feels good in the moment. She'll give me a half-ass apology later, and I'll probably accept it. Story of our entire friendship. And why am I so surprised about Ari? He's exactly who I thought he was that first night in the sleeping bag. A gross horndog. A total player.

"Are you KIDDING me?" I say anyhow.

They stop groping each other momentarily. Jem winces. "Sorry. You know I can't handle rejection," she explains. "I had to redeem myself. Prove I still have it. My bad. Forgive me?"

Ari pats the bed on the other side of him. "Hey, no need to fight over me, girls. There's more than enough to go around."

Jem giggles. "Truth!"

I roll my eyes. "Gross."

Those two deserve each other. I stalk out of the room, slamming the door behind me.

In the living room, Sam is curled up on the couch, snoring her cute little *wheep-a-wahnah*. She looks so young and innocent. A huge pang of regret washes over me. Coming to Vegas was my worst idea yet. Ever since we got here, it's been one shit show after another. Chandra trying to solve the huge problem that landed her in Camp Smiley by repeating her mistakes (I need to go find her before she gets herself in a brand-new world of trouble!). Sam feeling worse than ever about her adventures with fuckboy, and how it left her friend-less. Jack trying so hard to make sure everyone is okay and coming up short. And now, Jem hooking up with Ari even though she knew I liked him. Make that, *thought* I liked him. I am finally getting it through my thick skull that bad boys like Ari are plain old bad news, and with friends like Jem, who needs enemies?

I decide right then and there: I'M TAKING A STAND. Or maybe it's that I'm finally ready to start taking responsibility for my actions. Damn Camp Smiley for being right in so many ways. I want to try and fix everything I messed up for everyone before it's too late.

I rifle through my luggage and grab an outfit that hope-fully makes me look older—a silk shirt, blazer, dark-wash skinny jeans, and heels. I throw my hair into a messy bun. Swipe some more mascara on my lashes and gloss on my lips. Hopefully the guard will let me into the casino now that I look more presentable.

I give a soft knock on the bedroom door Jack retreated to. "I'm sleeping, Jem," he growls. But I know by now he's all bark, no bite.

"It's Lizzie," I say. "And I just wanted to tell you, I'm going to save Chandra from herself now. I can't let her screw up her life again."

He opens the door. His hair is tousled and wet and he has a towel wrapped around his waist. He smells clean and yummy. His body is looking obscenely perfect again. I try not to notice. I'm pretty sure he notices me trying not to notice. Mortifying.

"I'll come with you," he says. "Just a sec."

He shuts the door behind him and comes back out dressed a minute later. "So what's your plan?"

"Wing it, I guess," I tell him.

He gives me a funny little smile. "That hasn't exactly worked out for you in the past, has it?"

He's right. "You have a better suggestion?"

He shakes his head. "Nope. And just so you know, I'm going back to Camp Smiley after we find Chandra. I'm finishing out the program."

This shouldn't surprise me, but it still does. "Sounds like a better plan than winging it," I tell him.

We get in the elevator. Jack pushes the button for the lobby. He stares me straight in the eye. "I just think it's the right thing to do. Plus, I kind of like Lake. I feel like she's helping me. I don't mind the hiking and I'm not ready to face everyone back home yet. So yeah."

"I'll tell you what. I'll pay for your Uber ride if you take everyone else back with you," I say. "I'd feel much better knowing they weren't, like, getting in trouble, or worse, hurt or dead, and it's all my fault because I talked them into coming here."

"You're on," he says. "Thanks."

We get off the elevator and there's Chandra sitting in the lobby. Holding a stack of bills. She looks up and waves.

"Is that the wave of a winner?" I ask.

"I'm actually even," she says. "Not up, not down."

"That's good, right?"

She runs her fingers over the hundreds she's clutching in her palm. "What was I thinking? Even if I won back all the money I lost and more, it still wouldn't erase what I did. I'd still have to live with the fact that I cared more about what I wanted than the huge sacrifices my parents made for me. I'd still be a bad person."

Jack puts a hand on her shoulder. "You can't beat yourself up forever about it."

"Pot? Meet kettle," she says miserably.

"I mean, I know you're right," he says. "I'm telling you to do something I can't do myself. Which is just another reason we all need to go back to Camp Smiley. To figure our heads out."

"All of us? Even you, Lizzie?" she asks.

I look from Jack to Chandra and then down at my feet. What would be worse at this point: facing the music at Camp Smiley, or pissing my parents off forever by going to Greece with the worst best friend on the planet? I can't figure out the answer so I just shrug.

"So how did it feel?" Jack asks Chandra while I debate silently. "Gambling again, I mean?"

"I didn't actually play," Chandra mumbles.

"Good for you!" Jack exclaims. "I can't believe you resisted temptation like that!"

Chandra rolls her eyes. "No need to give me so much credit. The dealer asked for my ID when I tried to place my first bet, and when I didn't have it he kicked me out of the casino. So I never even got a chance to resist. Or not, as the case might've been. Who knows what I would've done."

We head back upstairs to collect Sam and Ari. I shake Sam awake and tell her the plan. She nods groggily. "Yeah. I'm down."

Ari, who has to be pried out of the bedroom with fake promises of more champagne, is not as easily convinced. "No way I'm going back to Camp Smiley. I'm coming with you ladies to Greece. I like the way you roll."

"The cruise is sold out," Jem tells him. It's no surprise she's done with him already. He was a shiny new toy and now that she's played with him, he's lost his appeal. "It's been sold out for months."

"Just go back to Camp Smiley," I tell Ari. "Be realistic. You don't have any money or anywhere to stay in Vegas."

"Maybe you should've thought of that before you dragged us all here," he says, scowling at me.

"Maybe I should have," I agree.

"I thought you said the room was paid for until tomorrow, Jem," he adds. "So I'll just stay the night and figure it out from there."

Chandra hands Jem back her gambling seed money. Jem hands it directly to Ari. "Here. A little nest egg for your new life in Vegas. Don't spend it all in one place."

"Jem!" I yell.

"What? If he wants to be a homeless dumbass, let him."

Ari tucks the bills in his pocket. "Thanks. Don't mind if I do."

Sam, Jack, Jem, and I head down to the lobby. Ari trails us. "What? I'm a gentleman like Jack. I'm seeing you all off."

Jem glances down at her phone. "We have to get going to the airport, Lizzie."

"Let me just talk to the Uber driver first," I tell her. "I want to make sure he knows where he's going and that he's not some weird creeper. I want all these guys getting back safe."

Jem rolls her eyes. "I'm not missing the plane because you want to hold your weird-ass friends' hands. We need to go now. They'll survive."

"You go now then. I'll meet you there," I argue.

"Fine," she says, whirling around, wheeling her luggage behind her. "Don't blame me if you can't get on the ship until Mykonos."

I know she thinks I'm going to follow her. And I probably would have, before Camp Smiley. But this time, I find myself wanting to stick with the people who have my back a little longer, not chase after the one who just stole the guy I liked because she cared more about getting some action than her lifelong friend's feelings.

"She's a trip," Jack says as Jem stalks away.

"Yeah, you kind of have to get to know her to really appreciate her quirks," I tell him.

"I guess," he says, looking unconvinced.

The Uber pulls up. The driver looks slightly shady to me. His car is a rattling old junker. I really don't want my friends to get in there and drive the four hours back to Camp Smiley. Who knows what might happen if they break down on the barren desert highway?

"I'm sorry, sir, we changed our minds."

He gives me the finger and roars off.

"What was that about?" Jack asks.

"His car didn't look safe," I say. "I just called for another one." I fail to mention that I've also sent a big email to Director Willis via Camp Smiley website contact form, taking full responsibility for making everyone leave and letting them know everyone is on the way back. I'll follow up with the new driver's name and number so Willis can track their return.

"Thanks, Grandma," Ari says, cracking himself up again. I give him a death stare. "Just joking, babe."

I whirl around. "I'm not your babe, and I never will be."

His hands fly up and he backs away. "Touchy, touchy."

The Uber is still five minutes away when my phone starts buzzing relentlessly. It's a series of texts from Jem. In all caps. Ruh-roh, Scooby.

Jem

> TOLD YOU YOU SHOULD'VE COME WITH ME.

> YOUR DAD CALLED MY MOM.

> SHE CHECKED MY CREDIT CARD CHARGES AND KNOWS I WAS AT THE BELLAGIO TODAY.

> PINGED FIND MY IPHONE TO CONFIRM.

> BENJAMIN IS ON HIS WAY.

> LEAVE NOW!

"You guys. Your driver's name is Dennis. He's in a black Suburban. He has the address," I say, words tumbling out in a rush on top of each other. "I have to go now or I'm completely busted. Good luck!"

"Have fun in Greece," Chandra says.

"Be good," Jack adds. "And if you can't be good—"

"Be careful." Sam finishes the thought for him.

"I was going to say, come with us instead." Jack laughs.

Chandra steps forward to give me a hug. Jack joins in. Then Sam. We're a tight circle of friends and I almost don't want to let go.

But I know I have to extricate myself so I do. I give one last squeeze and run out to where the bellhop is directing cars in and out of the driveway. Lucky for me, a limo is pulling up right as I get there. I'll figure I'll wait for whoever's inside to get out and then I'll jump in and say *to the airport, and step on it.*

The guy gets out. It's my dad.

"Hello, Lizzie," he says, the biggest frown I've ever seen on his face. "It looks like you've had quite a day."

"I can explain," I begin. "In fact, I already explained everything to Director Willis in an email. . . ."

"You're in a lot of trouble," he says. "You really outdid yourself this time."

My friends are just heading outside to catch the Uber. Even Ari is there, I guess to say sayonara, suckers. My dad waves them over too.

"How would you all like a ride back to Camp Smiley in this limo?"

"Thank you, sir, that would be great," Jack says, and slides inside. Chandra and Sam follow him in. Ari tries to just keep on walking by inconspicuously. My dad stares him down. "You too, son."

He slinks into the car without a word.

"I just want you to know, Dad, this was all my idea and all my fault," I say. I was already in trouble before we ever came to Vegas. I can at least try to spare my friends the kind of punishment I'm sure to get if I take the fall for everyone. "I totally bribed them to come here. That's why Ari has five hundred dollars in his pocket. You can check. I threatened terrible things if they didn't come with me and promised them all money if they did. So as you can see, they really had no choice in the matter."

My dad shakes his head sadly. "Money seems to be the root of all your problems, Lizzie."

You leaving is the real the root of all my problems, I think. But I don't say a word. I just slide in the back with Poochie, and let Dad slide in the front with the driver, and off we go. Back to Camp Smiley and for me to figure out how to clean up the mess I've made of my life.

And everyone else's.

BELLAGIO
LAS VEGAS

Guest   *Room & Rate*

Regina George/Gretchen Wieners   Chairman Suite
North Shore High School/Old Orchard Mall   Regular rack rate
Evanston, IL 60201
United States

DATE	DESCRIPTION	CHARGES
3-JULY	Suite with butler services	$5,000.00
3-JULY	Veuve Cliquot, 1 bottle	$150.00
3-JULY	Private cabana, daily rate	$275.00
3-JULY	Miami Vice, 32	$480.00
3-JULY	Cosmopolitan, 3	$70.00
3-JULY	Vodka club, 4	$50.00
TOTAL		**$6025.00**

chapter

20

I wake up on my seventeenth birthday to a horrible sense of dread multiplied by a crappy hangover. My meeting with D-R-period Willis, my dad, and Mom via speaker phone is happening in five minutes. Scarlet unlocks the door to the windowless cabin they made me sleep in all alone—and double-locked me into to avoid any more escape attempts—and leads me to the main office.

In I walk. Willis gestures to an empty chair. It's next to my dad's.

D-R-period clears his throat. "Considering your behavior and how you bullied the other campers into a mass escape, my first reaction is to say we can no longer have you at Camp Smiley. You're too much of a liability."

"I understand," I tell him, hanging my head. "You'll be happy to hear I learned a lot at Camp Smiley, most especially that I love my life and I'm very lucky to be living it the way I am. Thank you for that."

"Good to hear," my dad says. He's holding Poochie. She jumps off his lap and onto mine. "But not enough to clear the slate."

"Your email was appreciated as well. But it doesn't erase what you've done," Director Willis adds.

"We're very worried about you and your future, Lizzie," my dad says. "And we all want what's best for you."

"I know I messed up here. And I know I can't go on the service trip like I was supposed to," I say. "But maybe I could go home and finish the community service I was assigned by the peer jury instead? And volunteer at the animal shelter too?"

My dad and Willis stare at me. Neither says a word about my proposal. Which was both sincere and reasonable.

"Let's just get Mrs. Beauvier on speaker before we continue this discussion." D-R presses a button on the phone. It crackles with static. "Margot, are you there?"

"I am," she says, sounding perkier than usual for this time of the morning. Normally she'd still be in bed. I give her credit for hauling her ass up and being so coherent so early in the day.

"Great. Now I was just telling your daughter and husband—"

"—ex-husband," my mom corrects him.

"Ah yes. Ex-husband. As I was saying, my first instinct was to immediately dismiss Elizabeth from Camp Smiley for all the trouble she's caused here. Her suggestion was to come home and complete her community service along with volunteering at an animal shelter as an alternate possibility."

"Lizzie needs to know it's simply not possible for her to come home to New York at the moment," my mom replies.

My heart is pounding in my ears. My throat has a lump the

size of an orange in it. Why do things in my life always go so wrong? "Are . . . are you saying I'm no longer welcome at home?"

"That's not what your mother is saying at all," my dad says.

Director Willis jumps back in. "As I was saying, while my first reaction was to expel you from the program, after further thought, we all think the best thing for you to do is stick this out. To stay focused and finish what you've started. This is what all successful people do."

I think about all the times I've quit things: Camp Greenlake. Ballet. Spanish. Relationships with friends and boyfriends. Where would I be today if I'd tried even just a little harder? Who knows. Maybe I'd have a job as a counselor at my old camp this summer. Or be taking an intensive at the New York Ballet. Or doing a homestay in Barcelona, where I spoke the language every day.

"Okay," I finally say, my voice a whisper.

My dad doesn't look at me when he delivers this next gem. "That's not all. The trust that you've been expecting when you turn eighteen will be put on hold until a later date when we feel like you're ready for it."

"You mean until I'm like twenty-one or something?" I ask. That might not be so bad. I can do the poor college student thing. If everyone else can handle it, so can I.

"No, darling," my mom says through the speaker. "Until you're thirty. Or forty. Maybe forever. However long it takes for you to become a responsible, mature adult."

"For . . . ever?" They can't mean that. I'll show them. I'll go to Bowdoin, get decent grades, land a good job. That way I'll get my trust just when I need it to buy my own place in the city. It's all good.

"It all depends on you," my dad says.

"Deal," I tell him.

"I must say, I'm impressed at how maturely you're handling all this," Director Willis says. "Especially after all the immature things you did before this meeting. Though I want to, it's almost hard to believe you're sincere. Why the sudden change of heart?"

Maybe he's a little right: part of my agreeing is just wanting to get this over with, to tell the adults what they want to get them off my case. Who knows, they might cave later. But part is also realizing that maybe it's time I start taking something in my life seriously. Not everything, but some things. Like what I might want to do with my life after high school, beyond just getting in the best house and partying my face off in college.

"I guess hanging out with kids who actually know what they want to be when they grow up got me to thinking that maybe I should try to figure that out too," I tell him. "I kind of can't wait to get to Bowdoin and get started."

"Which leads us to the final consequence for your actions," my dad says. "I can't in good conscience pull any strings to get you into Bowdoin after everything that's happened. Wherever you go to college, it needs to be on your own merits."

Director Willis nods. "You have to earn your place in this life. Not be handed things without doing the hard work."

"MOM!" I yell. "You can't let him do this to me, especially after everything else he's done to us!"

"I love you too much to let you waste your life, Lizzie," my mom says.

I'm so upset now, the worst thing flies off my tongue before I can stop it. "This from a woman who is *always* wasted." I clap my hand over my mouth but it's too late. Guilt sinks in HARD.

"I'm busy working on me, Lizzie," my mom calmly says. "And I suggest you do the same for yourself."

"Hard at work how, Mom?" I ask, my tone still too sarcastic.

And that's when my mom drops a bomb. "I'm not there in person today because I'm in rehab, honey. Getting off the pills and learning how to manage my anxiety without them."

This is all just too much for me to handle at once. My entire life has changed. I bury my face in Poochie's fur and sob.

"Lizzie, someday you'll thank us for this," my dad says. "It's a gift and a blessing to find your purpose in life."

My dad and Willis stand up. I guess the meeting is over.

"Elizabeth, I suggest you be on your best behavior and put your most sincere effort into your time at Camp Smiley so we don't have to repeat another meeting like this," Willis says.

My dad holds his arms out like he wants a hug. I avert my eyes and try to walk by him.

"I just need Poochie before you rejoin your group," he says. I have no interest in letting her go, but even less interest in having her eaten on the trail by a bear or getting caught in a noose like I did. I put her in my dad's arms, grab my pack, and walk out the door.

Per usual, I can't imagine what to say to him so I say nothing at all. I'm his disappointment of a daughter, and he's my disappointment of a father. I'm sure we can both agree on that.

I don't say goodbye to my mom either, though I respect her tons more knowing she's doing what she's doing. She was honest and fearless on the phone, and that's saying a lot for someone who's terrified of pretty much everything. Rehab agrees with her.

Scarlet walks me to where the group is currently camped out. They're sitting in a circle by the dreaded tarp where this whole saga started. Everyone is silent.

"That was quite an adventure you had yesterday, Lizzie," Jed says.

I nod. It hardly seems worth it now, knowing I only ended up back here in more trouble than ever. My mind races with questions: Will my parents actually disinherit me permanently? Where would I go if I have no home to go to and no money to get my own place? Am I even going to be allowed to be a senior in the fall? I missed the last week of school and didn't take finals. If I have to repeat junior year, I might have to do it from a homeless shelter, or a cardboard box like that lady who hangs out in front of my favorite Fifth Ave boutique.

"We've discussed what happened and how you coerced your peers to join you on yesterday's ill-fated road trip," Scarlet says. "However, they are still responsible for their actions. And while we know you've already received severe consequences for your part in this scenario, Jed and I have decided that today, there will be silence on the trail. It's not a punishment. It's a time to reflect and meditate. We want everyone to think about why you each did what you did. How the way you've acted both yesterday and in the past stops you from reaching your goals."

"Remember, you are always the cause of your own problems, as well as the solution," Jed says.

Scarlet smiles at him. "That's so deep. Who said that?"

He grins back at her. "Me."

Relationship goals. I still wish I had a Jed. I no longer wish he was Ari, though. I deserve someone I can trust, and who likes me enough that he can resist cheating on me with any hot girl that comes along. Ahem, Jem.

And I've got way bigger worries on my mind than who my next boyfriend will be, or whether it might just be time to find a new BFF. *I don't even know who I am anymore*, I keep hearing over and over in my head. *I'm nobody. I've got no home, no place to go. No one loves me except Poochie.*

And they made me leave her with my dad until I graduate. If that ever happens. Do I even *want* it to happen if I have nothing to go home to—like, not even a home? I've probably never felt so lost in my whole life. Or maybe I have, twice: first when my dad left and then when my parents got divorced.

Only difference is that this time, I'm losing everything I've ever known—not just two parents who are together. I'm losing, like, ME. And how am I supposed to deal with that? I love how my mom and dad think making a spoon and hand jobbing a fire in the woods will solve this big of a problem.

Also, how both of them forgot it was my birthday.

CAMP SMILEY
WILDERNESS EXPLORATION AND EDUCATION EXPERIENCE

Transforming your child, renewing their smile!

• CAMPER DISCIPLINE MEETING •

In attendance:

Benjamin Finklestein, father

Margot Beauvier, mother (by phone)

Director Willis

Poochie (camper's dog)

1.	*Incident Date:* <u>7/2 - 7/3</u> Please enter the date the incident occurred.
2.	*First Name:* Elizabeth B. Finklestein
3.	*Complaint:* Camper violated rules by coercing group to leave the cabin and camp without permission, hitchhiking to town and then Las Vegas, and attempting to flee the country. Additional transgressions include underage drinking.
4.	*Disciplinary Action Taken:* <u>X</u> Consequences with reparations *Explain:* Camper must complete solo overnight before she can graduate. No limit on how many sessions this takes. Her trust has been rescinded until parents can discuss further how it should best be restructured. ____ Alternate placement (Move camper to alternate facility to address current drug, alcohol or mental health issues) <s>X</s> Explusion

chapter

21

We hike along for hours. By the time we make camp, I still have zero answers as to why or how I always seem to get in my own way, or how I can dig my way out of it. I'm just numb and exhausted.

We set up our tents. Wash up. Eat dinner. Awkward silence.

At Truth Circle, Scarlet and Jed tell us we can finally talk again. The topic for tonight's discussion: who we think we are.

"I'm a formerly nice guy with a terrible dark side," Jack offers. I stare at him across the fire, appreciating how the glow makes him look like a broody and handsome actor on a vampire show.

"Jack," Jed says gently. "Don't you think it's time you told everyone what happened?"

He shakes his head. "Nope."

"I assure you there's lots of light left in you, Jack," Scarlet says.

He shakes his head more and we move on.

"I'm . . . complicated, I guess," Sam says. "Like, I always thought I was a chocolate chip. You always know what you're getting with a chocolate chip, right? But it turns out I'm more like a raisin. With all sorts of hidden wrinkles and whatever. Which is such a bummer, because people definitely like chocolate chips more than shriveled-up grapes. Even I do."

"You're not a raisin," I tell her. "You're a beautiful lychee or something even more exotic. Unexpected. It's a good thing."

"I just wish my sexuality was as black and white as I always thought," she says, scraping a stick in the dirt. "Life was so much easier that way."

"You're unique," Jed tells her. "One of a kind."

"You do you," Scarlet adds. "Just be yourself, as hard as you can. That's all anyone can ever ask of you."

Be yourself, as hard as you can. I immediately start imagining how awesome graphic tees would look with that on it. Someday, some way, when I have my own fashion line. . . .

"I already AM myself, as hard as I can," Ari jumps in. "But, like, no one seems to think that's a good thing. Especially the 'rents."

Though Scarlet and Jed must be sick of repeating the same old message, they do. With great patience. "I don't think it's who you are your parents object to," Scarlet explains. "It's that your favorite activities are also illegal and will land you in jail one of these days."

"Major in art in college," Jed says. "I bet there's even schools that have classes in street art. Go legit, man. Make it a living, not a vocation."

Ari digs in his heels. "Legit defeats the purpose. Graffiti is punk. It's rebellion. I refuse to sell out. I'm not giving up on my dreams like every other adult seems to be okay doing. Not now, not ever."

"I kind of think I'm, like, pretty average," Chandra jumps in. "I know I did something out of the norm to be here, but the reasons why were beyond common. I mean, who doesn't want to go to, like, Harvard instead of Crap State?"

"Sounds awesome," Scarlet says. "Not Crap State, but being average. Like you'll fit right in no matter where you go to college, and find friends with lots in common with you."

Chandra gives her a look. "What do you mean, awesome? It sucks."

"Since when does normal equal sucks?" Jed wants to know.

"What's the opposite of a snap?" Sam asks. "You're YOU, you're pretty normal, and you're awesome. A little uptight, but awesome."

I snap my agreement. We all snap. We all laugh.

"So what about you, Lizzie?" Scarlet asks.

I give a little shrug. "I basically have no idea who I am anymore."

"Care to elaborate?" This from Jed.

"Well first, I was one-third of the Awesome Threesome. That's what my parents called our family when I was little. But then they got divorced and my father decided he'd rather go save endangered armadillo thingies in Africa than stay with me and my mom," I begin. "When the divorce settlement hit, the newspapers started calling me the Poor Little Rich Girl, which was perfect for how sad and small I felt. And right before I got here, the media decided to release a video of an embarrassing drunk tirade I'd rather have forgotten and started calling me the RBB. The Rich Bitch Billionairess. Today, my dad told me I'm cut off, maybe forever. My mom said I can't go home. So who am I now? Certainly not a poor little rich girl or rich bitch billionairess, considering I have no money anymore. So I basically have no clue."

Everyone around the Truth Circle starts snapping at the last part. It actually makes me feel weirdly good that I've finally done something right at Camp Smiley.

The snapping dies down. I notice Jack has his head in his hands. I can't tell whether he's mad or sad or both or what.

"What touched you about Lizzie's story, Jack?" Scarlet asks.

"I guess I just completely understand what it's like to lose your identity," he says, staring into the fire. "It really feels terrible."

Sam throws a stick into the fire. "Me too. But I'm pretty sure the whole point of being a teenager is trying to figure out who you are. It doesn't make you defective or anything."

Ari jumps in. "We're all gonna be fine. We're all ALREADY fine."

Chandra, who's been pretty quiet up until now, jumps back into the convo. "What if the things we *thought* defined us were actually keeping us from who we're supposed to be? Like, maybe all that other stuff was just our caterpillar phase and when we really figure it out we'll come out of our cocoons and turn into motherfucking butterflies!"

Scarlet shoots her a look. "Language, Chandra."

She claps a hand over her mouth and blushes. "Mother-*freaking* butterflies, I meant."

"That's a gorgeous observation, minus the swearing," Jed tells her, then turns back to me. "How does that make you feel, Lizzie?"

"I guess a little better. Thanks, Chandra."

"Welcome back, everyone," Jed intones, brushing sage smoke at me from that same old bundle of hay. "Welcome back to the fold of Camp Smiley, where you will be once again made full and whole. We love you and honor your struggle."

Scarlet stands and smiles. "I'd like to make an announcement. It's a special day today for Lizzie, because not only is she emerging as a butterfly as Chandra so astutely observed, but it's also her seventeenth birthday."

"HAPPY BIRTHDAY!" everyone says. It almost makes up for my parents blowing it off.

Sam toasts me a perfect marshmallow over the fire, puts it in the middle of two graham crackers with two little slabs of Hershey bar on either side, and presents it to me.

"Thanks!" I say, and inhale it. I'm still licking chocolate off my fingers when Jed pulls out his uke and plays happy birthday. Everyone sings. I blush.

"May I?" Jack asks when he's done.

Jed passes him the ukulele. Jack starts plucking, not strumming. As the first few notes hit the air, the hairs on my arms prickle until they're all standing on end. His voice is surprisingly good. Low and raspy.

"Blackbird singing in the dead of night, take these broken wings and learn to fly . . ."

On the next line, I join in with the harmony. My dad always told me the note to find is a third higher than the regular note, but who even knows what that is. I only remember how to do it because we used to sing this song together every night before I went to bed. "All your life, you were only waiting for this moment to arise."

Remembering how happy we used to be is a knife in my heart. I burst into tears. I can't stop.

"I'm sorry, Lizzie," Jack says, putting down the ukulele.

"Jack, why don't you take Lizzie for a walk so she can clear her head for reflective time and lights out," Jed tells him.

"Uh, sure."

He holds out a hand to me. I take it and he pulls me up. We walk in silence.

I'm gulping back heaving sobs. There's snot running down my face. My eyes sting. They're probably beet red.

But guess what? I don't really care. Bag ladies who eat Vaseline and live in cardboard boxes can't be bothered with how they look.

We get to a clearing in the woods. I stop to check out the view. Jack slings an arm around my shoulder. The weight of it feels nice. The sun is just starting to set and there are visible rays of light streaming through the clouds.

"When I was little, I used to think those were, like, actually God," I say, wiping my nose on my sleeve.

"Cute."

"At least I've still got that going for me."

Jack gazes out at the horizon. "I'm going to be honest here. You've got to stop feeling sorry for yourself. I really don't think you not being independently wealthy by the time you're eighteen is such a bad thing."

"You wouldn't feel sorry for yourself?"

He shrugs. "I guess what I'm saying is, you seem, like, more human without it. Tonight, everyone got what you said. It was deep. Everyone maybe got a look at the real *you* for the first time. You know?"

Somehow his hand finds its way into mine. I don't pull away. IDK why. I guess because whenever he's around I feel cared for and safe. I relax and rest my head against his arm.

"While we're being honest," I say. "You don't hit me as the cold-blooded killer type."

He sighs. "I honestly don't want to talk about it ever again. I wish I never even had to *think* about it. But every night before I go to sleep, that's the only thing I can think about. Sometimes I wonder if I'll ever forget what happened and be happy again."

I decide to TMI him. Why not. We'll never see each other again after graduation. "You know what *I* can't stop thinking about every night? And, like, makes me too scared to even sleep?"

"Tell me."

I start to giggle. It's nuts that I'm still sometimes terrified that a Disney villain lives under my bed. She's a cartoon. As in, not real. It's so dumb. "Ursula."

Jack looks down at me. His eyes melt into mine. I get lost in them. "Who?"

"Ursula the Sea Witch," I say. "From *The Little Mermaid*?"

Jack stares at me for a second longer, then starts cracking up. "You are one of a kind, Lizzie. Truly an original."

And then he leans down and kisses me. The sun dips below the horizon. It's like the God rays are blessing us.

"Happy birthday," he says, resting his forehead against mine. His eyes are sparkly again.

I silently thank whoever or whatever is out there that I'm alive and here. I might not know where I'm going, but I figure I'll know it when I get there. Until then, the good, the bad, the awesome, the truly crappy, and the roller-coaster butterflies—I want it all.

I almost think I might already *have* it all. Minus the money. But still.

chapter

22

Jack and I act kind of shy around each other the next day. We don't find ourselves alone again so we certainly don't get to reenact the romantic moment we had on our walk. But if the opportunity ever arises again—I'm all in. It just felt right.

We practice making fire after our hike in preparation for our solo overnights. I am totally dreading that, because well, solo and overnight. I hate being alone. Especially in the dark with no fire. For a whole day and night.

Besides, I'm no closer to getting one now than I was the first day Scarlet demonstrated how it's done. Still, I try. I put the long stick into the knotty hole and start twisting away.

Jed stands by, watching and offering encouragement. "Great effort. Keep it up."

My arms burn. I want to quit. But then I remember I'm trying not to do that anymore. So I don't.

"Maybe you could try holding the stick a little more firmly at the base and rubbing faster?" Scarlet suggests.

Sam snorts. Because of course she's probably thinking about how I call this hand-jobbing sticks, and Scarlet's instruction sounded like she was talking about an actual hand job. Pretty soon, we're both ROFLing.

Scarlet shakes her head and smiles. "I hope you two haven't eaten any of those wild mushrooms I saw on the trail earlier. They might be hallucinogenic, but they're also poisonous. You could die from that stuff."

"I didn't eat any 'shrooms," Sam assures her.

"Me neither," I say.

Scarlet waits until I start working the sticks again. At the end of what feels like an entire century, a little wisp of smoke appears.

"OHMYGOD!" I yell.

And in the amount of time it takes for me to say that, poof, the puff of smoke is gone. Just like my trust fund. *C'est la vie.*

Sam gets about a zillion puffs of smoke but just can't convert any of them into a flame. Ari gets nothing, but doesn't look like he's trying that hard, either. While the rest of us are busy getting blisters, Jack starts a roaring fire.

A half hour later, another round of franks and beans are served. Me, still without a spoon. I have barbecue sauce all over my face by the time I'm done eating. I kind of get the feeling Jack still thinks I'm cute.

The next morning, I wake up to find he already has a fire stoked. I grab the stick Sam gave me a long time ago from my backpack. I figure it's about time I stopped eating with my fingers. Plus, it's a perfect excuse to talk to Jack without it being so awkward.

"Hey," I say, my heart pounding against my ribs. It's both embarrassing and awesome to feel so nerdily nervous around a guy.

"Hey yourself," he says, his lips curving into a little smile.

I hold out my stick that is hopefully about to become a spoon. "Got a spare ember?"

He nods at the fire. "Of course. Have at it."

I step forward but can't figure out how to scoop one out with going up in flames myself.

"Do I just, like . . ." I motion like I'm about to dunk my whole arm in and grab a random coal. Even as I pantomime, it doesn't seem like the best idea.

"Use another stick to help you get it in there," he coaches me.

I pick up the longest, sturdiest one I can find and slowly, slowly scoot a smallish coal toward the outer circle of the fire. It looks like it's about the right size for a spoondentation. It also looks really freaking hot.

I look up at Jack for more instructions. He just says, "You got this, Lizzie."

It's cool how he just tells me to go for it. If my mom were here, she'd totally freak out and scream at me to be careful. My dad—if I'm remembering correctly—would probably walk me through each little step, so in the end I would feel like he made the spoon instead of me. But I actually want to do it for myself this time.

I turn the stick to the side and put it close to the coal, but not so close that I get burned. Then I take the longer branch and in one quick motion, flip the ember on top. It lands in just the right spot.

I blow and blow and blow. The coal glows orange and amber and red. When it seems like the hole is deep enough, I unload the ember back into the fire.

"*Muchas gracias,*" I say to Jack.

"*De nada.*"

I grab the pointiest rock I can find and start digging out the burnt part. It's hard work and my arm gets tired. But I don't quit. I don't even complain.

I keep trying my hardest to be a good friend and camper. I rub sticks. I hike faster. I climb another rickety ladder and zip-line over a river. I even help Chandra do it by giving her lots of encouragement.

I meet with Lake a few more times. I tell her things. Honest things. We play *Two Truths and a Lie.* Mine are:

1. I had to be medivaced out of Africa because I got bitten on the butt by a tsetse fly.
2. I matched with James Franco on Tinder.
3. I drank, danced, and accepted a ride home from a twenty-five-year-old who wasn't even my type, grabbed his stick shift while driving down the West Side Highway, and got arrested for it.

I have a lot of fun making Lake guess which one is the lie. I mean, they're all technically true, or at least I always thought so until my dad told me the bite on my butt was from an ordinary mosquito and in no way life-threatening. She laughs when I explain the situation, then gives me a motherly lecture about safe sex and just safety in general.

"Lake, I didn't sleep with the guy!" I laugh. "When I said I grabbed his stick shift, I mean an ACTUAL stick shift."

She laughs along with me, then starts explaining ways I might be able to manage my impulsiveness better. She says that even though I'm a teenager and I *want* to do crazy stuff, the problems that result from it—and all the stress they cause me—are probably what's triggering my IBS (and acne, though that doesn't seem to be a problem out here in the woods).

Basically, she says my "prefrontal cortex"—where decision-making is done in the brain—is fighting with my "amygdala," which is where emotions are. Lake is pretty reassuring that my prefrontal cortex will continue to mature into my twenties, and I won't always want to do things that sound like fun in theory but turn out to be a total shit show. Like making Brad swerve dangerously while we were driving down the West Side Highway, or the joy ride in Times Square with Jem where I almost ran over the Japanese tourists.

She says until then, though, I should get some coaching in executive function skills. That it would help me make more informed choices and pay better attention in school. I ask, *isn't that what Ritalin is for?* She laughs and tells me drugs are only a temporary fix and learning how to deal with my pre-frontal cortex without a pill will be better for me in the long run.

That night, I of course can't sleep. I toss and turn, but every time I start to drift off, I go right back into a nightmare where I'm living in the sewers of New York City, scrounging for change that people accidentally flush down the toilet. I shake myself awake time after time, trying not to freak about what might actually be in my future: diving for poop change. I have *got* to figure out a better plan.

I finally give up on any hope of sleeping and get up just as the sun starts to rise. The woods have a hazy, dewy glow that makes the world look like it picked the perfect selfie filter. I take out my sticks and start rubbing.

And rubbing. And rubbing. And rubbing.

Nothing happens. Zero. Nada. Zippo. Zilch.

I'm just about to give up, just like I have with every single other thing in my life when it gets too hard, when a tiny wisp of smoke appears. I'm not all that impressed. It's happened a few times before and nothing ever came of it. But what the hell, I'll blow and look like a total loser when the puff of smoke is gone in a puff of smoke. There's no one up yet to witness my most recent failure.

So I blow. And I blow. And I blow.

AND I GET A FIRE GOING.

My first thought is: *I am amazing!* My second is: *Poor Sam. She's been trying to get fire this whole time and it's just not working for her.* Third thought: *This will probably never happen again, so I better make the most of it.*

I stoke it into a great big roar, find the big communal cooking pot, and start making oatmeal for everyone. By the time my friends wake up, I've got breakfast waiting for them. Me. A girl who has never cooked anything before in her life. And it tastes damn good.

LIZZIE'S AWESOME CAMPFIRE OATMEAL

(adapted from Jack's original recipe)

1 ¾ cup water
1 ¾ cup Parmalat
2 cups old-fashioned oatmeal
Handful of almonds
Handful of chopped dried apricots
Handful of dried plums
2 crumbled oat and honey protein bars

☕ Slowly bring water and Parmalat to a boil. Be careful not to burn the weird, never-expiring milk-like substance!

☕ Add oats. Stir often, until gloopy and thick. (Like if you threw them at a wall, they would just stick there in a big ball.)

☕ Toss in the dried apricots and plums and stir. These will definitely make you fart/poop (dried "plums" is just a nice word for prunes), but they taste awesome, so it's worth the extra hole you might have to dig later.

☕ Top with almonds and crumbled protein bars. The whole thing tastes like cookies. Trust me.

chapter
23

Eat, hike, sleep, repeat. The days at Camp Smiley have a nice rhythm to them, and before long I feel like I know every little thing there is to know about Ari, Chandra, Sam, and Jack.

Except, of course, what actually happened during Jack's bungled murder attempt. That he still refuses to talk about. I still can't believe it actually happened.

I love the way sometimes I catch him looking at me with those blueberry eyes and ripple-y abs, and how it always seems like he's watching out for me. It's like I'm some rare and precious gift he doesn't want to lose. But I'm not going anywhere. Where would I go anyhow? My mom told me I have no home to go back to. Besides, I'm having a better time here in the woods with my friends.

DID I REALLY JUST THINK THAT?

I guess I did.

"Well, there's only one thing left for you guys to do," Scarlet announces one morning. "Your solo overnights. I'll take half of you and Jed will get the other two."

Scarlet heads off with Sam, Chandra, and Ari, leaving me and Jack with Jed as our guide.

"You guys wait here a sec," he says, grabbing his single-ply and shovel. "I'll be right back."

It's the first time we've hung out just the two of us since my birthday. Although we talk all the time when everyone else is around, we both get shy.

"So . . ." I say.

"So . . ." Jack says, staring up into the branches above our heads.

"So I was thinking," I try again. "Maybe you could, like, practice by telling me. You know, about what happened. So you know how to say it in front of everyone at Truth Circle."

He shakes his head. "I really don't want you to think differently of me. And you definitely would, if you knew."

"I don't think I will." I'm acutely aware of my disappearing feelings problem, and how there's no guarantee I'll feel the same after. But I'm pretty sure I can handle whatever he's about to say.

"You will," he insists. "I do."

"How about if I tell you one of my biggest secrets?" I rush ahead without waiting for him to answer. "Once, when I was in third grade, I forgot I had a book report due. So right before school, I grabbed a book I'd found under my parents bed when I was playing hide-and-go-seek by myself. Yes, I know that's stupid and pointless. Only child probz. Anyhow, I glanced at the title on the way to school—I thought it was called Caramel Sugar, but like in French or spelled fancy or something, and that it was a dessert cookbook. I figured I'd just improv a little, show a few pictures, no worries. Except, you know, it turned out to be the Kama Sutra, which is like an illustrated Indian sex guide. So I basically taught my third grade class how to get laid. All because I didn't want to actually read a book and give a report on it."

I'm glad I told him this story and not the one about how once in fifth grade I farted in class and blamed it on my "squeaky shoe" that I could never make squeak again after that. Everyone knew it was a lie, and I knew everyone knew it was a lie, but I just couldn't let it go and kept trying to make my shoe "fart" for like a week. Finally, Jem announced, "You'd be better off just actually farting again and blaming it on your shoe instead of the other way around." Everyone in class howled and I ran out of the room sobbing.

He laughs but still won't tell me his secret. So I actually DO tell him the squeaky shoe story. I figure he'll think it was even funnier than the Kama Sutra one, but when I'm done he just looks sad.

"I know she's your best friend, Lizzie," Jack says. "But she doesn't seem like a very good one to me."

"I've been thinking the same thing," I tell him. "I deserve better."

The thought has been hanging around in the back of my mind for a while, even before the video and her basically stealing Ari in Vegas. But saying it out loud solidifies what I've finally realized: real friends don't do that kind of stuff. I'm totally annoyed that being at Camp Smiley has taught me another "valuable lesson" but there's no denying it.

"Yeah, she pretty much sucks. But at least she didn't take a picture of the nerdiest kid ever jerking off in the bathroom stall at school and send it to her lax bros," he says so quietly I almost miss it.

I know how it feels to have everyone see you doing something embarrassing that you never wanted anyone to see, ever. Hello, dashcam video, turned into RBB video. How humiliating. "I mean . . . that was really shitty of you. But it's hardly attempted murder."

"It is if the kid tries to kill himself over it." His words come out hoarse and choked. "I only sent the picture to like three guys, but of course they sent it to three more. It spread like wildfire. The guy was so worried his parents would see it and disown him, or that the admissions counselors of all the colleges he was planning to apply to would, that he decided his life was over and tried to jump off a bridge. Thankfully someone saw him and talked him down in time, or I would've had to off myself too. There's no way I could live, knowing I'd caused someone else to *stop* living. You know what I mean?"

I'm surprised that my feelings don't take off for something as big as this, when they have for something as little as a bad haircut. "Jack. Listen to me. Yes, you made a mistake. A big one. And you hurt someone. A lot. Your amygdala won over your pre-frontal cortex. It's a teenage thing. Give yourself a break."

I explain Lake's brain theory. It doesn't have the impact I was hoping for so I try another tactic.

"Look, I know what it feels like to be exposed publicly like that," I tell him. "To have everyone in on your dirty little secret. You feel naked and ugly and like no one will ever see anything BUT that when they look at you, ever again. So I really and truly get that what you did sucks. But you didn't try to kill the guy."

He shrugs. "Semantics."

"Not semi-whatever that word you just used is," I tell him. "You're the future lawyer. You should know you couldn't be convicted of attempted murder when all you did was take a picture. Like, maybe you'd get busted for invading someone's privacy—though I don't really think a public bathroom can be considered private—or underage porn or something, but not murder."

He turns to me. His eyes are total Deadsville. No sparkles to be found. "Lizzie, you don't get it. I can never forgive myself."

"Maybe if you get the guy to forgive you, then you could?" I suggest.

"I've thought about apologizing a million times, but what would I say? I'm the total asshole who ruined your life so I could give my buddies a few laughs?"

I try to put words around my thoughts. "I think it's more about really meaning it than the actual words. I know I would feel a ton better if my dad apologized to me for leaving. I might even be able to forgive him if I had just like a SPECK of insight about why he did it and that he at least feels bad about abandoning us."

Jack's holding his head in his hands. It looks like it weighs ten jillion pounds. Almost as much as his guilt. Maybe what he said is true. Maybe he will never get over this.

"Do you forgive Jem for making that video about you?" he finally asks.

"Her apology wasn't exactly sincere."

"What if it was?"

"I mean, yeah. I think I would," I say. "Part of it's my fault too, because I never told her how crappy it made me feel. And honestly, that guy has to take responsibility for his part in what happened too. Like, please. Control yourself. Wait to jack off until you get home, right?"

I root around my heart, trying to gauge whether knowing Jack's secret changes how I feel about him. And the answer I keep coming up with is no. He's a good guy who did a bad thing, but he's not a bad person.

I lean down and kiss the top of his head, hoping he gets what I mean without me having to spell it out. *I believe in you* and *you can get past this* and *you're all good, really and truly.* He looks up at me and I kiss both his eyelids. And then I lay the softest one ever on his lips, something I've been wanting to do ever since that first time on my birthday.

We both fall into the kiss. He doesn't even try to grab a boob or put my hand down his pants or anything. He's a perfect gentleman. OMG. Is he actually the perfect guy?

The next thing I know, there's a lot of leaves crinkling and throat-clearing. Jack and I jump apart.

"Let's head out," Jed says. He has a huge smile on his face, which is confusing because I know we can get demerits or even not graduate for having "inappropriate sexual contact" with another camper.

"That wasn't what it looked like," I stutter.

"Yeah, I was trying to help Lizzie get something out of her eye. . . ." Jack adds.

"I have no idea what you two are talking about," he says. "Come on, follow me."

Jed drops me off at my solo campsite. Before he leaves, he hands me a little book with a green cover. It's called *Brave Enough*.

"I thought you might want some company tonight," he says.

"I would," I tell him. "Actual human company, though. I'm not much of a reader."

"Maybe this will change your mind," he says.

"Maybe," I tell him, but I know there's not a chance it will.

Jed and Jack take off and I'm on my own. We've been told we'll all be several miles apart and not to try and find each other. I still can't help wishing Jack and I were doing the solo as a duo.

I get to work on setting up camp. I assemble my tent. Hang my food so bears won't get it. Find rocks to make a circle to keep any fire I might succeed in stoking from spreading. And then, of course, the rubbing starts.

And continues until lunch with zero puffs of smoke.

I eat some leftover oatmeal, drink egg-fart water, and remember how awesome kissing Jack was. And what a nice guy he is. And how I want him to be able to get past what he did. I really think asking forgiveness is the place to start. If not, the whole ugly scene will just hang over his head, torturing him forever.

I take out my sticks and start twisting again. Which reminds me of how I nicknamed it hand-jobbing. Which makes me wonder if a lot of girls have done that to Jack. I decide he's not the man whore type.

Several hours later, I have two open blisters and very little hope of ever making fire. I guess that one time I did was a total fluke. I come close to throwing in the towel a few times. But I refuse to give up. I keep going.

Droplets of sweat fall from my face, ruining any chance at all of sparking up a spark, which it's looking more and more like I will never create. I sit back, sigh, and swipe an arm across my forehead. I hear a vaguely familiar clicking noise and look up to see my ex-BFF.

"Bandit, you little thief!"

He's holding my cup in one hand and the spoon I worked so hard to make in the other. Yeah, I probably shouldn't have left them out after lunch, but it just seemed like it would be so much more convenient once dinner rolls around. "Put those down this instant!"

He brings the cup to his cutie little nose and smells it. Then he makes a face and chucks it at a nearby tree.

"That's right, klepto, you just put everything back where you found it and no one will get hurt!"

He clicks some more. I swear he smiles at me. And then he kind of waves the spoon around in the air and takes off running. I sprint after him. I don't think I'd get passed over for graduation for not having my spoon anymore but you never know.

I crash around trees and through bushes and over streams trying to keep up with Bandit. I'm surprised that I'm not even the slightest bit out of breath, even though we're going fast and far. I guess I've kind of gotten in shape at Camp Smiley. Can I PLEASE stop thinking nice things about it here?

Bandit stops short at the base of a hollow tree and drops my spoon there. I know he can't talk or really communicate with me, but I swear his posture and expression say *Hey, thanks for the fun game of tag. Here you go. Maybe you want to clean the crusty oatmeal off this before you have dinner.*

I inch forward. Bandit doesn't move. I creep closer on my tiptoes. He stares at me. I stand completely still. He waves at me with his cutie little paws. And then I pounce.

"Gotcha!" I say, scooping up my precious spoon like it's vintage Tiffany, made of sterling silver and not some splintery wood.

Bandit grins.

"I have to get going now, little guy. Gotta finish this solo overnight so I can go home and . . . well, I don't actually know what I'll be doing once I go home. Or where home is really. But I have to finish this or I can't leave. Wait, why do I want to leave if I have nothing to go back to?"

Bandit cocks his head and nods. And then he disappears into a hole in the tree he's standing in front of.

"Well, okay then. It's been nice knowing you," I call after him. "Stay safe now, and don't get eaten by a mountain lion or anything."

I'm about to start heading back to my campsite when Bandit pops back out of the hole holding something familiar. I cannot even BELIEVE what I'm seeing. I squint and rub my eyes.

"BUDDY!" I scream.

Apparently, my whoop of joy startles Bandit. He lets go of my blankie and darts deeper into the recesses of the tree. Buddy flutters to the ground. I run over and scoop him up.

I gather my BFF to me, inhaling his special scent. Sure, there's a little bit of what smells like skunk funk on him. And he has a few new little holes, like Bandit has been rubbing him for comfort at night like I do. Whatever, BUDDY'S BACK!

By the time I find my way to camp, the sun is setting. I try a few more times to get a spark but my blisters and aching muscles are not cooperating. I give up on the idea of a hot dinner and munch on turkey jerky instead. It's really not so bad once you get used to it. Salty and meaty with just a little kick of honey for sweetness. Plus, it fills you up without weighing you down.

Maybe I could be in advertising, I think. *Making up TV commercials for jerky and baby blankets and camps for teenage screw-ups. I might be good at that.*

I've been thinking a lot lately about the kinds of colleges I can actually get into with my grades, and what I might want to study once I get there. What Ari said about majoring in something creative actually sounds like it fits me way more than regular liberal arts stuff, or pre-med or pre-law. I'll have to check out what my options are when I get back to . . . wherever it is I end up. Hopefully my cardboard box has Internet access.

The sun disappears. The God rays go with it. Even though the twilight is pretty, I'm dreading what comes next. Pitch black. Ursula city.

I rub Buddy's soft edges between my fingers and stare up at the sky. The darker it gets, the more stars appear. I wonder if my dad sleeps like this, out in the wild, in a little tent in Africa. And if the stars are as bright or even brighter there.

Does he ever sit there and wonder what I'm doing, or how I am? Does he ever regret how things turned out? Does he wish I spent the time there with him that I was supposed to, before the judge said I didn't have to? Would I even be here if I had?

I know I regret how things turned out. Of course my first instinct was to wish my parents would get back together. But life isn't *The Parent Trap,* and I don't have a long-lost twin somewhere no matter how awesome that would be. But maybe my second instinct should have been to admit to my mom that *she* was the one with PTSD over the fake tsetse fly bite. I was too young to realize the emergency flight was due to the fact she was worried I was dying; I actually thought flying home via medivac was strange and exciting at the time, and it remains a fun fact to pull out when people start telling "the craziest thing that ever happened to me" stories to this day.

My deep thoughts are interrupted by snarling and growling, multiplied by the crackling of branches and rustling of leaves. The good news is I know it can't be Ursula. We're nowhere near the ocean. The bad news is I'm about to get eaten anyhow, by something probably just as scary. My adrenalin pumps into high gear as I scramble around inside my backpack for my lame headlamp.

I strap it on and peer around. There's nothing out there.

Nothing.

Nothing.

Then, this. TWO GLOWING EYEBALLS STARING STRAIGHT AT ME.

"Go away!" I scream at Eyeballs. "Get out of here! I have a gun! And a knife! And . . . other stuff that can hurt you!"

Like temporary flip-flops and a roll of generic TP. Great. I'm as good as dead. The eyeballs come closer.

I throw a rock at them. They scamper away. But I'm not about to be a dumbass like all those chicks in the horror movies who assume they're safe and then get hacked into a jillion little pieces two seconds later. I need to stay on guard. I'm not convinced Eyeballs has actually left the area. I didn't hear enough twigs snapping in his retreat.

I'm still shaking and swiveling my head around in a one-hundred-and-eighty-degree arc trying to spot my predator what feels like hours later. I'm both completely on edge and totally spent, an uncomfortable combination of terror and exhaustion coursing through my veins. I want nothing more than to lie down and try to sleep but am worried if I do, I'll be dinner for Eyeballs.

I reach into my pack for a snack and my hand comes to rest on the book Jed gave me. Maybe I should give it a few pages. Reading is sure to be the ultimate insomnia cure.

It turns out to be a book of quotes. Sometimes just one sentence per page, and never more than a short paragraph. If all books had this few words, I'd read more of them. Turns out, there's something for everyone in here.

For Sam there's one about not wasting time being sad over an outdated idea you had about yourself that no longer fits.. She just needs to get used to the fact that she might not 100 percent know what kind of parts the next person she falls for will have. And really, truly know it's okay, because life's allowed to be mysterious like that.

For Ari, there's another about getting on a different path if the one you've been on isn't working for you anymore. He has to stop doing graffiti on every blank wall in town or he'll end up in jail for real next time. Which would be a waste of a perfectly cool person. I hope he'll consider Jed and Scarlet's art school suggestion. He's already really, really good. But I bet he'd get even better if he let someone teach him a thing or two.

For Chandra and Jack, it's all about forgiveness, and how that's not going to just come to them without a big effort. Because those two not only need to be forgiven by the people they wronged, but they also need to forgive *themselves*. And only they have the power to do that.

And last but not least, for me, a message about letting go of what used to be, and being okay with what is now. So my dad still went to live in Africa after my mom decided it was too dangerous for us to be there with him. So my parents got divorced. So they're never getting back together. I need to just accept what is, not what I wish or hope things would be.

I have to keep moving ahead instead of looking back.

chapter

24

I wake up to the sun beating down overhead. Birds chirping away. And Bandit staring down at me thoughtfully.

I look up at him and rub my eyes. "You shouldn't sneak up on people like that, Bandit. It scares us!"

He blinks his eyes. They catch the sunlight. They look like they're glowing.

"Hey, wait a minute," I say, sitting up. "Was that you last night?"

I swear he laughs at me.

I laugh along with him. "You're Eyeballs? I stayed up practically the whole night being scared of you?"

It occurs to me that most of the things that scare me in the middle of the night—Ursula, Eyeballs, living in a cardboard box—are probably not things I need to worry about at all. Will the revelations never end? Maybe that's why Camp Smiley thinks it's so important we finish a solo overnight before we graduate: so much time to think so many big thoughts.

Which reminds me: I made it through the solo! IT'S A CAMP SMILEY MIRACLE!

There's only one thing left to do, and that's make a fire. I'll be damned if I'm going to half-ass the overnight by not having one. I pop up, stumble to my feet, and see Scarlet way off in the distance.

I start hand-jobbing like crazy. The sticks throw an immediate spark, but even though I blow on it hard and quick, it goes out immediately.

Hand job, spark, bleh.

Hand job, spark, meh.

"What am I doing wrong?" I mutter to myself. I touch the bundle of twigs and leaves I was working with yesterday and know immediately. They're dewy and cold. I'm never going to make fire with wet kindling. I stroke Buddy while I try to figure out my next move. He's so comforting. So warm and dry.

SO FLAMMABLE.

I take Buddy by the corners and pull hard. He rips right smack down the middle. And at least I'll still have half of him when I'm done. I can't believe I just bifurcated Buddy. Which is a funny word that I only know because of my English teacher, the prudey Mrs. Lemelson. I guess she wasn't so bad at her job after all if I remembered that all the way out here in the woods.

I position half-Buddy in front of the sticks. And I rub until my fingers bleed. And guess what?

A PUFF OF SMOKE TURNS INTO SPARKS TURN INTO A FLAME TURNS INTO A FIRE.

"I did it!" I whisper to myself. "I actually finished what I started for once."

"It's wonderful to see you finally stopped fighting the light inside you that was always there, just waiting to come out," Scarlet tells me with a warm smile. "You made an incredible turnaround, Lizzie. You should be very proud of yourself."

"I am," I tell her.

On our way to pick up Sam, Scarlet asks about my plans for the future, and I explain to her how I think maybe Bowdoin wasn't really the right place for me anyhow. That I maybe want to do something relating to fashion in college, if that's possible. She gives me a few suggestions that I might even be able to try out starting this summer. I'm pumped.

When we get to Sam's campsite, Sam looks completely miserable. "I can't make a fire. I tried so hard, for so long."

"Don't quit," I urge her. "Try one more time."

She holds up her blistered hands. "No thanks."

I reach for another tactic. Which is busting her chops. "It's because you're a 5.99 on the Kinsey Scale, isn't it?"

She scowls. "What does that have to do with anything, Lizzie?"

I smile. "I'm just saying it's kind of unfair, expecting a homoflexible but 99.99 percent lesbian to know how to give a good hand job. It's almost like they should give you another task, like licking the jelly out of a donut or something. . . ."

Sam starts cracking up. "Fuck you, Elizabeth," she says, grabbing her sticks and starting to rub them together.

"Right back at ya, Samantha," I say, tossing the other half of bifurcated Buddy in front of where she's furiously rubbing.

She gasps. "No, Lizzie. You love that blanket. Don't sacrifice it for me. There's no reason to."

"You're worth it," I tell her. And she is. I can always buy another Buddy, if it's not too expensive. Or I guess I could ask for one for Christmas or Hanukkah. Maybe dad celebrates Kwanzaa now that he lives in Africa?

Suddenly, a spark flies off Sam's sticks and into Buddy. She kneels, she blows. There's fire. She puts both fists to the sky like Rocky and yells, "YES! FINALLY!"

I throw my arms around her. "It feels damn good to finish what you started, doesn't it?"

Coeur Canyon Animal Rescue
@ccar • Jul 5

Myth: Raccoons seen in daytime are rabid.

Fact: Raccoon kits aren't nocturnal yet, and often play in daylight hours while Mom naps.

chapter

25

"I'm so freaking nervous," Chandra says.

Sam, Chandra and I are getting ready for the grad ceremony in our cabin back at Outpost. We just finished taking
one final shower in the communal bathroom. We all have a
good laugh at how Chandra was so worried about being naked
in there the first time that she showered in her underwear.

"But I'm not worried anymore because my boobs are too big
and my butt is too small for you," Chandra teases Sam. "Or is
it the other way around?"

"Your nose is too perfect," she teases back. "It has no character at all."

I guess it's this big Camp Smiley tradition to send your
newly un-fucked up kid something to wear other than khakis,
fleece, and fake Timberlands for the ceremony. And so in the
nicest gesture ever Scarlet and Lake have put together a totally
rad outfit for me, paid for by my parents of course. My mom
can't shop from rehab so she gave them some ideas, and warned

them not to leave the picking to my dad since he's not the most fashion-forward dude on the planet. Both Scarlet and Lake have heard the Ginger Jewish Jesus story, so they knew my mom wasn't exaggerating. I also have back all the stuff that got confo'ed on my first day of Camp Smiley.

I check myself out in the not-glass funhouse mirror on the wall. I look warped and wiggly, yet still somehow glowing and great. I've blown dry and flat ironed my hair so it hangs straight and shiny down my back. My makeup is understated and subtle. I even blow dried, flat ironed, and made up both of my friends. Well, as much as Sam would let me. I got to apply the teensiest, tiniest bit of mascara and tinted chapstick on her. We all look hot together.

I'm wearing a clingy yet classy wrap dress paired with pretty high heels. I kind of can't believe how uncomfortable thongs are compared to granny panties, and how much cleavage a push-up reveals as opposed to even a Lulu sports bra. I'm sure I'll get used to being normal again, but for now it feels weird.

"You look great, Lizzie," Chandra tells me. She's still wearing her uniform. Her parents haven't sent her anything special to wear tonight. Either they haven't quite forgiven her yet, or they don't have the money to buy her new clothes even if they have. Or both. I can almost feel her disappointment, seeing that Sam and I both have "civilian" outfits on.

"You really do." Sam squints and turns her head to the side. "One suggestion, though?"

"Sure."

"Those shoes might be kind of hard to run in. And you know how they said everyone always goes sprinting to their parents after the final Truth Circle. . . ."

"I can pretty much guarantee you I won't be running any-where. My mom can't come because she's in rehab, and I just can't see me running into my dad's arms. So thanks, but I'm good."

But Chandra's still eyeing me. "Your outfit is so beautiful. I've never seen anything so gorgeous, especially not up close."

I look down at the dress. It's, like, perfect. I just know Jack's eyes will pop out when he sees me in it. But I'm also pretty sure he likes me no matter what I'm wearing. "You know what? You wear it."

Chandra puts her hands up in front of her. "Oh no, I couldn't!"

But I'm already stripping and handing the dress and shoes to her. "Can't let it go to waste, can we?"

She runs a hand down the silky fabric. "For real? Do you think it will fit me?"

"It's stretchy," I say, nodding. "And if there ever was a time for a sisterhood of the travelling dress, I'd say this was it."

She tears up. "That's the second nicest thing anyone's ever done for me. After giving me the Lulu leggings. Thanks for everything, Lizzie."

I'm about to put my uniform back on when I take another look at what's in my bag. There's a pair of, I don't know, some weird pajama pants, a white crop top, and black flat-form sandals in there. The pants are made of similar uber-soft material and have a repeating leaf pattern on them. There's a note: *There's even fashion in Africa too, believe it or not. Love, Dad.*

"Look at these pajamas my dad brought me back from Africa," I tell my friends.

Sam holds up the pants. They have a wide swath of elastic ribbing at the waist and ankles. Basically, they're genie pants. "Pretty sure everyone would buy these if they sold them at Urban Outfitters."

I give them another look. They're just bohemian enough to be trendy. Weirder things have happened. Jeggings were a thing once too. "Not really my style, but you're probably right. I can't believe he got the right top and shoes to go with them."

"Maybe he asked your mom for advice?" Sam says. She's basically wearing a fancier variation of our Camp Smiley uniform to graduation: Nantucket red Bermuda shorts, a white tank top with an unbuttoned, untucked pinstripe oxford shirt over it, sleeves rolled up, navy Sperry sneakers. She currently looks like an adorably preppy boy wearing a little mascara.

"Maybe," I say, putting on the ensemble. The roomy pants are. So. Soft. Stupidly comfortable. I pull the crop top over my head, strap on the flatforms, and do a little twirl.

"So what do you think?" I ask Sam.

"If I didn't know you, I'd totally hit on you," she says.

I stare into the wavy fake mirror and see that she's right on the money. The pants are cut so they make my waist look tiny and my legs appear longer, and show off my delicate ankles (now that the right one is no longer swollen and bruised). The crop top adds a touch of sex appeal with just a flash of skin, and the flatforms are totally on trend this season.

"You too," Sam tells Chandra. She looks stunning in the dress. Truly beautiful.

Sam holds out one arm to me and one to Chandra. "Ready?" We all lock elbows and we march out to our last Truth

Circle together. I can't believe how much has happened. How much my life has changed. How much my whole *outlook* on life has changed.

"Wow," Jack says when he sees me.

"Oh, these old things?" I say, grinning up at him. "They're just some weird pajamas my dad got me in Africa."

"Those are some damn sexy pajamas."

"I'd like to start tonight's Truth Circle by having everyone give their revised autobiographies. Jack, how about you go first?" Jed says.

Jack points at his chest. *Who me?*

Scarlet flashes him a peace sign. Jed hums a few bars of "Friend of the Devil." I squeeze his thigh and whisper *you can do this.*

"Hey everyone," Jack says, clearing his throat. He shifts nervously from one foot to the other. "I, uh . . . I came to Camp Smiley because I was so ashamed of myself. I thought I was worthless, lower than the lowest primordial ooze."

"When's he going to get to the killing part?" Sam whispers.

"Shhhhhhh. The man's trying to confess here. Give him a chance."

Jack keeps going. "I've been haunted by a really shitty decision I made before I came here, one that got me so messed up in the head I barely knew who I was anymore. I didn't want to talk about what happened. I didn't even want to think about it ever again, although that totally backfired. It's all I thought about, day and night. And I couldn't stop hating myself."

Jack pauses for a breath. The brief pause turns into a full minute of silence. I can tell he's really struggling, and hope I made it a little easier by not freaking out or pulling away when he told me his story out in the woods.

"You got this," I tell him, just like he did when I was trying to make my spoon.

"I guess I'm just trying to say, think before you act. Because you never know who you might be hurting for one little moment of pleasure or a cheap laugh."

"Can you please just spit it out, Jack," Sam says, no bullshit as always.

"Fine. I saw a guy at school in a . . . compromising position. Something best left private. And instead of letting it stay private, I took a picture of him and sent it to a few of my buddies, thinking it would be funny and that would be the end of it. Instead, they sent the pic on to more friends, and it just went viral from there. The kid understandably freaked out. He thought his life was ruined, so he decided to take it. Luckily someone stopped him, and he didn't die. But the fact remains that one stupid, thoughtless thing I did almost killed someone. So, like, just be kind to one another. Even the nerds of this world. Especially the nerds and the outcasts of the world. They have enough people bullying them. Just be nice, okay? That's my message."

Jack looks like he doesn't know whether to laugh or cry. Everyone snaps. A few people start clapping. As for me, I stand up and give him a hug. "Good job. I knew you could do it," I whisper in his ear.

"I wrote him a big, long, sincere apology letter today when we got back. Scarlet already mailed it for me. Thanks for the idea."

"I took my own idea too, and sent an apology note to the policemen I was so rude to. Feels good, right?"

He nods. I nod. We grin at each other like idiots. Make that, in love idiots. DID I JUST THINK THAT? I guess I did.

After everyone takes a turn, it's time for us to throw our lists of the bad habits we're leaving behind onto the fire. After much deep thought, mine says no more:

- Hooking up with randos on Tinder
- Sneaking out and getting shitfaced with randos in bars
- Grabbing a rando's stick shift while we're driving down the West Side Highway (to this I add a parenthetical note that says *no, that's not an innuendo if this doesn't burn . . . I'm talking about a literal stick shift*)
- Screaming rude stuff at the cops after I hand them my crappy fake ID instead of the real one
- Trying to hide/run away from my problems
- Not letting people know how much they've hurt me, or how much I care about them
- Being ungrateful for all the great things I have
- Being so unforgiving when I know everyone makes mistakes and does stuff they regret

I'm pretty sure Jack's has something on it about not using social media to ruin nerds' lives, and the next time he sees some guy whacking it in a bathroom stall, he'll just walk out and pretend he never saw a thing. I hope everyone else burns all the things that hold them back and plans to do whatever will move them forward from now on.

The fire lights up in a rainbow of purples, greens, and blues. Even though I know it's just the Mystical Fire powder again, it somehow seems not cheesy. Totally meaningful. Another sign of maturity? Seriously, I can't believe how frigging mature I've gotten since I turned seventeen.

Everyone tells everyone else what they love about each other. Ari tells Sam, *You're always so chill* and *Your hair looks cool like that.* Chandra tells Jack she admires his muscles and gorgeous eyes. I might be a little bit jealous now, but I still hold it together. Sam tells me, *I love how you're always willing to listen to everyone's problems.* Chandra tells me she thinks I'm really generous. Scarlet says, *You've got a great sense of style.*

Which gets me to thinking: what if I tried to market these ridiculously soft and comfortable and yet still somehow cool pants? Sam was right when she said if Urban sold them, everyone would want a pair. So why not just sell them myself? If they got popular enough, it might be enough to get me into a great school with fashion majors. I might even be rich again someday. ON MY OWN MERITS. Note to self: finally something I *want* to talk to Dad about—how to get more of these pants, stat.

And then it's time. The parents burst out of the teepee to congratulate their newly graduated sons and daughters. Everyone's laughing and running and hugging and crying. I walk forward slowly, trying to find my dad.

An adorable little girl jumps into Jack's arms and she buries her head in his shoulder. "I missed you so much!" she squeals.

Sam's mom slings an arm around Sam's shoulder and squeezes her tight. "Truce?"

"Truce," she says.

Chandra's parents seem reserved but happy to see her, and Ari's mom and dad fawn over him. My dad trots toward me. He's actually dressed like a normal human being in jeans and a T-shirt this time. He holds his arms out for a hug and, after a second of hesitation, I fall into it. "I'm so proud of you, honey," he says.

"Thanks." I'm surprised that I don't feel the same amount of anger toward him that I usually do. I mean, his leaving still hurts. But I'm done being pissed off all the time. I finally figured out that I had a part in how disconnected we are too. Maybe we both need to clear the air.

I resolve to start making an effort at fixing our relationship. It seems like my dad already is. My mom is making an effort by trying to get better. We're each doing the best we can. That's all you can ask of anyone.

"Your mother wanted to be here—" my dad starts.

"I know. I'm proud of her, actually."

"You should be," he says. "You're her inspiration, you know. She said if you could make positive changes in your life, so could she."

"Is being in rehab the only reason why she said I couldn't go home at the meeting? I've been really worried she was just, like, kicking me out for good."

"We'd never kick you out, honey," he says. "And of course you're coming home. With me. I'll be staying with you and Poochie in New York until your mom finishes the program. I'm sorry. I had no idea things had gotten so bad."

"How could you have known? You haven't been around in a really long time." I don't mean it as mean as it comes out, but, like . . . it's the truth. We have to deal with it. I'm done pretending things are okay when they're not. "Can I ask you a question?"

"Anything," he says.

"Why?" I ask, my voice catching on the words. Tears start pouring down my face. "How could you?"

Now my dad looks like he wants to cry too. "The way things turned out . . . that's not the way it was supposed to be, honey," he says. "The plan was always that we'd all be living in Africa and doing charitable work as a *family*. But your mom and I were having relationship problems by the time it came to launch the initiative, and she balked once she got there and it fully sunk in there was no Starbucks or Neiman Marcus nearby, or even Internet access very often. Everything about Africa made her anxiety worse than ever, and you getting that mosquito bite was the last straw. She flew you home and never looked back."

"You could've come with us," I mumble.

My dad shakes his head. "There were so many people relying on me to make the venture a success. So many lives that depended on me keeping the promises that I'd made. Your mom and I realized our differences were irreconcilable. And so we agreed you'd spend four months of the year with me, when you were on school breaks and in the summer, and I'd come home every other month during the other eight to make sure we stayed close. It seemed fair and like we'd both get quality time with you. But then you refused to come stay with me. The judge reinforced your decision. And every time I visited, it was like you'd slipped farther and farther away. You told me you hated me. I had no idea how to get your love and trust back."

"Every thirteen-year-old tells their parents they hate them! You're not supposed to believe it! You're supposed to fight for me!"

My dad hands me a thick hardcover book. Anyone who knows me at all knows I'm not a read-for-pleasure kind of girl. Or a read anything, ever kind of girl. The Caramel Sugar book report incident was an early tip off.

"Bottom line is, I love you and I'm so sorry it felt like I'd abandoned you. I want you to know that not a day has gone by in the last four years that I didn't think about you or write to you, Lizzie. I know you never opened any of my emails, but I thought if maybe I put them in book format, you might be in a better frame of mind to give it a try now. "

I glance at the title: *Letters to Lizzie.* I flip to the end. The thing clocks in at 529 pages. "Email? Who uses email anymore? Do I even *have* an email address?"

My dad cracks a smile. "A lot of old people like me still email," he tells me. "Along with people who don't have smartphones, like the villagers in the more remote areas I work in. Like, for instance, the ladies who made your pants—which are quite flattering on you, by the way—go to the local Internet café in town to check on online orders and email their distributors once or twice a month."

"Could we figure out how I can be their US distributor?" I ask my dad. "I was thinking I could maybe even give part of my profits to help save your precious pangolins or whatever?"

My dad's eyes get misty. "That's sounds like a great plan."

"Sounds like money to me," I say. "Which I'd like to start making for myself."

"About Bowdoin," he says. "I could probably still put in a good word with the dean if you can get your GPA up next semester, if you want me to. . . ."

"Thanks, but no thanks," I tell him. "I'm actually going to apply other places that are probably a better fit for me.

Lake told me today I got enough school credits for being at Camp Smiley to pass junior year. So as long as I kick it in first semester next year, I should be able to get in somewhere, right?"

"I'm sure you'll figure it out," he says, and hands me my phone. "Welcome back to civilization. I'm so glad to get this thing out of my pocket. It's been buzzing like crazy through the entire ceremony."

I take it from him and look at the screen. There's a text from my mom congratulating me on graduating. And then there are ten thousand from Jem, pictures of every fabulous port the cruise has stopped in, the fab jewelry and clothes she's bought, and a whole slew of tiny baby sea turtles.

I bet you have the worst FOMO right now, her last text says.

I throw my arm around my dad's shoulder and say, "Smile!"

I take a selfie of us grinning and text it to Jem. *Zero FOMO,* I tell her. *Life is good here too.*

"Come on, let's go say goodbye to your friends," my dad says.

"Wait, I want to tell you something first."

"Sure. You can tell me anything."

I take a deep breath. "The truth is, I *did* hate you for leaving," I tell him. "But I never stopped loving you, either. It was so confusing. I finally realized on my solo overnight that I was wrong too. I was stubborn and rude and unwilling to forgive. So I owe you an apology."

He wraps me in a hug. "You're forgiven, Lizzie."

"So are you," I whisper.

We walk back out to the fire. We run into D-R-period first.

"I have to say, I'm impressed, Elizabeth," he says, smiling at me warmly. "I wasn't sure you had it in you to graduate from

Camp Smiley and now look at you. Such a success story. I'm glad you proved me wrong."

I blush. So Director Willis actually IS a nice guy who's just a hard-ass for kids following the rules. He might even like me as a person? "I'm glad I proved you wrong too."

I run over to Sam and give her a huge hug. "You're tops, dude. Truly the best."

"Anyone who would shred her baby blanket for me is a lifelong friend," she tells me. "If you ever need anything, I'm there. Just say the word."

Chandra scoops me into the next hug. "Thanks for everything. I'll send the dress and shoes back to you when I get home. My parents already have the car packed and are waiting for me or I'd do it now. . . ."

"Nope," I tell her. "They're yours. You could probably even sell that outfit on eBay and make bank for tuition if you want to."

"No way, I'm keeping it forever," she tells me. She walks away, gets in her parents' car, and waves. I can't believe I'm saying this, but I'm going to miss her.

I feel a tap on my shoulder. It's Jack. "My little sister wants to meet you."

This adorable little creature with curly pigtails and Jack's humongous sparkly blue eyes is staring up at me. "I'm Chelsea," she says, holding out her tiny hand.

I shake it. "I'm Lizzie. Pleased to meet you, Chelsea."

She grins. "My big brother says you have a cute puppy. Can you please bring her over to play soon?"

"Absolutely. Real soon. I promise."

I mean, he only lives in Jersey. I'd go there for him.

Jack hugs me, plants the softest, sweetest, slowest kiss on me, then spins me around and heads me back toward my dad. I put my fingers to my lips, wanting to remember every last second, to feel this awesome feeling, to imprint this indelible night on my brain forever.

I turn around and wave one last goodbye to Camp Smiley as I get into the limo. Spartan never looked so comfortable. Bittersweet never tasted so good.

All your life, you were only waiting for this moment to be free.

Lizzie

My teacher for the Social Media Marketing and Branding summer class I'm taking at NYU just walked in.

Guess who he looks like?

Jack

I don't know.

Mark Zuckerberg?

Lizzie

Try James Franco.

Jack

Please tell me you're not going out for drinks with him after . . .

Jack

Lizzie

No way.

I have a date with my boyfriend.

And he's WAY cuter than Fake or James Franco, whichever this guy turns out to be.

Jack

<3. Can't wait to see you.

Lizzie

<3 <3 <3. I'm bringing Poochie so Chelsea can meet her.

You MUST know how much we like you if we're willing to trek all the way to Jersey for you guys ;)

Praise for Bapsi Sidhwa

"Pakistan's finest English-language novelist."
—*New York Times Book Review*

"Pakistan's leading female author."
—*Washington Post*

"A powerful and dramatic novelist."
—*London Times*

Praise for *Cracking India*

"In reducing the Partition to the perceptions of a polio-ridden child, a girl who tries to wrench out her tongue because it is unable to lie, Bapsi Sidhwa has given us a memorable book, one that confirms her reputation as Pakistan's finest English language novelist."—*New York Times Book Review*

"Sidhwa . . . is a rarity even in swiftly-changing Asia—a candid, forthright, balanced woman novelist. Her twentieth century view of Indian life can only be compared to V. S. Naipaul's."—*Bloomsbury Review*

"Much has been written about the holocaust that followed the Partition of India in 1947, but seldom has that story been told as touchingly, as convincingly, or as horrifyingly as it has been by novelist Bapsi Sidhwa."
—*Philadelphia Inquirer*

"A lively, compelling novel, ambitiously conceived, skillfully plotted and beautifully written."—*New York Newsday*

"A historical tragedy comes alive, yielding insight into both the past and the subcontinent's turbulent present."—*USA Today*

"A multifaceted jewel of a novel."—*Houston Chronicle*

"A mysterious and wonderful novel."—*Washington Post Book World*

Praise for *The Crow Eaters*

"A delightful and perceptive view of a Parsee family's rise from rags to riches. . . . A most intelligent and enjoyable novel."—*Seattle Times*

"[Bapsi Sidhwa's] roguish hero is a genuine charmer, and her book is as warm and vital as it is funny."—*Miami Herald*

"Fascinating. . . . The descriptions of Parsee customs and of life in Lahore, Bombay and London are rich in color, sound and aroma."—*Kansas City Star*

"Completely charming and very funny."—*New York Newsday*

"A picaresque, comic tale . . . [that] recalls the past in charming detail." —*Los Angeles Times*

"Wonderfully comic. . . . Lively and entertaining."—*Washington Post*

"An entirely refreshing, spicy and satirical book."—*Plain Dealer*

"A charming visit to India in the early 1900s. The wit is sparkling. The fragrances, sounds, and tactile aspects of Lahore are more entrancing than any travel brochure."—*San Diego Union-Tribune*

Praise for *An American Brat*

"Sidhwa's writing is brisk and funny, her characters painted so vividly you can almost hear them bickering."—*New York Times Book Review*

"The pluses and minuses of the prevailing American culture of individualism (and aversion to traditional ways) are given intelligent attention . . . and the novel takes a long, affectionate look at the exotic world of the modern Parsee community and its ancient Zoroastrian faith."—*Economist*

"An exceptional novel. . . . A remarkable sketch of American society as seen and experienced by modern immigrants."—*Los Angeles Times*

"Sidhwa writes with cunning knowledge of modern Lahore and its Parsee community."—*New York Newsday*

"Affecting, amusing, and profoundly enjoyable."—*Washington Post Book World*

CRACKING INDIA

A NOVEL

❀

Bapsi Sidhwa

❀

MILKWEED EDITIONS

© 1991, Text by Bapsi Sidhwa
(800) 520-6455
www.milkweed.org

Published 2006 by Milkweed Editions
Printed in the United States of America
Cover design by Christian Fünfhausen
Interior design by R. W. Scholes
The text of this book is set in Trajanus Roman.
12 13   9 8 7

ISBN-10: 1-57131-048-7 (paperback)
ISBN-13: 978-1-57131-048-4 (paperback)

Milkweed Editions, a nonprofit publisher, gratefully acknowledges support from Anonymous; Emilie and Henry Buchwald; Bush Foundation; Patrick and Aimee Butler Family Foundation; Cargill Value Investment; Timothy and Tara Clark Family Charitable Fund; Dougherty Family Foundation; Ecolab Foundation; General Mills Foundation; Kathleen Jones; D. K. Light; McKnight Foundation; a grant from the Minnesota State Arts Board, through an appropriation by the Minnesota State Legislature, a grant from the National Endowment for the Arts, and private funders; Sheila C. Morgan; Laura Jane Musser Fund; an award from the National Endowment for the Arts, which believes that a great nation deserves great art; Navarre Corporation; Debbie Reynolds; Cynthia and Stephen Snyder; St. Paul Travelers Foundation; Ellen and Sheldon Sturgis; Surdna Foundation; Target Foundation; Gertrude Sexton Thompson Charitable Trust (George R. A. Johnson, Trustee); James R. Thorpe Foundation; Toro Foundation; Weyerhaeuser Family Foundation; and Xcel Energy Foundation.

The Library of Congress has cataloged the first edition as follows:

Sidhwa, Bapsi.
    [Ice-candy-man]
    Cracking India : a novel / Bapsi Sidhwa.
        p. cm.
    Previously published as: Ice-candy-man.

    1. India—History—1947—Fiction. I. Title.
    PR9540.9.S53I34 1991
    823—dc20   91-12967

MINNESOTA
STATE ARTS BOARD

40th
ANNIVERSARY

NATIONAL
ENDOWMENT
FOR THE ARTS
Established 1965

This book is printed on acid-free paper.

For the Kermanis
Zerses, Cambayses and Behram
Baku and Koko
And Deepa Mehta

CRACKING INDIA

Chapter 1

Shall I hear the lament of the nightingale, submissively lending my ear?
Am I the rose to suffer its cry in silence year after year?
The fire of verse gives me courage and bids me no more to be faint.
With dust in my mouth, I am abject: to God I make my complaint.
Sometimes You favor our rivals then sometimes with us You are free,
I am sorry to say it so boldly. You are no less fickle than we.
                    —Iqbal: "Complaint to God"

My world is compressed. Warris Road, lined with rain gutters, lies
between Queens Road and Jail Road: both wide, clean, orderly
streets at the affluent fringes of Lahore.

Rounding the right-hand corner of Warris Road and continuing on Jail Road is the hushed Salvation Army wall. Set high, at
eight-foot intervals, are the wall's dingy eyes. My child's mind is
blocked by the gloom emanating from the wire mesh screening the
oblong ventilation slits. I feel such sadness for the dumb creature I
imagine lurking behind the wall. I know it is dumb because I have
listened to its silence, my ear to the wall.

Jail Road also harbors my energetic Electric-aunt and her
adenoidal son. . . large, slow, inexorable. Their house is adjacent to
the den of the Salvation Army.

Opposite it, down a bumpy, dusty, earth-packed drive, is the
one-and-a-half-room abode of my godmother. With her dwell her
docile old husband and her slavesister. This is my haven. My refuge
from the perplexing unrealities of my home on Warris Road.

A few furlongs away Jail Road vanishes into the dense bazaars
of Mozang Chungi. At the other end a distant canal cuts the road
at the periphery of my world.

11

Lordly, lounging in my briskly rolling pram, immersed in dreams, my private world is rudely popped by the sudden appearance of an English gnome wagging a leathery finger in my ayah's face. But for keen reflexes that enable her to pull the carriage up short there might have been an accident, and blood spilled on Warris Road. Wagging his finger over my head into Ayah's alarmed face, he tut-tuts: "Let her walk. Shame, shame! Such a big girl in a pram! She's at least four!"

He smiles down at me, his brown eyes twinkling intolerance.

I look at him politely, concealing my complacence. The Englishman is short, leathery, middle-aged, pointy-eared. I like him.

"Come on. Up, up!" he says, crooking a beckoning finger.

"She not walk much . . . she get tired," drawls Ayah. And simultaneously I raise my trouser cuff to reveal the leather straps and wicked steel calipers harnessing my right boot.

Confronted by Ayah's liquid eyes and prim gloating, and the triumphant revelation of my calipers, the Englishman withers.

But back he bounces, bobbing up and down. "So what?" he says, resurrecting his smile. "Get up and walk! Walk! You need the exercise more than other children! How will she become strong, sprawled out like that in her pram? Now, you listen to me . . . " He lectures Ayah, and prancing before the carriage which has again started to roll says, "I want you to tell her mother . . . "

Ayah and I hold our eyes away, effectively dampening his good-Samaritan exuberance . . . and wagging his head and turning about, the Englishman quietly dissolves up the driveway from which he had so enthusiastically sprung.

The covetous glances Ayah draws educate me. Up and down, they look at her. Stub-handed twisted beggars and dusty old beggars on crutches drop their poses and stare at her with hard, alert eyes. Holy men, masked in piety, shove aside their pretenses to ogle her with lust. Hawkers, cart-drivers, cooks, coolies and cyclists turn their heads as she passes, pushing my pram with the unconcern of the Hindu goddess she worships.

Ayah is chocolate-brown and short. Everything about her is

12

eighteen years old and round and plump. Even her face. Full-blown cheeks, pouting mouth and smooth forehead curve to form a circle with her head. Her hair is pulled back in a tight knot.

And, as if her looks were not stunning enough, she has a rolling bouncy walk that agitates the globules of her buttocks under her cheap colorful saris and the half-spheres beneath her short sari-blouses. The Englishman no doubt had noticed.

We cross Jail Road and enter Godmother's compound. Walking backwards, the buffalo-hide water-pouch slung from his back, the waterman is spraying the driveway to settle the dust for evening visitors. Godmother is already fitted into the bulging hammock of her easy chair and Slavesister squats on a low cane stool facing the road. Their faces brighten as I scramble out of the pram and run towards them. Smiling like roguish children, softly clapping hands they chant, "*Langer deen! Paisay ke teen! Tamba mota, pag mahin!*" Freely translated, "Lame Lenny! Three for a penny! Fluffy pants and fine fanny!"

Flying forward I fling myself at Godmother and she lifts me onto her lap and gathers me to her bosom. I kiss her, insatiably, excessively, and she hugs me. She is childless. The bond that ties her strength to my weakness, my fierce demands to her nurturing, my trust to her capacity to contain that trust—and my loneliness to her compassion—is stronger than the bond of motherhood. More satisfying than the ties between men and women.

I cannot be in her room long without in some way touching her. Some nights, clinging to her broad white back like a bug, I sleep with her. She wears only white khaddar saris and white khaddar blouses beneath which is her coarse bandage-tight bodice. In all the years I never saw the natural shape of her breasts.

Somewhere in the uncharted wastes of space beyond, is Mayo Hospital. We are on a quiet wide veranda running the length of the first floor. The cement floor is shining clean.

Colonel Bharucha, awesome, bald, as pink-skinned as an Englishman, approaches swiftly along the corridor. My mother springs up from the bench on which we've been waiting.

He kneels before me. Gently he lifts the plaster cast on my dangling right leg and suddenly looks into my eyes. His eyes are a complex hazel. They are direct as an animal's. He can read my mind.

Colonel Bharucha is cloaked in thunder. The terrifying aura of his renown and competence are with him even when he is without his posse of house surgeons and head nurses. His thunder is reflected in my mother's on-your-mark attentiveness. If he bends, she bends swifter. When he reaches for the saw on the bench she reaches it first and hands it to him with touching alacrity. It is a frightening arm's-length saw. It belongs in a woodshed. He withdraws from his pockets a mallet, a hammer and a chisel.

The surgeon's pink head, bent in concentration, hides the white cast. I look at my mother. I turn away to look at a cloudless sky. I peer inquisitively at the closed windows screening the large general ward in front of me. The knocks of the hammer and chisel and the sawing have ceased to alarm. I am confident of the doctor's competence. I am bored. The crunch of the saw biting into plaster continues as the saw is worked to and fro by the surgeon. I look at his bowed head and am arrested by the splotch of blood just visible on my shin through the crack in the plaster.

My boredom vanishes. The blood demands a reaction. "Um . . . ," I moan dutifully. There is no response. "Um . . . Um . . . ," I moan, determined to draw attention.

The sawing stops. Colonel Bharucha straightens. He looks up at me and his direct eyes bore into my thoughts. He cocks his head, impishly defying me to shed crocodile tears. Caught out I put a brave face on my embarrassment and my nonexistent pain and look away.

It is all so pleasant and painless. The cast is off. My mother's guilt-driven attention is where it belongs—on the steeply fallen arch of my right foot. The doctor buckles my sandal and helps me from the bench saying, "It didn't hurt now, did it?" He and my mother talk over my head in cryptic monosyllables, nods and signals. I am too relieved to see my newly released foot and its valuable deformity intact to be interested in their grown-up exclusivity. My mother takes my hand and I limp away happily.

It is a happy interlude. I am sent to school. I play "I sent a letter to my friend..." with other children. My cousin, slow, intense, observant, sits watching.

"Which of you's sick and is not supposed to run?" asks the teacher: and bound by our telepathic conspiracy, both Cousin and I point to Cousin. He squats, distributing his indolent weight on his sturdy feet and I shout, play, laugh and run on the tips of my toes. I have an overabundance of energy. It can never be wholly released.

The interlude was happy.

I lie on a white wooden table in a small room. I know it is the same hospital. I have been lured unsuspecting to the table but I get a whiff of something frightening. I hate the smell with all my heart, and my heart pounding I try to get off the table. Hands hold me. Colonel Bharucha, in a strange white cap and mask, looks at me coolly and says something to a young and nervous lady doctor. The obnoxious smell grows stronger as a frightening muzzle is brought closer to my mouth and nose. I scream and kick out. The muzzle moves away. Again it attacks and again I twist and wrench, turning my face from side to side. My hands are pinned down. I can't move my legs. I realize they are strapped. Hands hold my head. "No! No! Help me. Mummy! Mummy, help me!" I shout, panicked. She too is aligned with them. "I'm suffocating," I scream. "I can't breathe." There is an unbearable weight on my chest. I moan and cry.

I am held captive by the brutal smell. It has vaporized into a milky cloud. I float round and round and up and down and fall horrendous distances without landing anywhere, fighting for my life's breath. I am abandoned in that suffocating cloud. I moan and my ghoulish voice turns me into something despicable and eerie and deserving of the terrible punishment. But where am I? How long will the horror last? Days and years with no end in sight...

It must have ended.

I switch awake to maddening pain, sitting up in my mother's bed crying. I must have been crying a long time. I become aware of the new plaster cast on my leg. The shape of the cast is altered from the last time. The toes point up. The pain from my leg radiates all over my small body. "Do something. I'm hurting!"

My mother tells me the story of the little mouse with seven tails.

"The mouse comes home crying." My mother rubs her knuckles to her eyes and, energetically imitating the mouse, sobs, "'Mummy, Mummy, do something. The children at school tease me. They sing: "Freaky mousey with seven tails! Lousy mousey with seven tails!" ' So, the little mouse's mother chops off one tail. The next day the mouse again comes home crying: 'Mummy, Mummy, the children tease me. "Lousy mousey with six tails! Freaky mousey with six tails! " ' "

And so on, until one by one the little mouse's tails are all chopped off and the story winds to its inevitable and dismal end with the baby mouse crying: "Mummy, Mummy, the children tease me. They sing, 'Freaky mousey with no tail! Lousy mousey with no tail!' " And there is no way a tail can be tacked back on.

The doleful story adds to my misery. But stoically bearing my pain for the duration of the tale, out of pity for my mother's wan face and my father's exaggerated attempts to become the tragic mouse, I once again succumb to the pain.

My mother tells my father: "Go next door and phone the doctor to come at once!" It is in the middle of the night. And it is cold. Father puts on his dressing gown and wrapping a scarf round his neck leaves us. My screaming loses its edge of panic. An hour later, exhausted by the pain and no longer able to pander to my mother's efforts to distract, I abandon myself to hysteria.

"Daddy has gone to fetch Colonel Bharucha," soothes Mother.

She carries me round and round the room stroking my back. Finally, pushing past the curtain and the door, she takes me into the sitting room.

My father raises his head from the couch.

The bitter truth sinks in. He never phoned the doctor. He never went to fetch him. And my mother collaborated in the betrayal. I realize there is nothing they can do and I don't blame them.

The night must have passed—as did the memory of further pain.

As news of my operation spreads, the small and entire Parsee community of Lahore, in clucking clusters, descends on the Sethi household. I don't wish to see them. I cry for Godmother. I feel only she can appreciate my pain and comfort me. She sends her obese emissary, Mini Aunty, who with her dogged devotion to my mother—and multiplicity of platitudes—only aggravates. "My, my, my! So here we are! Flat on our backs like old ladies!" She clicks her tongue. "We've no consideration for poor Mummy, have we?" As if I've deliberately committed surgery on my foot and sneaked my leg into a cast!

But, preceded by the slave, Godmother comes.

She sits by my bed stroking me, smiling, her eyes twinkling concern, in her gray going-out sari, its pretty border of butterflies pinned to iron strands of scant combed-back hair. The intensity of her tenderness and the concentration of her attention are narcotic. I require no one else.

All evening long Mother and Father sit in the drawing room, long-faced and talking in whispers, answering questions, accepting advice, exhibiting my plastered leg.

When Colonel Bharucha makes his house call at dusk he is ushered through the sitting room—hushed by his passage into the nursery by the officiating and anxious energy of Electric-aunt. Father, cradling me like a baby, carries me in.

The visiting ladies form a quiet ring round my cot as with a little mallet the doctor checks my wrist, knees, elbows and left ankle for reflexes, and injects a painkiller into my behind. Cousin, watching the spectacle, determines seriously to become a doctor or a male nurse. Any profession that permits one to jab pins into people merits his consideration.

Taking advantage of Colonel Bharucha's brief presence Mother reads out her list of questions. Should she sit me out in the sun? Massage like this . . . or that? Use almond or mustard oil? Can she give me Mr. Phailbus's homeopathic powders? Cod-liver oil?

"I'm to blame," she says, "I left her to the ayahs . . . "

A month later, free of pain, I sit in my stroller, my right leg stuck straight out in front on account of my cast, as Ayah propels me to the zoo. I observe the curious glances coming my way and soak in the commiserate clucking of tongues, wearing a polite and nonchalant countenance. The less attention I appear to demand the more attention I get. And, despite the provocative agitation of Ayah's bouncy walk, despite the gravitational pull of her moon-like face, I am the star attraction of the street.

When we stop by the chattering monkeys in the zoo, even they through their cages ogle me. I stare at the white plaster forcing my unique foot into the banal mold of a billion other feet and I ponder my uncertain future.

What will happen once the cast comes off? What if my foot emerges immaculate, fault-free? Will I have to behave like other children, slogging for my share of love and other handouts? Aren't I too old to learn to throw tantrums—or hold my breath and have a fit? While other children have to clamor and jump around to earn their candy, I merely sit or stand, wearing my patient, butter-wouldn't-melt . . . and displaying my calipers—and I am showered with candy.

What if I have to labor at learning spellings and reciting poems and strive with forty other driven children to stand first, second or third in class? So far I've been spared the idiocy—I am by nature uncompetitive—but the sudden emergence from its cocoon of a beautifully balanced and shapely foot could put my sanguine personality and situation on the line.

I flirt, briefly, with hope. Perhaps, in his zeal, Colonel Bharucha has over-corrected the defect—and I see myself limping gamely on the stub of my heel while the ball of my foot and my toes waggle suspended.

I am jolted out of my troublesome reverie when I realize that Ayah is talking to Sher Singh, the slender Sikh zoo attendant, and I have been rolled before the lion's cage. There he lies, the ferocious beast of my nightmares, looking toothless and innocent . . . lying in wait to spring, fully dentured, into my dreams.

Chapter 2

Father stirs in the bed next to ours. "Jana?" Mother says softly, propping herself up on an elbow.

I lie still pretending sleep. She calls him Jan: life. In the faint glow of the night-light I see him entirely buried beneath his quilt like in a grave. Mother hates it when he covers his face, as if he is distancing himself from her even in his sleep. She knows he is awake. "Jana?" she says again, groping for his head. "Don't cover your face like that . . . You'll suffocate."

"So?" says Father drowsily, hanging on to the heavy cotton quilt and unveiling only his eyes. "You'll be a merry widow. You'll blow every pice I've saved."

I can almost feel a languorous happiness settle in my mother's flesh. He sounds teasing, affectionate, as she says he did in the first year of their six-year-old marriage.

"Don't say that, Jana. Even as a joke," Mother says, her voice plaintive, grateful, husky. She rolls over and molding herself to his back makes small burrowing, yearning movements. Father turns and lifting the quilt buries his head in the breasts she has inherited from a succession of bountifully endowed Parsee grandmothers.

Having polio in infancy is like being born under a lucky star. It has many advantages—it permits me access to my mother's bed in the middle of the night.

"Baijee? Wake up." Ayah taps Mother's hand urgently. *"Baijee?"*

My lids fly open. Mother looks startled and her eyes, still glazed with dreams, stare fixedly at Ayah.

"Something's happened to Papoo . . . I've put her in the nursery," whispers Ayah. "You'd better come."

In one starting movement Mother pushes away the quilt and

swings her feet to the icy floor. Her calves gleam creamily in the pale light seeping in through the narrow windows. Shanta, my eighteen-year-old ayah, pushes the red felt slippers towards her mistress's feet and holds out Mother's pashmina shawl.

I sit up, whimpering, and Ayah swings me up and places me on her hip. I know I am heavy with my cast.

It is warmer in my nursery. A thin woolen dhurrie covers the brick floor and the sweeper's daughter is lying on it in front of the glowing rods of an electric heater. She is three years older than me, a bit taller, but she weighs less I'm sure.

Ayah places me in my cot and squats beside my kneeling mother. I feel a sickening lurch of fear—and fury. From the way she lies, ashen, immobile—the right side of her dark cheek and small mouth slightly askew, a thread of saliva stretched to a wet spot on the dhurrie—I think that there is something terribly wrong with Papoo. "Has Muccho beaten her again?" I ask fiercely.

Ayah looks up at me, shivering in the sleeveless cardigan worn over her cotton sari. Her hair is disheveled and her large eyes are dilated with anger too. "Shush," she says. "She'll be all right." The shawl she has flung aside earlier lies in a heap on the floor.

"Papoo," Mother says, smoothing back her straight, sun-bleached hair, "open your eyes, child. You're safe. Come?"

But the girl, normally so responsive, lies absolutely still. She looks unbearably ill: shrunken, her small features barely defined, showing milky crescents beneath her lids.

"We'd better get her to the hospital," Mother says, standing up. "I'll tell Sahib to mind Lenny."

Papoo remains in the hospital two whole weeks. She has a concussion. Her mother says she fell off her bed, but we know she's lying. Muccho maltreats her daughter.

When Papoo returns from the children's ward of the Ganga Ram Hospital she is sprightly, defiant, devilish and as delightful as ever.

My parents sit on wood-bottomed chairs in Colonel Bharucha's consulting room. Mother holds me. I've been inflated to twice my size by knitted underwear, pullovers, a five-foot Kashmir shawl and a quilt.

Colonel Bharucha is applying a stethoscope to the emaciated chest of an infant. A woman in a shabby black burka holds the child. The infant coughs so severely that his mother has to hold him upright.

Colonel Bharucha removes the stethoscope from his ears and lets it hang from his neck like a talisman. "How long has he had this cough?" he asks.

The father, standing deferentially to one side, bends towards his wife. She turns her veiled face to him and whispers.

"For a week, doctor sahib," the man says. His head and neck are wrapped in a muffler and his gaunt face is careworn.

"How often does he throw up?" asks the doctor.

Again the man stoops and, relaying his wife's words, says: "Quite often, sir."

"Once a day? Twice a day? Ten times a day?" the doctor booms impatiently. I feel Mother's arm twitch.

This time the woman addresses the doctor directly, looking at him through the netting covering her eyes. "He vomits every time he has milk. . . five, six times a day." Her voice is incredibly young. She couldn't be more than twelve, I think, surprised.

"Why didn't you bring him earlier?" the doctor roars.

"I'm sorry, sir," the man says. "She didn't tell me."

"She didn't tell you? Are you a father or a barber? And you all want Pakistan! How will you govern a country when you don't know what goes on in your own house?"

The man, shivering slightly in a short, scruffy jacket and cotton trousers, hangs his head and smiles sheepishly.

His patients understand Colonel Bharucha. The more he roars and scolds the more likely he is to effect a cure. They have as much faith in his touch as in his mixtures.

"Take this to the dispenser," Colonel Bharucha says, handing him a prescription. "He won't charge you for the medicine."

22

"Your fees, sir?" The man fishes out a handful of grubby one-rupee notes from his coat pocket. "No need," Colonel Bharucha says with a dismissive gesture, and turning to us, asks, "Well?"

The man salaams and shepherds his wife out of the tiny room.

"It's Lenny," says Mother. "You said you'd remove her plaster today? She has a cold...I don't know if you should..." Her voice trails off on a quavering note.

I quake. The news comes as a complete shock. I thought I was seeing the doctor for my cold. Misinterpreting my devotion to the cast which conceals my repaired foot, Mother thinks I'm merely scared of being hurt and has kept the true purpose of the appointment from me.

"No!" I scream, unable to bear the thought of an able-bodied future. The suspense—although it has given my forehead premature wrinkles of worry—is preferable to the certainty of an altered, laborious and loveless life.

I open my mouth wide and bawl as loudly as I am able and cleave to my mother.

"It won't hurt, *mai*," soothes Father gently.

"Don't you remember? It didn't hurt at all last time," carols Mother brightly. "Dr. Bharucha would never let you hurt."

Father waves a crisp ten-rupee note before my nose as I turn my face from side to side to abjure temptation and establish disdain. It is a touching gesture of extravagance on Father's part. I would appreciate it in any other circumstance.

But trade my future for ten rupees?

Colonel Bharucha moves his spindly chair closer and looks eloquently at me, implying: Now what's all this fuss about? I won't tolerate nonsense.

But my terror is genuine and the doctor compromises. "I only want to have a look at the plaster," he says, and displays hands innocent of saw, chisel or hammer. "See? I have nothing."

He shifts his eyes to Mother. "How do you expect me to examine her through all this quilting?" And standing up from his desk, tall and stooping, directs: "Bring her to the table."

Mother briskly removes the quilt and hands it to Father. She unwinds the shawl, removes my coat and trousers and lays me on the hard and treacherously narrow table that is covered only by an iodine-stained white sheet.

"Take her clothes off, woman!" the doctor hollers.

"She has such an awful cold and fever...," says Mother hesitantly.

"Then take her home and broil her! If you know what's good for her, why bring her to me?"

Mother and Father hastily strip me of my pullovers and knitted underwear, sparing only my cotton knickers.

The doctor applies his cold stethoscope. I'm still trembling from the thunder of his angry roars—and now I shiver also from the cold. "She hasn't got a fever," the doctor declares severely. He signals to Mother and she covers my naked and trembling torso with the shawl. At the direction of a swift and secret signal I miss, Father and Mother move to either side of me and firmly stroke my arms and shoulders: and, at my instant alarm, make soothing noises.

"Lie still!" the doctor orders, and petrified by his tone, I lie still.

Colonel Bharucha saws, hammers and chisels at my cast, and using both hands, tears it apart.

"See? No pain," he says, moving his eyes close to mine. "Have a look," he offers, helping me sit up. Mother hastily winds the shawl round my shoulders and I examine the doctor's handiwork.

I let go my breath in a massive sigh of relief. My right leg looks dead: pathetically thin, wrinkled and splotched with dis-colored and pale patches. The shape of my ankle has definitely changed. It joins my foot at a much more reasonable angle. On the whole I'm surprisingly pleased. My leg looks functional but it remains gratifyingly abnormal—and far from banal!

I am dressed and stood on my bare feet. My heel still clears the floor. Colonel Bharucha tries briefly to press my heel down.

"Much better!" he announces, looking up. "See the differ-ence?"

My parents' twinge of initial disappointment is at once

replaced by readjusted expectations. They nod their heads with admiring smiles of satisfaction.

"Mind you, she must wear her calipers for some time," says the doctor, and turning to me he adds, "We'll get you new ones." I could hug him. "She still needs care . . . Massage, ultraviolet rays, physical therapy." He raises my right arm and bends my torso to the left. "Her right side is affected: she will have to exercise and stretch her waist like this!"

Mother's eyes are brimming with tears, her beautiful mouth working.

Colonel Bharucha places his arm around her. "What's here to worry now?" he says gruffly, surprised at Mother's agitation. "By the time she grows up she'll be quite normal."

Mother blows her nose in a daintily embroidered cambric handkerchief and taking the doctor's hand presses it to her eyes. Father sniffs and clears his throat.

"What about her schooling?" he asks, masking his emotion. I can't tell if he is inordinately pleased by the condition of my leg— or inordinately disappointed.

"She's doing fine without school, isn't she?" says the doctor. "Don't pressure her . . . her nerves could be affected. She doesn't need to become a professor." He turns to me. "Do you want to become a professor?"

I shake my head in a firm negative. "She'll marry—have children—lead a carefree, happy life. No need to strain her with studies and exams," he advises, thereby sealing my fate.

Mother's mouth is again working—her eyes again brimming. And driven by unfathomable demons, again her guilt surfaces. "I don't know where I went wrong," she says. "It's my fault . . . I neglected her—left her to the care of ayahs. None of the other children who went to the same park contracted polio."

"It's no one's fault really," says Colonel Bharucha, reassuring her as usual. "Lenny is weak. Some child with only the symptoms of a severe cold could have passed the virus." And then he roars a shocking postscript: "If anyone's to blame, blame the British! There was no polio in India till they brought it here!"

As far as I'm concerned this is insurgence—an open declaration of war by the two hundred Parsees of Lahore of the British Empire! I am shocked because Colonel Bharucha is the president of our community in Lahore. And, except for a few designated renegades, the Parsees have been careful to adopt a discreet and politically naive profile. At the last community dinner, held on the roof of the YMCA building on the Mall, Colonel Bharucha had cautioned (between the blood-chilling whines of the microphone): "We must tread carefully . . . We have served the English faithfully, and earned their trust . . . So, we have prospered! But we are the smallest minority in India . . . Only one hundred and twenty thousand in the whole world. We have to be extra wary, or we'll be neither here nor there . . . " And then, surmounting his uncharacteristic hesitancy, and in thunderous voice, he declaimed: "We must hunt with the hounds and run with the hare!"

Everybody clapped and gravely said: "Hear! Hear!" as they always do, reflexively, every time anyone airs a British proverb in suitably ringing tones.

"The goddamn English!" I think, infected by Colonel Bharucha's startling ferocity at this "dastardly" (one of Father's favorite words, just as "plucky" is Mother's) instance of British treachery. "They gave us polio!" And notwithstanding the compatible and sanguine nature of my relationship with my disease, I feel it is my first personal involvement with Indian politics: the Quit-India sentiment that has fired the imagination of a subject people and will soon sweep away the Raj!

Chapter 3

Ayah and I, arrested by a discordant bugle blast, come to a dead stop outside Godmother's gate. There is a brief roll of drums. The tall tin-sheet gates of the Salvation Army compound open and the band and marchers emerge from the leafy gloam of neem trees fermenting behind the walls.

It is always a shock to see the raw hands and faces of the English exposed to the light of day; and as the column moves away my mind transforms it into a slick red and white caterpillar, its legs marching, marching, its hundred sightless eyes staring ahead.

At startling intervals the caterpillar bursts into sound. Drums, bugles and tambourines clash—and as it curves out of sight round a bend in Jail Road it manufactures a curious vibration, like a unison of muzzled voices raised in song.

I stand transfixed, waiting for the creature's return. Ayah tries to drag me away but I resist, and she leans resignedly—and attractively—against the white-washed gatepost.

When the caterpillar returns, now marching on our side of the road, the red jackets and white saris separate to take the alien shapes of Englishmen and -women. Observed in microscopic dissection the head of the centipede is formed by a strutting Englishman holding the stout pole of a red flag diagonally across his chest. Of its own volition his glance slides to Ayah and, turning purple and showing off, he wields the flag like an acrobatic baton.

Close behind, orifices glued to convoluted brass horns, strut two red jackets: and on their heels, forming the shoulder and chest of the creature, a tight-packed row of red jackets beating drums, cymbals and tambourines, their leaden eyes attracted to the magnet leaning against the gatepost.

The saviors move away and the bits and pieces of Englishmen and -women fit together again to form the elongated and illusionary caterpillar of Jail Road.

27

✤

We no longer use the pram to visit Godmother's house: it is a short ten minute walk. But when Ayah takes me up Queens Road, past the YWCA, past the Freemasons' Lodge, which she calls "The Ghost Club," and across the Mall to the Queen's statue in the park opposite the Assembly Chambers, I'm still pushed in a pram. I love it.

Queen Victoria, cast in gunmetal, is majestic, massive, overpowering, ugly. Her statue imposes the English Raj in the park. I lie sprawled on the grass, my head in Ayah's lap. The Faletti's Hotel cook, the Government House gardener, and an elegant, compactly muscled head-and-body masseur sit with us. Ice-candy-man is selling his popsicles to the other groups lounging on the grass. My mouth waters. I have confidence in Ayah's chocolate chemistry . . . lank and loping the Ice-candy-man cometh . . .

I take advantage of Ayah's admirers. "Massage me!" I demand, kicking the handsome masseur. He loosens my laces and unbuckles the straps gripping my boots. Taking a few drops of almond oil from one of the bottles in his cruet set, he massages my wasted leg and then my okay leg. His fingers work deftly, kneading, pummelling, soothing. They are knowing fingers, very clever, and sometimes, late in the evening, when he and Ayah and I are alone, they massage Ayah under her sari. Her lids close. She grows still and languid. A pearly wedge gleams between her lips and she moans, a fragile, piteous sound of pleasure. Very carefully, very quietly, I maneuver my eyes and nose. It is dark, but now and then a dart of twilight illuminates a subtle artistry. My nose inhales the fragrance of earth and grass—and the other fragrance that distills insights. I intuit the meaning and purpose of things. The secret rhythms of creation and mortality. The essence of truth and beauty. I recall the choking hell of milky vapors and discover that heaven has a dark fragrance.

Things love to crawl beneath Ayah's sari. Ladybirds, glow-worms, Ice-candy-man's toes. She dusts them off with impartial nonchalance. I keep an eye on Ice-candy-man's toes. Sometimes, in the course of an engrossing story, they travel so cautiously that both Ayah and I are taken unawares. Ice-candy-man is a raconteur. He is also an absorbing gossip. When the story is extra good, and the tentative toes polite, Ayah tolerates them.

Sometimes a toe snakes out and zeroes in on its target with such lightning speed that I hear of the attack only from Ayah's startled "Oof." Once in a while I preempt the big toe's romantic impulse and, catching it mid-crawl or mid-strike, twist it. It is a measure to keep the candy bribes coming.

I learn also to detect the subtle exchange of signals and some of the complex rites by which Ayah's admirers coexist. Dusting the grass from their clothes they slip away before dark, leaving the one luck, or the lady, favors. I don't enjoy the gardener's turn because nothing much happens except talk. He talks and Ayah talks, and he listens and Ayah talks. I escape into daydreams in which my father turns loquacious and my mother playful. Or to heroics in which I rescue Godmother from the drooling jaws of her cannibalistic brother-in-law who is a doctor and visits from way beyond the perimeter of my familiar world.

I learn fast. I gain Ayah's goodwill and complicity by accommodating her need to meet friends and relatives. She takes me to fairs, cheap restaurants and slaughterhouses. I cover up for her and maintain a canny silence about her doings. I learn of human needs, frailties, cruelties and joys. I also learn from her the tyranny magnets exercise over metals.

I have many teachers. My cousin shows me things.

"You want to see my marbles?" he asks, and holds out the prettily colored glass balls for me to admire and touch—if I so wish, to play with. He has just returned from Quetta where he had a hernia operation. "Let me show you my scar," he offers, unbuttoning his fly and exposing me to the glamorous spectacle of a stitched scar and a handful of genitals. He too has clever fingers. "You can touch it," he offers. His expression is disarming, gallant. I touch the fine scar and gingerly hold the genitals he transfers to my palm. We both study them. "I am also having my tonsils removed," he says.

29

I hand back his genitals and look at his neck. I visualize a red, scalloped scar running from ear to ear. It is a premonition.

Sometimes I spend days and nights with my limber electric-aunt and my knowing and instructive cousin. "See this pillow?" he asks one night—and as it moves nearer it resembles a muzzle. I scream. Frightened, he covers my scream with the pillow and sits on it. I struggle madly at first and then feebly, and cautiously he allows me to emerge, screamless.

The next day, when we are alone, my cousin's face looms conspiratorially close and he says, "Come on. I'll show you something."

He leads me through wire-mesh doors to the back veranda. He drags a wooden stool close to the whitewashed wall and climbing on it points to a hole in a small white china object stuck to the wall. "See this?" he asks. "Put your finger there and see what happens." He jumps down and almost lifts me to the stool. He is a couple of years older than me. I raise my hand, index finger pointed, and look down at him expectantly. He nods. I poke my finger into the small depression and an AC current teaches me everything I will ever need to know about gullibility and shock. Though my faculties of reason, deduction and logic advance with the years, my gullibility and reaction to shock remain the same as on the day I tumbled screaming, hair, nerves and limbs spread-eagled, into my cousin's arms.

My electric-aunt is a resourceful widow addicted to quick decisions and swift results. The speed at which she moves from spot to spot—from dawn to dusk—have earned her a citation. She is called, in moments of need and gratitude, *bijli*: a word that in the various Indian languages, with slight variations, stands for both electricity and lightning.

She is also addicted to navy blue. She and her son share a bedroom. It has navy-blue curtains, navy-blue bedspreads and navy-blue linen doilies on the dressing table. It is, depending on my mood, either a restful or a gloomy room. The night of my lesson in gullibility and shock I find it gloomy. My cousin and I spread mattresses and sleep on the carpeted floor of the cheerful sitting room next to the bedroom.

That night I have the first nightmare that connects me to the pain of others.

Far away I hear a siren. Tee-too! Tee-too! it goes, alarming my heart. The nocturnal throb and shrieking grow louder, closing in, coming now from the compound of the Salvation Army next door. Its tin-sheet gates open a crack to let out a long khaki caterpillar. Centipedal legs marching, marching, it curves, and as it approaches Electric-aunt's gate it metamorphoses into a single German soldier on a motorcycle. Roaring up the drive the engine stops, as I know it must, outside Electric-aunt's doorstep. The siren's tee-too tee-too is now deafening. My heart pounds at the brutality of the sound. The soldier, his cap and uniform immaculate, dismounts. Carefully removing black gloves from his white hands, he comes to get me.

Why does my stomach sink all the way to hell even now? I had my own stock of Indian bogeymen. *Choorails*, witches with turned-about feet who ate the hearts and livers of straying children. Bears lurking, ready to pounce if I did not finish my pudding. The zoo lion. No one had taught me to fear an immaculate Nazi soldier. Yet here he was, in nightmare after nightmare, coming to get me on his motorcycle.

I recall another childhood nightmare from the past. Children lie in a warehouse. Mother and Ayah move about solicitously. The atmosphere is businesslike and relaxed. Godmother sits by my bed smiling indulgently as men in uniforms quietly slice off a child's arm here, a leg there. She strokes my head as they dismember me. I feel no pain. Only an abysmal sense of loss—and a chilling horror that no one is concerned by what's happening.

Chapter 4

I pick up a brother. Somewhere down the line I become aware of his elusive existence. He is four—a year and a month younger than me. I don't recall him learning to crawl or to walk. Where was he? It doesn't matter.

My brother is aloof. Vital and alert, he inhabits another sphere of interests and private thoughts. No doubt he too is busy picking up knowledge, gaining insights. I am more curious about him than he about me. His curiosity comes later. I am skinny, wizened, sallow, wiggly-haired, ugly. He is beautiful. He is the most beautiful thing, animal, person, building, river or mountain that I have seen. He is formed of gold mercury. He never stands still enough to see. He turns, ducks, moves, looks away, vanishes.

The only way I know to claim his undivided attention is to get him angry. I learn to bait him. His name is Adi. I call him Sissy. He is too confused to retaliate the first few times I call him by his new name. At last: "My name is Adi," he growls, glowering.

The next day I persist. He pretends not to notice. In the evening, holding up a sari-clad doll I say, "Hey, Sissy, look! She's just like you!"

Adi raises his head and looks squarely from the doll to me. His jet eyes are vibrant. His flushed face holds the concentrated beauty and venom of an angry cobra. And like a cobra striking, in one sweep he removes a spiked boot and hurls it at me. I stare at him, blood blurring my vision. And he stares back communicating cold fury and deathly warning.

It's not that he doesn't want to play with me. It's just that I can't hold his attention for more than a few seconds. His unfathomable thoughts and mercurial play pattern absorb him. Squatting before corners or blank walls, head bent, fingers busy, he concentrates on trains, bricks, mudballs, strings. Quickly he shifts to another heap of toys and garbage in another corner; or out the doors into the garden, or vegetable patch, or servants' quarters at the back of the house.

At night he's into his nightsuit and fast asleep while I'm still soaking my chilblained toes in scalding salt water—or standing on a stool brushing my teeth. We sleep in outsize elongated cots. Like our loosely tailored clothes with huge tucks and hems, our cots are designed to last a lifetime. (My brother outgrew his cot. I still fit into mine.) Ayah tucks in the mosquito net and switches off the faint light.

Is there anything to compare with the cozy bliss of snuggling beneath a heavy quilt with a hot-water bag on a freezing night in an unheated room? Particularly if you've just dashed from the bathroom over a bare brick floor? And you're five years old? And free to go over the excitements and evaluate the experience of the day and weave them into daydreams that drift into sleep? That is, provided the zoo lion does not roar. If he roars—which at night is rare—my daydreams turn into quaking daymares: and these to nightmares in which the hungry lion, cutting across Lawrence Road to Birdwood Road, prowls from the rear of the house to the bedroom door, and in one bare-fanged leap crashes through to sink his fangs into my stomach. My stomach sinks all the way to the bottom of hell.

Whether he roars at night or not, I awake every morning to the lion's roar. He sets about it at the crack of dawn, blighting my dreams. By the time I dispel the fears of the jungle and peep out of my quilt, Adi is already out of bed. A great chunk of his life is lived apart: he goes to a regular school.

Spring flowers, birds and butterflies scent and color the air. It is the end of March, and already it is hot in the sun. Cousin and I come indoors and see my brother, embedded in the sag of a charpoy, fast asleep. We gently turn him on his back and propped on elbows scrutinize his face.

"He's put on lipstick," Cousin says.

"Yes," I agree.

His face has the irresistible bloom of spring flowers. Turn by turn Cousin and I softly brush our lips and cheeks against his velvet face, we pry back a sleek lick of dark brown hair and kiss his forehead and the cushioned cleft in his chin. His vulnerability is breathtaking, and we ravish it with scrutiny and our childish kisses. Carried away by our ardor we become rough. Adi wakes up and opens indulgent, jewel-jet eyes. They are trusting and kind as a saint's.

"You've put on lipstick?" I ask, inviting confidence.

"No," he says mildly.

"Of course he has!" says Cousin.

"No, I've not," says Adi.

"Can I rub some tissue and find out?" I ask courteously.

"Okay," he says.

I stroke the Kleenex across his lips and look at it. It is unblemished. I moisten it with my tongue and rub harder. Cousin is armed with his own tissue. Adi withstands our vigorous scouring with the patience of the blameless. I notice blood on the Kleenex. The natural red in his lips has camouflaged the bleeding. Astonished, we finally believe him.

"He should have been a girl," says Cousin.

By now Adi is fully awake. I watch helplessly as mercurial preoccupation veils his eyes. He becomes remote. His vulnerability vanishes. He kicks out, pushing back our hands with the tissues. He is in control.

Passing by, Ayah swoops down on him and picks him up. After hugging him and nuzzling his face she abruptly puts him down again, saying: "He is my little English baba!"

Last evening Ayah took us for a walk in Simla-pahari and a passerby, no doubt impelled by her spherical agitation into spouting small talk, inquired: "Is he an English's son?"

"Of course not!" said Ayah imperiously. However, vanity softening her contempt, she added: "Can any dough-faced English's son match his spice? Their looks lack salt!"

Ayah is so proud of Adi's paucity of pigment. Sometimes she takes us to Lawrence Gardens and encourages him to run across the space separating native babies and English babies. The ayahs of the English babies hug him and fuss over him and permit him to romp with their privileged charges. Adi undoes the bows of little girls with blue eyes in scratchy organdy dresses and wrestles with tallow-haired boys in the grass. Ayah beams.

On bitterly cold days when ice sales plummet, Ice-candy-man transforms himself into a birdman. Burdened with enormous cages stuffed with sparrows and common green parrots he parades the paths behind the Lahore Gymkhana lawns and outside the Punjab Club. At strategic moments he plants the cages on the ground and rages: "I break your neck, you naughty birds! You do too much *chi chi!* What will the good memsahibs think? They'll think I no teach you. You like jungly lions in zoo. I cut your throat!"

He flourishes a barber's razor. It is an infallible bait. Clutches of tenderhearted Englishwomen, sporting skirts and tennis shoes, abandon their garden chairs and dainty cucumber and chicken tea sandwiches to rush up and scold: "You horrid man. Don't you dare cut their throats!"

"Them fresh parrots, memsahib. They not learn dirty words yet. I catches them today," coaxes Birdman, plunging his crafty hands into the cages. "They only one rupee for two birds."

His boneless fingers set up such a squawking and twittering among the parrots and the sparrows that the ladies become frantic. They buy the birds by the dozen, and, cooing, "You poor little itty-bitty things," snuggle them to their bosoms.

After the kissing and the cuddling, holding the stupefied birds aloft, they release them, one by one. Their valiant expressions and triumphant cries enthrall the rapt crowd of native gawkers as they exclaim: "There! Fly away, little birdie. Go, you poor little things!"

Squatting on his heels Birdman surveys the tearful and spirited mems with open-mawed and marveling admiration. Conjuring rueful little nods and a catch to his voice, he remarks: "It go straight to mama-papa." Or, sighing heavily, "It fly to hungry little babies in nest."

And today, foreshadowing the poetic impulse of his future, wiping tears and pointing at a giddily spinning and chirping sparrow, Ice-candy-man says: "Look! Little sparrow singing, 'See? See? I free!' to mad-with-grief wife!"

Ayah, Adi and I watch the performance with concealed glee. Every now and then we heighten the histrionics and encourage sales by shouting, "Cut their throats! Cut their throats!" We cheer and clap from the sidelines when the birds are released.

Ice-candy-man resorts to his change in occupation only two or three times a year, so his ingenuity works. He usually clears a packet. And if the sale has been quick and lucrative, as on this Saturday afternoon just before Christmas, he treats us to a meal at Ayah's favorite wayside restaurant in Mozang Chungi.

We are regulars. The shorn proprietor acknowledges us with a solemn nod. He is a *pahailwan*: a wrestler. Covering his massive torso with a singlet in deference to Ayah's presence, he approaches. Despite the cold, his shoulders gleam with sweat and a striped lungi clings to his buttocks and legs.

We are directed to sit on a narrow backless bench. Opposite us Ice-candy-man drapes his lank and flexible length on another bench, and leaning across the table ogles Ayah. He straightens somewhat when an urchin-apprentice plonks down three tin plates heaped with rice and a bowl of vegetable curry. The rice is steaming and fragrant. We fall to it silently. Ayah's chocolate fingers mold the rice into small golf balls which she pops into her mouth. She eats with her right hand while her left hand reposes in her lap.

Halfway through the meal I sense a familiar tension and a small flurry of movement. Ice-candy-man's toes are invisibly busy. I glance up just as a supplicating smile on his face dissolves into a painful grimace: and I know Ayah's hand is engaged in an equally heroic struggle.

Meanwhile the mounds of rice steadily diminish. Outwardly calm, systematically popping golf balls, Ayah signals the proprietor for another helping.

After the meal, as we descend the rickety wooden steps into the crowded gully, Ayah tries, tactfully, to get rid of Ice-candy-man. But he hoists Adi onto the seat of his bicycle and persists in walking with us to Warris Road.

At the gate of our house, less tactfully, Ayah says: "You'd better go. I have chores."

"What chores?" asks Ice-candy-man, reluctant to let Ayah go.

"A ton of washing. . . And I haven't even dusted *Baijee's* room!"

"Let me help you," says Ice-candy-man.

"You gone crazy?" Ayah asks.

Imagine Ice-candy-man working alongside Ayah in our house. Mother'd throw a fit! He's not the kind of fellow who's permitted inside. With his thuggish way of inhaling from the stinking cigarettes clenched in his fist, his flashy scarves and reek of jasmine attar, he represents a shady, almost disreputable type.

"Okay, I'll go," Ice-candy-man temporizes reluctantly, "but only if you'll come to the cinema later."

"I told you I've work to do," says Ayah, close to losing patience. "And I dare not ask *Baijee* for another evening off."

"Talk to me for a while. . . Just a little while," pleads Ice-candy-man so piteously that Ayah, whose heart is as easily inclined to melt as Ice-candy-man's popsicles, bunches her fingers and says, "Only ten minutes."

Aware of the impropriety of entertaining her guest on the front lawn Ayah leads us to settle on a bald patch of grass at the back near the servants' quarters. The winter sun is diffused by the dust and a crimson bank of clouds streaks the horizon. It is getting uncomfortably chilly and my hair already feels damp. Ayah notices it and, drawing me to her, covers my head with her sari *palloo*.

"Now talk," she says to Ice-candy-man. "Since you're so anxious to talk, talk!"

Ice-candy-man talks. News and gossip flow off his glib tongue like a torrent. He reads Urdu newspapers and the *Urdu Digest*. He can, when he applies himself, read the headlines in the *Civil and Military Gazette*, the English daily.

Characteristically, Ice-candy-man starts by giving us news of the world. The Germans, he informs us, have developed a deadly weapon called the V-bomb that will turn the British into powdered ash. A little later, drifting close to home, he tells us of Subas Chandra Bose, a Hindu patriot who has defected to the Japanese side in Burma. "Bose says the Japanese will help us liberate India from the *Angrez*," Ice-candy-man says. "If we want India back we must take pride in our customs, our clothes, our languages . . . And not go mouthing the got-pit sot-pit of the English!"

Obviously he's quoting this Bose. (Sometimes he quotes Gandhi, or Nehru or Jinnah, but I'm fed up with hearing about them. Mother, Father and their friends are always saying: Gandhi said this, Nehru said that. Gandhi did this, Jinnah did that. What's the point of talking so much about people we don't know?)

Finally, narrowing his focus to our immediate surroundings, he says to Ayah, "Shanta *bibi*, you're Punjabi, aren't you?"

"For the most part," Ayah agrees warily.

"Then why don't you wear Punjabi clothes? I've never seen you in shalwar-kamize."

Though it has never struck me as strange before—I'm so accustomed to Ayah only in a sari—I see the logic of his question and wonder about it.

"*Arrey baba*," says Ayah spreading her hands in a fetching gesture, "do you know what salary ayahs who wear Punjabi clothes get? Half the salary of the Goan ayahs who wear saris! I'm not so simple!"

"I've no quarrel with your saris," says Ice-candy-man disarmingly demure, "I was only asking out of curiosity."

And, catching us unawares, his ingenuous toe darts beneath Ayah's sari. Ayah gives a start. Angrily smacking his leg and smoothing her sari, she stands up. "*Duffa ho!* Go!" she says. "Or I'll get *Baijee* to V-bomb you into ash!" Applying all his strength, Adi restrains Ice-candy-man's irrepressibly twitching toe.

"*Arrrey!*" says Ice-candy-man holding his hands up as if to stave off Ayah's assault. "Are you angry?"

"Then what?" Ayah retorts. "You have no sense and no shame!"

Grinning sheepishly, groveling and wriggling in the grass to touch the hem of Ayah's sari, he says, "I'm sorry, forgive me. I won't do it again . . . Forgive me."

"What for?" snaps Ayah. "You'll never change!"

Ice-candy-man coils forward to squat and, threading his supple arms through his calves from the back, latches on to his earlobes. It is a punishing posture called "the cock," used in lower-class schools to discipline urchins. He looks so ridiculous that Ayah and I laugh.

But Adi, his face grim, dispenses a totally mirthless and vicious kick to his ankle.

Ice-candy-man stands up so abruptly that his movements are a blur.

And, my eyes popping, I stare at Adi dangling in the air at the end of his rangy arm. Ice-candy-man has a firm grip on the waistband of Adi's woolen trousers and Adi looks like an astonished and stocky spider plucked out of his web and suspended above the level of my eyes.

"I'm going to drop him," Ice-candy-man says calmly. He takes a loping step and, holding Adi directly above the brick paving skirting the grass, raises his arm. "If you don't go to the cinema with me I'll drop him."

I can't believe he means it.

But Adi does. His face scarlet, he lets out a terrified yell and howls: "He'll drop me! Save me . . . someone save me!"

"I'm going to drop him," repeats Ice-candy-man.

Ayah's round mouth opens in an "O," her eyes stare. Seeing her expression, my wiggly hair curls tighter. I look in horror upon the distance separating Adi from the brick. Adi kicks, crawls and squirms in the air and yells: "Save me! Save me! *Bachao! Bachao!*"

And Ayah shouts: "Put him down at once, oye, badmash! I will go to the cinema."

Ice-candy-man carefully lowers Adi—face down and dribbling spit—on the grass.

Ayah deftly pulls off a sandal and, lunging wildly, strikes Ice-candy-man wherever she can. Ice-candy-man cowers; and gathering his lungi above his knees, snatching up his slippers, manages to move out of her reach. Ayah chases him right out of the gate.

Chapter 5

Rich men's wives and children soar to the Simla or Kashmir Hills in summer. We also soar, but to the lesser Murree Hills at the foot of the Himalayas.

Adi is perched on a tall pony. I am on a donkey. My donkey trots alongside and I perceive just how short it is. My legs stick out beneath the safety ring on the saddle. I grip the ring resentfully. The donkey-man holds the reins. I am not spared even this indignity! My donkey perch is ludicrous.

I am about to shake heaven and earth to set things right when an astonishing tidal wave of relief and frivolity barrels over the world. Shopkeepers on the Murree Mall have picked out a few words from the static of their 1944 radios and happiness strikes all hearts. Men, women, beast, mountain, tall pony and short donkey all exult. Simultaneously we know that the war is over. We have won! Victory! The war is over! Faces around me are wreathed in smiles. Incredibly Father is blowing a whistle that uncoils a foot-long paper tongue. God! I have never been so happy. I who have subversively hoped that the defector Bose and the Japanese enemy win the war. All the same I am swept by a sense of relief so unburdening that I realize I was born with an awareness of the war: and I recall the dim, faraway fear of bombs that tinged with bitterness my mother's milk. No wonder I was a colicky baby.

The gaiety on people's faces is infectious. My mother's face swims up with a smile I never again see; and plucking paper cups, streamers and whistles from the air she gives them to Adi and me.

Father seldom visits Murree for more than two or three days at a time. He returns to Lahore. A week later we catch a bus and follow him down into the plains which the sun has scorched and pulverized into a dusty hell. We pant under ceiling fans. And now the temperatures soar.

Our stay in Murree has been cut short because the Parsees of Lahore are holding a Jashan prayer to celebrate the British victory.

On the day of the Jashan the temperature is 116°F in the shade. A tonga waits in the porch. Hollow-eyed and dazed with heat we pile perspiring into the tonga. Mother and Ayah in the back and Adi and I up front with the tongaman. We sit back to back on a bench divided by a quilted backrest. A flimsy canvas canopy shelters us from the sun. The tonga is held together by two enormous wooden wheels on either side of the shaft and is balanced by the harnessed horse. Up front we are more secure—unless the horse falls.

Scarcely out of our gate, the horse falls. Adi and I shoot over the guard and spill onto Warris Road. Mother and Ayah are suspended high in the air, clinging for all they are worth to the other end of the seesaw. Adi and I get up and scamper to one side. The tongaman picks himself off the horse cursing: and the Birdwood Barracks' sepoy abandons his post and runs forward to render help. Ayah's presence galvanizes men to mad sprints in the noon heat. It is a pity she has no such effect on animals though.

The tongaman and the sepoy lift the shafts and assist the harnessed horse to stand upright. Adi pats the horse's rump. The animal swishes his bristly tail and blows wind in our faces. The sepoy makes an encouraging sucking noise with his tongue and pushes one of the enormous wooden wheels to start the tonga. Straining and quivering under the dual burden of passengers and heat, the shaken animal drags us past the barracks, the barricading walls of the Lucy Harrison School for girls next to it, up Queens Road, past the pretty pink spread of the Punjab High Court and behind the small-causes court to the Fire Temple.

We leave the tongaman and Ayah to gossip and doze beneath whatever shade they can find.

The main hall of the temple is already full of smoke. Two priests, sitting cross-legged and swaying slightly, face each other across a fire altar. They are robed in a swollen froth of starched white muslin. They wear cloth masks like the one Colonel Bharucha wore in the hospital. Their chanting voices rise and boom in fierce competition and the mask prevents specks of spittle from profaning the fire. They sit on a white sheet amidst silver trays heaped with fruit—grape, mango, papaya—and flowers. And the *malida* cooked by the priest's wife. Adi and I join the children sitting patiently on a wooden bench—our collective mouths drooling.

The priests cannot be hurried. They go through a ritual established a millennium ago. They stoke the fire with silver tongs and feed it with sandalwood and frankincense.

It is comparatively cool beneath the high ceiling. My eyes are getting accustomed to the dark but smart with smoke. Mother has found a seat in the front row. There is an empty chair between her and Colonel Bharucha. He must have grown taller, because his pink scalp thrusts higher above his hairline than before. Godmother sits next to him, fanning herself and the doctor with a slow, rotary motion of her palm-leaf punkah. She catches my watering eye and winks. Only I ever see her wink. Her dignified bearing and noble features preclude winking. She only relaxes her guard with me. No one sees her as I do. Slavesister is snatching a few blessed minutes of sleep in the last row. Godmother knows she's asleep. She knows everything. Slavesister sleeps peacefully because she knows Godmother will not mind. Godmother, after all, is not unreasonable.

Both priests stand up, smoothing their beards and garments. Chairs squeak as the ladies greet each other and gradually converge on the fruit trays. Slavesister waddles plumply forward on painful bunions, smiling her patient, obliging smile, securing her sari border to her hair. The women shoo us from the benches and sit down to peel and cut the fruit.

Mother stands talking to Colonel Bharucha. She is tense, alert, anxious to please. Electric-aunt joins them, also tense. Her quick, intelligent eyes scan the room. I know she is looking for me. Godmother releases me and I run up to them.

"What is this?" says Colonel Bharucha. Copying and exaggerating my limp he lurches halfway across the room like a tipsy giraffe. "Put your heel down! You must remember to."

Mother purses her shapely mouth and looks at me sternly.

Electric-aunt frowns, her thin lips a tight, anxious line beneath her sharp nose.

Colonel Bharucha stoops and pushing down on the contracted tendon presses my heel to the floor. "Massage the back of her leg down: like this," he says, kneading and stretching my stubborn tendon.

He straightens, pats my back and dismisses me. I know they are beaming behind my back, pleased with my progress since the operation. Cousin is waiting for me to be free of the grown-ups.

"I want to show you something," he says, drawing me to a window in the wings. He reaches into the pockets of his shorts and pulls out scraps of cardboard. He lifts off one layer and reveals a pressed butterfly, its colors turned to powder, its wings awry.

"Hold out your hand," he commands. I withhold my hand. There are certain things I'll hold and certain things I won't. Cousin gropes for my hand and, "No," I say. "Don't!"

"But it's for you," says Cousin.

"I don't want it!"

Cousin is, for once, confounded.

There is a drift now towards the inner sanctum. Electric-aunt beckons Cousin and Mother signals me. We step into the inner room and I can see through two barred windows and an open archway the main fire altar. It is like a gigantic silver eggcup and the flames are dancing above a bed of white ashes.

I kneel before the altar and touch my forehead to the cool marble step beyond which I cannot go. Except for the priests who tend the fire and see that it never goes out, no one can enter the inner sanctum. Mother kneels beside me. I ask God to bless our family and Godmother and all our servants and Masseur and Ice-candy-man . . . until Mother says, "That's enough! The meeting's about to start. Hurry!"

And Adi hisses, "Don't hog God!"

We enter the main hall. The chairs have been rearranged. Colonel Bharucha is standing before the mike, testing it with practiced snaps of his fingers. "Hello hello," he says, and knocks on it with his knuckles. He struggles with both hands to stretch the rod. Mr. Bankwalla, an officer at the Central Bank of India, his slight body crisp and dependable in sweatless white shirt and white trousers, rushes up obligingly. Between them they adjust the mike to suit the colonel's height.

The banker moves back, fleet and unobtrusive beneath his maroon skullcap, to his seat in the aisle next to his jolly wife. (His wife is so indefatigably jolly that it is said after the initial burst of grief she even wisecracked at her son's funeral. Later I heard she cracked jokes on her deathbed and prepared to meet Ahura Mazda with jests, and sly winks at the mourners, whose appreciative laughter turned to inconsolable grief when the will was read. She left everything to the Tower of Silence in Karachi.)

By the time Colonel Bharucha clears his throat, and it is an impressive throat-clearing, we are all settled in our chairs.

Colonel Bharucha tells us: "We are gathered here, etc., etc. To thank God Almighty, etc., etc."

The mike has transformed him from a plain-speaking doctor into a resounding orator. But his rhetoric has a cadence that makes my mind wander.

Suddenly I hear him declare: "Gandhi says, we must stop buying salt. We should only eat salt manufactured from the Indian Ocean!"

The colonel pauses, dramatically, and my loafing mind becomes attentive. The pause, shrewdly timed to permit just that tiny license so dear to a Parsee audience, is snapped up. "Who does this Gandhi think he is?" shouts an obliging wag promptly from somewhere in the middle. "Is it his grandfather's ocean?"

Colonel Bharucha, smiling amiably, explains that the British government is charging an unfair salt tax and, as a protest, we should not buy it. Gandhijee plans to walk a hundred miles to the ocean to make salt for us. He is even prepared to go to jail to make his point!

"And what do we do while he's in jail? Walk around with goiters for lack of salt?" shouts the wag.

"Go to jail for us!" snorts Dr. Manek Mody. (He is God-mother's brother-in-law, and is here on one of his periodic visits from Rawalpindi.) "Big deal!" he booms. "There's such a demand for A-class in jails that there's no room left for folk like us!"

(Even though I cannot see him I can tell it's Dr. Mody by the amazing volume of his voice. He is a short, chubby man, with a totally bald and brown head.)

"Yes," chimes in the first wag. "The Congress gangsters provoke the police and get rewarded with free board and lodging. It's a shame! I propose that the Parsee Anjuman lodge a formal protest with the Inspector General of Police. Why should we be left out of everything?"

"Hear! Hear!" agrees the congregation, and thumps the armrests of its chairs and wooden benches.

"Let us march to jail now!" the wag says, jumping to his feet. He is a paunchy man with very dark skin.

Colonel Bharucha raises a restraining hand. "No doubt the men in jail are acquiring political glory . . . But this shortcut to fame and fortune is not for us. It is no longer just a struggle for Home Rule. It is a struggle for power. Who's going to rule once we get *Swaraj*? Not you," says the colonel, pointing a long and accusing finger at us as if we are harboring sinful thoughts. "Hindus, Muslims and even the Sikhs are going to jockey for power: and if you jokers jump into the middle you'll be mangled into chutney!"

Wise heads nod—Godmother's, Electric-aunt's, Slavesister's—although Slavesister's can hardly be called wise.

"I hope no Lahore Parsee will be stupid enough to court trouble," continues the colonel. "I strongly advise all of you to stay at home—and out of trouble."

"I don't see how we can remain uninvolved," says Dr. Mody, whose voice, without aid of mike, is louder than the colonel's. "Our neighbors will think we are betraying them and siding with the English."

"Which of your neighbors are you not going to betray?" asks a practical soul with an impatient voice. "Hindu? Muslim? Sikh?"

"That depends on who's winning, doesn't it?" says Mr. Bankwalla. "Don't forget, we are to run with the hounds and hunt with the hare."

"No one knows which way the wind will blow," thunders the colonel, silencing everyone with his admirable rhetoric. "There may be not one but two—or even three—new nations! And the Parsees might find themselves championing the wrong side if they don't look before they leap!"

"Does it matter where they look or where they leap?" enquires the impatient voice. "If we're stuck with the Hindus they'll swipe our businesses from under our noses and sell our grandfathers in the bargain: if we're stuck with the Muslims they'll convert us by the sword! And God help us if we're stuck with the Sikhs!"

"Why? Which mad dog bit the Sikhs? Why are you so against them?" says Dr. Mody contentiously.

"I have something against everybody," declares the voice, impartial and very hurt.

"Order! Order!" says Mr. Bankwalla. And Colonel Bharucha clears his throat so effectively that the questions, answers and wisecracks subside.

"I'll tell you a story," the colonel says, and susceptible to stories the congregation and I sit still in our seats.

"When we were kicked out of Persia by the Arabs thirteen hundred years ago, what did we do? Did we shout and argue? No!" roars the colonel, and hastily provides his own answer before anyone can interrupt. "We got into boats and sailed to India!"

"Why to India?" a totally new wit sitting at the end of my bench enquires. "If they had to go some place, why not Greece? Why not to France? Prettier scenery..."

"They didn't kick us hard enough," says Dr. Mody, with hearty regret. "If only they'd kicked us all the way to California... Prettier women!"

There is an eruption of comments and suggestions. The meeting is turning out to be much more lively than I'd anticipated. Godmother's brother-in-law restores order with his built-in microphone. "Shut up!" he bellows, startling us with the velocity of his voice.

Colonel Bharucha continues as if he's not been interrupted at all.

"Do you think it was easy to be accepted into a new country? No!" he booms. "Our forefathers were not given permission even to disembark!"

"What about our foremothers?" someone enquires.

"And our foreskins?" an invisible voice pipes up from the back.

"Mind! There are ladies here!" says the colonel sternly. There is a long pause no one dares interrupt. Satisfied by our silence, the colonel continues: "Our forefathers and foremothers waited for four days, not knowing what was to become of them. Then, at last, the Grand *Vazir* appeared on deck with a glass of milk filled to the brim." He looks intently at our faces. "Do you know what it meant?"

Knowledgeable heads nod wisely.

"It was a polite message from the Indian Prince, meaning: 'No, you are not welcome. My land is full and prosperous and we don't want outsiders with a different religion and alien ways to disturb the harmony!' He thought we were missionaries.

"Do you know what the Zarathushtis did? God rest their souls?"

Knowing heads nod, and among them I spy Cousin's. I feel annoyed. I am not privy to information that is rapidly being revealed as my birthright. Even if Godmother, Mother, Slavesister and Electric-aunt did not tell me, Cousin ought to have!

Colonel Bharucha, again answering his own question, continues: "Our forefathers carefully stirred a teaspoon of sugar into the milk and sent it back.

"The Prince understood what that meant. The refugees would get absorbed into his country like the sugar in the milk. . . And with their decency and industry sweeten the lives of his subjects.

"The Indian Prince thought: what a smart and civilized

people! And he gave our ancestors permission to live in his kingdom!"

"*Shabash!* Well done!" say the Parsees, regarding each other with admiration and congratulatory self-regard.

"But as you see, we have to move with the times," roars the colonel, his oratorical capacities in full form. "Time stands still for no one!"

"Hear hear! Hear hear!"

Even I applauded on cue.

"Time and tide wait for no man!"

Thunderous applause.

"Let whoever wishes rule! Hindu, Muslim, Sikh, Christian! We will abide by the rules of their land!"

A polite smattering of Hear hears! The congregation, wafted on self-esteem and British proverbs, does not want to be brought back to earth.

"As long as we do not interfere we have nothing to fear! As long as we respect the customs of our rulers—as we always have— we'll be all right! Ahura Mazda has looked after us for thirteen hundred years: he will look after us for another thirteen hundred!"

Like English proverbs, Ahura Mazda's name elicits enthusiasm.

"We will cast our lot with whoever rules Lahore!" continues the colonel.

"If the Muslims should rule Lahore wouldn't we be safer going to Bombay where most Parsees live?" asks a tremulous voice weakened by a thirteen-hundred-year-old memory of conversions by the Arab sword.

A slight nervousness stirs amidst the timorous. There is much turning of heads, shifting on seats and whispering.

"We prospered under the Muslim Moguls didn't we?" scolds Colonel Bharucha. "Emperor Akbar invited Zarathushti scholars to his *darbar*: he said he'd become a Parsee if he could . . . but we gave our oath to the Hindu Prince that we wouldn't proselytize—and the Parsees don't break faith! Of course," he says, "those cockerels who wish to go to Bombay may go."

"Again Bombay?" says the man sitting at the end of my bench

who had objected to our coming to India in the first place. "If we must pack off, let's go to London at least. We are the English king's subjects aren't we? So, we are English!"

The suggestion causes an uproar: drowned, eventually, by Dr. Manek Mody's remarkable voice. "And what do we do," he asks, "when the English king's *Vazir* stands before us with a glass full of milk? Tell him we are brown Englishmen, come to sweeten their lives with a dash of color?"

Mr. Bankwalla, precise as the crisp new rupee notes he handles at the bank, says, "Yes. Tell him, we came across on a coal steamer . . . and drop a small lump of coal in the milk. That will convey the unspoken message of love and harmony."

"As long as we conduct our lives quietly, as long as we present no threat to anybody, we will prosper right here," roars the colonel over the mike.

"Yes," says the banker. "But don't try to prosper immoderately. And, remember: don't ever try to exercise real power."

The wag at the back, who's been champing at the bit to butt in, stands up and irrelevantly shouts: "Those who want four wives say aye! Those who want vegetarian bhats and farts say nay!"

There is a raucous medley of ayes and nays. There is nothing like a good dose of bathroom humor to put us Parsees in a fine mood. It is impossible to conduct the meeting after this.

We emerge into the sun's brassy blast and our faces crinkle in self-defense. Mother reminds us to rub the ash from our foreheads. Ayah looks as if she is melting. The tongaman removes the horse's feed sack and we pile into the tonga.

Chapter 6

I sit on the small wooden stool and Ayah's soapy hands move all over me. Water from the tap fills the bucket. Ayah, squatting before me, rubs between my toes. I'm ticklish. Deliberately she rubs the soles of my feet and, screaming, I fall off the stool and wiggle on the slippery floor. She pins me to the cement with her foot and douses me with water from the tin bucket. By the time I'm dried, powdered and lifted to the bed Ayah is drenched.

Now it is Mother's turn. Ayah calls her and she appears: willing, conscientious, devout, her head covered by a gauzy white scarf and smelling of sandalwood. She has been praying.

Ever since Colonel Bharucha tugged at my tendon and pressed my heel down in the Fire Temple, Mother massages my leg. I lie diagonally on the bed, my small raised foot between her breasts. She leans forward and pushes back the ball of my foot. She applies all her fragile strength to stretch the stubborn tendon. Her flesh, like satin, shifts under my foot. I gaze at her. Shaded by the scarf her features acquire sharper definition. The tipped chin curves deep to meet the lower lip. The lips, full, firm, taper form a lavish "M" in wide wings, their outline etched with the clarity of cut rubies. Her nose is slender, slightly bumped: and the taut curve of her cheekbones is framed by a jaw as delicately oval as an egg. The hint of coldness, common to such chiseled beauty, is overwhelmed by the exuberant quality of her innocence. I feel she is beautiful beyond bearing.

Her firm strokes, her healing touch. The motherliness of Mother. It reaches from her bending body and cocoons me. My thighs twitch, relaxed.

Her motherliness. How can I describe it? While it is there it is all-encompassing, voluptuous. Hurt, heartache and fear vanish. I swim, rise, tumble, float, and bloat with bliss. The world is wonderful, wondrous—and I a perfect fit in it. But it switches off, this motherliness. I open my heart to it. I welcome it. Again. And again. I begin to understand its on-off pattern. It is treacherous.

Mother's motherliness has a universal reach. Like her involuntary female magnetism it cannot be harnessed. She showers material delight on all and sundry. I resent this largesse. As Father does her unconscious and indiscriminate sex appeal. It is a prostitution of my concept of childhood rights and parental loyalties. She is my mother—flesh of my flesh—and Adi's. She must love only us! Other children have their own mothers who love them . . . Their mothers don't go around loving me, do they?

A portion of our house at the back is lent to the Shankars. They are newly married, fat and loving. She is lighter skinned than him and has a stout braid that snuggles down her back and culminates in a large satin bow, red, blue or white. At about five every evening Shankar returns from work. He trudges up the drive, up along the side of our house, and somewhere in the vicinity of our bathroom lets loose a mating call.

"Darling! Darling! I've come!"

No matter where we are, Ayah, Adi and I rush to the windows and peer out of the wire netting.

"My life! My Lord! You've come!" rejoices Gita, as if his return is a totally unexpected delight.

At his mate's answering call Shankar puffs out, and further diminishing a slender leather briefcase he carries under his arm, breaks into a thudding trot.

Because theirs is an arranged marriage, they are now steamily in love. I drop in on Gita quite often. She is always cooking something and mixed up with the fumes of vegetables and lentils is the steam of their night-long ecstasy. It is very like the dark fragrance Masseur's skillful fingers generate beneath Ayah's sari. Gita is always smiling, bubbling with gladness. She is full of stories. She tells me the story of Heer and Ranjah, of Romeo and Juliet.

Ayah, too, knows stories. Sitting on the lawn in front of the house she stretches her legs and dreamily chews on a blade of grass. Hari the gardener, squatting in his skimpy loincloth, is digging the soil around some rosebushes. He moves on to trim the gardenia hedge by the kitchen. It is the middle of the day in mid-February.

Pansies, roses, butterflies and fragrances—the buzz of bees and flies and of voices drifting from the kitchen. The occasional clip-clop of tonga horses on Warris Road, and bicycle bells and car horns. Hawks wheeling and distantly shrieking beneath a massive blue sky. I think of God, I pick up a dandelion and blow. "He loves me—he loves me not. He loves me—he loves me not . . ."

Ayah hums. I recognize the tune.

"Tell me the story of Sohni and Mahiwal," I say.

Ayah's hum becomes louder and she half croons, half speaks the Punjabi folktale immortalized in verse. We drift to rural Punjab—to a breeze stirring in wheat stalks and yellow mustard fields. To village belles weaving through the fields to wells.

Ayah's eyes are large and eloquent, rimmed with kohl, soft with dreams. "Beautiful Sohni—handsome Mahiwal . . ."

Their love is defiant, daring, touching. Their families bitter enemies. Sohni is not allowed to meet Mahiwal.

The wide Chenab flows between their villages, separating the lovers. But late one night, slipping furtively from her village, risking treacherous currents and fierce reprisal, Sohni floats across on an inflated buffalo hide to her lover.

Mahiwal's delight is boundless. He celebrates in rapturous outbursts of verse. But he is distraught when he discovers he has nothing in the house to feed his Sohni.

It is too late to send for sweets—the bazaar is closed. "But such is the strength of his passion—the tenderness of his love," says Ayah lowering her lids over her faraway and dreamy eyes, "that he cuts a hank of flesh from his thigh, and barbecuing it on skewers, offers his beloved kebabs!"

Ayah cannot speak any more. Her voice is choked, her eyes streaming, her nose blocked.

"Does she eat it?" I enquire, astonished.

"She gobbles it up!" says Ayah, sobbing. "Poor thing, she doesn't know what the kebabs are made of . . . "

In the end the doomed lovers die.

A shout, a couple of curses, a laugh, break away from the hum of voices coming from the kitchen. And then a receding patter of bare feet.

They are after the gardener's dhoti.

Ayah and I jump up from the grass and following the pattering feet run along the side of the house and past Gita's window.

"What's happening?" Gita calls from within.

"They're after Hari's dhoti!" I shout.

We approach the servants' yard and, sure enough, see the ragged scuffle around Hari. Hari's spare, dark body is almost hidden. Ayah stops to one side and I dive into the tangle of limbs yelling for all I'm worth, contributing my mite of rowdyism to the general row.

Yousaf the odd-job man, Greek-profiled, curly-haired, towers mischievously over Hari. Everybody towers over the gardener—even the sweeper Moti. I, of course, am still far from towering. As is Papoo, the sweeper's daughter, who comes galloping and whooping from the servants' courtyard, an infant wobbling dangerously on her hip, and brandishing a long broom. Her wide, bold mouth flashing a handsome smile she plunges herself, the insouciant babe, and the fluffy broom into the scuffle.

Yousaf has a grip on Hari's hand—which is hanging on to the knot at his waist. Yousaf casually shakes and pulls the hand, trying to loosen its hold on the loincloth, and Hari's slight, taut body rocks back and forth and from side to side.

Imam Din, genial-faced, massive, towers behind Hari. He is our cook. His dusty feet, shod in curly-toed leather slippers, are placed flat apart. He drums his chest, flexes his muscles and emits the fierce *barruk* cries with which Punjabi village warriors bluff, intimidate and challenge each other. "*O vay!*" he roars. "I'll chew you up and I won't even burp!" Majestically, good-naturedly, he lunges at the cloth between the gardener's legs.

Hari is having a hard time fending off the cook's hand with his spare arm, and also coping with Moti's sly attacks, and Papoo's tickling broom. The washerman, who has brought our laundry for the week, has also joined the melee. We are like a pack of puppies, worrying and attacking each other in a high-spirited gambol.

But we play to rules. Hari plays the jester—and he and I and they know he will not be hurt or denuded. His dhoti might come apart partially—perhaps expose a flash of black buttock to spice the sport—but this happens only rarely.

It is a good-natured romp until suddenly three shrill and familiar screeches blast my ears. "Bitch! *Haramzadi!* May you die!" And Muccho's grasping hand reaches for the root of her daughter's braid. The gaunt, bitter fingers close on the hair, yanking cruelly, and Papoo bows back and staggers backwards at an improbable angle. She falls sitting on her small buttocks, her legs straight out; still holding the jolted and blinking infant on her hip and the broom in her hand.

"*Haram-khor!* Slut! Work-shirker! Move my eyes from you, and off you go!" shrieks Muccho in ungovernable rage, raining sharp, hard slaps on Papoo's head and back.

Ayah swoops down to snatch the infant to safety, and with an outstretched leg tries to fend off the blows. We abandon Hari. And the men, Hari included, group around Papoo, setting up a protective barrier of arms and hands, and muttering: "Forgive her, Muccho, she's just a child... You're too hard on her..."

They cannot physically restrain Muccho. Handling a woman not related to them would be an impropriety. Her husband, Moti, dares not interfere either. Muccho would make his life intolerable. Submissive in all other respects, Muccho's murderous hatred of their daughter makes her irrational.

Despite the intervening arms, Muccho manages to pound her daughter with her fists and with swift vicious kicks. Her hands protecting her head Papoo roils in a ragged ball in the dust, screaming, "*Hai*, I'm dead."

I hate Muccho. I cannot understand her cruelty to her own daughter. I know that someday she will kill her. From the improbable angle of Papoo's twisted limbs, I'm sure she has already done so.

Papoo lies deathly still, crumpled in a dusty heap. Ayah, holding Muccho's son on her hip, dips her *palloo* into a mug of water and sponges the dust from Papoo's lifeless face. "I don't know what jinn gets into her every time she sees Papoo," she declares. "Even a stepmother would be kinder... After all, what's the innocent child done that's so terrible?"

"What do you know?" Muccho screams. "She's no innocent! She's a curse-of-a-daughter... Disobedient, bone lazy, loose charactered... she'll shame us. She'll be the death of me, the whore!"

"How can she be your death? You've already killed her!" says Imam Din.

Imam Din rarely shows anger and his harshness intimidates Muccho. Afraid she might have gone too far, she shakes Papoo's shoulder roughly, as if to awaken her from sleep. "She'll be all right: don't carry on so," she tells Imam Din.

"Oye, Papoooo... Oye, doll," she says with affected affection. "Come on, get up."

She lays Papoo's head on her thigh and pinching her cheeks forces her mouth open. Papoo shows the whites of her eyes as Muccho pours water between her teeth from the mug Ayah brought.

Suddenly Muccho curses—and shies as if blinded. Papoo is spitting a fine spray of water straight into her face. As Muccho raises her hand to lash out Papoo leaps up, miraculously whole. Skipping nimbly from her mother's lunges, Papoo jerks her boyish hips and makes dark, grinning faces and rude and mocking sounds and gestures. All at once she pretends to go limp and, again rolling her eyes up to show their whites, crumples defenseless to the ground; and then spinning like a bundle of rags in a gale, flinging her limbs about, twists away from Muccho's eager clutches; dodging, jeering, now tantalizingly close, now just out of reach. Papoo is not like any girl I know. Certainly not like the other servants' children, who are browbeaten into early submission. She is strong and high-spirited, and it's not easy to break her body... But there are subtler ways of breaking people.

"Wait till I fix you, you *shaitan!* You *choorail!*" Muccho screams vindictively. "You've got a jinn in you... but I'll knock it out or I'm not your mother! Just you see what I have in store for you... It'll put you right! You'll scream to the dead... May you die!"

We laugh at Papoo's feigning—and her funny faces and her mother's ranting. The men start to drift away and Papoo, followed by a cursing, shrieking Muccho aiming stones at her, imitates my limp—and lurching horribly, runs out on the road.

Papoo, recognizing the manipulative power of my limp—and perhaps empathizing with my condition, sometimes affects it. She never does so out of any malice. Besides she knows it aggravates Muccho to no end.

Chapter 7

Ayah calls Imam Din the Catcher-in-the-kitchen. He sits in a corner on a wicker stool near the open pantry door and grabs anything soft that enters the kitchen. Sitting it, him, or her, on his lap he gently rocks. Ayah, I, Adi, Papoo, stray hens, pups, kittens and Rosy and Peter from next door have all had our turn. Rosy and I are bewildered by Imam Din's behavior. Adi and Peter, belonging perhaps to the same species, are less confused and more aggressive.

One day I come upon a dazed Rosy rocking dizzily on Imam Din's lap and I pull her off. "Don't do that, you damn fool!" I say, unleashing my bottled-up fury. "Why do you do that!"

Imam Din gives a sheepish grin, genially pulls us both squirming on his lap, offers us puffs from his hookah and proceeds to tell us we should not mind. It is what he playfully calls only a little *"masti"*—a bit of naughtiness.

And he tells me, "Lenny baby, don't swear—swearwords don't become you."

I know. Adi can swear and it's a big joke. Rosy can curse and look cute. Papoo can let fly a string of invective, compared to which the tongawallah's invective sounds like a lullaby, and manages to appear stunningly roguish. And I cannot even say a damned "damn fool" without being told it does not suit me!

Imam Din possesses a sixth sense—a sensitive antenna that beams him a chart of our movements. And no matter how stealthily Ayah or I sneak into the kitchen, he is ready to pounce. He knows exactly who it is and he never pounces on Mother or Yousaf or Hari. Or us, if we are followed by any of them.

Imam Din is tolerated because of the gray bristles in his closely cropped hair. They permit him to get away with liberties that in a younger man would provoke, if not the wrath of God, at least dire consequences from Ayah. As it is, God looks the other way and Ayah merely pulls away from him saying, "Have you no shame? Look at your gray hairs . . . Fear God, at least!"

Imam Din is tall, big-bellied, barrel-chested, robust: he bicycles twenty miles to and from his village once a month to impregnate his fourth wife. Happily he is three times widowed and four times wed. He is the most respected elder in his village; and his benign temperament and wisdom have earned him a position of respect in our house and among the other servants on Warris Road. He is sixty-five years old. Now you see why he is allowed a certain latitude? Indulged even, you might say?

Rocking apart, I like him and take my complaints to him. So does Ayah. He is a fair and imaginative arbitrator—and when Adi grows up a bit, and I grow, and Adi resolutely peeps through a crack in the bathroom door with a single-minded determination that is like an elemental force, Imam Din is the only one who can handle him.

Twice Imam Din has taken me to his village. I have only a vague recollection of pleasurable sensations. I was too young then.

It is not yet winter. I have been badgering Imam Din for the past week to take me on his next junket to his village home.

"Lenny baby, I'm not going to my village," he says, sighing heavily. "I need to go to my grandson, Dost Mohammad's, village. It's too far . . . Pir Pindo is way beyond Amritsar . . . Forty miles from Lahore as the crow flies!"

"It may be too far for a little crow; but it's not too far for a strong old ox like you," says Ayah. She is toasting *phulkas* (miniature chapatties) on the glowing coal fire and deftly flipping them with tongs. "Poor child," she says. "She wants so much to go . . . It won't break your back to take her."

"Not only my back, my legs too!" says Imam Din. "I'm not so young anymore . . . I'll have a heart attack merely conveying myself there."

"Go on with you!" says Ayah. "You should talk of growing old! I'll know that when I know that!"

"I'll never be too old to bother you," murmurs Imam Din,

sighing, pushing his hubble-bubble away and advancing from his corner on Ayah.

Ayah whirls, tong-handed, glowing iron pointed at Imam Din.

"*Arrey baba . . . ,*" says Imam Din hunching his shoulders and holding his hands out defensively in front. "I still haven't recovered from the last time you scarred me. Aren't you ashamed . . . burning and maiming a harmless old man like me?"

"I know who's harmless and who isn't! Go on, sit down!" she commands.

Imam Din collapses meekly in his corner and drawing deeply on the hookah, causing the water in the smoke filter to gurgle, offers her a puff.

But Ayah is in a determined mood. "Will you take her with you or not?" she demands, tongs in hand: and Imam Din capitulates.

"*Arrey baba,* you're a Hitler! I'll take her. Even though my back snaps in two! Even though my legs fall off! I'll take her."

"She weighs less than this *phulka,*" says Ayah turning her back on us and tossing a thin disk of wheat on the fire until it is swollen with trapped air.

The next morning Ayah wakes me up when it is still night. She helps me to dress quietly: wrestling my arms into last year's coat and my ears into a horrible pink peaked cap Electric-aunt knitted me two years ago. Imam Din and Ayah have a small altercation in the kitchen. Rather, Ayah scolds and Imam Din only protests and pacifies affably. I don't know what the argument is about, but I can guess. Imam Din must have attempted with some part of his anatomy the seduction Ice-candy-man conducts with his toes—with less audacity perhaps, and perhaps with less ingenuity—but, at last, Ayah is appeased—and properly apologized to—and we cycle down our drive with the first faint smudge of dawn diluting the night.

I sit on a small seat attached to the bar in front of Imam Din and his legs, like sturdy pistons, propel us at a staid and unaltering pace through the gullies and huddled bazaars behind Queens Road, then along the Mall past the stately pink sprawl of the High Court, and the constricted alleys running on one side of Father's shop. It is an illuminating experience—my first glimpse of the awakening metropolis of two million bestirring itself to face a new day.

At the crack of dawn, Lahore, the city known as the garden of the Moguls, turns into a toilet. Creeping sleepily out of sagging tenements and hovels the populace squats along alleyways and un-paved street edges facing crumbling brick walls—and thin dark stains trickle between their feet halfway down the alleys.

Cycle bell ringing, Imam Din and I perambulate through the profusion of bared Lahori bottoms. I hang on to the handlebars as we wobble imperturbably over potholes past a view of backsides the dark hue of Punjabi soil—and the smooth, plump spheres of young women who hide their faces in their veils and bare their bottoms. The early risers squat before their mugs, lost in the private contemplative world of their ablutions, and only the children face the street unabashed, turning their heads and bright eyes to look at us.

Past Data Sahib's shrine, past the enormous marble domes of the Badshahi mosque floating in a gray mist, and just before we cross the Ravi bridge we rattle through the small Pathan section of town. Now I see only fierce tribesmen from the northern frontiers around the Khyber and Babusar Passes who descend to the plains in search of work. They leave their families behind in flinty im-poverished valleys concealed in the arid and massive tumult of the Karakorams, the Hindu Kush and the Himalayas. They can afford to visit them only every two or three years. The tribesmen's broad, bared backsides are much paler, and splotched with red, and strong dark hair grows down their backs. In place of mugs there are small mounds of stone and scraps of newspaper and Imam Din sniffs: "What manner of people are these who don't clean their arses with water?"

A particularly pale bottom arrests Imam Din's attention. The skin is pink, still fresh and tingling from cold mountain winds.

"So. We have a new Pathan in town!" he muses aloud.

At that moment the mountain man turns his head. He does not like the expression on our faces. Full of fury he snarls and spits at us.

"Welcome to Lahore, brother," Imam Din calls.

Months later I recognize the face when I see Sharbat Khan, still touchy and bewildered, bent intently over his whirring machine as he sharpens knives in the Mozang Chawk bazaar.

The sun is up, dispelling the mist. Filthy with dust, exhausted, we roll into Wagah, a village halfway to Amritsar. We have covered sixteen miles. I've stopped talking. Imam Din is breathing so hard I'm afraid he really will have a heart attack. He pedals slowly down the rutted bazaar lane and, letting the cycle tilt to one side, stops at a tea stall.

After a breakfast of fried *parathas* and eggs we get a ride atop a stack of hay in a bullock-cart. Imam Din stretches an arm across his bicycle, and lulled by the creaking rhythm of wooden wheels, we fall asleep. Two miles short of Pir Pindo the cart driver prods us awake with his whip.

We rattle along a path running between irrigation ditches and mustard fields. As we cut through a cornfield a small boy, followed by three barking dogs, hurtles out of the deepening light gathered in the stalks. He chases us, shouting, "Oye! Who are you? Oye! What're you up to? Oye! Corn thief! Corn thief!"

The cycle wobbles dangerously. Cursing, Imam Din kicks out. A ribby pup yelps and backs away. Imam Din roars: "Oye, turd of Dost Mohammad! Don't you recognize your great-grandfather?"

Ranna stops short, peering at us out of small, wide-set eyes. He bends to scrape some clay from the track and throws it at the dogs, shooing them away. He approaches us gingerly, awkwardly. He is a little taller than me. His skin is almost black in the dusk. He already has small muscles on his arms and shoulders. A well-proportioned body. But what attracts me most is his belly button. It protrudes an inch from his stomach, like a truncated and cheeky finger. (Later, when he sees me walk, I can tell he is equally taken by my limp.)

As soon as Ranna is within range Imam Din ministers two quick spanks to his head; and, the punishment dispensed, introduces us. "Say salaam to your guest, oye, mannerless fellow!"

Ranna stares at me, his mouth slack. His teeth are very white, and a little crowded in front.

"Haven't you seen a city girl before?" Imam Din raps Ranna's head lightly. Ranna flinches. "Why aren't you wearing a shirt, oye? Shameless bugger . . . Go tell your mother we are here. We want supper. Tell Dost Mohammad we're here." Both Dost Mohammad and Chidda are Imam Din's grandchildren. Muslim communities like to keep their girls in the family; so marriages between first cousins are common.

Ranna appears to fly in his skimpy drawers, the pale soles of his feet kicking up dust as he dissolves down the path.

In Ranna's village we dwell close to the earth. Sitting on the floor we eat off clay plates, with our fingers, and sleep on mats spread on the ground, breathing the earth's odor.

The next morning Ranna and I romp in the fields, and Ranna, fascinated, copies my limp. I know, then, that like Papoo, he really cares for me. I let him limp without comment. In return, he shows me how to mold a replica of his village with dung. And, looking generously and intently into my eyes, he permits me to feel his belly button. It even feels like a finger.

His sisters, Khatija and Parveen, barely two or three years older than us, already wear the responsible expressions of much older women. Like the other girls in the village, they affect the mannerisms and tone of their mother and adults. They are pretty girls, with large, serene eyes and a skin inclined to flush. Painfully shy of me, they are distressed—and perplexed—by the display of my twig-like legs beneath my short dress. (I don't wear my calipers as much now.) They don't know what to make of my cropped hair either. Busy with chores, baskets of grain stuck to their tiny hips, they scuttle about importantly.

Every short while Ranna suspends play to run to his mother. Chidda is cooking at the clay hearth in their courtyard; she feeds her son and me scraps of chapatti dipped in buttermilk.

Later in the blue winter afternoon a bunch of bearded Sikh peasants, their long hair wrapped in loose turbans or informally displayed in topknots, visit Pir Pindo. They are from Derra Tek Singh, a neighboring village. The men of Pir Pindo—those who are not out working in the fields—come from their barns and courtyards and sit with the Sikhs in a thick circle beneath a huge *sheesham* in a patch of wild grass.

The rough grass pricks my bottom and thighs. Ranna has sidled into his father's lap. Prompted by Imam Din, he wears a buttonless shirt he has clearly outgrown. I sit between Dost Mohammad and Jagjeet Singh, a plump, smiling bowlegged Sikh priest, a *granthi*. Khatija and Parveen, looking like miniature women of eight and nine, their heads modestly covered, bring us piles of fragrant cornbread fried in butter and a steaming clay pot of spicy mustard-greens. I see the wisdom of their baggy shalwars and long kamizes as I fidget in the grass, tugging at my dress.

The Sikh *granthi*, gray-bearded and benign, beckons the girls, and, sly eyes lowered, they come to him. He strokes their covered heads and says, in Punjabi, "May the True Guru bless you with long lives." He draws them to him affectionately. "Every time I see you, you appear to have grown taller! We'll have to think about arranging your marriages soon!" He leans across me and addresses Dost Mohammad. "Don't you think it's time their hands were painted yellow?"

Jagjeet Singh has alluded to the henna-decorated hands of Muslim brides. The sisters duck their heads and hide their mouths in their veils. Ranna finds the suggestion outrageously funny. Slipping from his father's lap, his belly button pointed at them like a jabbing finger. he jumps up and down. "Married women!" he chortles. "Ho! Ho! Married women!"

Already practiced in the conduct they have absorbed from the village women, the girls try not to smile or giggle. They must have heard their mother and aunts (as I have), say: "*Hasi to phasi!* Laugh (and), get laid!" I'm not sure what it means—and I'm sure they don't either but they know that smiling before men can lead to disgrace.

We have eaten and belched. The hookah, stoked with fresh tobacco, is being passed among the Muslim villagers. (Sikhs don't smoke.) In the sated lull the village mullah clears his throat. "My brothers," he says. And as our eyes turn to him, running frail fingers through his silky white beard, he says, "I hear there is trouble in the cities... Hindus are being murdered in Bengal... Muslims, in Bihar. It's strange... the English *Sarkar* can't seem to do anything about it."

Now that he has started the ball rolling, the mullah raises his white eyebrows in a forehead that is almost translucent with age. He looks about him with anxious, questioning eyes.

The village *chaudhry*—sitting by Imam Din and the mullah— says, "I don't think it is because they can't... I think it is because the *Sarkar* doesn't want to!" He is a large man, as big-bellied and broad-beamed as Imam Din, but at least twenty years younger. He has large, clear black eyes and an imposing cleft in his chin. As he talks, he slowly strokes his thick, up-twirled moustache: without which no village headman can look like a *chaudhry*. "But all that is in the cities," he continues, as if he has considered the issue for some time. "It won't affect our lives."

"I've not come all this way without a reason," says Imam Din. The villagers, who are wondering why he is visiting them, look at him attentively. He rubs his face with both hands; as if it pains him to state the reason. "I don't think you know how serious things are getting in the towns. Sly killings; rioting and baton charges by the police... long marches by mobs... The Congress-wallahs have started a new stunt... they sit down on the rail tracks—women and children, too. The police lift them off the tracks... But one of these days the steam engines will run over them... Once aroused, the English are savages...

"Then there is this Hindu-Muslim trouble," he says, after a pause. "Ugly trouble... It is spreading. Sikh-Muslim trouble also..."

The villagers, Sikh and Muslim, erupt in protest.

"Brother," the Sikh *granthi* says when the tumult subsides, "our villages come from the same racial stock. Muslim or Sikh, we are basically Jats. We are brothers. How can we fight each other?"

"*Barey Mian*," says the *chaudhry*, giving Imam Din his due as a respected elder, "I'm alert to what's happening... I have a radio.

But our relationships with the Hindus are bound by strong ties. The city folk can afford to fight...we can't. We are dependent on each other: bound by our toil; by Mandi prices set by the Banyas—they're our common enemy—those city Hindus. To us villagers, what does it matter if a peasant is a Hindu, or a Muslim, or a Sikh?"

Imam Din nods. There is a subtle change in his face; he looks calmer. "As long as our Sikh brothers are with us, what have we to fear?" he says, speaking to the *granthi*, and including the other Sikhs with a glance. "I think you are right, brothers, the madness will not infect the villages."

"If needs be, we'll protect our Muslim brothers with our lives!" says Jagjeet Singh.

"I am prepared to take an oath on the Holy Koran," declares the *chaudhry*, "that every man in this village will guard his Sikh brothers with no regard for his own life!"

"We have no need for oaths and such," says the mullah in a fragile elderly voice. "Brothers don't require oaths to fulfil their duty."

Later, when the mullah's voice calls the evening prayer, and the Sikhs have begun to saunter across the fields to their village, Dost Mohammad carries his son to a small brick mosque with a green dome in the center of Pir Pindo. I stay back with the women.

We are due to leave in an hour. Chidda has awakened early to prepare breakfast. I sit on the floor crosslegged, eating my *paratha* and omelette. Parveen shuffles closer to me. With extreme delicacy, her face flushed and confiding, she whispers into my ear. It takes me a while to realize, she is asking if my hair was cut on account of lice.

"Of course not!" I say. I don't care who hears me. "It's the city fashion." I glare at her. "Even my mother's hair is short."

Chidda, squatting by the hearth, summons her daughter.

Rapping her on the head she says: "Who told you to be uncivil? Who told you to ask questions? Haven't I taught you to mind your tongue? Go! Get out of my sight!" she says. Ranna quickly grabs his sister's share of the breakfast.

A bunch of villagers accompanies us for a mile, wheeling Imam Din's bicycle for him as we walk. I leave Pir Pindo with a heavy heart and a guilty conscience.

Chapter 8

When I return from Imam Din's village to the elevated world of chairs, tables and toilet seats, Imam Din continues his efforts to keep on the right side of Ayah. She is the greatest involuntary teacher ever. He plies her with beautifully swollen *phulkas* hot off the griddle, slathered with butterfat and sprinkled with brown sugar. He prepares separate and delicious vegetarian dishes for her. In fact he is, to a large extent, responsible for her spherical attractions. Where would she be without his extra servings of butter, yogurt, curry and chapatti? Wouldn't she look like all the other stringy, half-starved women in India whom one looks at only once —and never turns around to look at twice?

He continues to appease Adi and me with dizzying inhalations from his hookah; and chicken giblets and liver, turn by turn, on those occasions when my parents have guests and he cooks chicken.

My parents entertain often: and when guests are expected we are fed early. Adi and I sit across the oilcloth on a small table against the wall, away from the silver cutlery and embroidered dinner cloth. Yousaf folds the starched white napkins into fancy peacocks and stuffs their props into long-stemmed crystal glasses. Flowers blaze in silver vases.

Glitter and glory, but very little food. We know the guests will be served delectable but small portions.

We have already shared the chicken liver, and today it is my turn for the single giblet. I place it on a side plate, saving it for the end when I can chew and suck on it for long uninterrupted moments. I notice the movement of Adi's eyeballs under his lids as they sneak to the corners, peer at the giblet and slip back. This only enhances the quality of my possession. I am at peace—there is honor even among thieves—and the fear of reprisal. I casually place my left hand above the plate and maneuver it to shield the giblet. I don't wish to put undue strain on Adi's honor.

As it happens, the precaution is unnecessary. I raise a glass of water to my lips and Adi's swift hand strikes. The giblet is jammed into his mouth and swallowed whole. His throat works like a boa constrictor's and his face turns red. I grab at his mouth and he opens it wide, saying "Aaaaaa!"

There is nothing left to retrieve.

What hurts me most is him swallowing my giblet like a pill. Not even tasting it. It is an affront to my sense of fair play. I grab his hair and let out a blood-curdling shriek that brings Mother rushing from the drawing room and Yousaf, Imam Din and Ayah from the kitchen.

Mother spanks Adi, and Adi, cursing and fighting back, is picked up by Yousaf and spirited away into the darkness outside.

Ayah carries me screaming into the kitchen and proceeds to splash my face at the sink. Imam Din pops a chicken heart into my mouth. Yousaf carries Adi back to the kitchen. Adi's mouth is working. It too has had something popped into it. I wonder what? An uneasy truce is contemplated as we scrutinize each other's ruminating mouths. A short while later when everyone is busy preparing dinner we slip unobserved beneath the dinner table, friends again.

We have done this innumerable times. One would imagine that someone might think to look under the table and chase us away before dinner is served.

The table is supported by stands of polished wood. The stands are held to by a beam which runs six inches above the floor. We roost quietly on the beam in cloth-screened twilight, amidst a display of trouser cuffs, sari borders, ankles, shoes and a medley of fragrance.

Rosy and Peter's parents are present: we can tell by their legs. His are crossed at the ankles, smell frankly of cow dung and are prone to shake in and out at the knees. Hers are planted solidly side by side beneath her sari. Peter's father is a turbaned and bearded Sikh. He is not permitted to cut his hair or shave—not even the hair of his armpits or crotch. Peter has told us this.

Their mother is American. She ties her blond hair back in a severe knot and always wears a white cotton sari with wide borders. Sometimes I feel she doubles as one of the marching Salvation Army band-women. She is green-eyed and very white and placid and otherworldly. She carries on with whatever she is doing—which is for the most part a mystery—and pays scant attention to the world. Nothing that her children, or her husband, do can wipe the placid look from her face or disturb her unhurried movements.

Her husband is not a bad man. Mr. Singh does not beat her or white-slave traffic in her. But he has habits that would drive Mother up the wall. . . I've heard her say so. He roams on long hairy legs in loose cotton drawers, barefoot. He milks his water buffalo himself. He converses loudly in vituperative Punjabi and he clears his throat and spits around—generally conducting himself like a coarse Jat in a village. Mother expects more refined conduct from a man married to an American woman.

They are infrequent guests.

This appears to be an evening dedicated to neighborly brotherliness. The other guests are from the Birdwood Barracks: Inspector General of Police and Mrs. Rogers. He is tall, colorless, hefty-moustached, pale-eyebrowed; and she, soft, pretty, plump and submissive—with a fascinating proclivity to clean out and around her children's ears with a handkerchief dampened with spit.

Their two children are younger than us. The only reason we countenance them at all is because of their glowing ears.

There are only four guests to dinner tonight, plus my parents—which makes six. Father calculates six portions to a chicken. Hence the single giblet.

Meanwhile Father has launched his emergency-measures joke.

A British soldier and a turbaned native find themselves sharing a compartment. They are traveling by the Khyber Mail to Peshawar. The Indian lifts a bottle of Scotch to his mouth frequently. He does not offer any to the soldier. When the Indian leaves the compartment for a moment the soldier steals a hasty draught from the bottle.

Again the Indian goes out, and the tommy sneaks another swig.

They get to talking. The soldier confides he took a draw or two from the Indian's bottle of Scotch. "Since you didn't offer it to me, old chap, I helped myself!" he says companionably.

The native is aghast.

"But that is my urine in the bottle!" he exclaims. "My *hakim* prescribed it as a cure for syphilis . . ."

Poor soldier.

Father and Mother hoot with laughter. Their Sikh guest is in guffaws. And twice, unable to constrain his appreciation, Mr. Singh inserts two fingers in his mouth and emits piercing whistles. His American wife, I think, titters.

I cannot see them but I doubt if the Rogers manage even a smile. All I see—and barely escape—is a vicious little kick the Inspector General of Police gives the beam. His boots, smelling faintly of horse dung and strongly of shoe polish, keep stabbing the wood.

Father adds a postscript: "You know—I learned the other day—there was no syphilis in India until the British came . . ."

"You won't be able to blame everything on us for long, old chap," says Inspector General Rogers. "That old bugger, Gandhi, is up to his old bag of tricks."

"We will have *Swaraj!*" declaims Mr. Singh in deafening belligerence. As if the Englishman, instead of hinting at the premature departure of the British, has just denied him Home Rule.

"You think you'll be up to it, old chap?" says Mr. Rogers snidely.

"Why not?" shouts Mr. Singh as if he is arguing with the Inspector of Police across a hockey field. "I am up to ruling you and your Empire! You recruit all our Sikh soldiers into your World War Number Two and we win the war for you! Whyfore then you think we cannot do Home Rule?"

Mr. Singh's broad Punjabi accent and loud voice never fail to annoy Mother. She must have indicated her displeasure with some gesture because Mrs. Singh placidly says, "Don't shout, dear."

"I am not shouting!" hollers Mr. Singh. "I'm telling this man: Quit India! Gandhijee is on a fast," he warns the police officer. "If he dies, his blood will be on your head!"

"That wily Banya is an expert on fasting unto death without dying," says the heftily moustached policeman demurely.

"And what if he dies?" questions Mr. Singh righteously. "You mark my word. One day he will die! Then what you will do?"

"I'll tell you what I'll do. I'll celebrate!" says the Inspector General, losing his patience.

"You will not celebrate! You know why? Because rivers of your blood will flow in our gutters!" says Mr. Singh in a sarcastic singsong. He shakes his knees in and out in an engaging rhythm and bangs his fist on the table. I can tell by the swift little stabs of the Inspector General's shoe on the wood that he too is angry.

"Rivers of blood will flow all right!" he shouts, almost as loudly as Mr. Singh. "Nehru and the Congress will not have everything their way! They will have to reckon with the Muslim League and Jinnah. If we quit India today, old chap, you'll bloody fall at each other's throats!"

"Hindu, Muslim, Sikh: we all want the same thing! We want independence!"

Inspector General Rogers recovers his Imperial phlegm. "My dear man," he intones, "Don't you know the Congress won't agree on a single issue with the Muslim League? The Cabinet Mission proposed a Federation of the Hindu and Muslim majority provinces. Jinnah accepted it; Gandhi and Nehru didn't!

"They even rejected Lord Wavell's suggestion for an interim government with a majority Congress representation! They're like the three bloody monkeys! They refuse to hear, or see that Jinnah has the backing of seventy million Indian Muslims! Those arrogant Hindus have blown the last chance for an undivided India . . . Gandhi and Nehru are forcing the League to push for Pakistan!"

"And where will this so-called Pakistan be?" enquires our Sikh neighbor with withering and snickering sarcasm.

"They want the Muslim majority provinces: Punjab, Sind,

Kashmir, the North West and Bengal," replies the police officer, as if coaching a backward child. I can imagine the haughty flare of his English nostrils.

"They are only saying that to be in a better bargaining position and you are stringing them along because of your divide-and-rule monkey tricks!" accuses Mr. Singh. "You always set one up against the other... You just give Home Rule and see. We will settle our differences and everything!"

"Who will? Master Tara Singh?" It is a contemptuous, curl-of-the-lip tone of voice.

"Yes. He is my leader. I will obey him!" Mr. Singh says this so quietly and firmly that for a moment I wonder if someone else has spoken in his stead.

The Inspector General makes a very peculiar sound. Then he says, "The Akalis are a bloody bunch of murdering fanatics!"

Even I can tell it's a tactless thing to say.

Mr. Singh's rhythmically knocking knees grow perfectly still. In one quick movement, drawing his legs to his chair, almost knocking it over, he stands up. Everybody's feet make erratic moves. Adi and I, terrified of discovery, retract our legs and cower in hunched-up bundles.

Father has stood up also. I hear him say in Punjabi: "Oye, sit down, Sardarjee... I say, *yaar*, don't mind the *Angrez* Sahib. He doesn't know..."

But before Father can finish the sentence Mr. Singh cuts in: "Oh yes? He knows very well!" and one of his legs completely disappears. There is a clatter of crockery, a heavy thump over our heads, and three variously pitched feminine "Oh"s! Mr. Singh must have leaned clear across the table.

"Jana! Take the fork away!" Mother shouts.

"Don't you dare touch him!" screams Mrs. Rogers hysterically. "Oh! He'll blind him!"

"Put that fork away, dear," says Mrs. Singh, her voice quavering in the effort to sound firm.

I realize with a little thrill of excitement running up my spine that Mr. Singh has tried to stab the Englishman's eyes with a fork: and since Mr. Rogers has not cried out, the attempt has failed. No blood has so far been shed.

Father's legs skittle behind Mr. Singh's solitary leg. There is a brief scuffling sound. A piece of cutlery falls clattering on the table-top. Mr. Rogers remains disappointingly quiet. Obviously Mr. Singh has been de-forked. Then Mr. Singh's wide butt pounds down on the cane-bottomed dining chair.

"Tell him to apologize!" He roars, almost wailing, shuffling on his seat.

"Go to hell, you fat hairy slob!" spits the police officer, his short breath betraying his jolted nerves.

"Please," pleads Mother. "Please apologize."

I can visualize Mother's hand on the Inspector's arm. None, except Father, can resist her touch.

There is a tense pause.

"Oh, all right . . . I'm sorry, old boy! I shouldn't have said that," says the Englishman gruffly.

In sandaled feet Father toddles back to his own seat, and Mr. Singh's muscular thighs commence their rhythmic twitching with renewed vigor.

Mother and Mrs. Rogers chatter excessively about the weather. Suddenly they become quiet.

"You know, old chap," Inspector General Rogers has just said to Mr. Singh, "if you Sikhs plan to keep your lands in Lyallpur and Montgomery, you'd better start fraternizing with the Muslim League. If you don't, the Muslims will throw you off your rich lands."

"That motherfucker isn't born who can throw us out! We will throw them out! and you out!" Mr. Singh bashes his fist on the table with such force that the cutlery and crockery jangle.

"Who wants pudding?" trills Mother shrilly, loudly banging a spoon against her glass.

In the startled silence that follows, Mrs. Rogers enthusiastically warbles: "Oh, I'd love some pudding!"

And Mrs. Singh, mustering all the emphasis of which she is capable, says, "Me too!"

In a determined effort to flood with oil the precariously tranquilized waters, Mother tells Father, "Janoo, you must tell everybody that joke about the cannibals and the padre's wife that you told me! About breakfast in bed..."

Since when did Father start telling Mother jokes? Mother has this habit of voicing her fantasies... If she persists in her visions of conjugal bliss, I'm afraid she will lose touch with reality.

There are other jokes. Father and Mother crack up with hoots that I'm sure can be heard by the lion in his zoo. Beneath the table Adi and I mimic their laughter, taking care to time the whoops and blend our voices. Mr. Singh is breathless with laughing. He stamps his feet, here and there, unaware of the havoc he is causing beneath the table.

After they are through with the pudding, and the thimblefuls of liqueurs, Adi pinches Mrs. Singh's calf and I pinch Mrs. Rogers's. Even the imperturbable Mrs. Singh shrieks. Their feet fly up to our chests and chins. The tablecloth is raised and six bewildered faces poke under.

We emerge. Mother is angry. Apprehensive. She glances at Father and, taking her cue from his amused countenance, relaxes. She beams at us in that way I have begun to notice and resent: her "other-people-are-around" way. Father looks pleasant and even makes indulgent sounds. Yousaf gathers us by the ears and propels us to bed.

Father's dinner party jokes never fail. The Rogers have scarcely eaten. Over the years it saves thousands of rupees' worth of chicken, lamb, caramel custard and other party fare.

Half asleep I can still hear them laugh. Was that really Father? that communicative person making "pooch-pooch" noises with his lips and kindly saying, "Get along you two!" as Yousaf took us from the room? and that hooting, rollicking woman my remote and solemn mother?

At about this time I become aware of a secondhand Morris Minor in our midst. It has a crank up front to start the engine, a radiator that consumes countless kettles of boiling water, and a five-manpower crew to push-start the eight-horsepower motor.

The snap of the crank now features as one of the regular noises of the morning. Together with the lion's roar, the bustle of domestic activity to provide Father with his newspaper and cups of tea—and the battle Muccho wages with Papoo—it awakens me. In my nightsuit, barefoot, I go to the veranda. The crank changes hands every five minutes. Imam Din is at it. One hand on the car hood, a duster wrapped round the handle for a firm grip, he lurches mightily and the engine burps. He straightens and presses the small of his back.

Hari takes over. Stooping before the handle like a frisky terrier he energetically turns the crank with both hands.

Adi bursts out of the dining room door in his pyjamas, holding his toothbrush, followed by Ayah's shouts and then by Ayah. He too has a crack at the crank.

I help Ayah pry him loose and Moti takes over.

I go to greet Father. He is in the bathroom, enthroned on the commode. With a great rustling of newspaper, preoccupied and mute, he sits me on his bare thigh.

Father is in a good mood. So, Mother too is in a good mood. She gives me a hug. She puts toothpaste on Father's toothbrush. She tells me to take Father's empty cup and saucer to the pantry. But Father latches on to me with such a show of speechless anguish and consternation at the thought of being parted from me that Mother says, "Let it be. Yousaf will take them."

She smiles indulgently: as if she could cross my father if she had a mind to.

Father has a twenty-minute nap after lunch. Not nineteen, not twenty-one, precisely twenty. He knots a kerchief tightly round his eyes and lies down flat on the bed with his sandals on. Mother removes his sandals, his socks if he is wearing socks, blows tenderly between his toes, and with cooing noises caresses his feet.

With a stern finger on her lips she hushes the household, until Father's internal alarm clock causes him to jump out of bed, and within four minutes on to his bicycle.

After lunch on a luminous November Saturday I'm idling on my cot, filling my tedium with dreams, when a hushed rush of sound comes from my parents' bedroom. Not the harsh angry sounds that still me with dreadful apprehension, but the kind of noises signifying Father's frolicsome mood. Father takes a longer break some Saturdays.

I leap from my bed and burst into their room.

Mother and Father are standing at the opposite ends of their joined beds. "Janoo! Don't tease me like this . . . I know you've got it: I saw it!"

Mother's voice teeters between amusement and a wheedling whine. She is a virtuoso at juggling the range of her voice and achieving the exact balance with which to handle Father. Father has the knack of extracting the most talented performances from us all—and from all those who work for him.

"Jana!" Mother says in throaty exasperation, "you know I'm going to get you!" and she lunges around the bed.

Father, limber in his striped cotton nightsuit and maroon dressing gown, maintains a strategic distance. "Don't be foolish," he says with fake and *sotto-voce* irritability. Conscious of the servants, my parents squabble in low voices and, being a more private person, Father is more particular. Outside their window Yousaf is shaving the leaves from the trees with a scythe, assisting the half-hearted Lahori fall to complete its task.

Mother clutches the headboard and tries to dodge, taking a step this way and that. Then, climbing on their bed, she scrambles across the mattress on all fours.

Father skips away easily. "Stop pestering me," he says, "I'm getting late for work."

"I won't let you go, Jana," says Mother in a voice so tearfully childish that it cannot possibly present a threat to Father's authority. Turning appealingly to me, her bosom heaving, she enlists my support.

"Lenny, catch him."

"Stop acting like a child," Father says disgustedly. He spreads his hands to show that he is not concealing anything.

But Mother, an expert at reading his face, says, "I know you are smiling under your moustache, Jana. I love it when you are this way." And attuned to the nuance underlying his disgusted voice, she knows she can persist. "I'll get my hands on the money, or my name isn't Bunty."

I run round the bed, exaggerating my modified limp, and grab hold of Father's leg.

"One minute. One minute," he coaxes, loosening my grip and misleading me. The instant I release his leg he vaults through the curtains into the narrow study, and, swiftly shutting the doors, draws the bolt.

"Jana! Let me in, Jana," Mother cries, shaking the door and rattling the loose iron bolt. I bang on it. Yousaf and his scythe have moved to shave another tree and the wintry sun shines through its bared branches.

"You will break the door, stupid twit!" cries Father in a harsh, hushed voice. Uncomfortably aware of the ubiquitous servants, he pulls the bolt and opens the door.

Mother and I rush him excitedly. Expecting the charge, Father staggers back and plonks down on the settee with Mother and me on top of him. Mother's searching hands move all over his dressing gown, and beneath it, probing his pockets, crotch and other crannies.

Knowing now I'm looking for money, I also stroke and pat his clothes.

"You've hidden it, Janoo," cries Mother in dismay. "But I'll find it! I'm not about to give up!"

Heaving herself off Father, determinedly and methodically Mother opens and shuts drawers in a rickety old desk and in a steel filing cabinet. Father lounges on the settee looking smug. But when Mother strides towards the large teak cupboard at the far end of the room he bounds forward and, spreading his hands, stands before it. The heavy panels on the top half of the almirah conceal a neat array of narrow drawers, and the lower half is composed of two sets of deeper drawers.

We fling ourselves at Father. My wiry Father is strong, but Mother has the advantage of her voluptuous weight. In the tug of war that ensues we manage to open the door panels—and to keep them open—despite Father's desperate efforts to dislodge us.

Mother, breathing heavily, plunges her hands here and there and with a triumphant cry sprints out of the room, her stubby fingers closed on a large wad of notes.

"Oye, *uloo!*" Father says, rushing after her. "It's not my money, you crazy! I'll bring you your housekeeping money from the office."

"I'll take only what I have to," Mother shouts, locking herself into the bathroom. "I haven't even paid Lenny's physiotherapist yet . . . I've to buy the children's clothes for Christmas and New Year." (Christmas, Easter, Eid, Divali. We celebrate them all.)

"Oye, madwoman," hisses Father through the door, ostensibly mindful of the servants' ears. "Show some sense. I owe the money. I have to return it on my way to the office. Give it back at once."

"I'll give it after I've taken what I need, Jana," Mother warbles and suddenly opening the door shoves the bundle at my father.

Before she's had time to move to her cupboard Father has flicked through the notes and counted them. "*Arrey!* You've taken far too much!" he exclaims as if shaken to the core and bankrupted by the banditry. But I am also schooled to read between the lines of my father's face. His heart is not in his anguish. Mother must have withdrawn a very meager and reasonable sum indeed!

"She's bent on destroying us," Father grumbles, striking his forehead again and again. "Money Money Money Money! From morning to night. Money Money Money Money! I'm fed up."

But Mother, with dew in her eyes and a misty smile, blows him kisses. And, having locked the money in her cupboard, she goes about her business of picking up Father's clothes and tidying the beds and getting dressed.

Chapter 9

To our left is the Singhs' large bungalow. The compound wall we share is partially broken by the sloping trunk of a eucalyptus tree near our kitchen. This is where Rosy, Peter, Adi and I, and sometimes Cousin, gather to discuss world affairs, human relationships, Mr. and Mrs. Singh's uncut hair and Rosy's sister's impending baby.

"I'll tell you how babies come," says Rosy.

"Oh, we know," I say, "Ayah's already told us."

"How?" challenges Rosy. "The stork brings them?"

Rosy sighs, rolling her eyes. "I'll tell you how they are made," she persists; "my sister's told me everything."

Rosy is obnoxiously smug and swollen these days. She may walk about with a grown-up air—but her cotton knickers, I notice, remain wet. Her big sister unquestionably pumps her with questionable knowledge.

"If your sister knows so much, how come she could not even pass her Matric exam?" I ask.

Rosy has picked up a reasonable way of talking which gives me goose bumps. "Passing Matric exams has nothing to do with having babies," she explains sweetly. "She has a husband who she loves—and who loves her..."

"She's got to have a husband, stupid! She's married isn't she?" Adi butts in, "and married people have babies! That's all there is to it!"

"You're much too young to understand such things," says Rosy.

"I'll show you who's too young," says Adi, pushing her back and jumping the wall after her and knocking her down and throwing himself upon her. They argue with their limbs and voices, churning dust. How is Rosy to know that just that morning Cousin settled an argument with Adi by shoving him off Skinny-aunt's veranda saying: "You're too small to know anything, stupid. Scram!"

The kitchen door banging shut, Yousaf emerges to investigate the row. He snatches Adi up and Rosy, dragged to her feet by her hair, emits a bloody yell that curdles the milk in Mr. Singh's buffaloes. Yousaf carries Adi kicking and cursing into the kitchen.

For the moment at least Adi has knocked the stuffing out of Rosy's intolerable grown-uppishness. Red-faced, bawling, martyred, wet knicker bottoms caked with mud and arms outstretched, Rosy totters in slow motion towards her veranda.

Putting on a straight face I jump the wall after Rosy. I place a hypocritical arm protectively round her shoulders and console her all the way up the veranda steps to her room.

"What is it, Rosy? What is the matter, dear?" warbles Mrs. Singh in her cool-water-in-a-jug American voice from somewhere in the house.

Rosy bawls something indecipherable and Mrs. Singh, apparently satisfied, asks no more questions.

The three miniature glass jars wink at me!

Leaving Rosy to cope with her hurt feelings and bruised flesh, I crouch before them. One by one I lift the fragile jars and remove their tiny crystal stoppers. They gleam, reflecting rainbow hues— insinuating questions... What is eternity? Why are the stars? Where do cats lay their eggs? And why don't hospitals have flushing bedpans built into the beds?

Rosy never even looks at the jars unless I am there. If they were to fall this minute and smash to smithereens she would be sad—the destruction of beauty is depressing—but she wouldn't miss them among all her little pots and pans and cups and saucers. Would it be stealing then? Taking away something Rosy doesn't want anyway?

I cannot bring myself to ask her to give them to me. She might refuse. It's an unthinkable risk. I know when you want something very much it gives people power over you. I will not give

Rosy that power to withhold—or to grant. Too many people have it as it is.

Silently Rosy gets up and leaving a damp indentation of her dusty bottom on the bedspread goes out of the room.

My hands feel weak. I cannot stir out of my crouched position. I force my mind to be rational. Hundreds of thousands of people steal. . .

Suddenly my brain clicks. My eyes locate the fireplace. My hands spring to life, deft and obedient, and I bury the jars in a bed of ashes. It is almost summer. No one will kindle a fire for months. I can leave the jars there till Rosy forgets they ever existed.

Rosy returns bearing a saucer and my heart sinks. On the saucer are small mounds of sugar, rice and red pepper. It is an offering. A maneuver to shore up my shaky allegiance; and a silent testimony of her worth. She knows I love filling the jars, like their enormous counterparts in the kitchen, with sugar and rice.

There is no help for it. While Rosy fills the toy teapot with water from the bathroom I pry out the jars from the ashes and fill them with rice and sugar.

I could weep. Any time I maneuver a set of circumstances to suit me this happens. Fate intervenes. There is no other word for it. Fated! Doomed! No wonder I have such a scary-puss of a conscience.

Ayah has acquired two new admirers: a Chinaman and the Pathan.

Mother wonders why we are suddenly swamped with such a persistent display of embroidered bosky-silk and linen tea cozies, tray-cloths, trolley sets, tablecloths, counterpanes, pillowcases and bedsheets.

Twice a week the Chinaman cycles up our drive, rattling and bumping over the stones, a huge khaki bundle strapped to the carrier.

Our drive is made of packed earth. Every year, worn by traffic and eroded by monsoons, the drive lays bare patches of brick rubble.

The Chinaman is dapper, thin, brusque and rude. He parks his bicycle in the porch, removes the cycle-clips from his khaki trousers and heaves his bundle to the veranda. "Comeon, comeon, Chinaman come!" he shouts, squatting before his bundle and sorting out his wares for display. "Comeon Memsahib, comeon Ayah. Comeon, comeon, Chinaman come!"

Mother yells from inside: "Tell him to get out! What is this nonsense? Coming every day! Ayah? Yousaf? Is anyone there?"

Ayah comes to the veranda. "Go, go!" she says in tart English. (Besides Cantonese, the Chinaman speaks only a smattering of English.) "Memsahib no want. Go, Go!"

But the Chinaman has sprung his trap with cunning. Ayah's attention is snared by the shimmering colors. Her eyes wander to the silks.

"Comeon, comeon," he coaxes, getting up. He reaches for Ayah's arm and pulls her to his silks. "See?" he says, stroking his free hand over the bosky and then over her arm. "It silky like your skin. See? See?" he says burying her hand in the soft heap.

Ayah knows well how to handle his bold tilted eyes and his alien rudeness. "Oh-ho," she says, all singsongy. "I have no munneeey—how I buy?"

"You sit," coaxes the Chinaman, pulling Ayah to squat beside him and, retaining his hold, engages her in a staccato and desultory conversation. When Ayah's restiveness becomes uncontrollable he introduces a bribe: "Now, what I can give you?" he muses. "Let me see . . . Sit, sit," he says and Ayah's restiveness succumbs to the dual restraints of hand and promises.

Although Ayah has been allotted quarters, she dwells and sleeps in our house. Soon the tabletops, mantelpieces, sideboards and shelves in our rooms blossom with embroidered, bosky-silk doilies.

The attentions of Ayah's Pathan admirer also benefit our household. All our kitchen knives, table knives, Mother's scissors and paper-knife and Hari's garden shears and Adi's blunt penknife suddenly develop glittering razor edges. And it is not only our household the Pathan services. Gita Shankar's, Rosy-Peter's, Electric-aunt's and Godmother's houses also flash with sharp and efficient cutting implements. Even the worn, stubby knives in the servants' quarters acquire redoubtable edges, for the Pathan is a knife-sharpener.

I have often noticed him in the bazaar, plying his trade before streetside shops. He pushes a pedal on his machine and a large and slender wheel turns dizzily round and round. With great dexterity and judgment he brings the knife blades to the wheel, and in the ensuing conflagration of sparks and swift steel-screeches, the knives are honed to jewel edges. He wraps the loose end of his floppy turban about his mouth like a thug—to filter out the fine steel and whetstone dust.

It is only when I see him in a sidewalk brawl with the restaurant-wrestler, looking bewildered and furious, his face no longer covered like a thug's, that I recognize the face and connect it to the pink and tingly bottom we cycled past on our way to Imam Din's village.

The Pathan's name is Sharbat Khan. He too cycles up our long drive, steel clattering and wheels wobbling over the rubble that sticks out of the mud. The cycle looks like a toy beneath the man from the mountains and involuntarily Adi and I grow tense, expecting the pistol-shot-like report of a punctured tire. It is late in the afternoon and we stand on the veranda, hypnotized by his approach.

Sharbat Khan wears drawstring pantaloons so baggy they put to shame Masseur's shalwar—and over them a flared tunic that flaunts ten yards of coarse white homespun. He cycles past our bedroom and Gita Shankar's rooms to the back of the house. Adi and I scoot after him.

Sharbat Khan parks his cycle against a tree and squatting by it waits for Ayah.

Ayah comes.

Ayah is nervous in his presence, given to sudden movement; her goddess-like calm replaced by breath-stopping shyness. They don't touch. He leans across his bicycle, talking, and she shifts from foot to foot, smiling, ducking and twisting spherically. She has taken to sticking a flower in her hair, plucked from our garden. They don't need to touch. His presence radiates a warmth that is different from the dark heat generated by Masseur's fingers—the lightning strikes of Ice-candy-man's toes.

Sharbat Khan tells her of his cousin who has a dry fruit and *naswar* (mixture of tobacco and opium) lean-to in Gowalmandi. It is a contact point for the many Pathans from his tribe around the Khyber working in Lahore. He gives Ayah news of the meat, vegetable, tea and kebab stall owners and of their families, whose knives he sharpens. He is doing well. And not only at sharpening knives.

Sharbat Khan cautions Ayah: "These are bad times—Allah knows what's in store. There is big trouble in Calcutta and Delhi: Hindu-Muslim trouble. The Congresswallahs are after Jinnah's blood . . ."

"What's it to us if Jinnah, Nehru and Patel fight? They are not fighting our fight," says Ayah, lightly.

"That may be true," says Sharbat Khan thoughtfully, "but they are stirring up trouble for us all."

Sharbat Khan shifts forward, his aspect that of a man about to confess a secret. Ayah leans closer to him and I slide into her lap.

He glances at me dubiously, but at a reassuring nod from Ayah, says, "Funny things are happening inside the old city . . . Stabbings . . . Either the police can't do anything—or they don't want to. A body was stuffed into a manhole in my locality . . . It was discovered this morning because of the smell: a young, good-looking man. Several bodies have been found in the gutters and gullies of the Kashmiri, Lahori and Bhatti Gates and Shalmi . . . They must have been dumped there from different neighborhoods because no one knows who they are."

"Are they Hindus?" asks Ayah, her carefree mood dispelled.

"Hindu, Muslim and Sikh. One can tell they are from prosperous, eating-drinking households . . ."

"There have also been one or two fires . . . I don't like it . . ."

We fall into a pensive silence.

Ayah sighs, *"Arrey Bhagwan."* She pushes me off her lap and unties a knot in her sari that serves as her wallet. She holds out a small bundle of tightly folded notes. "Look," she says, shaking her head to dispel the somber mood. "I've saved my whole salary this month... forty rupees!"

Sharbat Khan takes the money from her and, removing his turban, tucks it inside its rancid-smelling interior. His hair, matted to his head, is brown and falls from a center parting to his ears.

Sharbat Khan loans money as a side business like most Pathans. He carries out transactions on Ayah's behalf and gives her the profits. Often he wears a gun. There are few defaulters.

I listen as Sharbat Khan talks to Ayah of the crops and sparse orchards in his mountain village. Now it is the apple season and the season for apricots. It is also time to cash the rice crop, the maize crop, and hoe the potatoes... He is going to his tribal village for a month or so to help his folk wrest the harvest from the gritty, unyielding soil of his land. There are leopards in the granite ravines and stony summits surrounding his village. He has encountered them on mountain trails, their eyes gleaming emerald by night, their spots camouflaged by the filtered sunlight dappling the underbrush by day.

"Hai Ram!" exclaims Ayah, her lips trembling with concern. "Don't they attack?"

"Only if they're shown disrespect," says Sharbat Khan. "We mountain folk know what to do. We touch our foreheads and courteously say *"Salaam-alekum mamajee* [uncle]" and they let us alone."

"I'd never have the nerve to say that!" says Ayah. "I'd faint right away!"

"Then he'd think you very rude and eat you up!"

"Arrey baba, I'd never go to your village," says Ayah firmly.

Sharbat Khan grins, his eyes shining with love. "Then I must bring the mountains to you! What would you like?" he asks Ayah. "Almonds? Pistachios? Walnuts? Dried apricots?" Sharbat Khan wears silver rings on his fingers roughly embedded with turquoise and uncut rubies. "Ah, the taste of those nuts!" he sighs, raising his fingers to his lips and smacking them, and sliding his warm tiger-eyes in a way that leaves Ayah so short of breath that she can barely say, "Bring me pistachios."

Sharbat Khan leans forward. "What?" he asks, aware of his effect on her. "I didn't hear you."

Ayah shuffles her bare feet and fidgets with her sari. Her eyes are shy, full of messages. "Bring me pistachios," she says again. "And almonds: they are good for the brain."

"And what are pistachios good for?" asks Sharbat Khan knowingly, and Ayah lowers her head and fiddles with the scarlet rose anchored to the tight knot in her hair and says, "How should I know?" And Sharbat Khan sighs again, and his eyes turn so radiant they shine like amber between his bushy lashes.

Something happens within me. Though outwardly I remain as thin as ever, I can feel my stomach muscles retract to create a warm hollow. "Take me for a ride—take me for a ride," I beg and Sharbat Khan, tearing away his eyes from Ayah, places me on the cycle shaft. He gives me a turn round the backyard, grazing past the buffalo, the servants' quarters and the Shankars' veranda. He smells of tobacco, burnt whetstone and sweat. He brings me back and offers Ayah a ride.

"Sit in front: it's safer," he says.

"*Aiiii-yo!*" she says in a long-drawn way, as if he has made an improper suggestion, and turning her face away covers her head with her sari.

Sharbat Khan coaxes her again, and with a great show of alarm Ayah wiggles on to the shaft in front and Sharbat Khan takes her off on a circuit of the backyard. He pretends to lose his balance: and as the front wheel swings wildly, "*Hai*, I'll die!" cries Ayah. The inhabitants of the servants' quarters pop out to watch the *tamasha* and applaud. Adi laughs and claps. Laughing, Sharbat Khan releases Ayah back under the trees.

He gives Adi a ride, and depositing him outside the kitchen, cycles down the drive like a mountain receding.

✿

I hear the metallic peal of Father's cycle bell and rush out to welcome him. Mother rushes out of another door. It is almost three in the afternoon: Father is late for lunch. Together we slobber all over him as Father, with a phony frown and a tight little twist of a smile beneath his moustache, places the cycle on its stand and removes the ledgers clamped to the carrier.

Mother removes his solar topi and slips off the handkerchief tied round his forehead to keep the sweat from his eyes. She brushes his wet curls back. As I reach up to kiss him Father bends and puts his arm round me. Mother relieves him of the ledgers and taking hold of his other arm winds it about herself, making little moaning sounds as if his touch fills her with exquisite relief. With me clinging to his waist and Mother hanging on to his arm, Father labors up the veranda steps.

Making affectionate sounds we accompany Father to the bathroom. He washes his hands and empties his bladder and we accompany him to the dining table.

Mother and I sit with him. Mother talks while he chomps wordlessly on his food and looks at her out of the assessing and disconcerting eyes of a theater critic. Mother chatters about friends and supplies political tidbits filtered through their consciousnesses: Colonel Bharucha says that Jinnah said... And Nehru said that... And oh, how I laughed when Mehrabai (that's the mirthsome Mrs. Bankwalla) said this about Patel... and that about...

Unflagging, she gives a résumé of the anxious letters from sisters and sisters-in-law in Bombay and Karachi, who have heard all sorts of rumors about the situation in the Punjab and are exhorting us to come to them.

A little later, mention of Adi's hostile antics causes Father to scowl. Leaning forward to shovel a forkful of curried rice into his mouth he crumples his forehead up, and out of sharp and judgmental eyes gazes acutely at Mother.

Switching the bulletin immediately, Mother recounts some observations of mine as if I've spent the entire morning mouthing extraordinarily brilliant, saccharinely sweet and fetchingly naive remarks. "Jana, you know what Lenny told me this morning? She said: 'Poor Daddy works so hard for us. When I grow up, I will work in the office and he can read his newspaper all day!' "

Peals of laughter from Mother. A smile from Father.

And when Mother pauses, on cue, I repeat any remarks I'm supposed to have made: and ham up the performance with further innocently insightful observations.

Father rewards me with solemn nods, champing smiles, and monosyllables.

And as the years advance, my sense of inadequacy and unworth advances. I have to think faster—on my toes as it were... offering lengthier and lengthier chatter to fill up the infernal time of Father's mute meals.

Is that when I learn to tell tales?

Chapter 10

Instead of school I go to Mrs. Pen's. Her house is next to God-mother's on Jail Road—opposite Electric-aunt's—and I walk there with Ayah or with Hari. Channi, her slight but stately sweeper, takes out a small table and two chairs and we sit in the garden under bare February trees and lukewarm sunshine. Mr. Pen lounges on the veranda in an easy chair.

A parrot might relish reciting tables. I do not.

> "Two twos are four
> Two threes are six
> Two fours are eight
> Etc., etc."

By the time I reach the five-times table I am resting my head on my arms stretched flat out on the table, peering sideways at Mrs. Pen. My jaws ache—my mind wanders—I hear Mr. Pen snore...

He is much darker than Mrs. Pen. He is Anglo-Indian.

Mrs. Pen is fair, soft, plump, English.

I have a trick. My voice drones on, my mind clicks off. I take time out to educate myself. I watch the trees shed their leaves and sprout new buds...and the predatory kites swoop on pigeons. And the crows, in ungainly clusters, attack the kites...

And I sniff a whiff off Mrs. Pen as it drifts up from under the table, its moldy reality percolating the dusting of cheap talcum powder.

Despite her efforts to clutter my brain with the trivia and trappings of scholarship, I slip in a good bit of learning. The whiff off Mrs. Pen enlightens me. It teaches me the biology of spent cells and aging bodies—and insinuates history into my subconscious...

of things past and of the British Raj . . . of human frailties and vulnerabilities—of spent passion and lingering yearnings. Whereas a whiff off Ayah carries the dark purity of creation, Mrs. Pen smells of memories.

Mrs. Pen reads aloud prosaic English history.

I turn my head the other way. I observe Mr. Pen's fingers. They are long, fat and large. His legs are huge tubes encased in flannels and beneath them, visible through a hole in his socks, plops his mordant toe. I feel sorry for Mrs. Pen. I can't imagine his fingers working the subtle artistry of Masseur's fingers—or his sluggish toe conveying the dashing impulses of Ice-candy-man's toes.

After Mrs. Pen's I go to Godmother's.

Godmother rents rooms in the back of a bungalow. She has a large room, and a small room with a kerosene stove and a dangerous Primus stove. The small room serves as kitchen/pantry. And off it, a bathroom with three commodes.

I go straight to the kitchen. Slavesister, short and squat, is slaving over the kerosene stove. I follow her as she walks on painful bunions to the water trough at the back of the compound and watch her scour the heavy pans and brass utensils with ash and mud. I help her carry them back .

Every now and then Slavesister serves Godmother strong half-cups of steaming tea which Godmother pours into her saucer and slurps. I too take an occasional and guilty sip. Drinking tea, I am told, makes one darker. I'm dark enough. Everyone says, "It's a pity Adi's fair and Lenny so dark. He's a boy. Anyone will marry him."

Yesterday I carried a gleaming image of the jars in my mind. Something darker lurks in their stead today—fear and guilt.

The three jars are in my possession.

I glance about the room. There is not a single hiding place when I want one. When I don't need them they abound, secreting away things.

I tuck the jars in an old pair of felt slippers beneath a tangle of neglected toys in the bottom drawer of our dresser.

Adi breezes in and makes a beeline for the dresser. He opens and closes drawers, running among the wrecked cars, trains, nursery books, gutless badminton rackets, and celluloid dolls. He grabs the deflated football he's looking for and I let my breath go. I need a safer hiding place.

Next morning I transport the jars to Mrs. Pen's, wrapped in toilet paper and tucked in my schoolbag. After my tuition I transport them to Godmother's. She is propped up on three white pillows that are cement-hard and as heavy. I recline beside her on her cot, propped almost upright.

My eyes wander all over the room. Another string-cot, smaller and sagging, lies in front of the almirah with the three doors. Squeezed between two cupboards, fitting one into the other, are three more cots. Oldhusband sits hunched and still on a bentwood chair before a heavy mahogany desk. Chairs with cane seats, tin trunks and leather suitcases are stacked against the walls. My eyes, like happy roaches, crawl into the abundance of crevices and crannies.

Slavesister goes into the kitchen. When she calls Godmother to light the Primus I quickly slip the jars between two stacks of trunks covered by dhurries.

I hear Godmother pump the spirit stove: koochuck, koochuck, koochuck, koochuck. I see her, white-saried, bent forward in concentration, vulnerable and heroic.

The technology involved in starting the Primus is too complex for Slavesister to handle. Godmother exposes herself to grave risk every time she starts the stove. Like Russian roulette, any one of the pumps might trigger the Primus to blow up in her face.

There is a fierce hissing. It is now safe to peek in. The ring of flame from the Primus is like a fierce blue storm.

I lie back on Godmother's pillows, absent-mindedly listening to her scold Slavesister. When she approaches I make room for her. She settles in the hollow of the bed and I wind myself about her like a rope.

She calls to Slavesister. Her voice is still stern from the scolding: "I want that Japanese kimono Mehrabai brought me two years back. That red one. I want to give it to Bachamai's Rutti. Do you remember where it is?"

No answer.

She raps her punkah on the wall to attract her sister's attention, and raising her voice to accommodate the hissing stove, repeats the text, adding: "Do you hear me?"

Still no answer.

"Oh? We are sulking, are we?"

No comment.

"We are getting all hoity-toity today?"

Godmother blinks exaggeratedly, and makes a haughty, naughty face and holds her long pointed fingers in such a supercilious and dainty manner that I burst into giggles. Godmother shakes with suppressed chuckles.

Catching her breath and sobering up, she says: "Will you look for the kimono—or do I have to get up?"

The bed creaks as Godmother slowly heaves herself up and lowers her feet, and Slavesister comes in flapping her slippers noisily and saying, "I'm coming, I'm coming. . . Really, Rodabai, you have no patience, have you? I can't cook and look for the kimono at the same time too, can I?"

Godmother caricatures her expression and pantomimes her martyred movements behind her rotund back.

"I know what you're doing. Go ahead: do it in front of the child! As it is she doesn't respect me. I have asked you so often not to. You never consider how you humiliate me, do you?"

Godmother continues her performance, pantomiming Slavesister's gestures, opening and shutting her mouth in a dumb charade.

Godmother nudges me. Slavesister has commenced mumbling.

Godmother sets up an imitative hum. As Slavesister peers into boxes and suitcases looking for the kimono, she mumbles louder and Godmother says, "Some people don't like being scolded. If they don't like being scolded they shouldn't hover around Primus stoves when I'm pumping them!"

"Mumble—grumble." A lifting and shutting of trunk lids. A puzzled expression on Slavesister's face, a wad of toilet paper in her hands. "What's this?"

"Careful! It's glass! It's mine," I say, scampering off the cot.

Balancing her bifocals on the tip of her rubbery and shapeless nose, Slavesister examines the tiny jars admiringly. "Where did you get them?"

"Rosy gave them to me."

Perhaps I hesitate a fraction too long. Or my body signals contrarily. The moment the sentence is out I can tell Godmother knows I have stolen the jars. I leap back to my original roost, not able to meet her eyes, and hide my face in her sari.

"You have stolen the jars, haven't you?" she asks.

"No," I say, shaking my head vehemently against her khaddar blouse.

"Don't lie. It doesn't suit you."

There it is again! Lying doesn't become me. I can't get away with the littlest thing.

"Why not?" I howl. "Why doesn't it suit me? No one says that to Adi, Ayah, Cousin, Imam Din, Mother, Father or Rosy-Peter!"

"Some people can lie and some people can't. Your voice and face give you away," says Godmother.

"But I can't even curse," I howl, sitting up.

Adi can swear himself red in the face and look lovable—Rosy can curse steadily for five minutes, going all the way from "*Ullu-kay-pathay*" to "asshole," from Punjabi swear words to American, and still look cute. It's okay if Cousin swears—but if I curse or lie I am told it does not suit the shape of my mouth. Or my personality. Or something!

"Everybody in the world lies, steals and curses except me!" I shout, choked with self-pity. "Why can't I act like everybody?"

"Some people can get away with it and some can't," says

Godmother. "I'm afraid a life of crime is not for you. Not because you aren't sharp, but because you are not suited to it."

A life sentence? Condemned to honesty? A demon in saint's clothing?

I was set firmly and relentlessly on the path to truth the day I broke a Wedgwood plate and, putting a brazen face on my mischief, nobly confessed all before Mother. I was three years old. Mother bent over me, showering me with the radiance of her approval. "I love you. You spoke the truth! What's a broken plate? Break a hundred plates!"

I broke plates, cups, bowls, dishes. I smashed livers, kidneys, hearts, eyes... The path to virtue is strewn with broken people and shattered china.

Gandhijee visits Lahore. I'm surprised he exists. I almost thought he was a mythic figure. Someone we'd only hear about and never see. Mother takes my hand. We walk past the Birdwood Barracks' sepoy to the Queens Road end of Warris Road, and enter the gates of the last house.

We walk deep into a winding, eucalyptus-shaded drive: so far in do we go that I fear we may land up in some private recess of the zoo and come face to face with the lion. I drag back on Mother's arm, vocalizing my fear, and at last Mother hauls me up some steps and into Gandhijee's presence. He is knitting. Sitting cross-legged on the marble floor of a palatial veranda, he is surrounded by women. He is small, dark, shriveled, old. He looks just like Hari, our gardener, except he has a disgruntled, disgusted and irritable look, and no one'd dare pull off his dhoti! He wears only the loincloth and his black and thin torso is naked.

Gandhijee certainly is ahead of his times. He already knows the advantages of dieting. He has starved his way into the news and made headlines all over the world.

Mother and I sit in a circle with Gita and the women from Daulatram's house. A pink-satin bow dangling from the tip of her stout braid, Gita looks ethereal and content—as if washed of all desire. I notice the same look on the faces of the other women. Whatever his physical shortcomings, Gandhijee must have some concealed attractions to inspire such purified expressions.

Lean young women flank Gandhijee. They look different from Lahori women and are obviously a part of his entourage. The pleasantly plump Punjabi women, in shalwar-kamizes and saris, shuffle from spot to spot. Barely standing up, they hold their veils so that the edges don't slip off their heads as they go to and from Gandhijee. The women are subdued, receptive; as when one sits with mourners.

Someone takes Mother's hand, and hand in hand we go to Gandhijee. Butter wouldn't melt in our mouths. Gandhijee politely puts aside his knitting and increases his disgruntled scowl; and with an irrelevance I find alarming, says softly, "Sluggish stomachs are the scourge of the Punjabis. . . too much rich food and too little exercise. The cause of India's ailments lies in our clogged alimentary canals. The hungry stomach is the scourge of the poor and the full stomach of the rich."

Beneath her blue-tinted and rimless glasses Mother's eyes are downcast, her head bowed, her bobbed hair—and what I assume is her consternation—concealed beneath her sari. But when Gandhijee pauses, she gives him a sidelong look of rapt and reverent interest. And two minutes later, not the least bit alarmed, she earnestly furnishes him with the odor, consistency, time and frequency of her bowel movements. When she is finished she bows her head again, and Gandhijee passes his hand over her head: and then, absently, as if it were a tiresome afterthought, over mine.

"Flush your system with an enema, daughter," says Gandhijee, directing his sage counsel at my mother. "Use plain, lukewarm water. Do it for thirty days. . . every morning. You will feel like a new woman.

"Look at these girls," says Gandhijee, indicating the lean

women flanking him. "I give them enemas myself—there is no shame in it—I am like their mother. You can see how smooth and moist their skin is. Look at their shining eyes!"

The enema-emaciated women have faint shadows beneath their limpid eyes and, moist-skinned or not, they are much too pale, their brown skins tinged by a clayish pallor.

Gandhijee reaches out and suddenly seizes my arm in a startling vise. "What a sickly-looking child," he announces, avoiding my eye. "Flush her stomach! Her skin will bloom like roses."

Considering he has not looked my way even once, I am enraged by his observation. "An enema a day keeps the doctor away," he crows feebly, chortling in an elderly and ghoulish way, his slight body twitching with glee, his eyes riveted upon my mother.

I consider all this talk about enemas and clogged intestines in shocking taste, and I take a dim and bitter view of his concern for my health and welfare. Turning up my nose and looking down severely at this improbable toss-up between a clown and a demon, I am puzzled why he's so famous—and suddenly his eyes turn to me. My brain, heart and stomach melt. The pure shaft of humor, compassion, tolerance and understanding he directs at me fuses me to everything that is feminine, funny, gentle, loving. He is a man who loves women. And lame children. And the untouchable sweeper—so he will love the untouchable sweeper's constipated girl-child best. I know just where to look for such a child. He touches my face, and in a burst of shyness I lower my eyes. This is the first time I have lowered my eyes before man.

It wasn't until some years later—when I realized the full scope and dimension of the massacres—that I comprehended the concealed nature of the ice lurking deep beneath the hypnotic and dynamic femininity of Gandhi's non-violent exterior.

And then, when I raised my head again, the men lowered their eyes.

Chapter 11

The April days are lengthening, beginning to get warm. The Queen's Park is packed. Groups of men and women sit in circles on the grass and children run about them. Ice-candy-man, lean as his popsicles and as affable, swarming with children, is going from group to group doing good business.

Masseur, too, is going from group to group; handsome, reserved, competent, assured, massaging balding heads, kneading knotty shoulders and soothing aching limbs.

I lie on the grass, my head on Ayah's lap, basking in—and intercepting—the warm flood of stares directed at Ayah by her circle of admirers. The Faletti's Hotel cook, the Government House gardener, a sleek and arrogant butcher and the zoo attendant, Sher Singh, sit with us.

"She is scared of your lion," drawls Ayah, playfully tapping my forehead. "She thinks he's let loose at night and he will gobble her up from her bed."

Sher Singh, wearing an outsize blue turban and a callow beard, sits up. Delighted to be singled out by Ayah, he looks at me earnestly: "Don't worry. I'll hang on to his leash," he boasts, stammering slightly. "He won't dare eat you!"

I'm not the least bit reassured. On the contrary, I am terrified. This callow youth with a stem-like neck hold the zoo lion?

"What kind of leash?" I ask.

"A-an iron ch-chain!"

It's much worse than I'd imagined. A lion roaring behind bars is bad enough. But a lion straining on a stout leash held by this thin, stuttering Sikh is unthinkable. I burst into tears.

"Now look what you've done," says Ayah in her usual good-natured manner. Gathering me in her arms and hugging me she rocks back and forth. "Don't be silly," she tells me. "The lion is never let out of his cage. The cage is so strong a hundred lions couldn't break it."

"And," says Ramzana the butcher, "I give him a juicy goat every day. Why should he want to eat a dried-up stick like you?"

The logic is irrefutable during daylight hours as I sit among friends beneath Queen Victoria's lion-intimidating presence. But alone, at night, the logic will vanish.

Masseur and Ice-candy-man drift over to us and join the circle. Masseur is raking in money. He has invented an oil that will grow hair on bald heads. It is composed of monkey and fish glands, mustard oil, pearl dust and an assortment of herbs. The men listen intently, but Masseur stops short of revealing the secret recipe. He holds up the bottle and Ayah reaches out to touch the oil.

"Careful," says Masseur, whipping the bottle away. "It'll grow hair on your fingertips."

"*Hai Ram!*" says Ayah, quickly retracting her fingers, and rolling her eyes from one face to the next with fetching consternation.

We all laugh.

Not to be outdone, Ice-candy-man says he has developed a first-class fertility pill. He knows it will work but he has yet to try it out.

"I'll give it a try," offers the Government House gardener.

"Your wife's already produced children, hasn't she?"

"Tch! Not for her, *yaar*. For myself. I feel old sometimes," confesses the graying gardener.

"It is not an aphrodisiac. It's a fertility pill for women," explains Ice-candy-man. "It's so potent it can impregnate men!"

There is a startled silence.

"You're a joker, *yaar*," says the butcher.

"No, honestly," says Ice-candy-man, neglectful of the cigarette butt that is uncoiling wisps of smoke from his fist. He too will rake in money.

Masseur clears his throat and, breaking the spell cast by the fertility pill, enquires of the gardener: "What's the latest from the English *Sarkar's* house?"

The gardener, congenial and hoary, is our prime source of information from the British Empire's local headquarters.

"It is rumored," he says obligingly, rubbing the patches of black and white stubble on his chin, "that Lat Sahib Wavell did not resign his viceroyship."

He pauses, dramatically, as if he's already revealed too much to friends. And then, as if deciding to consecrate discretion to our friendship, he serves up the choice tidbit.

"He was sacked!"

"Oh! Why?" asks Ice-candy-man. We are all excited by a revelation that invites us to share the inside track of the Raj's doings.

"Gandhi, Nehru, Patel... they have much influence even in London," says the gardener mysteriously, as if acknowledging the arbitrary and mischievous nature of antic gods. "They didn't like the Muslim League's victory in the Punjab elections."

"The bastards!" says Masseur with histrionic fury that conceals a genuine bitterness. "So they sack Wavell Sahib, a fair man! And send for a new Lat Sahib who will favor the Hindus!"

"With all due respect, malijee," says Ice-candy-man, surveying the gardener through a blue mist of exhaled smoke, "but aren't you Hindus expert at just this kind of thing? Twisting tails behind the scene... and getting someone else to slaughter your goats?"

"What's the new Lat Sahib like? This Mountbatten Sahib?" asks Ayah.

She, like Mother, is an oil pourer. "I saw his photo. He is handsome! But I don't like his wife, *baba*. She looks a *choorail!*"

"Ah, but Jawaharlal Nehru likes her. He likes her *vaaary much!*" says Ice-candy-man, luridly dragging out the last two words of English.

"Nehru and the Mountbattens are like this!" the gardener concurs, holding up two entwined fingers. His expression, an attractive blend of sheepishness and vanity, reinforces the image of a seasoned inside tracker.

"If Nehru and Mountbatten are like this," says Masseur, "then who's going to hold our Jinnah Sahib's hand? Master Tara Singh?"

Masseur says this in a way that makes us smile.

"Ah-ha!" says Ice-candy-man as if suddenly enlightened. "So that's who!" He slaps his thigh and beams at us as if Masseur has proposed a brilliant solution. "That's who!" he repeats.

The butcher snorts and aims a contemptuous gob of spit some yards away from us. He has been quiet all this while and as we turn our faces to him he gathers his stylish cotton shawl over one shoulder and says: "That non-violent violence-monger—your precious Gandhijee—first declares the Sikhs *fanatics!* Now suddenly he says: 'Oh dear, the poor Sikhs cannot live with the Muslims if there is a Pakistan!' What does he think we are—some kind of beast? Aren't they living with us now?"

"He's a politician, *yaar,*" says Masseur soothingly. "It's his business to suit his tongue to the moment."

"If it was only his tongue I wouldn't mind," says the butcher. "But the Sikhs are already supporting some trumped-up Muslim party the Congress favors." He has a deadpan way of speaking which is very effective.

The Government House gardener, his expression wary and sympathetic, gives a loud sigh, and says: "It is the English's mischief. . . They are past masters at intrigue. It suits them to have us all fight."

"Just the English?" asks Butcher. "Haven't the Hindus connived with the *Angrez* to ignore the Muslim League, and support a party that didn't win a single seat in the Punjab? It's just the kind of thing we fear. They manipulate one or two Muslims against the interests of the larger community. And now they have manipulated Master Tara Singh and his bleating herd of Sikhs!" He glances at Sher Singh, his handsome, smooth-shaven face almost expressionless.

Sher Singh shifts uncomfortably and, looking as completely innocent of Master Tara Singh's doings as he can, frowns at the grass.

"*Arrey,* you foolish Sikh! You fell right into the Hindus' trap!" says Ice-candy-man so facetiously that Sher Singh loses part of his nervousness and smiles back.

The afternoon is drawing to a close. The grass feels damp. Ayah stands up, smoothing the pleats in her limp cotton sari. "If all you talk of is nothing but this Hindu-Muslim business, I'll stop coming to the park," she says pertly.

"It's just a discussion among friends," says Ice-candy-man, uncoiling his frame from the grass to sit up. "Such talk helps clear the air . . . but for your sake, we won't bring it up again."

The rest of us look at him gratefully.

There is much disturbing talk. India is going to be broken. Can one break a country? And what happens if they break it where our house is? Or crack it further up on Warris Road? How will I ever get to Godmother's then?

I ask Cousin.

"Rubbish," he says, "no one's going to break India. It's not made of glass!"

I ask Ayah.

"They'll dig a canal . . . ," she ventures. "This side for Hindustan and this side for Pakistan. If they want two countries, that's what they'll have to do—crack India with a long, long canal."

Gandhi, Jinnah, Nehru, Iqbal, Tara Singh, Mountbatten are names I hear.

And I become aware of religious differences.

It is sudden. One day everybody is themselves—and the next day they are Hindu, Muslim, Sikh, Christian. People shrink, dwindling into symbols. Ayah is no longer just my all-encompassing Ayah—she is also a token. A Hindu. Carried away by a renewed devotional fervor she expends a small fortune in joss-sticks, flowers and sweets on the gods and goddesses in the temples.

Imam Din and Yousaf, turning into religious zealots, warn Mother they will take Friday afternoons off for the Jumha prayers. On Fridays they set about preparing themselves ostentatiously. Squatting atop the cement wall of the garden tank they hold their feet out beneath the tap and diligently scrub between their toes.

They wash their heads, arms, necks and ears and noisily clear their throats and noses. All in white check prayer scarves thrown over their shoulders, stepping uncomfortably in stiff black Bata shoes worn without socks, they walk out of the gates to the small mosque at the back of Queens Road. Sometimes, at odd hours of the day, they spread their mats on the front lawn and pray when the muezzin calls. Crammed into a narrow religious slot they too are diminished, as are Jinnah and Iqbal, Ice-candy-man and Masseur.

Hari and Moti-the-sweeper and his wife Muccho, and their untouchable daughter Papoo, become ever more untouchable as they are entrenched deeper in their low Hindu caste. While the Sharmas and the Daulatrams, Brahmins like Nehru, are dehumanized by their lofty caste and caste-marks.

The Rogers of Birdwood Barracks, Queen Victoria and King George are English Christians: they look down their noses upon the Pens who are Anglo-Indian, who look down theirs on the Phailbuses who are Indian-Christian, who look down upon all non-Christians.

Godmother, Slavesister, Electric-aunt and my nuclear family are reduced to irrelevant nomenclatures—we are Parsee.

What is God?

All morning we hear Muccho screeching at Papoo. "I turn my back; the bitch slacks off! I say something; she becomes a deaf-mute. I'll thrash the wickedness out of you!"

"I don't know what jinn's gotten into that woman," says Ayah. "She can't leave the girl alone!"

I have made several trips to the back, hanging around the quarters on some pretext or other, and with my presence protecting Papoo.

Papoo hardly ever plays with me now. She is forever slapping the dough into chapatties, or washing, or collecting dung from the road and plastering it on the walls of their quarters. The dried dung cakes provide fuel.

In the evening she sweeps our compound with a stiff reed *jharoo*, spending an hour in a little cloud of dust, an infant stuck to her hip like a growth.

Though she looks more ragged—and thin—her face and hands splotched with pale dry patches and her lips cracked, she is as cheeky as ever with her mother. And forever smiling her handsome roguish smile at us.

Late that evening Ayah tells me that Muccho is arranging Papoo's marriage.

I am seven now, so Papoo must be eleven.

My perception of people has changed.

I still see through to their hearts and minds, but their exteriors superimpose a new set of distracting impressions.

The tuft of *bodhi*-hair rising like a tail from Hari's shaven head suddenly appears fiendish and ludicrous.

"Why do you shave your head like that?" I say disparagingly.

"Because we've always done so, Lenny baby, from the time of my grandfather's grandfathers . . . it's the way of our caste."

I'm not satisfied with his answer.

When Cousin visits that evening I tell him what I think. "Just because his grandfathers shaved their heads and grew stupid tails is no reason why Hari should."

"Not as stupid as you think," says Cousin. "It keeps his head cool and his brain fresh."

"If that's so," I say, challenging him, "why don't you shave your head? Why don't Mother and Father and Godmother and Electric-aunt and . . ."

Cousin stops my mouth with his hand and as I try to bite his fingers and wiggle free, he shouts into my ears and tells me about the Sikhs.

I stop wiggling. He has informed me that the Sikhs become mentally deficient at noon. My mouth grows slack under his palm.

He carefully removes his hand from my gaping mouth and, resuming his normal speaking voice, further informs me: "All that hair not only drains away their gray matter, it also warms their heads like a tea cozy. And at twelve o'clock, when the heat from the sun is at its craziest, it addles their brains!"

It is some hours before I can close my gaping mouth. Immediately I rush to Imam Din and ask if what Cousin says is true.

"Sure," he says, pushing his hookah away and standing up to rake the ashes.

"Just the other day Mr. Singh milked his cow without a bucket. He didn't even notice the puddle of milk on the ground . . . It was exactly two seconds past twelve!"

Cousin erupts with a fresh crop of Sikh jokes.

And there are Hindu, Muslim, Parsee and Christian jokes.

I can't seem to put my finger on it—but there is a subtle change in the Queen's Garden. Sitting on Ayah's crossed legs, leaning against her chocolate softness, again the unease at the back of my mind surfaces.

I fidget restlessly on Ayah's lap and she asks: "What is it, Lenny? You want to do soo-soo?"

I nod, for want of a better explanation.

"I'll take her," offers Masseur, getting up.

Masseur leads me to the Queen's platform. Squatting beneath the English Queen's steely profile, my bottom bared to the evening throng, I relieve myself of a trickle.

"Oye! What are you gaping at?" Masseur shouts at a little Sikh boy who has paused to watch. His long hair, secured in a topknot, is probably already addling his brain.

Masseur raises his arm threateningly and shouts: "Scram!"

The boy flinches, but returning his eyes to me, stays his ground.

The Sikhs are fearless. They are warriors.

I slide my eyes away and, pretending not to notice him, stand up and raise my knickers. As Masseur straightens the skirt of my short frock I lean back against his legs and shyly ogle the boy.

Masseur gropes for my hand. But I twist and slip away and run to the boy and he, pretending to be a steam engine, "chook-chooking" and glancing my way, leads me romping to his group.

The Sikh women pull me to their laps and ask my name and the name of my religion.

"I'm Parsee," I say.

"*O kee?* What's that?" they ask: scandalized to discover a religion they've never heard of.

That's when I realize what has changed. The Sikhs, only their rowdy little boys running about with hair piled in topknots, are keeping mostly to themselves.

Masseur leans into the group and placing a firm hand on my arm drags me away.

We walk past a Muslim family. With their burka-veiled women they too sit apart. I turn to look back. I envy their children. Dressed in satins and high heels, the little Muslim girls wear make-up.

A group of smooth-skinned Brahmins and their pampered male offspring form a tight circle of supercilious exclusivity near ours.

Only the group around Ayah remains unchanged. Hindu, Muslim, Sikh, Parsee are, as always, unified around her.

I dive into Ayah's lap.

As soon as I am settled, and Ayah's absorption is back with the group, the butcher continues the interrupted conversation:

"You Hindus eat so much beans and cauliflower I'm not surprised your yogis levitate. They probably fart their way right up to heaven!" He slips his palm beneath his armpit and, flapping his other arm like a chicken wing, generates a succession of fart-like sounds.

I think he's so funny I laugh until my tummy hurts. But Ayah is not laughing. "Stop it," she says to me in a harsh somber whisper.

Sher Singh, who had found the rude sounds as amusing,

checks himself abruptly. I notice his covert glance slide in Masseur's direction and, looking a little foolish, he suddenly tries to frown.

I twist on Ayah's lap to look at Masseur. He is staring impassively at the grinning butcher, and Butcher's face, confronted by his stolid disfavor, turns ugly.

But before he can say anything, there is a distraction. A noisy and lunatic holyman—in striking attire—has just entered the Queen's Garden. Thumping a five-foot iron trident with bells tied near its base, the holyman lopes towards us, shouting: *"Ya Allah!"* A straight, green, sleeveless shift reaches to his hairy calves. His wrists and upper arms are covered with steel and bead bangles. And round his neck and chest is coiled a colossal hunk of copper wiring. Even from that distance we can tell it's the Ice-candy-man! I've heard he's become Allah's telephone!

A bearded man, from the group of Muslims I had noticed earlier, goes to him and deferentially conducts him back to his family. As Ice-candy-man hunkers down, I run to watch him.

A woman in a modern, gray silk burka whispers to the bearded man, and the man says, "Sufi Sahib, my wife wants to know if Allah will grant her a son. We have four daughters."

The four daughters, ranging from two to eight, wear gold high-heeled slippers and prickly brocade shirts over satin trousers. Frightened by Ice-candy-man's ash-smeared face and eccentric manner, they cling to their mother. I notice a protrusion in the lower half of the woman's burka and guess that she is expecting.

His movements assured and elaborate, eyeballs rolled heavenwards, Ice-candy-man becomes mysteriously busy. He unwinds part of the wire from the coil round his neck so that he has an end in each hand. Holding his arms wide, muttering incantations, he brings the two ends slowly together. There is a modest splutter, and a rain of blue sparks. The mad holyman says "Ah!" in a satisfied way, and we know the connection to heaven has been made. The girls, clearly feeling their distrust of him vindicated, lean and wiggle against their mother, kick their feet up, and whimper. Their mother's hand darts out of the burka, and in one smart swipe, she spanks all four. Nervous eyes on Ice-candy-man, the girls stick a finger in their mouths and cower quietly.

Holding the ends of the copper wire in one hand, the holyman stretches the other skywards. Pointing his long index finger, murmuring the mystic numbers "7 8 6," he twirls an invisible dial. He brings the invisible receiver to his ear and waits. There is a pervasive rumble; as of a tiger purring. We grow tense. Then, startling us with the volume of noise, the muscles of his neck and jaws stretched like cords, the crazed holyman shouts in Punjabi: "Allah? Do You hear me, Allah? This poor woman wants a son! She has four daughters. . . one, two, three, four! You call this justice?"

I find his familiarity alarming. He addresses God as "tu," instead of using the more respectful "tusi." I'm sure if I were the Almighty I'd be offended; no matter how mad the holyman! I distance myself from him mentally, and observe him stern-faced and rebuking.

"Haven't You heard her pray?" Ice-candy-man shouts. Covering the invisible mouthpiece with his hand, in an apologetic aside, he says: "He's been busy of late. . . You know; all this Indian independence business." He brings the receiver to his ear again.

Suddenly he springs up. Thumping his noisy trident on the ground, performing a curious jumping dance, he shouts: "Wah Allah! Wah Allah!" so loudly that several people who have been watching the goings-on from afar, hastily get up and scamper over. Sikhs, Hindus, Muslims form a thick circle round us. I notice my little Sikh friend. I can tell from the reverent faces around me that they believe they are in the presence of a holyman crazed by his love of God. And the madder the mystic, the greater his power.

"Wah, Allah!" shouts Ice-candy-man. "There is no limit to your munificence! To you, king and beggar are the same! To you, this son-less woman is queen! Ah! the intoxication of your love! The depth of your compassion! The ocean of your generosity! Ah! the miracles of your cosmos!" he shouts, working himself into a state. And, just as suddenly as he leapt up to dance before, he now drops to the ground in a stony trance. Our ears still ringing from his shouts, we assume his soul is in communion with God.

The woman in the burka, believing that the holyman has interceded successfully on her behalf, bows her body in gratitude and starts weeping. The bearded man fumbles in the gathers of his trousers and places two silver rupees bearing King George's image at the holyman's entranced toes.

Holding the holyman's pious finger, feeling privileged, I return to our group.

"*Aiiay jee, aiiay!* Sit, Sufi Sahib; sit! We are honored!" exclaim the men in half-awed, half-mocking welcome, making room for Ice-candy-man between the Government House gardener and Masseur. Laying his trident aside, lighting a cigarette and assuming his customary, slouching pose on the grass, the holyman becomes Ice-candy-man.

The Government House gardener places his hand affectionately on Ice-candy-man's thigh, and says, "Sufijee, have you heard the latest about the Lucknow Muslims?" In his quiet way, he is getting his own back for Butcher's wisecracks about the levitating vegetarian Hindus.

The overly polite Lucknow Muslims are notorious for endlessly saying: "After you, sir," and "No, sir, after you!" My attention is riveted. The Government House gardener relates his joke.

Two Muslim gentlemen arrive at a public toilet at the same time.

One insists, "After you, sir."

"No, sir, you first! After you!" insists the other.

Until, eventually, one of them resignedly says: "You might as well go first, sir . . . I've been."

Ayah becomes breathless laughing and almost rolls on the grass. Her sari slips off her shoulders and her admirers relish the brown gleam of her convulsed belly beneath her skimpy blouse, and the firm joggle of her rotund bosoms.

A clutch of Hindu children with caste-marks on their foreheads, curious at the burst of laughter, run up timidly and suddenly yell: "Parsee Parsee, crow eaters! Crow eaters! Crow eaters!"

"We don't! We don't! We don't!" I scream.

The gardener, threatening to get up, throws his turban at them and they scamper in squealing disarray.

"Why do they say that?" I ask fiercely.

"Because y'all do 'kaan! kaan!' at the top of your voices like a rowdy flock of crows," says Ayah.

Ice-candy-man tucks his green shift between his legs as if he's wearing a dhoti, and acting like a timid Banya, declaims:

"We were only seventeen; they were a gang of four!
How we ran; how we ran; as we'd never run before!"

It is so apt to the occasion that my anger vanishes.

I have heard this couplet before. A glimpse of four Sikhs, Muslims or Parsees is supposed to send a mob of Banyas scurrying.

Chapter 12

A strange black box makes its appearance in my parents' bathroom.

It is Saturday and Cousin is visiting for the day. Mother, the indefatigably mirthsome Mrs. Bankwalla, Mrs. Singh and Maggie Phailbus, the schoolteacher who also lives on Warris Road, are sitting on the veranda. Having drawn their chairs close to the marble-topped coffee table they talk in hushed voices that fade into silence when we pass. Even Mrs. Bankwalla's explosive conviviality is subdued. I've noticed a lot of hushed talk recently. In bazaars, restaurants and littered alleys men huddle round bicycles or squat against walls in whispering groups.

We are playing kick-the-can in the garden. Cousin, Adi and Peter form one team and Rosy, Ayah, Papoo-with-babe-on-hip and I the other. It's girls versus boys, and having Papoo on our side compensates for Rosy's erratic play.

Abruptly Cousin puts his hand on his fly and, awkwardly shuffling his feet, dashes away. The game is suspended.

When Cousin returns we can tell by his studied nonchalance he has something to tell. We gather about him. After sliding his eyes this way and that, he looks at us out of the wide and innocent eyes he displays whenever he has something to hide. He signals with a sly tilt of his head, and Adi, shoving Ayah from the back, rushes her out of the garden. Ayah good-naturedly disappears into the kitchen.

"I have seen something strange," confides Cousin portentously. "Follow me."

In a furtive group we move past the portico to the side of the house. Cousin pushes open the bathroom door. We get a whiff of Dettol and, as we crowd the steps, I immediately see the black wooden box. It is heavy-looking, about a foot high, long and narrow. Like a coffin for a very thin man. Rosy, turning pale, whispers, "Someone is dead."

We are agreed it is a coffin. It looks sinister enough. But the species of the corpse baffles us. Adi and Peter squat to examine the stays.

"It's locked," says Cousin, who has already examined the locks. Without a word he attempts to lift the box. I give a hand. Rosy shies away. The box is heavy, and in the constricted space we are only able to lift it a foot or so. We try to shake it and tilt it. There is a very slight, heavy and dull movement.

"Definitely a corpse," declares Peter.

"As if you can tell," I say.

"What else can there be in a coffin, stupid!" says Adi.

We hear Mother's voice. Footsteps in the bedroom. We exchange alert glances and scamper into the garden to resume our game.

Cousin kicks the misshapen can distractedly, and our pursuit of him is half-hearted and abstracted.

But no one tells us what's in that box.

"A snake? A skeleton? A corpse?"

The servants don't know. The other adults maintain a maddening silence. We are not to be inquisitive: it belongs to Father and it's nobody's business but his.

We wander about with glazed, preoccupied eyes and pinched faces. We waste away.

Electric-aunt has begun to force-feed Cousin. She pinches his nostrils, and when he opens his mouth to breathe, pops in a tablespoon of food. She releases his nostrils only after he swallows the morsel.

Mother begins to sit with us at our small table with the oilcloth and, beguiling us with fairy tales, charming us with her voice, slips spoonfuls into our mouths.

Muccho chases Papoo with a broom shouting: "Hai, my fate! If that accursed slut dies on me, how will I show my face to

Jemadar Tota Ram?"

Tota Ram is Papoo's prospective husband . . . An almost mythical figure no one's seen.

Even Mrs. Singh has begun to supervise her offspring's feed.

Gandhijee too is off his feed, we hear. There is a slaughter of Muslims in Bihar—he does not want it to spread to Bengal.

It doesn't.

Inspired by Gandhijee, we launch a more determined fast.

We turn sallow, hollow-eyed, pot-bellied. Electric-aunt's frenzied anxiety becomes chronic. Mother turns into a prophetess of doom. "Mark my words," she says eerily, "you'll remain weaklings the rest of your lives!"

Muccho has taken to beating her hollow breasts and crying: "What face will I show Tota Ram?" And Mrs. Singh is moved to wring her hands!

Their strategies change. Cousin is force-fed chocolates and carry-home ice cream by my resourceful aunt. They are easier to force-feed than food. He goes about with stuck nostrils and an open mouth. Mother's fairy tales turn into horror stories and every time we form our lips in an "O" and suck in our horrified breaths, we unwittingly also suck in food. Their American mother is so upset when she sits before Rosy-Peter's hollow cheeks and full plates that she bursts into tears: and Rosy-Peter, astounded by this spectacle of maternal emotion, permit her to pour food into their gaping mouths. Muccho has started sweet-talking and spoon-feeding her stupefied and incredulous daughter.

Colonel Bharucha gives us calcium-and-glucose injections.

If they want to get Gandhijee to eat the next time he fasts they should send for Muccho and Electric-aunt and Mother and Colonel Bharucha. And even the unformidable Mrs. Singh.

As mysteriously as it has appeared, the box disappears.

While I lead the life of a spoilt little brat with pretensions to diet, forty miles east of Lahore, in a Muslim village, Ranna leads the unspoilt life of a village boy shorn of pretensions. While Ayah shovels spoonfuls of chicken into my mouth as I doodle with Plasticine, Chidda, squatting by the clay hearth, feeds her son scraps of chapatti dipped in buttermilk. All day, baked by the sun, Ranna romps in the fields and plays with dung. And—when I close my eyes and I wish to—I see us squatting beneath the buffalo, our mouths open and eyes closed, as Dost Mohammad directs squirts of milk straight from the udder into our mouths—and I can still taste its foddery sweetness.

It is a little over a year since my visit to Ranna's village. Imam Din, who feels that the tension in the cities will spread to the villages, and is concerned for his numerous kin in Pir Pindo, decides to pay them another visit. When I excitedly protest and exclaim that I *will* go with him, he surprises me by agreeing at once, in a preoccupied way, that I can if Mother consents.

Mother consults Father, her friends, Ayah; and finally gives her hesitant permission—provided we go by train. Trains don't go to Pir Pindo, but we can get off at Thokar, and hire a tonga for the two remaining miles.

We have been in Pir Pindo for two days. On Baisakhi, the day that celebrates the birth of the Sikh religion and of the wheat harvest, we go to Dera Tek Singh. I ride on Imam Din's shoulders, Ranna on his father's—at the head of a procession of nephews, uncles, cousins, brothers, grandsons and great-grandsons. The women and girls—except for me, because I am insistent, and from the city—stay behind as always. The men go to the Baisakhi Fair every year: before Ranna was born—before his great-grandfather was born!

Dost Mohammad is walking in front of us. His head wrapped in a crisp white puggaree, his lungi barely clearing the mud behind his squeaky-new curly-toed shoes, a hookah swinging in his right hand, he looks like a prosperous landlord: and, riding atop his

Father's shoulders, Ranna imagined that the other villagers looked at them in awe and said among themselves (as Punjabis—even little ones—are wont to imagine), "Wah! There goes that fine-looking zemindar; walking at the head of his family with his handsome son on his head!"

It is the thirteenth of April. The wheat has been harvested; the spring rains have spent themselves, and the earth is powdery. From on top of Imam Din's head I see the other groups of villagers converging on Dera Tek Singh: Hindu, Muslim, Sikh—as they raise their own majestic trails of dust.

The festival is already in full swing when we arrive. A group of four fierce-looking Sikhs, their hair tied in turbans and wearing calf-length shirts over tight *churidar* pajamas, perform the *Ghadka* before drifting waves of admirers. Wielding long swords and staves, clashing them to the beat of drums, the dancers lunge, parry, and twirl to the accompaniment of folk singers extolling the valor of ancient Sikh warriors. The singers shriek, their voices hoarse from the dust, and the effort to be heard above the uproar. There are several such groups.

Dost Mohammad leads us to the heart of the fair, to the rides and food stalls. Frying onion *pakoras*. A bubbling, spicy stew of chickpeas. Pink and yellow clouds of spun-sugar candy. Helium-filled balloons. Our every step deflected by aromas. The family scatters. Ranna and I spend most of our small allowance on food; stuffing ourselves on syrupy *gulab-jamans* and *jalebis*. We scramble for seats on the creaking Ferris wheel, its six wooden trays swaying from six wooden spokes. Each tray is jammed with children, and the stones that are juggled from one tray to another to balance them. Agile attendants scramble among the spokes like acrobats to turn the wheel with the weight of their bodies. Dost Mohammad lifts us into a tray. I don't trust the shallow railing guarding us; and as we orbit, our delighted limbs cramped, our eyes narrowed against the wind, I cling to Ranna. Holding the rickety edge of the swaying tray with one hand, he supports me with the other.

We ride the merry-go-rounds with metal seats and the seesaws. And despite the gaiety and distractions, Ranna senses the chill spread by the presence of strangers, their unexpected faces harsh and cold. A Sikh youth whom Ranna has met a few times, and who has always been kind, pretends not to notice Ranna. Other men, who would normally smile at Ranna, slide their eyes past. Little by little, without his being aware of it, his smile becomes strained and his laughter strident. "What's the matter?" I ask him. "Nothing," he says, surprised.

In the afternoon Dost Mohammad takes us with him to visit Jagjeet Singh. He has his hookah with him so he waits outside the Gurdwara while we go in to summon the *granthi*. Jagjeet Singh is sitting cross-legged in front of an open Granth Sahib. It is resting on an elaborately carved walnut stand. I have never seen a book so large. Surely, if God dwells in books, He dwells in one as large! Later that night Ranna told me that he had wished that the holy Koran their mullah occasionally displayed was larger.

Jagjeet Singh leads us to his charpoy beneath a young banyan already spreading its tender shade over part of the temple wall. He shouts to a Sikh boy washing utensils at a well to fetch tea. Dost Mohammad asks the *granthi*'s permission to light his hookah.

Dost Mohammad has noticed the presence of strangers too. After the boy hands us our tea, and we settle down to blowing into and sipping from the steaming brass mugs, he asks, "Jagjeet Singh-jee, you have a large number of visitors to the fair this year... All those stalwarts in blue turbans with staves and long *kirpans*...?"

The *granthi*'s genial face becomes uncommonly solemn. He rubs the puffy skin around his eyes and I notice how old and tired he looks. "I don't know what to say," he says, bowing his head. "They are Akalis... The Immortals... Maharaja Ranjeet Singh formed the sect when he conquered the Punjab a hundred years ago." And, though there is no one else that I can see—the Sikh boy is in any case too far away to hear—he moves closer to Dost Mohammad. Lowering his voice, he says: "I visit the Golden Temple at Amritsar from time to time... The Akalis swarm around it like angry hornets in their blue turbans... I wish they'd remain there!" He pauses; then, scratching his curly beard and frowning, he says: "They talk of a plan to drive the Muslims out of East Punjab. . . To divide the Punjab. They say they won't live with the Mussulmans if there is to be a Pakistan. Owlish talk like that! You know city talk. It's madness. . . It can't amount to anything. . . but they've always been like that. Troublemakers. You'll have to look out till this evil blows over."

I don't know where Imam Din is. I wish to God he were here! It is, almost exactly, what he's been telling the villagers for the past two days. Dost Mohammad appears to have sunk lower into the charpoy. He is quiet for so long that the *granthi* turns to look at him anxiously. I feel Dost Mohammad's thigh twitch against mine. He raises his head slowly, and at last he says, "We'll look out. . . Don't worry Jagjeet Singh-jee. . . We keep track of things on our *chaudhry*'s radio."

"May the Ten Gurus help us," the *granthi* sighs. "*Wah Guru!*"

A short while later, pressing the small of his back, and acting old, Imam Din lumbers up, sighing, "*Ya Allah! Ya Rahman! Ya Rahim!*" Seeing our mugs, he asks for tea. Other men, Sikh and Hindu friends and a few villagers from Pir Pindo, stroll up in twos and threes, and group around the *granthi*'s cot. They talk of everything but the intrusive presence of the Akalis. Before dusk Dost Mohammad's younger brother, Iqbal, joins us. He has bought some land in a village four miles west of Pir Pindo and had moved there. His wife is Ranna's favorite aunt. He loves going to their village to play with his cousins and to be spoilt by his Noni *chachi*. She always has something special for him to eat or wear, he tells me. His uncle tosses a knitted skullcap into Ranna's lap, saying, "Here's something from your Noni *chachi*, *pahailwan!*" He calls Ranna *pahailwan*, wrestler. It is an affectionate form of address. Ranna wears the cap at once and his uncle laughs and musses his hair.

"You'd better leave before it gets dark," Jagjeet Singh says quietly to Dost Mohammad; the other men are talking among themselves. "There's no telling who's about these days. . . and not all of them are your friends."

The sun has set, but it is still light enough to see. Ranna was leaning against his father when the *granthi* spoke. The tone of the

116

granthi's voice, the sadness, and the resignation in it, turned the heaviness in Ranna's heart into the first stab of fear. Even in retrospect, these isolated impressions didn't add up to a reliable warning. Pir Pindo was too deep in the hinterland of the Punjab, where distances are measured in footsteps and at the speed of bullock-carts, for larger politics to penetrate.

The Sikhs of Dera Tek Singh escort us halfway to Pir Pindo.

That evening we crowd into the *chaudhry*'s courtyard to listen to his radio. The Congress and Muslim League spokesmen, the announcer says, warn the peasants not to heed mischievous rumors. Even Master Tara Singh, the leader of the Akali Sikhs, tells the peasants—especially the Muslims—to remain where they are. No one will disturb them.

A few days later, in Lahore, we hear of attacks on Muslim villages near Amritsar and Jullundur. But the accounts are contrary—and the details so brutal and bizarre that they cannot be believed. Imam Din tells Yousaf and Ayah that he is sure it is Akali propaganda, calculated to scare the Muslim peasants. And even if it does scare them, he asks, what good will it do the Akali Sikhs? Where can the scared Muslim villagers go? There are millions of them. Even supposing Dost Mohammad and his family leave Pir Pindo, which they can't. . . how can they abandon their ancestors' graves, every inch of land they own, their other kin? How will they ever hold up their heads again? Suppose every single person in Pir Pindo can hold his own someplace else—even then millions of Mussulmans will be left in East Punjab! Where will they go? No, he says, I have seen for myself; they cannot throw the Mussulmans out!

A fortnight after the Baisakhi Fair, late in the afternoon, an army truck disgorges a family of villagers outside our gate. Hearing the noise, I run to the kitchen. Imam Din is standing in the open door, staring at a string of men, women and children as they troop up our drive. I recognize some of the faces from Pir Pindo; they are distant kin—not of his immediate family—cousins, nephews or great-grandnephews thrice removed. I wonder how he will accommodate them all in his quarters. Ayah has one look at his face and says, "Go, greet them. I'll prepare the tea and *parathas*." Yousaf and Hari, followed by Imam Din, welcome the villagers and lead them to the quarters at the back.

The women and children are distributed among Imam Din and Ayah's quarters. The men will sleep in Hari and Yousaf's. There is a steep fall in the temperature at night, and it is still too cold to sleep out. It is difficult to count them; the babies all look alike. Excluding the tiny babies, there are at least fifteen guests. As the men squat in the courtyard, eating from a common tray as Muslims do, they tell us what happened the night before. They tell the story vividly, in the way of peasants, repeating the dialogue, presenting each detail of expression and movement, transporting us to the village.

Late in the evening three military lorries had lumbered into Pir Pindo gouging deep ruts in the fields and laying waste swathes of sugarcane. They were Gurkha soldiers come to evacuate them.

"Those Mussulmans who want to go to Pakistan had better get into the truck," a soldier shouted through a megaphone. He was short and stocky like most of his race, and his small Tibetan features appeared frighteningly alien to the villagers. "We will leave at dawn."

"What?" the puzzled villagers asked. "Is Pakistan already there?"

"Who knows," said the Gurkha. "I'm telling what I'm told to say."

The villagers gathered in the open yard of their mosque. They squatted in a tight arc round the mullah and the *chaudhry*. I imagine their faces: obstinate, dazed. And the *chaudhry*'s as, smiling wryly, attempting with sarcasm and wisdom to mask his panic, he says: "Do you expect us to walk away with our hands and feet?

What use will they serve us without our lands? Can you evacuate our land?" he asks cunningly. And the villagers, as if they are at a debate where their *chaudhry's* wit is scoring points, nod their heads and say: "Wha! Wha! Well said! What answer do you have to that, *Hawaldar* Sahib?"

They peppered the Gurkhas with formidable questions. "And what about our harvest?" they asked. "And the crop we have just sown? And our cattle? Who will evacuate them?"

The soldiers, unimpressed by the sarcasm and indifferent to the villagers' confusion and troubles, shrugged and said, "We're just here to evacuate you: hands, feet and heads. Nothing else. We've told you why we're here; the rest is up to you."

"Do you expect us to leave everything we've valued and loved since childhood? The seasons, the angle and color of the sun rising and setting over our fields are beautiful to us, the shape of our rooms and barns is familiar and dear. You can't expect us to leave just like that!"

The soldiers were weary. They stood up. "You're not the only village we are to evacuate, you know," one of them said.

The *chaudhry* remained quiet and the silence settled like a black cloud over their heads, blocking out the stars. At last the *chaudhry* said: "If we have to go, if it's Allah's will, we will go when the time comes... The right time..."

"Yes... When the time comes, we shall see...," said the villagers.

The trucks left at dawn. Five families, who like our visitors were poor relatives and hired hands, with no land in the village, left Pir Pindo, not caring one way or the other where the sun rose or set.

Chapter 13

The times have changed; the world has changed its mind.
The European's mystery is erased.
The secret of his conjuring tricks is known:
The Frankish wizard stands and looks amazed.

—Iqbal

Already it is winter. I am never warm. I feel coldest in the misty mornings when, holding Hari's calloused hand with my chilblained fingers, I walk on chilblained toes to Mrs. Pen's.

The colder it gets the more reserved Hari becomes. I know he is secretly shivering. Cold turns me weepy and Hari secretive and Mrs. Pen indulgent. She lets me off early.

At Godmother's I go straight to the kitchen. I am hungry. Slavesister warms some leftover curry and gives me the news that the Inspector General of Police, Mr. Rogers, is dead. Murdered. His mutilated body discovered in the gutter.

For a moment I cannot breathe. I feel I might fall.

I know of death: a grandfather died in Karachi and his remains were consigned to the Tower of Silence. Moti's relatives are forever dying... But they weren't murdered. Or mutilated. And they weren't people I knew!

"How mutilated?" I ask, shocked.

"Never you mind," says Slavesister.

I have seen goats slaughtered at the end of the Muslim fast on Eid. I've watched them being disemboweled and, with the other children, lined up to blow into their moist windpipes and inflate their lungs. But those were goats. Not tall men with moustaches and haughty voices and polished shoes and submissive wives...

"Will he go to heaven?" I ask breathlessly, clutching at straws.

"To hell!" says Mini Aunty with unexpected viciousness:

giving me another shock. "All Englishmen will burn in hell for the trouble they've started in the Punjab! And let me tell you. The Christian hell is forever!"

The relish in her voice is ghoulish. I feel so upset at the awful fate awaiting Mr. Rogers's mutilated carcass that I collapse on a stool. I cannot face the curry. I recall the police inspector's chilly blue eyes that so narrowly escaped mutilation by Mr. Singh's fork and the spit-polished ears of his orphaned children.

I start sobbing. Godmother sits up in bed and calls: "Hey! What's the matter?"

"Mr. Rogers is dead," I say, choking on the words. "He will burn in hell forever!"

"Who said that?" demands Godmother, knowing very well who.

"Mini Aunty." (That's Slavesister's pet name. I've never heard her real name.)

"I know who's going to roast forever if they don't watch out!" says Godmother. "Don't listen to Mini. She has no more sense than a twit!"

"After the Mountbatten plan to tear up the Punjab . . . how can you . . . ," mumbles Slavesister, shaking her head at the stove and looking martyred.

"If your mutilated body was discovered in the gutter, then you'd know how it feels! Badmouthing a dead man!"

Slavesister clicks her tongue and peers into a steaming pan and extra sweetly smiles because she is on the verge of tears. Her pale brown lips, that despite their clear outline and generous width are flat, flatten further and stretch moistly.

"Will they put Mr. Rogers into the Tower of Silence?" I ask, coming to the slave's rescue—and attempting to get the derailed conversation back on track.

"He's Christian. They'll bury him," says Godmother.

It occurs to me that I don't know enough about the Tower. Perhaps I was too young when I first heard of it . . . The shock of Mr. Rogers's demise makes me curious about all aspects of dying. "What is the Tower of Silence?" I ask.

"We call it *Dungarwadi*, not Tower of Silence. The English have given it that funny name. . . Actually it is quite a simple structure: just a big round wall without any roof," says Godmother.

"So?" I persist.

"So nothing!" interjects the ungrateful slave crankily. "When little girls ask too many questions their tongues drop off!"

"I wasn't asking you," I retort, and poking my tongue at her, pointedly turn to Godmother. Godmother never talks down to me like that.

"The dead body is put inside the *Dungarwadi*," explains Godmother. "The vultures pick it clean and the sun dries out the bones."

I must look frightful because Godmother pats the bed and says, "Come here."

I sit down, facing her, and drawing me close she says: "Mind you . . . It's only the body that's dead. Instead of polluting the earth by burying it, or wasting fuel by burning it, we feed God's creatures. The soul's in heaven, chatting with God in any case . . . Or broiling in hell like Mini's will."

I feel curiously deprived. Here's an architectural wonder created exclusively by the charitable Parsees to feed God's creatures and I haven't even seen it. And I don't want to wait until I'm dead! Mr. Rogers's murdered and mutilated body is forgotten and my eyes stop tearing.

"I want to see it," I demand.

"We don't have one in Lahore," says Godmother. "There are too few Parsees: the vultures would starve. But when you go to Karachi or Bombay you can see it from the outside. Only pallbearers can go in . . . We have a graveyard in Lahore."

"Thank God!" says Mini Aunty so emphatically that Godmother—who views all emphatic statements from Mini Aunty as direct challenges to her authority—rears up from her pillows demanding: "Why? What's there to thank God for?"

"I prefer to be buried."

"Oh? Why?"

"You know why! It gives me the creeps . . . The thought of

vultures smacking their beaks over my eyeballs!"

"You'd rather have your eyeballs riddled by maggots? Would you like me to post a sign over your body stating, Maggots only. No vultures allowed?"

"Really, Rodabai! I don't want to talk or think about it. Please forget I ever..."

"I don't know what you have against the poor vultures... favoring the maggots and worms over them! I'd be ashamed to call myself a Zoroastrian if I were you."

"Being devoured by vultures has nothing to do with the religion... Surely Zarathustra had more important messages to deliver..."

"Since when have you become an authority on Zarathustra?" demands Godmother. "Haven't you heard of Parsee charity? Only last month Sir Eduljee Adenwalla had his leg amputated in Bombay. Sick as he was, he sat in a wheelchair all through the ceremonies and had his leg deposited in the *Dungarwadi!* And what do you think happens when Parsee diabetics' toes are cut off? Do you think they discard them in the wastebasket and deprive the vultures?"

Holding the dripping ladle aloft Mini Aunty covers her ears with her plump and muscular arms and says, "I don't want to know!"

Even I'm feeling queasy. Godmother looks at me and holds her peace; and Mini Aunty, pressing her advantage, says, "I must say, you can be ghoulish sometimes. I wish you wouldn't talk such nonsense before the child..."

"What do you mean, nonsense?" challenges Godmother. "Who was the one talking about eternal roastings in hell?"

"You know what I mean, Roda... Now don't..."

"Who's Roda? Who's permitted you to call me Roda? Since when have you become my elder sister?"

"You know I didn't mean it that way."

"Which way did you mean it, then?"

Slavesister, almost on tiptoe, hovers quietly over the stove. Her wet smile is flattening. Her eyes do not dare to shift from the bubbling contents of the pan she is stirring.

"Some people are getting too big for their boots... Some people are becoming quite airy-fairy!"

Slavesister mumbles, "Only my bunion's getting too big... I'll cut it off and mail it to the *Dungarwadi*."

"What?" queries Godmother. "What is your Highness mumbling?"

"Oh! All right, all right! Carry on... you must have everything your way, Rodabai... filling the child's mind with such notions... mumble, mumble."

"Don't you all right, all right me! I'll have your carcass flown straight to the vultures!"

Slavesister doesn't answer. Only shakes her head and mutters. She will not answer back now. She too has learned from experience.

"Small mouth, big talk!" grumbles Godmother as if to herself, but loud enough for Slavesister to hear. "Little minds should not attempt to weigh in big fish!"

Still poised for attack, eyes bright, Godmother waits to see if Slavesister will respond.

But Slavesister's insurgence has been effectively squashed. She maintains a strategic silence, suppressing even her mumbles.

Godmother makes a magically triumphant face. She holds her pointy fingers in a "V" for victory, winks at me and leans back on her concrete pillows.

I go into the kitchen to finish my curry but I cannot eat. Mr. Rogers's English toes and kidneys float before my disembodied eyeballs...

And the vision of a torn Punjab. Will the earth bleed? And what about the sundered rivers? Won't their water drain into the jagged cracks? Not satisfied by breaking India, they now want to tear the Punjab.

Yousaf comes to fetch me. The sun has had time to warm the afternoon. It is balmy. "Let's go through the Lawrence Gardens," I urge, and Yousaf, unable to deny anyone, makes the detour

124

through the gardens. We stop along a trimmed gardenia hedge to look at the sunken rose garden; and we clamber up the slopes of artificial hills and run down bougainvillea valleys ablaze with winter flowers. Casting long shadows we take a path leading to where Yousaf has parked his cycle.

Our shadow glides over a Brahmin Pandit. Sitting cross-legged on the grass he is eating out of a leaf-bowl. He looks at Yousaf—and at me—and his face expresses the full range of terror, passion and pain expected of a violated virgin. Our shadow has violated his virtue. The Pandit cringes. His features shrivel into arid little shrimps and his body retracts. The vermillion caste-mark on his forehead glows like an accusing eye. He looks at his food as if it is infected with maggots. Squeamishly picking up the leaf, he tips its contents behind a bush and throws away the leaf.

I am a diseased maggot. I look at Yousaf. His face is drained of joy, bleak, furious. I know he too feels himself composed of shit, crawling with maggots.

Now I know surely. One man's religion is another man's poison.

I experience this feeling of utter degradation, of being an untouchable excrescence, an outcast again, years later when I hold out my hand to a Parsee priest at a wedding and he, thinking I am menstruating beneath my facade of diamonds and a sequined sari, cringes.

Late that evening there is a familiar pattern of sound.

Again they're after Hari's dhoti. But instead of the light, quick patter of bare feet there is the harsh scrape and drag of leather on frozen earth.

It doesn't seem quite right to toy with a man's dhoti when it is so cold. It is a summer sport.

Someone shouts, "Get him before he gets into his quarters!" I hear Imam Din's bullying, bluff barruk as he bellows: "Aha-hurrr! A-vaaaaaaay!" And, closer to his quarry, Yousaf's provocative bubbly

"Vo-vo-vo-vo-vo-vo," as running he taps his mouth in quick succession. Curses! Hair all over my body creeps aslant as I hear Hari's alarmed cry.

Snatching me up and straddling me on her hip Ayah flings open the bathroom door and runs out. I am struck by the cold, and the approach of night casts uneasy shadows over a scene I have witnessed only in daylight. Something else too is incongruous. The winter shawl wrapped around Hari.

Yousaf is twirling his plume of hair and tugging at it as if he's trying to lift him. I feel a great swell of fear for Hari, and a surge of loathing for his *bodhi*. Why must he persist in growing it? And flaunt his Hinduism? And invite ridicule?

And that preposterous and obscene dhoti! Worn like a diaper between his stringy legs—just begging to be taken off!

My dread assuming a violent and cruel shape, I tear away from Ayah and fling myself on the human tangle and fight to claw at Hari's dhoti.

Someone pulls off his shawl and it is trampled underfoot. Hands stretch and pull his unraveling mauve lady's cardigan (Mother's hand-me-down) and rip off his shirt. His dhoti is hanging in ragged edges and, suddenly, it's off!

Like a withered tree frozen in a winter landscape Hari stands isolated in the bleak center of our violence: prickly with goose bumps, sooty genitals on display.

With heavy, old-man's movements, Imam Din wrenches the shawl from under our feet and throws it at the gardener, and the tattered rag that was his dhoti. "Cover up, you shameless bugger," he says, attempting his usual bantering manner, but there is a gruff uncontrollable edge to his voice. He is not at ease with cruelty.

I look back. The Shankars stand on their veranda like fat shadows. Ayah has turned her face away. I run to her. I dig my face in her sari and stretch up my hands. Ayah tries to lift me but her fluid strength is gone. Her grip is weak. I hug her fiercely. Her heart beneath her springy breasts is fluttering like Ice-candy-man's nervous sparrows. She raises frightened eyes from my face and, turning to follow her gaze, I see an obscured shape standing by the compound wall. Stirred by a breeze, the shadows cast by a eucalyptus tree shift and splinter, and define the still figure of a man.

The man moves out of the darkness, and as he approaches I am relieved. It is only Ice-candy-man.

Chapter 14

Ayah is seeing more of Masseur. So, so am I. When Ayah's work is done, and she stretches out in the afternoon sun, massaging butter into her calves and smooth shins, she hums a new tune and sighs: *"Siski hawa ne lee: Har pati Kanp oothi.* The breeze sucked in his breath... The leaves trembled, breathless." It's Masseur's song. He sings it in a rumbling, soulful baritone, and he sings often.

I am seeing more of Lahore, too. Ayah and I roam on foot and by bus: from Emperor Jehangir's tomb at Shahdara to Shahjehan's Shalimar Gardens. From the outskirts of the slaughterhouse to the banks of the Ravi in low flood. We amble through the tall pampas grass—purposefully purposeless—and sniffing the attar of roses, happen upon Masseur: his creamy bosky-silk shirt, his strong forearms and broad ankles stretched out on a dhurrie on the gray sand.

His cruet set of oils beside him, Masseur turns, making room for Ayah, and his eyes, full of honey, shower her with his maddening dreams. They lie, side by side, a stalk of grass stuck at a thoughtful angle between Masseur's teeth as he traces with a skillfull finger Ayah's parted lips.

I get up and Masseur says, "Lenny baby, don't go far." His voice is gravelly with desire and it makes something happen in my stomach, as when Sharbat Khan, radiant with love, ogles Ayah.

I know Ayah is beyond speech—her will given over to a maestro's virtuosity. Masseur's consummate arm circles Ayah...

Caressing me through the pampas, the breeze moans with love—and brings to me Masseur's song:

> "Spring bloomed in moonlit wildernesses—
> Heady with sap the flowers swayed—
> And a rose, bubbling,

Dancing in the breeze,
Attracted a bumblebee—
Floating, frolicking, the bumblebee came—
Strutting among the flowers, strumming love."

And so, the bumblebee courts the rose. I listen to the words unfolding the rose's tragic story and wait intently for the change in Masseur's voice.

"And then one day [he sings in a very low and urgent key]
When all was hushed—
No stars, and in the sky no moon—
The bee stole the rose's youth—"

There it is. The fearful and tragic climax! The rose awakens, weeps, shrivels, swoons! And nature, in all its marvelous tenderness, commiserates:

"The breeze sucked in his breath—
The leaves trembled breathless—
Moist-eyed the stars winked out—"

I wait a while, watching the shallow boats drift sluggishly on the shallow Ravi. The men in them, still as the dead, remain comatose as the boats, bumping along the shoals, right themselves and float slowly downstream.

We hear Masseur's song calling from the fountains, cypresses and marble terraces of the Shalimar Gardens. We hear him singing from the giddy heights of the minarets looming above Emperor Jehangir's tomb—directing his voice like a shower of petals to summon Ayah.

Ayah comes. And with her, like a lame limpet, come I.

We find Masseur waiting for us on the artificial hill behind the zoo lion's cage and by the chattering monkeys and among the peacocks. The heavy pleats of his Multanisilk lungi fall in slender folds to his ankles as leaning against the paling he waits for Ayah. And when she comes, the peacocks spread their tail feathers. And Masseur's movements unfold the rich pleats in his checked lungi.

Where Masseur is, Ayah is. And where Ayah is, is Ice-candy-man.

I sense his presence.

While Masseur's voice lures Ayah to the dizzy eminence of one minaret, it compels Ice-candy-man to climb the winding stairs to the other minaret. On the riverbank I sense his stealthy presence in the tall clumps of pampas grass. He lurks in the dense shade of mangoes in the Shalimar Gardens and in the fearsome smells skirting the slaughterhouse . . . He prowls on the other side of the artificial hill behind the zoo lion's cage, and conceals himself behind the peacocks when they spread their tail feathers and open their turquoise eyes: he has as many eyes, and they follow us.

In the evenings he visits Ayah and squatting like an ungainly bird in his cotton shawl astounds her with his knowledge of our wanderings. And when his driven toes are too weary to perform their amazing seduction, his glib tongue takes over. Ayah, wide-eyed, wrapped in the silken web of his gossip, draws closer . . .

Ice-candy-man has an inexhaustible fund of gossip.

"Our lion tamer got rid of his tenants at last!" he announces one sultry afternoon in Electric-aunt's garden. He has followed us there. My aunt is busy inside filing her accounts in neat figures beneath the credit and debit columns. We are sitting outside so as not to disturb her while we wait for Cousin to return from school.

"How did he get rid of them? Did he win a case?" asks Ayah. "Did he get the police to throw them out?"

"If you await court decisions, you wait forever," says Ice-candy-man with such contempt and authority that my faith in the judicial system is forever shattered.

"I told Sher Singh to take matters in hand," he continues. "I told him: Why go through all the rigmarole of courts and notices when we have time-honored remedies at hand?"

Ayah and I lean closer. Ayah is positively within striking distance. Ice-candy-man's toe twitches, but it is a weary, footsore little twitch and its impulse easily checked. I merely glance its way sternly and the twitch ceases.

"At first Sher Singh hemmed and hedged," says Ice-candy-man. "Then he said: 'You're a Mussulman... The tenants are Mussulmans... Why should you help a Sikh?' "

His raconteur's gift places us in Sher Singh's shoes and we look at him with the same questions in our eyes.

" 'Oye, you donkey,' I told him. 'So what if you're a Sikh? I'm first a friend to my friends... And an enemy to their enemies... And then a Mussulman! God and the politicians have enough servers. So, I serve my friends.' "

Now he has us in his shoes. Ayah has an animated look on her rapt face. "Tell us... what happened then?" she asks breathlessly.

"Lenny child, be a good girl," says Ice-candy-man, snapping his fingers to flick the ash from his cigarette. "Ask the cook to make me a strong cup of tea. Go: *putch-putch*." (Kissing noises used to wheedle children dispatched on trivial errands.)

"No," I say. "I'm not going anywhere: I also want to listen to you."

He glances at Ayah. Since Ayah appears content to have me stay, he says: "Well, Sher Singh, his brothers Prem and Pratab, and one or two cousins—all strapping fellows... and I. Armed with hockey sticks we went to their tenants' house while the men were at work. We made a bit of *hulla-goolla* outside the building. Waved our hockey sticks and shouted: 'Come to your windows, pretty ladies: don't hide. We have something to show you.' "

Ayah and I, our eyes round, our lips parted, scarcely breathe.

"We attracted a crowd. There were quite a few dazzling eyes at some of the other windows in the building... But the ladies for whose benefit we were staging the show were more bashful.

"When I was sure we had their attention—and they were peeping at us through their reed blinds—as one man we opened our lungis! In such a way as to shield our rears: and in front our dangling dingdongs!"

Taking my cue from Ayah, I too wear a faintly scandalized, faintly amused expression.

"We exposed ourselves so that only they could see us. The crowd behind us guessed what was happening. There were one or two curses—one or two coarse remarks—but no interference. We made a few suggestive gestures...you know...It lasted only five minutes...

"But what a *hulla-goolla!* The women screamed and cursed... You'd have thought we'd raped them!

"We got wind the police were coming. By the time they appeared we'd wrapped our lungis back on and cleared out!" Ice-candy-man, half standing, moves his body and his arms like a magician conjuring images.

"I hear the men swore vengeance and what not. But this morning they cleared out!"

The triumph on his face is infectious: he sees it reflected in ours, and his teeth show increasingly white as his lips stretch and stretch into a smile in his narrow face. He crushes the stub of his cigarette into the grass—and I hear the school bus squeak to a halt as it deposits my cousin outside the gate.

Next evening when Ice-candy-man comes to our house I notice his toe is more vigorous. It is rested. We didn't wander far today. Only went to Godmother's.

Masseur massages Oldhusband every Thursday. Ayah was content to sit on her haunches and watch as, before our very eyes, beneath his supple fingers, Oldhusband acquired a youthful glow!

Later, when Electric-aunt and Cousin also came to Godmother's, Cousin informed me that Ice-candy-man's bicycle was parked outside Godmother's gate. In fact Cousin had purchased and devoured a raspberry popsicle. He showed me the inside of his raspberry-stained lower lip and drew my attention to a pale red stain on his khaki shorts.

Cousin is like that. Even when I believe him, he shows me, shows me, shows me things...

"Did you hear about Bhagwandas the tailor?" Ice-candy-man asks, settling down cross-legged on a mat on the servants' veranda outside Ayah's quarters. Ayah has just washed her long hair and, having brought it forward over her shoulder, is running a combative wooden comb through the wet tangles.

"Lenny baby," Ice-candy-man tells me, almost burying his head in his cupped hands as he lights one of his smelly cigarettes, "get me a glass of water. Tell Imam Din it's for me and he will put a bit of ice in it."

"No," I say, leaning firmly on his toe. "I'm not going anywhere. I also want to know about the tailor. Tell me!"

"Let her be," says Ayah, who is as curious as me. Bhagwandas is her tailor too.

"Well, he ran off with the Mission padre's wife!" Ice-candy-man pushes his pillbox cap forward rakishly and looks at Ayah out of the corners of his gleaming light brown eyes.

"*Hai!* No!" says Ayah, looking appropriately grave and scandalized and for a moment permitting the comb to cease its struggle with the tangles.

"Yes," says Ice-candy-man, grinning into our avid faces. "You know how it is when you women visit tailors... This is loose, that is tight. Alter this, alter that. The tailor's fingers touch here, smooth the cloth there..." Ice-candy-man's hand strays to Ayah's knees, and as he raises it to her shoulder his fingers brush her bosom. Ayah's eyes flash a warning and Ice-candy-man's serpentine arm floats away. He shifts his eyes from us and stares ingenuously into the fading day.

"The padre, poor fellow, still doesn't know what happened," he says dreamily. "He's a man of God. You know how they are. Simple. But the tailors are a sly lot. Never trust them, Lenny baby, with their measuring tapes, needles and threads—and smoothing fingers."

"Where's your wife?" I ask. I've never thought to ask him before.

"In the village, with her mother."

"What if she runs away?"

"She won't. They have no tailors in the village. No masseurs either. . . with their cunning fingers taking liberties!"

Ayah looks startled. So do I. This is the first time he has openly expressed his jealousy of Masseur. Although we have been conscious of the undercurrent of hostility between them, neither Ayah nor I realized its development into the acrimony Ice-candy-man's bitter voice has just expressed.

It changes the complexion of the evening. I become aware of the dusk that has gathered in shadows on the dung-plastered veranda and is thick behind the open door of Ayah's quarters. The earth floor, compressed and sprinkled with water and swept clean, and her small string-cot, large tin trunk, and pictures and statues of gods and goddesses in the niches are all obscured.

"Why don't you ever bring your wife here? I want to see her. Please bring her here," I plead, fretting him, trying to talk away my misgivings.

And, having at the same time to restrain his refreshed toes, I sit on them.

"What'll she do here, Lenny baby?" says Ice-candy-man, once again far-away-eyed and in control. "She's used to village ways, and to her folk there. . . She doesn't like to stay in the city. . . so I leave her there."

"Is she your only wife?" I ask.

But Ayah is restive and clamps my mouth shut with her hand. "Stop asking so many questions," she says with unaccustomed irritability. "Men don't like so much talk about their womenfolk."

"Oh, I don't mind. Let her be," says Ice-candy-man, pushing his cap back now that the impressive bit of gossip has been related. He musses my hair and, opening his thermos, reaches for a popsicle.

"Raspberry!" I demand, hoping there is still some raspberry left.

There is. Relinquishing my seat on his toes I stand up.

"Oof!" says Ayah suddenly, her comb caught painfully in her tangled hair.

Chapter 15

The periphery of my world extends to Mozang and Temple Road. Every Sunday we accompany the Shankars to the Daulatrams' two-story brick house for an evening of classical Indian music. The singers all make faces and strange noises but Israr Ahmed is my favorite singing boy. We sit on carpets and the singers on white sheets facing us. The accompanists—a harmonium player and a tabla-drum player—wiggle their toes and chew betel nut.

Israr Ahmed, a nondescript, unassuming, middle-aged clerk, is transformed into a dervish when he takes his turn on the white sheet. He flings his arms about, opens wide his mouth, displays *paan*-stained molars and makes noises that would turn the zoo animals green with envy. He gargles up and down the scale! He roars! He dislocates his jaw and hoists his mouth to one side—and then to the other.

Adi, Cousin and I cannot contain ourselves. In our fervor to acquire classical culture we copy his movements, contort our faces, twist our necks and are slapped and shushed for our pains.

Processions are becoming a part of the street scene. A youth holds aloft a stick with a green rag, bellows a slogan, and a group of rowdy urchins rally to the cry.

Adi and I slip past the attention of our vigilants and join the tiny tinpot processions that are spawned on Warris Road. We shout ourselves hoarse crying, *"Jai Hind! Jai Hind!"* or *"Pakistan Zindabad!"* depending on the whim or the allegiance of the principal crier. Within half an hour the processions disintegrate. The ragged flag holders, their trousers gray with washing, their singlets peppered with holes and grease spots, make a few desultory attempts to rally the stragglers. Then, lowering the banner, which reverts to becoming a lowly rag on a twig, the rabble-rouser usually climbs a mulberry tree for its fruit and we sneak back unnoticed.

We are gradually withdrawing from the shadow cast by the Queen's statue in the park. As the British prepare to leave, we meet less and less at the park and more often at the wrestler's restaurant.

Adi and I climb the rickety wooden steps behind Ayah and pick our way between the empty tables to our crowd. It is still a bit early for the regular diners. Our friends are sitting at the back, on either side of two narrow tables joined together. They are arguing. Everybody appears to be quarreling these days.

The wrestler shouts to Chotay, a skinny twelve-year-old in a skimpy lungi, to place wooden stools at either end of the tables. Adi and I sit on the stools, at the head and tail of the table, and Ayah sits down next to Masseur on the bench opposite the butcher.

Chotay hangs around, waiting for our order, and Ayah, with princessly authority and indulgence, orders three plates of vegetable biryani. "See that it's hot," she says, adopting Mother's tone with servants, "or I'll see to you!"

Like all urchins apprenticed to such establishments Chotay is bullied, teased and slapped around.

Continuing the conversation—and the feeding—our arrival has interrupted, Masseur says: "If the Punjab is divided, Lahore is bound to go to Pakistan. There is a Muslim majority here . . . "

"Lahore will stay in India!" says the Government House gardener, cutting him short. He is sitting next to the butcher. "There is too much Hindu money here," he says in his quiet, seasoned way. "They own most of the property and business in the city and . . . "

"But there are too many Mussulmans!" insists Masseur.

"So what? People don't matter . . . Money does!"

We look his way, startled by the unexpected cynicism, as he tucks a gob of rice into his mouth.

"It won't be hard to put the fear of God up the rich Hindus' dhoties—money or no money," says the butcher in a coarse, harsh voice.

"It just might be the other way round," murmurs the gardener.

In the tense silence that follows this exchange, only Adi and I look at them. The rest avert their eyes and appear to be preoccupied with their food.

Chotay appears with our plates, holding all three in one hand, and places them before us with a noisy clatter.

The butcher raps his plate on the table to indicate he wants another helping. The boy picks up the empty plate and the butcher, turning sharply, slaps his shaven head. It is a tempting target.

"Oye! You gone stupid?" says the butcher belligerently. "D'you know what I want?"

"The same?" Chotay says, wincing. His bared, narrow chest makes him look frighteningly vulnerable.

The butcher spanks his head again. "Did I ask for the same?"

Chotay stares at him foolishly.

"Bring me chops!" says Butcher as if he's just taught Chotay an invaluable lesson.

"You heard him, oye!" says the wrestler, also lightly spanking the boy's head. "What're you staring at our faces for? Hurry, or I'll break your bottom!" He exchanges a concurring glance with the butcher, showing his appreciation of the pains his friend has taken to smarten up the boy.

Chotay, ducking out of range of their hands, scampers away, dutifully saying, "Be right back, *janab!*"

"What d'you mean, put the fear of God up the rich Hindus' dhoties?" says Ice-candy-man, turning his suspiciously innocent, olive-oil eyes on the butcher.

"You know what I mean, *yaar,*" says the butcher impassively.

I close my eyes. I can't bear to open them: they will open on a suddenly changed world. I try to shut out the voices.

All at once the Sikh zoo attendant shouts, "And what about us?" so loudly that my eyes pop open. "The Sikhs hold more farm land in the Punjab than the Hindus and Muslims put together!"

"They don't!" says the butcher flatly.

"Are you calling me a liar?" Sher Singh's voice cracks with excitement and his agitated fingers disperse bits of rice in his beard.

"The only way to keep your holdings, Sardarjee, is to arrive at a settlement with the Muslim League," intervenes Masseur, smoothing the quarrel with his voice. He dusts the rice from Sher Singh's beard. "If you don't, the Punjab will be divided... That will mean trouble for us all."

"Big trouble," concurs Sher Singh portentously: as if he has secret knowledge he could disclose.

"You're what? Only four million or so?" asks Masseur. "And if half of you are in Pakistan, and the other half in India, you won't have much clout in either place."

"You don't worry about our clout!" says Sher Singh offensively. "We can look out for ourselves... You'll feel our clout all right when the time comes!"

"The British have advised Jinnah to keep clear of you bastards!" says the butcher just as offensively. "The *Angrez* call you a 'bloody nuisance'!"

"We don't want to have anything to do with you bastards either," roars the puny Sikh, sounding more and more like the tiger in his name.

"History will repeat itself," says the restaurant-owning wrestler phlegmatically. He slowly lowers his arm, and stretches it across the table. "Once the line of division is drawn in the Punjab, all Muslims to the east of it will have their balls cut off!"

His quietly spoken words have the impact of an explosion. And, as in the aftermath of a blast, the silence excludes all extraneous sound... The shrill voices of the children in the gully, the noise of traffic from the Chungi. Only Ice-candy-man's voice as if from a distance, saying: "Oye! You gone crazy? you son-of-an-owl!"

And the wrestler, quietly saying, "My cousin's a constable in Amritsar District... he says the Sikhs are preparing to drive the Muslims out of East Punjab—to the other side of the Ravi."

"But those are Muslim majority districts," says Masseur.

"The Sikhs are the fighting arm of the Hindus and they're prepared to use it . . . like when they butchered every single Mussulman from Ambala to Amritsar a century ago, during the Mogul empire's breakup."

"Behold! The savage arm of the murderous Sikh!" says Masseur, holding aloft and dangling Sher Singh's puny arm; his fingertips showering curried rice. Masseur places his arm around the Sikh and hugs him affectionately.

"It's fit only for bangles now!" says the butcher contemptuously. He tosses the gnawed skeleton of a lamb chop over his shoulder. "The Sikhs have become soft living off the fat of the land!"

"Don't fool yourself. . . They have a tradition of violence," says the wrestler. "Haven't you seen the portraits of the gurus holding the dripping heads of butchered enemies?"

"Shut up, *yaar*," says Masseur, his face unusually dark with a rush of blood. "It's all *buckwas!* The holy Koran lies next to the Granth Sahib in the Golden Temple. The shift Guru Nanaik wore carried inscriptions from the Koran. . . In fact, the Sikh faith came about to create Hindu-Muslim harmony!" He looks around the table to see how we are taking his impassioned plea for reason. "In any case," he continues more mildly, "there are no differences among friends. . . We will stand by each other."

"Of course, *yaar*," agrees the off-duty sepoy. (I can't tell what faith he belongs to.) "Who are we to quarrel? Let the big shots fight it out!"

"You're right, brother," says the Government House gardener. "The politicians will say anything in times like these to suit their purpose. . . But the English *Sarkar* won't let anything like that happen. . . You saw how they clamped down on the Independence movement."

There is an instant hum of agreement and disagreement.

"The English are not to be relied on, *yaar*," interposes Ice-candy-man, pushing his empty plate away to show he's done with eating. "They're too busy packing off with their loot to care what

140

happens. . . But that Nehru, he's a sly one. . . He's got Mountbatten eating out of his one hand and the English's wife out of his other what-not. . . He's the one to watch!"

He should know. He's working in the Government House as a *chaprassi* these days. And given his inquisitive nature and wily ways—

"Don't underestimate Jinnah," says the off-duty sepoy. "He will stick within his rights, no matter whom Nehru feeds! He's a first-rate lawyer and he knows how to attack the British with their own laws!"

"Jinnah or no Jinnah! Sikh or no Sikh! Right law, wrong law, Nehru will walk off with the lion's share. . . And what's more, come out of it smelling like the Queen-of-the-*Kotha!*" Ice-candy-man speaks with an assurance that is prophetic.

They go on and on. I don't want to hear them. I slip into Ayah's lap and, closing my eyes, hide my face between her breasts. I try not to inhale, but I must; the charged air about our table distills poisonous insights. Blue envy: green avidity: the gray and black stirrings of predators and the incipient distillation of fear in their prey. A slimy gray-green balloon forms behind my shut lids. There is something so dangerous about the tangible colors the passions around me have assumed that I blink open my eyes and sit up.

Some instinct makes me count us. We are thirteen.

I am not too young to know it is an uneasy number. I count us again, using my fingers like Mother does. There is Ice-candy-man, Masseur, Government House Gardener, Butcher, Sher Singh, the sepoy from the barracks, the wrestler, Yousaf and Hari who've been listening quietly, the Faletti's Hotel cook, me, Adi and Ayah.

"Why is thirteen an unlucky number?" I ask Mother.

"Who told you it's unlucky? There are no unlucky numbers, dear—only lucky numbers."

I ask Godmother.

"People say it's lucky—I don't know. Ask Mini: she should know."

"It's unlucky," says Mini Aunty, promptly and definitely and nodding her head. "I know. I was born on the thirteenth of March."

I ask Cousin.

"Something to do with Jesus Christ. . . He had a farewell party, you know. Something to do with that."

I ask Mrs. Pen. She tells me that the farewell party was called the Last Supper. She tells me about Christ, the twelve apostles and about Judas's betrayal and Christ's crucifixion.

From the distance, drawing stridently nearer, clamors the "tee-too, tee-too" of the dread siren. The sound shrivels time—the way Hari's genitals shriveled. I am back in the factory filled with children lying on their backs on beds. Godmother sits by me, looking composed, as competent soldiers move about hammering nails into our hands and feet. The room fills with the hopeless moans of crucified children—and with their collective sighs as they breathe in and out, in and out, with an eerie horrifying insistence.

I awaken to a distant, pulsating sound. The chant of slogans carried to me on gusts of wind.

Chapter 16

We leave early. Master Tara Singh is expected to make an appearance outside the Assembly Chambers, behind the Queen's Garden. Except for Muccho and her children, who remain behind in the servants' quarters, our house is deserted. Mother and Father left before us with the Singhs and the Phailbuses.

There is no room for us in the Queen's Garden. Seen from the roof of the Faletti's Hotel—the Faletti's Hotel cook has secured a place for us—it appears that the park has sprouted a dense crop of humans. They overflow its boundaries on to the roads and sit on trees and on top of walls. The crowd is thickest on the concrete between the back of the garden and the Assembly Chambers. Policemen are holding the throng from surging up the wide, imperious flight of pink steps.

There is a stir of excitement, an increase in the volume of noise, and Master Tara Singh, in a white *kurta*, his silken beard flowing creamily down his face, appears on the top steps of the Assembly Chambers. I see him clearly. His chest is diagonally swathed in a blue band from which dangles a decoratively sheathed *kirpan*. The folds of his loose white pajamas fall about his ankles: a leather band round his waist holds a long religious dagger.

He gets down to business right away. Holding a long sword in each hand, the curved steel reflecting the sun's glare as he clashes the swords above his head, the Sikh soldier-saint shouts: "We will see how the Muslim swine get Pakistan! We will fight to the last man! We will show them who will leave Lahore! *Raj karega Khalsa, aki rahi na koi!*"

The Sikhs milling about in a huge blob in front wildly wave and clash their swords, *kirpans* and hockey sticks, and punctuate his shrieks with roars: "*Pakistan Murdabad!* Death to Pakistan! *Sat Siri Akaal! Bolay se nihaal!*"

And the Muslims shouting: "So? We'll play Holi-with-their-blood! Ho-o-o-li with their blo-o-o-d!"

And the Holi festival of the Hindus and Sikhs coming up in a few days, when everybody splatters everybody with colored water and colored powders and laughs and romps...

And instead the skyline of the old walled city ablaze, and people splattering each other with blood! And Ice-candy-man hustling Ayah and me up the steps of his tenement in Bhatti Gate, saying: "Wait till you see Shalmi burn!" And pointing out landmarks from the crowded tenement roof:

"That's Delhi Gate... There's Lahori Gate... There's Mochi Darwaza..."

"Isn't that where Masseur lives?" Ayah asks.

"Yes, that's where your masseur stays," says Ice-candy-man, unable to mask his ire. "It's a Muslim *mohalla*," he continues in an effort to dispel his rancor. "We've got wind that the Hindus of Shalmi plan to attack it—push the Muslims across the river. The Hindus and Sikhs think they'll take Lahore. But we'll surprise them yet!"

"*Hai Ram!* That's Gowalmandi isn't it?" says Ayah. "*Hai Ram*... How it burns!"

And our eyes wide and somber.

Suddenly a posse of sweating English tommies, wearing only khaki shorts, socks and boots, runs up in the lane directly below us. And on their heels a mob of Sikhs, their wild long hair and beards rampant, large fevered eyes glowing in fanatic faces, pours into the narrow lane roaring slogans, holding curved swords, shoving up a manic wave of violence that sets Ayah to trembling as she holds me tight. A naked child, twitching on a spear struck between her shoulders, is waved like a flag: her screamless mouth agape, she is staring straight up at me. A crimson fury blinds me. I want to dive into the bestial creature clawing entrails, plucking eyes, tearing limbs, gouging hearts, smashing brains: but the creature has too many stony hearts, too many sightless eyes, deaf ears, mindless brains and tons of entwined entrails...

144

And then a slowly advancing mob of Muslim *goondas*: packed so tight that we can see only the tops of their heads. Roaring: *"Allah-o-Akbar! Yaaaa Ali!"* and *"Pakistan Zindabad!"*

The terror the mob generates is palpable—like an evil, paralyzing spell. The terrible procession, like a sluggish river, flows beneath us. Every short while a group of men, like a whirling eddy, stalls—and like the widening circles of a treacherous eddy dissolving in the mainstream, leaves in its center the pulpy red flotsam of a mangled body.

The processionists are milling about two jeeps pushed back to back. They come to a halt: the men in front of the procession pulling ahead and the mob behind banked close up. There is a quickening in the activity about the jeeps. My eyes focus on an emaciated Banya wearing a white Gandhi cap. The man is knocked down. His lips are drawn away from rotting, *paan*-stained teeth in a scream. The men move back and in the small clearing I see his legs sticking out of his dhoti right up to the groin—each thin, brown leg tied to a jeep. Ayah, holding her hands over my eyes, collapses on the floor, pulling me down with her. There is the roar of a hundred throats: *"Allah-o-Akbar!"* and beneath it the growl of revving motors. Ice-candy-man stoops over us, looking concerned: the muscles in his face tight with a strange exhilaration I never again want to see.

Ramzana the butcher and Masseur join us. Ayah sits sheathing her head and form with her sari, cowering and lumpish against the wall.

"You shouldn't have brought them here, *yaar*," says Masseur. "They shouldn't see such things. . . Besides, it's dangerous."

"We are with her. She's safe," says Ice-candy-man laconically. He adds: "I only wanted her to see the fires."

"I want to go home," I whimper.

"As soon as things quiet down I'll take you home," says Masseur reassuringly. He picks me up and swings me until I smile.

Ice-candy-man offers me another popsicle. I've eaten so many already that I feel sick. He gathers the empty tin plates strewn about us. The uneaten chapatti on Ayah's plate is stiff: the vegetable curry cold. Ice-candy-man removes the plate.

"Look!" shouts the butcher. "Shalmi's started to burn!"

We rush to the parapet. Tongues of pink flame lick two or three brick buildings in the bazaar. The flames are hard to spot: no match for the massive growth of brick and cement spreading on either side of the street.

"Just watch. You'll see a *tamasha!*" says Ice-candy-man. "Wait till the fire gets to their stock of arsenal."

As if on cue, a deafening series of explosions shakes the floor beneath our feet. Ayah stands up hastily and joins us at the parapet. The walls and balconies of a two-story building in the center of the bazaar bulge and bulge. Then the bricks start slowly tumbling, and the dark slab of roof caves into the exploding furnace . . .

People are pouring into the Shalmi lanes from their houses and shops. We hear the incredibly prompt clamor of a fire brigade. The clanking fire engine, crowded with ladders, hose and helmeted men, maneuvers itself through the street, the truck with the water tank following.

The men exchange surprised looks. Ice-candy-man says: "Where did those motherfuckers spring from?"

The firemen scamper busily, attaching hoses, shoving people back. Riding on the trucks they expertly direct their powerful hoses at the rest of the buildings on either side of the road.

As the fire brigade drives away, the entire row of buildings on both sides of the street ignite in an incredible conflagration. Although we are several furlongs away, a scorching blast from a hot wind makes our clothes flap as if in a storm. I look at Ice-candy-man. The astonishment on his features is replaced by a huge grin. His face, reflecting the fire, is lit up. "The fucking bastards!" he says, laughing aloud, spit flying from his mouth. "The fucking bastards! They sprayed the buildings with petrol! They must be Muslim."

The Hindus of Shalmi must have piled a lot of dynamite in their houses and shops to drive the Muslims from Mochi Gate. The entire Shalmi, an area covering about four square miles, flashes in explosions. The men and women on our roof are slapping each other's hands, laughing, hugging one another.

I stare at the *tamasha*, mesmerized by the spectacle. It is like a gigantic fireworks display in which stiff figures looking like spread-eagled stick-dolls leap into the air, black against the magenta furnace. Trapped by the spreading flames the panicked Hindus rush in droves from one end of the street to the other. Many disappear down the smoking lanes. Some collapse in the street. Charred limbs and burnt logs are falling from the sky.

The whole world is burning. The air on my face is so hot l think my flesh and clothes will catch fire. I start screaming, hysterically sobbing. Ayah moves away, her feet suddenly heavy and dragging, and sits on the roof slumped against the wall. She buries her face in her knees.

"What small hearts you have," says Ice-candy-man, beaming affectionately at us. "You must make your hearts stout!" He strikes his out-thrust chest with his fist. Turning to the men, he says: "The fucking bastards! They thought they'd drive us out of Bhatti! We've shown them!"

It is not safe to leave until late that evening. As the butcher drives us home in his cart, the moonlight settles like a layer of ashes over Lahore.

In a rush I collect the dolls long abandoned in bottom drawers and toy chest and climb stools to retrieve them from the dusty tops of old cupboards. I line them up against the wall, on my bed, and Adi, intrigued by my sudden interest in dolls, stands by quietly watching.

I can't remember a time when I ever played with dolls: though relatives and acquaintances have persisted in giving them to me. China, cloth and celluloid dolls variously stuffed, sized and colored. Black golliwogs, British baby dolls with pink complexions, Indian adult dolls covered in white cloth, their faces painted on.

147

I pick out a big, bloated celluloid doll. I turn it upside down and pull its legs apart. The elastic that holds them together stretches easily. I let one leg go and it snaps back, attaching itself to the brittle torso.

Adi moves closer. "What're you trying to do?" he enquires.

I examine the sari- and dhoti-clad Indian dolls. They are unreal, their exaggerated faces too obviously painted, their bodies too fragile. I select a large lifelike doll with a china face and blinking blue eyes and coarse black curls. It has a sturdy, well-stuffed cloth body and a substantial feel.

I hold it upside down and pull its pink legs apart. The knees and thighs bend unnaturally, but the stitching in the center stays intact.

I hold one leg out to Adi. "Here," I say, "pull it."

"Why?" asks Adi looking confused.

"Pull, damn it!" I scream, so close to hysteria that Adi blanches and hastily grabs the proffered leg. (He is one of the few people I know who is fair enough to blanch—or blush noticeably.) Adi and I pull the doll's legs, stretching it in a fierce tug-of-war, until making a wrenching sound it suddenly splits. We stagger off balance. The cloth skin is ripped right up to its armpits spilling chunks of grayish cotton and coiled brown coir and the innards that make its eyes blink and make it squawk "Ma-ma." I examine the doll's spilled insides and, holding them in my hands, collapse on the bed sobbing.

Adi crouches close to me. I can't bear the disillusioned and contemptuous look in his eyes.

"Why were you so cruel if you couldn't stand it?" he asks at last, infuriated by the pointless brutality.

How long does Lahore burn? Weeks? Months?

We climb to the roof of the Daulatrams' two-story house to watch. The Daulatrams flee.

The Shankars, too, go. The back portion of our house is untenanted. The Shankars' abandoned belongings are stored by Mother in empty servants' quarters. Gita, with her short fat plait and satin bows, and her steamy, bellowing mate, have disappeared.

Still we go to the Daulatrams' abandoned house to see Mozang Chawk burn. How long does Mozang Chawk burn . . . ?

Mozang Chawk burns for months . . . and months . . .

Despite its brick and mortar construction: despite its steel girders and the density of its terraces that run in an uneven high-low, broad-narrow continuity for miles on either side: despite the small bathrooms and godowns and corrugated tin shelters for charpoys deployed to sleep on the roof and its doors and wooden rafters—the buildings could not have burned for months. Despite the residue of passion and regret, and loss of those who have in panic fled—the fire could not have burned for . . . Despite all the ruptured dreams, broken lives, buried gold, bricked-in rupees, secreted jewelry, lingering hopes . . . the fire could not have burned for months and months . . .

But in my memory it is branded over an inordinate length of time: memory demands poetic license.

And the hellish fires of Lahore spawn monstrous mobs. These no more resemble the little processions of chanting urchins that Warris Road spawned—and that Adi and I shouted ourselves hoarse in—than the fires that fuse steel girders to mortar resemble the fires that Imam Din fans alive in our kitchen grates every morning.

Chapter 17

Playing British gods under the ceiling fans of the Faletti's Hotel—behind Queen Victoria's gardened skirt—the Radcliff Commission deals out Indian cities like a pack of cards. Lahore is dealt to Pakistan, Amritsar to India. Sialkot to Pakistan. Pathankot to India.

I am Pakistani. In a snap. Just like that.

A new nation is born. India has been divided after all. Did they dig the long, long canal Ayah mentioned? Although it is my birthday no one has time for me. My questions remained unanswered even by Ayah.

Mother makes a disappointing little fuss over me that lasts for about three minutes. She wishes me happy birthday and kisses me and instructs Imam Din to make sweet vermicelli with fried currants and almonds and hands Ayah a cup of milk afloat with rose petals to pour over my head before my bath.

Father hugs me, asks how old I am. I tell him I'm eight. (Yes, time has flown forward. It will fly back yet.)

"Good, good," says Father absentmindedly. He doesn't even say, "You're a big girl now," as he did last year. I hang around him feeling bored, while he sits on the commode absorbed in newsprint.

I go to the kitchen and announce my birthday. "So what?" says Adi, resuming his unseemly clamor for the sugar bowl. Imam Din and Yousaf say: "How nice. How nice. Greetings, Lenny baby." But they are preoccupied. Ayah hauls me off for a bath. I have to remind her to douse me with the milk-and-rose-petals.

It's the same at Godmother's. I get hugged and kissed, but insufficiently. Godmother is busy in the kitchen. She moves to and fro, looking like an upended whale in her white sari with her sloping shoulders and broadening torso and the sari narrowing round her ankles. She has the same noble bearing and alert, accommodating air of that intelligent mammal. As she moves to and fro, Godmother directs a nonstop stream of instruction and criticism at

Slavesister. Just so's to keep her on her toes and in fair working order. Besides, Godmother is in a hurry. Left to her own assessment of priorities and speed, Slavesister can bog down to a stop.

"Have you soaked the rice yet?" Godmother enquires. "After you've soaked it I want you to knead the chapatti dough. And I told you to tighten the cot strings yesterday . . . Did you? Well then, you may have the pleasure of sleeping on it tonight! Give yours to Manek! Will you hurry up? Half the day's gone," says Godmother, briskly putting Slavesister through her paces. "If you don't pick up your feet you'll cut off my nose! Manek will be at our door any minute! I hate to think what he'll tell Piloo about the disorder in this house . . . And I haven't even started preparing the halva for him."

Dr. Manek Mody is married to their middle sister, Piloo. Despite the loudspeaker in his throat, he is easygoing and genial and hardly the type to tattle to his wife about a disorderly house.

I am hurt. I thought the preparations for the sweet at least were on my account. I say so. "Aren't you making the halva for my birthday?"

"Of course," says Godmother preemptorily. "It's for you. Who else?"

"Of course," says Slavesister. Ever the opportunist, she adds, "But we mustn't be selfish, must we? It's for you, and to sweeten Manek Uncle's mouth in welcome and, don't forget, we have to celebrate the new arrival yet!"

Godmother and I look at her blankly. "Somebody has a baby I don't know of?" asks Godmother suspiciously.

"Have you forgotten already?" says Slavesister with reproof. "We've all produced a baby . . . We've given birth to a new nation. Pakistan!"

"You *are* silly," says Godmother crossly. But without the devastating artillery fire such an absurd way of putting things might be expected to provoke.

Godmother is a head taller than Slavesister. Standing on tiptoe she reaches for the semolina. "Where is the rose water?" she asks, peering into the top shelf. "And where is the sugar? Can't anything ever be in place?"

"Everything is in place . . . If you'd only bother to look, Rodabai."

"Is that so? The sugar and the rose water jumped last night? And, now, where's the tea? Where's the tea?"

"Under your nose. Right under your nose. If you'd only look properly!" says the worm, turning!

Godmother locates the box of tea literally under her nose. She doesn't say anything. I can't believe it.

I am so astonished my jaw hangs open (ever since, I've had trouble with my mandibular). Hung-jawed I go to Oldhusband, and standing before him in a daze, say, "It's my birthday."

Oldhusband emerges from his habitually sour-faced stupor and kisses my forehead. Like a somnambulist I receive from him a small packet wrapped in tissue paper.

I open the packet. It is an autograph book with colored pages, and it falls open on a yellow page with writing on it. I look at Oldhusband. He takes the book from my hand and reads aloud in resounding tones:

> "To my dear Lenny,
> 'The lives of great men all remind us
> How to make our lives sublime;
> And departing leave behind us
> Footsteps on the sands of time!' "

He must have been quite something when young! I am unutterably impressed! I've never seen him so animated.

"Will you leave your footsteps on the sands of time?" he asks.

I imagine a series of footsteps, obscured by litter, on the gray sand by the muddy Ravi. Ayah's, Masseur's and mine. I nod gravely, awed and overcome by the thunder of the words.

The only one who properly countenances my birthday is Cousin.

When Ayah takes me and Adi across the road from Godmother's to Electric-aunt's he comes galloping to the gate shouting,

"Happy birthday! Happy birthday!" And then, very seriously, like in films, he cautiously holds me by my shoulders and puckers his mouth. I read the intent in his eyes and, being theatrically inclined myself, I close my eyes and readily bunch my lips. I feel Cousin's wet, puckered mouth on my bunched-up lips. I know I'm supposed to feel a thrill, so, I muster up a little thrill.

The thrill comes and goes but Cousin's mouth remains in exactly the same position, exerting exactly the same pressure as at the moment of impact. The muscles of my mouth begin to ache. I open my eyes and discover Cousin's bewildered eyes gazing directly into mine. He doesn't know if he is doing it right. Or when to stop. The kissing scenes in the films go on much longer. But I can tell at that alarming proximity that the muscles in Cousin's jaws are trembling. My neck, too, is beginning to ache at that awkward angle. Kissing, I'm convinced, is overrated. Trust Cousin to enlighten me. When our mutual agony becomes unbearable, Ayah suddenly slaps Cousin hard on his back, thereby ungluing our stalemate, and scolds: "Oye! What is this badmashi? Shame on you!"

Cousin totters off balance and looks sheepish. And becomes defensive when Ayah casually spanks him again. I think she is repaying me for minding Ice-candy-man's toes.

Electric-aunt appears on her veranda and holding hands we gallop up to her, trailed unenthusiastically by Adi and good-naturedly by Ayah.

"What? No party?" says Electric-aunt, raising her scanty eyebrows and rubbing it in. She bares a white row of tiny teeth, as neatly packed and even as a goat's, in a bright smile.

Cousin looks at me pityingly: "We'll have one right here!" he volunteers gallantly.

While Ayah makes hard-boiled-egg sandwiches, Cousin tears Electric-aunt's cook away from the radio. They take off on their cycles to buy a cake and potato chips. Electric-aunt, compensating for her lack of charm with an abundance of energy and thrift, briskly opens a locked cupboard in her store and removes paper napkins, plates, party hats and streamers that have already served

Cousin's birthdays on two occasions. She counts out eight little candles from an economy-sized box of fifty.

Cousin returns with brown paper bags and a dented cardboard cake box. I blow out the candles and cut the squashed cake. And then we sit around the radio listening to the celebrations of the new Nation. Jinnah's voice, inaugurating the Constituent Assembly sessions on August 11, says: "You are free. You are free to go to your temples. You are free to go to your mosques or any other place of worship in the State of Pakistan. You may belong to any religion or caste or creed, that has nothing to do with the business of State . . . etc., etc., etc. *Pakistan Zindabad!*"

Chapter 18

Mr. Singh, long hair knotted on top of his head, on long hairy legs, in his yellow pajama-shorts and wearing his *kirpan*-dagger, carrying a hockey stick and trailed by his modest American wife and two sweaty and subdued children, comes up our drive just as the huge red sun rests on the top of the house opposite ours.

The family settles in wicker chairs on the veranda beneath the slowly squeaking ceiling fan. Mother, her young face grave and composed behind her tinted glasses, greets them with a stylish handshake—which Mr. Singh stands up to receive. Mother's touch ignites men. Mr. Singh's beard glows and his forehead turns incandescent.

Mr. Singh is obviously uncomfortable perched on the dainty wicker chair. He would prefer to sit cross-legged but manages to keep both dusty, slippered feet firmly on the floor. I signal to Rosy-Peter to come inside, but they shake their heads and sit listlessly on their chairs.

"The Mehtas have gone! The Malothras have gone! The Guptas have gone!" says Mr. Singh, coming straight out with what is uppermost in his mind. He is not a man for preliminary niceties.

"The Guptas too? When?" asks Mother, her voice throbbing with concern.

"About two hours back. They are joining an escorted convoy of cars."

Mother's eyes grow moist. Mrs. Singh discreetly wipes the tears that have rolled into the recently acquired indigo smudges beneath her eyes. Rosy gets up and, exposing her damp cotton knickers, which look absurd on her eight-year-old bottom, scrambles on to her mother's lap. Mrs. Singh smooths her daughter's hair.

Mr. Singh clears his throat. "I don't think there are any Hindu families left on Warris Road," he says.

"There aren't," Mother agrees.

"Just two Sikh families. The Pritam Singhs and us."

We hear a cycle rattle up the drive and the continuous peal of a cycle-bell as Father pedals slowly and laboriously into the portico. Smiling and nodding at our visitors, he parks the cycle on its stand next to the Morris and locks it. Father has reverted to going to work on his cycle, leaving the Morris for Mother.

Mr. Singh, noticeably relieved by Father's presence, shakes hands affably and Father, tucking his shirt into his flaring knee-length khaki shorts, sits down with a questioning countenance.

Alerted by the cycle-bell, Yousaf brings Father a frosted glass of water on a tray and takes away his khaki solar topi. There is silence as Father tips his head and drains the glass. He pushes back a short fringe of curls plastered to his forehead and removing his spectacles wipes the perspiration from the deep indentations on either side of his nose.

"Gurdaspur's gone to India," he remarks, settling into his chair and cleaning his glasses with a damp handkerchief.

"Yes! That's a surprise," says Mrs. Singh unexpectedly. The fact she has spoken out her thoughts indicates the measure of her inner turmoil. "I hear they had hoisted the green Pakistani flag and all. There's bound to be trouble," she says, making what is for her a remarkably pertinent statement.

Father nods significantly. He snaps his fingers to summon Yousaf, and turning his thumb down mutely indicates his wish for more water.

Now that Father is here, Mr. Singh spreads his thighs comfortably and, placing his hands on his knees, leans forward: "Sethi Sahib, we have just received orders from our leaders... We are to leave Lahore forever!"

Father raises surprised, questioning eyebrows and Mr. Singh continues: "I'm meeting them tonight. They've worked out plans for a complete Sikh evacuation. We'll form our own armed escort. I'll take our buffaloes... And whatever essentials we can pile into a truck. Each family is allotted a truck."

Father's sharp eyes grow severely comprehending and

sympathetic. He frowns and clears his throat. "Is there anything we can do?"

"Can you store a few things for us? Furniture and what we can't take?" says Mr. Singh. "You know, houses are being looted. Empty ones especially. They haven't come to the better neighborhoods yet, but who knows? I'll come back for them later. Things have to subside." Mr. Singh spreads his hands in a confused and helpless gesture.

"Sure," Father nods.

As always economical, Father makes the single word work on both counts: that he will be glad to store anything for Mr. Singh; and that things must subside.

"Of course!" says Mother warmly. "Bring anything! We'll keep it with the Shankars' things. You can leave it with us for as long as you want!"

Mr. Singh's and Father's eyes glisten in the dusk. The sun has disappeared. Mr. Singh hawks and directs his spit in a long arc into the portico, near some flowerpots with ferns. Father directs a commiserating gob of spit to nestle next to Mr. Singh's.

A sob escapes Mrs. Singh. Mother's mouth twitches and she sniffs. "Go and play outside! Or inside!" she says sternly to me, indicating Rosy and Peter with her quivering chin. She gets up to switch on the lights.

We go into the kitchen to Imam Din for chapatties with sugar and butter. Imam Din sprinkles a more generous helping of sugar than usual, and flapping his arms and crowing pretends to be a rooster to amuse Rosy-Peter. They are amused.

They follow me to the back of the house where I go looking for Ayah.

Things have become topsy-turvy. We've stopped going to the Queen's Garden altogether. We've also stopped going to the wrestler's restaurant. There is dissension in the ranks of Ayah's admirers. In twos and threes, or singly, they come instead to our house and sit with Ayah on the patch of lawn at the back or, as on this evening when Rosy-Peter and I join them, on the Shankars' neglected veranda. Ayah comes and goes, as duty or Mother calls, and the visitors talk among themselves. Butcher and the restaurant wrestler have ceased to visit.

Tonight, illuminated by the dusty yellow veranda light, we are grouped around a radio. Masseur is there. Also Hari, Sher Singh and the Government House gardener. Imam Din and Yousaf are still catering to the demands of my parents and their visitors. Adi is clinging to Ayah's back, rocking her to and fro and pulling strands of hair out of her bun. Rosy, Peter and I settle down on the brick floor to listen. The broadcast is fragmented by static.

"So! Gurdaspur's gone to India after all," says the zoo attendant, shaking his outsize, turbaned head.

"Shush!" says the Government House gardener, cupping his hand behind his hoary ear to listen better.

The radio announces through the crackling: "There have been reports of trouble in Gurdaspur. The situation is reported to be under control."

"Which means there is uncontrollable butchering going on in Gurdaspur," says the gardener flatly, reflecting the general opinion. "It is the Kali-*yuga*, no doubt about it," he says to a collective and resigned sigh of assent.

Masseur turns the radio off. Moti and his untouchable wife Muccho have silently joined the group. They sit on the veranda steps, just a little bit apart.

"If the worst comes to the worst, you can go to Gurdaspur— or to Amritsar," says Masseur to the Sikh youth.

"I'm not going anywhere," says Sher Singh, bristling. But he sounds more obstinate than determined.

"I said, if the worst comes to the worst," says Masseur mildly.

"Whoever must go, will go," says the Government House gardener, leaning forward laboriously to pick up his curly-toed slippers. He taps them on the floor to shake off the dried manure and picks off bits of grass adhering to the sides.

"*Aeeee!* You rascal!" groans Ayah, tugging her hair out of Adi's fists and tumbling him forward on her lap. "I'll teach you to be-

158

have, you badmash!" She grins and holds Adi struggling in the powerful vise of her thighs. Raising her arms she calmly plaits her hair.

We stir and stretch, preparing to break up for the evening. And just then, in the muted rustle, we hear the rattle of a bicycle hurtling up our drive at an alarming speed. We grow still, expectant. And emerging from the night like a blundering and scraggy bird, scraping his shoe on the veranda step to check the heedless velocity of his approach—Moti and Muccho scramble out of his way—Ice-candy-man comes to an abrupt and jolted halt. He is breathless, reeking of sweat and dust, and his frantic eyes rake the group. They rest for an instant on the Sikh, and flutter back to us. "A train from Gurdaspur has just come in," he announces, panting. "Everyone in it is dead. Butchered. They are all Muslim. There are no young women among the dead! Only two gunny-bags full of women's breasts!" Ice-candy-man's grip on the handlebars is so tight that his knuckles bulge whitely in the pale light. The kohl lining his eyes has spread, forming hollow, skull-like shadows: and as he raises his arm to wipe the perspiration crawling down his face, his glance once again flits over Sher Singh. "I was expecting relatives... For three days... For twelve hours each day... I waited for that train!"

What I've heard is unbearable. I don't want to believe it. For a grisly instant I see Mother's detached breasts: soft, pendulous, their beige nipples spreading. I shake my head to focus my distracted attention on Ice-candy-man. He appears to have grown shades darker, and his face is all dried up and shriveled-looking. I can see that beneath his shock he is grieving.

Instinctively I look at the zoo attendant. Sher Singh is staring at the popsicle man. His pupils are black and distended. His checked shirt is open at the throat, and his narrow pigeon-chest is going up and down, up and down, in the eerie veranda light.

A crowd has gathered in the narrow alley in front of the tobacco-*naswar* shop. If it is one thing I am, it's inquisitive. I slip

159

away from Ayah, and sliding between the thicket of legs ease my way into the center. I see the Pathan. Sharbat Khan has returned from the mountains!

I shout, *"Saalam ailekum, Khan Sahib!"* But busy pushing the pedal on his scraping and sparking machine he doesn't hear me. People are holding out to him their knives, choppers, daggers, axes, staves and scythes. And in the clamor, nose to the grindstone, Sharbat Khan sharpens one blunt edge after the other.

The crowd swells as more and more people get to know that Sharbat Khan is back. Children, sent by their mothers and grand-mothers, run up with an assortment of kitchen knives and meat cleavers and circle the crowd trying to squeeze in. Some are good-naturedly picked up and passed through, but for the most part the men appear nervous and so anxious to get their own implements sharpened that they threaten and abuse the children. They must have a lot of wood to chop. A lot of meat to cut. A lot of grass to mow with their scythes.

I spot Sher Singh. He is struggling towards Sharbat Khan with a tangled armload of daggers and swords. He has to be carrying the entire stock of his family's religious arsenal! He has a touchy, defensive look that I have noticed on his face of late. It makes me want to bring him into our house and ask everybody to be nice to him. Ayah, too, is very careful how she talks to him. He bristles even at her mildly flirtatious teasing. She handles him with the caution Sher Singh lavishes on the nervous little lion cubs in the zoo. He has taken us to see the cubs. It's all very well to see them romp and mew, but within a year they will roar their way into my nightmares and sink their fangs in me. Kittens are drowned. Why not them?

A hand suddenly grips my arm and yanks me out. It is Mas-seur's unerring hand. "What are you doing in this crowd?" he asks. "You could get hurt."

We spot Ayah. She appears panicked. And when she sees us she rushes up to me and picks me up and fusses over me as if I've been lost and found.

"It's all right," I say, wishing to reassure her, "I was only looking at Sharbat Khan."

"Oh," she says. "He's back?"

"Yes," I say, pointing at the crowd. "He's sharpening their knives."

That evening Sharbat Khan visits us, bringing Ayah almonds, pistachios and dried apricots tied in a square of red satin. "How long've you been back?" asks Ayah, undoing the knots in the bundle with her teeth and examining the contents with her fingers.

"Two days," he says, his voice honeyed with adoration. "I would've come earlier but there was such a rush of business. I never knew there were so many daggers and knives in Lahore!"

"If you'd waited much longer my presents would have rotted," says Ayah.

I am surprised. Ayah appears to have lost her sense of awe and excitement in Sharbat Khan's presence. She is not the least bit awkward. Instead of hiding her face and fidgeting with her sari she looks at him out of calm and bemused eyes.

Masseur, perfumed and primed, comes half an hour later. He is wearing a long creamy silk shirt over his heavy linen lungi and his moustache is oiled and gleaming. The men appraise each other with cautious suspicion as Masseur, hitching up his lungi, hunkers down on the floor.

"You've been away for quite some time," drawls Masseur, twirling the pointed tips of his moustache with a significance I miss. "Three months or so?"

"Yes," says Sharbat Khan, pensively smoothing the thick growth of hair, cropped like a rug, on his upper lip. "And you've been here all that time?"

"Obviously," says Masseur coolly.

They look as if each is a whiskered dog circling the other—weighing in and warning his foe.

Ayah, meanwhile, is cracking the almonds with her small strong teeth and chewing them with appreciative smacks. She offers the kernels to me and then to Masseur. Masseur smiles and shakes his head, no. He lifts his shirt and withdraws from a knot tied in his elegant lungi a small packet of prepared *paan*. He holds the betel leaf out to Ayah. Ayah looks at the succulent *paan*, plump with cardomom, and then at Masseur's mouth. Her face reflects an answer. And Sharbat Khan turns away his face, honorably conceding the round.

Enough is enough! They have stared at each other and secretly communicated until Ayah's mouth is red with *paan*, and I am fit to scream. Sharbat Khan carefully places the gold *kulla*—around which his turban is wrapped—on his head and stands up. Without a word he mounts his bicycle and wobbles away with his machine clattering dejectedly behind him.

His departure brings to mind the Chinaman. It occurs to me that I haven't seen him for a long time. "Where is he? Tell me. Tell me," I shout into Ayah's ears, and holding her by them, force her to turn to me.

"The Chinaman?" she asks absently. "Oh, he went away at the first smell of trouble," she says, with melodious indulgence for the cowardly Chinaman.

"What trouble?"

"This Pakistan-Hindustan business. . . "

"Where did he go?" I ask.

"Oh, I don't know," says Ayah. "Probably back to his China."

Masseur's been with Ayah practically all evening, yet there's no sign of Ice-candy-man. I wonder about it.

The next evening Masseur has Ayah all to himself. And the next. Still no sign of the popsicle vendor.

I am disturbed. So is Ayah. "Where is everybody?" she asks Masseur: meaning the Government House gardener, the wrestler, the butcher, the zoo attendant, Ice-candy-man and the rest of the gang. Even Yousaf and Imam Din appear to have become less visible.

Chapter 19

Papoo and I are helping Hari bathe the buffalo in the afternoon when Adi walks up in the slush and, maneuvering himself between me and the buffalo, stands absolutely, intensely still. As if this alone is not enough to rivet my attention, he murmurs in my ear: "Follow me!"

He turns and casually walks away. I can tell he is wild with excitement and has exercised all his self-control not to break into a run. I'd follow him to the ends of the earth to discover the cause of his excitement.

When we are outside the Shankars' empty rooms, he turns to me his shining eyes. He has no right to look like this . . . As if lit up from within. Regardless—I'd follow him to the ends of the earth.

"What is it?" I whisper in a frenzy.

"The black box is back in the bathroom."

It is a rare occasion: Adi-made-of-mercury standing still, and confiding in me.

Not only is the black box back, says Adi, but he also knows what's in it.

"What? What? Tell me," I plead.

But Adi, like a cat playing with the poor tail-less mousey, says: "See for yourself."

I tiptoe up the bathroom steps and approach the long box. It is as sinister as ever. I take Adi's word for it that it is open but I dare not lift the lid. I have no wish to be scared out of my wits: What if it's a grinning, skeletal corpse?

Adi puts a cautioning finger on his lips and lifts the lid. Nestled in scarlet velvet, in a depression specially carved for it, like a dark jewel in its setting, is an enormous double-barreled gun. I feel its smooth barrels and its polished wood.

No wonder we couldn't carry the box. The gun is heavy.

Between us we carry the gun, Adi cautiously leading at the barrel end, and me at the other. Nervous that we might be discovered, or that the gun might fire its double barrels into Adi's behind, we at last reach the gate.

Adi takes first turn. I help him stand up the gun and he looks like a diminutive Gurkha with a cannon.

I don't know how long we take turns holding the gun. An hour—perhaps two. We hear the ubiquitous chanting of the mobs in the distance: *"Allah-o-Akbar!"* comes the fragmented roar from the Muslim *goondas* of Mozang. *"Bole so nehal: Sat siri akal!"* from the Sikh *goondas* of Beadon Road. Standing at attention with the gun I feel ready to face any mob.

There is little traffic; a few tongas, half a dozen cyclists. A group of prisoners, the chains along their arms and legs clanking, eye the gun speculatively and the policeman shepherding them prudently crosses the road. No one talks to us. The presence of the dual barrels is intimidating.

Luckily it's not my turn when Father cycles up and comes to a grim halt in front of Adi. Not loquacious at his calmest, Father is rendered speechless. He glares at Adi. "Put it back at once!" he says at last. He slaps Adi for the first time in his life.

Pushing the cycle with one hand Father comes to me and thumps my back. As thumps go it is a half-hearted thump—unlike Mother's whole-hearted whacks that cause us to stagger clear across rooms—but no beating of Mother's ever hurt so much.

After dinner Father sits us on his lap and explains: "Your lives weren't worth two pice when you showed off with that gun."

The black box again disappears.

Ice-candy-man visits at last. Once again we are gathered on the Shankars' abandoned veranda. I cannot believe the change in him. Gone is the darkly grieving look that had affected me so deeply the evening he emerged from the night and almost crashed into us with the grim news of the trainload of dead Muslims.

Ice-candy-man has acquired an unpleasant swagger and a strange way of looking at Hari and Moti. He is full of bravado—and still full of stories. "You remember Kirpa Ram? That skinflint we all owe money?" he asks, barely bothering to greet anyone as he settles among us, chomping on a *paan*. His mouth, slimy and crimson with betel juice, bloated—as if he's become accustomed to indulging himself.

"That money-lender would squeeze blood from a fly!" he says, bending over to spit betel juice into a flowerpot holding a delicate tracery of ferns. "Well," he continues, "Kirpa Ram's packed his family off to Delhi. But can he bear to part from those of us he's been fattening on? No! So, he stays. He thinks he's that brave!" Ice-candy-man's mouth curls in a contemptuous sneer. "But the instant we entered his house I saw his fat dhotied tail slip out of the back door! Ramzana the butcher noticed a damp patch on one of the walls. It had been hastily whitewashed. He scraped the cement and removed a brick. What d'you think he found? Pouches with nine hundred guineas sewn into them! Nine hundred golden guineas!"

Ice-candy-man studies us, moving his swaggering eyes triumphantly from face to face.

Ayah, the Government House gardener, Hari and Moti stare back with set, expressionless faces. Masseur frowns. Yousaf scowls at the naked veranda bulb. Imam Din gets up, leaning heavily on the Government House gardener, and invoking Allah's mercy and blessings and sighing, heads for the kitchen.

"Show me your hand," says Ice-candy-man to Ayah.

Ayah, surprised into thinking he wants to read her future, opens her plump palm and shows it to Ice-candy-man. I also think he is initiating seduction through palmistry. Instead he places a gold coin in her hand. Ayah studies it minutely and bites it to test the gold.

It is bitten and passed from hand to hand and on to me. I examine Queen Victoria's embossed profile with fascination. Despite the difference in the metals it is the same profile she displays in her statue.

Ayah returns the coin to Ice-candy-man.

"Keep it. It's for you," he says grandly, folding her fingers over it.

"No," she says, shaking her head and hiding her hands behind her back.

She's like me. There are some things she will not hold.

"But I brought it specially for you! Please accept it," pleads Ice-candy-man, for the first time sounding like his old ingratiating self.

Ayah averts her face. "Where's Sher Singh?" she suddenly asks. As if the zoo attendant is somewhere he ought not to be.

There is no reply.

"He's left Lahore, I think," says Yousaf at last, glancing at Ice-candy-man.

Ice-candy-man makes a harsh, crude sound. "There's natural justice for you!" he says, spitting the red juice into the ferns again. "You remember how he got rid of his Muslim tenants? Well, the tenants had their own back! Exposed themselves to his womenfolk! They went a bit further. . . played with one of Sher Singh's sisters. . . Nothing serious—but her husband turned ugly. . . He was killed in the scuffle," says Ice-candy-man casually. "Well, they had to leave Lahore sooner or later. . . After what one hears of Sikh atrocities it's better they left sooner! The refugees are clamoring for revenge!"

"Were you among the men who exposed themselves?" asks the Government House gardener. His tone implies more a mild assertion than a question.

"What's it to you, oye?" says Ice-candy-man, raising his voice and flaring into an insolent display of wrath. "If you must know, I was! I'll tell you to your face—I lose my senses when I think of the mutilated bodies on that train from Gurdaspur. . . that night I went mad, I tell you! I lobbed grenades through the windows of Hindus and Sikhs I'd known all my life! I hated their guts. . . I want to kill someone for each of the breasts they cut off the Muslim women. . . The penises!"

In the silence that follows, the gardener clears his throat. "You're right, brother," he says. I feel he cannot meet Ice-candy-

166

man's eyes. He is looking so deliberately at the floor that it appears as if he is hanging his head. "There are some things a man cannot look upon without going mad. It's the mischief of Satan... Evil will spawn evil... God preserve us." His voice is gruff with the burden of disillusion and loss. "I've sent my family to Delhi. As soon as the *Sarkar* permits I will join them." The gardener turns his weary gaze upon Hari. "Have you made plans to go, brother?" he asks.

"Where to?" says Hari, shaking his head and wiping his eyes with his arm. "I'll ride the storm out. I've nowhere to go."

"You'll find someplace to go," says the Government House gardener. "When our friends confess they want to kill us, we have to go..." He makes no move to wipe the tears running in little rills through his gray stubble and dripping from his chin. The red rims of his eyes are blurred and soggy and blend into the soft flesh as if he has become addicted to weeping.

Moti and Papoo are sitting bowed and subdued on the veranda steps. "What about you two?" Masseur asks. "Are you leaving?"

After a pause, during which we hear Moti's knuckles crack as he presses his fingers against his palm, speaking hesitantly and so low that I can barely hear him, he says, "I talked to the padre at the Cantonment Mission... We're becoming Christian."

Ice-candy-man, appearing restless, nods casually. "Quite a few of your people are converting," he says. "You'd better change your name, too, while you're at it."

The longer I observe Ice-candy-man the more I notice the change wrought in him. He seems to have lost his lithe, catlike movements. And he appears to have put on weight. Perhaps it's just the air of consequence on him that makes him appear more substantial.

"The Faletti's Hotel cook has also run away with his tail between his legs!" he informs us, unasked. And once again he appears bloated with triumph... and a horrid irrepressible gloating.

It is very late. The frogs are croaking again. We might have some rain yet. Except for Masseur, everyone has gone. We move to the patch of grass near the servants' quarters. There is a full moon out but it is pitch dark where we sit under a mulberry tree. There is no breeze. And except for the occasional rustle in the leaves caused by a restless bird, or the indiscernible movement of a frog, the night is still.

Ayah is crying softly. "I must get out of here," she says, sniffing and wiping her nose on her sari-blouse sleeve. "I have relatives in Amritsar I can go to."

"You don't need to go anywhere," says Masseur, so assuredly possessive that I feel a stab of jealousy. "Why do you worry? I'm here. No one will touch a hair on your head. I don't know why you don't marry me!" he says, sighing persuasively. "You know I worship you . . ."

"I'm already yours," says Ayah with disturbing submission. "I will always be yours."

"Don't you dare marry him!" I cry. "You'll leave me . . . Don't leave me," I beg, kicking Masseur.

"Silly girl! I won't leave you . . . And if I have to, you'll find another ayah who will love you just as much."

"I don't want another ayah . . . I will never let another ayah touch me!"

I start sobbing. I kiss Ayah wherever Masseur is not touching her in the dark.

Chapter 20

Rosy-Peter have gone. The Government House gardener has gone...

And the gramophones and speakers mounted on tongas and lorries scratchily, endlessly pouring out the melody of Nur Jehan's popular film song that is now so strangely apt:

> *Mere bachpan ke sathi mujhe bhool na jana—*
> *Dekho, dekho hense na zamana, hanse na zamana.*
> Friends from our childhood, don't forget us—
> See that a changed world does not mock us.

Instead, wave upon scruffy wave of Muslim refugees flood Lahore—and the Punjab west of Lahore. Within three months seven million Muslims and five million Hindus and Sikhs are uprooted in the largest and most terrible exchange of population known to history. The Punjab has been divided by the icy card-sharks dealing out the land village by village, city by city, wheeling and dealing and doling out favors.

For now the tide is turned—and the Hindus are being favored over the Muslims by the remnants of the Raj. Now that its objective to divide India is achieved, the British favor Nehru over Jinnah. Nehru is Kashmiri; they grant him Kashmir. Spurning logic, defying rationale, ignoring the consequence of bequeathing a Muslim state to the Hindus, while Jinnah futilely protests: "Statesmen cannot eat their words!"

Statesmen do.

They grant Nehru Gurdaspur and Pathankot, without which Muslim Kashmir cannot be secured.

Nehru wears red carnations in the buttonholes of his ivory jackets. He bandies words with Lady Mountbatten and is presumed to be her lover. He is charming, too, to Lord Mountbatten. Suave,

Cambridge-polished, he carries about him an aura of power and a presence that flatters anyone he compliments tenfold. He doles out promises, smiles, kisses-on-cheeks. He is in the prime of his Brahmin manhood. He is handsome: his cheeks glow pink.

Jinnah is incapable of compliments. Austere, driven, pukka-sahib accented, deathly ill: incapable of cheek-kissing. Instead of carnations he wears a karakuli cap, somber with tight, gray lamb's-wool curls: and instead of pale jackets, black *achkan* coats. He is past the prime of his elegant manhood. Sallow, whip-thin, sharp-tongued, uncompromising. His training at the Old Bailey and practice in English courtrooms has given him faith in constitutional means, and he puts his misplaced hopes into tall standards of upright justice. The fading Empire sacrifices his cause to their shifting allegiances.

Mother shows me a photograph: "She is Jinnah's wife," she says. "She's Parsee."

The woman in the photograph is astonishingly beautiful. Large eyes, liquid-brown, radiating youth, promising intelligence, declaring innocence, shining from an oval marble-firm face. Full-lipped, delighting in the knowledge of her own loveliness: confident in the knowledge of her generous impulses. Giving—like Ayah. Daring—like Mother. "Plucky!" Mother says.

For the lady in the photograph is daring: an Indian woman baring her handsome shoulders in a strapless gown in an era when such unclothing was considered reprehensible. Defying, at eighteen, her wealthy knighted father, braving the disapproval of their rigid community, excommunicated, she marries a Muslim lawyer twenty-two years older than her. Jinnah was brilliant, elegantly handsome: he had to be to marry such a raving beauty. And cold, too, he had to be—to win such a generous heart.

"Where is she?" I ask Mother.

Mother's eyes turn inwards. Her lips give a twitch: "She died at twenty-nine. Her heart was broken..."

Her daring to no account. Her defiance humbled. Her energy

extinguished. Only her image in the photograph and her innocence—remain intact.

But didn't Jinnah, too, die of a broken heart? And today, forty years later, in films of Gandhi's and Mountbatten's lives, in books by British and Indian scholars, Jinnah, who for a decade was known as "Ambassador of Hindu-Muslim Unity," is caricatured, and portrayed as a monster. The man about whom India's poetess Naidu Sarojini wrote:

> . . . the calm hauteur of his accustomed reserve masks, for those who know him, a naive and eager humanity, an intuition quick and tender as a woman's, a humor gay and winning as a child's—pre-eminently rational and practical, discreet and dispassionate in his estimate and acceptance of life, the obvious sanity and serenity of his worldly wisdom effectually disguise a shy and splendid idealism which is of the very essence of the man.

Chapter 21

Hari has had his *bodhi* shaved. He has become a Muslim.

He has also had his penis circumcised. "By a barber," says Cousin, unbuttoning his fly in Electric-aunt's sitting room. Treating me to a view of his uncircumcised penis, he stretches his foreskin back to show me how Hari's circumcised penis must look.

I recall Hari's dark genitals, partially obscured by the dust and dusk and crumpled with fear as he stood in the circle of his tormentors. My imagination presents unbearable images. I shake my head to dispel them and revert my attention to Cousin's exposed flesh.

His genitals have grown since I last examined them three years ago—after he'd had his hernia operation. The penis is longer and thicker and gracefully arched—and it seems to be breathing.

"Feel it," offers Cousin.

I like its feel. It is warm and cuddly. As I squeeze the pliant flesh it strengthens and grows in my hand.

"Hey!" I say. "What's this!"

Cousin has a funny look in his eyes that I don't trust.

"I have become a honeycomb," he says. "Lick me, here, and see what happens."

I lick the tip gingerly. Nothing. No honey.

"You've got to suck out the honey." Cousin arches his back and maneuvers his penis to my mouth.

"Suck it yourself!" I say, standing up.

"I can't," says Cousin.

I see the absurdity of my suggestion. I shrug away.

I like Cousin. I've even thought of marrying him when we grow up, but this is a side of him I'm becoming aware of for the first time, and I don't like it.

"All right, I'll show you anyway," says Cousin in a conciliatory voice. "Just look: I'll show you something."

Cousin pumps and pumps his penis and it becomes all red and I think he will tear himself, and I say, "Stop it! You'll bleed," but he pumps and pumps and I begin to cry.

Cousin, too, is close to crying. He mopes around for the rest of the afternoon with his fly looking stuffed. I haven't been able to keep my eyes off flies since, intrigued by the fleshy machinery.

Hari has adapted his name to his new faith: he wants us to call him Himat Ali. He has also changed his dhoti for the substantial gathers of the drawstring shalwar.

I spend the night after my birthday at Godmother's. Late in the evening her room resembles the barracks dormitory we peep into from the servants' quarters roof. Five cots are laid out at all angles and there is hardly any space to walk.

I lie on my cot, between Godmother and Dr. Manek Mody. Oldhusband is already snoring gently from the direction of our feet. Only the kitchen light is on and Slavesister is softly laying out the cups and saucers for the morning's tea.

"Hurry up and go to sleep, Lenny," says Dr. Mody, so gleefully that I become suspicious and ask, "Why?"

"Because I want to pounce on your Roda Aunty and eat her up. I'm hungry."

There he goes again.

Godmother is silent. I reach out my hand and tap the wooden frame of her charpoy in the dark and she holds my hand tight.

Dr. Mody makes a "slurp-slurp" sound and rubs his hands together in the dark.

"Don't be silly. You can't eat people," I say.

"Go to sleep, can't you?" he says, ignoring my comment. "Now, where do I start?... Roast leg of Aunty or barbecued ribs? Of course! I'll make a nice jelly from her trotters! Seasoned with cinnamon and orange juice—slurp-slurp. Just like Imam Din's jelly."

Imam Din makes a delicious jelly—but out of sheep's trotters.

Dr. Mody's cot creaks as he sits up, and I see his pajama-suited silhouette and bald head shining menacingly in the faint light from the kitchen. I spring out of bed and wrap my limbs about God-mother. She lies within my small arms and legs like a trusting and tremulous whale in her white garments. "If you touch her, I will kill you!" I scream. "I have a double-barreled gun!"

"I think I will start with crumbed chops à la Roda," says the doctor undeterred.

The light is blocked briefly as Slavesister comes through the door, carefully balancing a saucer of hot tea for Godmother. She notices the seated doctor and asks, "Can I get you a nightcap?"

"Yes, please. I'd love a hot cup of blood à la Roda: with salt and pepper."

I have a brilliant idea. "You can have Mini Aunty. She is fat-ter."

"Thank you very much!" says Mini Aunty.

"I don't want Mini. I'm in the mood for a tough old thing I can chew on."

"You're a ghoul!" I screech sternly.

"Oh, no. I'm only a vampire."

"Now, now. No more of that," intervenes Slavesister. "Someone will have nightmares... And then someone might wet her bed."

"Someone will not wet her bed!" I say firmly, using the tone Godmother uses to squash her.

"Never mind your cheek. Get back to your charpoy. You should be fast asleep," says Slavesister, completely unabashed, and patiently holding out Godmother's saucer of hot tea.

"Chi, chi, chi! She wets her bed?" says Dr. Mody, holding his nose. "Chi, chi, chi! Don't sleep next to me."

"She does not wet the bed," says Godmother, rising gallantly to the occasion—and to take her saucer of tea.

"You wouldn't know. You don't wash the sheets," says Slavesister recklessly. She's probably counting on the inch Godmother allowed her when, bemused by the events of that historic day, she let Slavesister get away with insubordination on my birthday. But her lucky break has gone the way of all such breaks and Godmother, rearing up on her pillows, retaliates: "Don't think I've not been observing your tongue of late! If you're not careful, I'll snip it off! Then you'll probably learn not to be rude in front of guests. I hate to think what Manek will tell our middle sister about your behavior before your elders!"

"Really, Rodabai! How long will you treat me like a child?"

"Till you grow up! God knows, you've grown older and fatter—but not up! This child here has more sense than you. Now stop eating our heads. Say your prayers and go to sleep."

Slavesister retreats to the kitchen and commences mumbling.

Dr. Manek Mody represses his cannibalistic prowling and lies down quietly.

It's lovely to have someone fight your battles for you. Specially when you're little. I adore Godmother. I latch on to her tighter, and kiss her rough khaddar nightgown. The pantry light goes out. Slavesister gropes her way to her sagging charpoy and continues her mumbles in the vicinity of our heads.

"Um! Um!" warns Godmother.

The mumbles stop.

I know Dr. Mody is only teasing. After all, I'm eight!

When will they stop treating me like a baby? And I'm fed up of being called Lenny baby, Lenny baby, Lenny baby . . .

When Godmother comes out of her bath the next morning, clattering into the kitchen on wooden thongs, her dolphin shape wrapped in only her sari, one shoulder bare, hair dripping—all dewy and fresh—she looks like a dainty young thing. As if the water has whittled away her age.

By the time Slavesister emerges from her bath, looking like melting tallow and oozing moisture from powdered pores, Godmother has put on her bodice and blouse and velvet slippers and pumped alive the hissing Primus stove. She appears accepting of life. Conscious of her irrepressibly youthful spirit—raring to go.

"What took you so long in the bath?" she says, getting the day off to a flying start. "You know Manek has to go out early. You know there's so much to be done—the boys are coming in the evening—and you retire to splash from the bucket like Cleopatra!"

Slavesister is too sedated from her bath to react. Oozing moisture, she moves about gathering the ingredients for the omelettes and begins chopping the onions and green peppers.

Dr. Mody, anxious not to miss the chatter, bursts into the kitchen in his striped pajamas. And as if his loud voice were not enough, he claps hands to gain attention: "Where's breakfast? Where's breakfast? I'm so hungry I could eat Rodabai! Such a pity Lenny's here . . . ," he says, grinning from ear to ear—and nicely fanning banked fires.

"If Bathing Beauty didn't take hours wallowing in her bath like Cleopatra, you'd have breakfast! Come on. Come on. Move your fingers!"

"Yes, Mini! Move it. Move it," says the doctor, putting his short arms round Slavesister's heavy shoulders and hugging her affectionately.

"Mind you don't cut yourself," cautions Godmother.

"It's not the first time I'm using a knife, Rodabai," says Aunt Mini reasonably.

"I said 'mind.' I have enough worries without your adding to them!"

"Yes, yes! Mind you don't chop off your fat little fingers," says Dr. Manek Mody, echoing Godmother.

"Now, don't you go joining hands with her," says Mini Aunty.

"Her? Her?" asks Godmother, looking confusedly at her brother-in-law and at me. "Who's her? Where's her?"

Slavesister chops the tomatoes silently.

"Yes? Who's her?" asks her brother-in-law.

Oldhusband emerges from the bathroom. He is, as always, dry and brittle, and irritated.

"His Sourship's had his bath. Manek, you'd better take your turn before Cleopatra decides to settle down to her business on the commode."

"Really, Rodabai...I hate to say it, but you really are going too far," says Slavesister.

"Oh? Where to? Where am I going?"

"Don't make me say something you'll regret..."

"Come on. Out with it! I'd like to know where I'm going... and where I stand!"

"Yes. Out with it! Where are you packing my Rodabai off to?"

"Manek, you'd be wise to keep out of this," says Slavesister solemnly. "Don't aggravate the situation...It's bad enough without your encouraging her."

"Is that so?" Godmother is in good form. "May I ask who you are to tell Manek not to meddle? Are you somebody? Queen Cleopatra of Jail Road, perhaps?"

"You know! I'm nothing...nobody..."

"Then who does your Nobodyship think she is ordering about? You meddle all you want, Manek! You are married to our sister. You have every right to encourage whom you wish to in this house!" Godmother turns to face her stoic kid sister. "And he's only asking what I wish to know! How far, exactly, am I going?"

"I hate to say it...but, you are becoming...vulgar!"

"Oh? Is that so? And what do you think you are becoming... when you loll on the commode all morning spreading perfumes?"

"Chi, chi, chi!" says Dr. Mody, holding his fleshy nose.

"I'll chop off your nose, you *chi-chi-chiwalla!*" says Mini Aunty. She often acts the spoilt sis-in-law with him.

"No wonder Mrs. Pen asked the other morning if the garbage cart had been to us. No wonder! I feel so embarrassed...," says Godmother batting her eyes.

"If it's constipation, I can help her out," says the professional medicine-man.

"Is that what it is?" asks Godmother, all intelligent and alert and concerned. "Is she constipated, do you think? Could you prescribe her a strong purgative?"

"I can give her a horse's dose, if you wish."

"So good of you, Manek," says Godmother. "People will stop

taking us for the neighborhood manure dump."

Slavesister wipes her face on her sleeve. Her lips are moist and flattened: they appear to be moving.

"Are you muttering?" demands Godmother. "Kindly permit us to share your mutters."

"No . . . it's just the onions . . . ," Slavesister manages to say. "The omelette *masala* is ready. Where do you want me to make the omelette?"

Slavesister has wisely elected to sound docile and matter-of-fact.

Oldhusband shuffles out of the kitchen and settles with his prayerbook in the bentwood chair. The white stubble on his cheeks quivers as he silently mumbles his prayers.

Godmother has invited four students from the King Edward Medical College dorms to tea. Their parents, who have at some point in time known either Godmother or one of her kin, have requested her to keep an occasional eye on them.

Godmother invites them whenever her brother-in-law visits Lahore. She feels it is good for the fledglings to be in the company of a full-fledged doctor. Though, as far as I can tell, they diligently compete in setting each other a bad example.

Only two students, Yakoob from Peshawar and Charles Chaudhry, an Indian Christian from Multan, show up that evening.

"Prakash and his family have migrated to Delhi," says Yakoob, explaining the absence of the Hindu boy.

We are sitting in the drive in a rough circle; Godmother in her easy chair and I on her lap.

"Roshan Singh left for Amritsar only last Monday," says Yakoob, explaining the absence of the Sikh student. "Some *goondas* from Bhatti were after his sisters. We escorted them, and the whole family, to a convoy."

Slavesister, sitting on her low stool with her podgy knees spread beneath her sari, clucks mournfully and shakes her head.

"It's to be expected, I suppose," says Godmother, sighing.

"Pretty girls?" enquires Dr. Manek Mody. "Sikh girls have beautiful eyes," he states, airing his eye fetish.

"Oh yes!" says Charles Chaudhry with bated breath. "Light eyes. Hazel. Greenish. . . You can get lost in them, man!"

Ayah helps Mini Aunty serve tea.

"Your a-y-a-h has the most enormous eyes I've ever seen," says the doctor to me in English. "Gorgeous! Ravishing!"

People spell out the letters thinking Ayah will not understand the alphabet. This occurs so frequently that she'd have to be a real nitwit not to catch on.

Ayah, aware she is the star attraction, rolls and slides her thickly fringed eyes to glamorous effect as she passes the tea. She goes in and fetches a plate of almond fudge and sweet lentil *ladoos*.

"Look out! There's a fly on the *ladoos*," says Dr. Mody.

Being a doctor he is more agitated by the fly's presence than we are.

"Are you bothered by such a little fly?" says Ayah, peeking at the bald doctor from the corners of her teasing eyes. "Let it be: it will hardly eat anything."

Dr. Mody looks at her, surprised: too taken aback to comment.

Then he springs out of his chair and flutters his small hand over the *ladoos*, saying: "Shoo, shoo!" The disturbed fly lifts sluggishly and the doctor, in a swift brown movement, catches it in his fist. He puffs up and surveys us as if he's caught a lion.

"Well done!" says Mini Aunty: ever the sycophant.

"Why don't you eat it," I tell him. "You're always hungry!"

Dr. Mody slaughters the fly with a loud clap. "No, I'll save it for you," he says, stepping up to me and shoving his hand with the dead fly towards my mouth.

I scream and bury my face in Godmother's blouse. She fends him off with one hand and holds me protectively with the other. I feel her movements as she chuckles and flays.

Dr. Mody sits down laughing; and when I turn to look at him he makes a straight face and pretends to eat the fly.

"You're a pig!" I say.

But once launched, Dr. Mody cannot be distracted long from his fetish. He peers at me acutely: "Why do you have such an unfortunate pair of eyes?" he enquires. "You're a bit cross-eyed, aren't you?"

"No. I'm not!" I protest loudly.

"Not cross-eyed," says Slavesister, and treacherously adds, "She only squints."

"No!' I shout. "I don't!"

"Don't shout," says my traitorous aunt, covering her ears. "We're not deaf."

"I don't understand it," says the spiteful cannibal. "Your mother has such sweet chinky little eyes—such a pity her daughter's eyes are like this." He crosses his index fingers.

I ignore him.

"What about your Rosy-Peter's American mother? How is she?" the doctor suddenly asks. It's hard to keep track of his abrupt shifts in conversation.

"They left long ago," I say. Caught off guard, I'm civil.

"Another set of green eyes gone!" laments the doctor, sadly shaking his head. "I'd follow them to the ends of the earth!"

If one keeps his single track in mind the doctor is not so hard to follow after all. The woolly, ruminative silence that succeeds the doctor's soulful sighs is abruptly shattered by Oldhusband.

"What's all this business about eyes! eyes! eyes!" he explodes. "You can't poke the damn thing into their eyes!"

Slavesister gasps, shocked out of her hostess smile. The boys titter sheepishly. Dr. Manek Mody looks completely confounded.

I have never seen Oldhusband so awesome—not even when he thundered Longfellow at me.

"He's quite right!" says Godmother, standing by her matter-of-fact spouse.

Oldhusband has been hauled through the book, zombielike, in his cane-bottomed chair, white-stubbled, unprepossessing. . . He has been dragged, disgruntled, from the earliest pages to sit mute on the drive with Godmother and Slavesister while they chatter and fight and clap hands and sing: "Lame Lenny! Three for a penny!" He has been compelled to snore at our feet—and to spout verse and shuffle his feet. All so that he may in the end confound the carnivorous doctor with his testy outburst!

Now that he's had his say, he can peaceably pass away...

Of course, I only appreciated what Oldhusband had said years later.

Chapter 22

Mother develops a busy air of secrecy and preoccupation that makes her even more remote. She shoots off in the Morris, after Father drudges off on his bicycle; and returns late in the afternoon—and scoots out again. Electric-aunt often accompanies her, her thin lips compressed in determined silence, her efficient eyes concentrated on inward thoughts.

Our bewildered faces again grow pale as we ponder their absences. We eat less. We are fretful.

They aren't the least bothered.

"What can they be up to?" wonders Cousin on a warm April afternoon, lying face down on the cool living-room floor of the Singhs' empty rooms.

"Why don't they take us?" I say, hurt at being deprived of drives while my mother and my aunt gallivant God knows where.

"I know where they go. I know everything," says Adi, with a transparence that convinces us he knows absolutely nothing.

Ayah, almost as mystified as us, volunteers an intriguing bit of information. "Get a look in the car's dicky sometime."

"Why?" I demand, surprised.

"Because it is full of petrol cans!" she confides. And on this dramatic note attempts to slip away.

But Cousin grabs the end of her sari. And I jump up to block her exit. And as she tries to escape, the sari unravels. Giggling, turning giddily on the balls of her feet like a gaudy top, she wraps herself back in and bounces down among us. *"Toba, toba!"* she says, and touching the tips of her ears in quick succession saying, "I've never seen such badmash children! Who's going to iron your mother's sari? You?"

Mother and Father are going out to dinner later. Four hours

later! The sari can wait. Matters of more moment—like the dickyful of petrol—have to be considered first.

The car dicky is always locked. I accept Ayah's statement on faith, but cousin is suspicious. "How do you know about the petrol?" he asks, permitting mistrust to shade his voice.

"I know!" says Ayah, buttoning up.

Cousin can be silly sometimes. Here we are, on the brink of a revelation, and he insults Ayah.

"If Ayah says there is petrol in the car's dicky, there is petrol in the car's dicky!" I say.

Adi holds Ayah by her ears and, shaking her head like a coconut, says: "Come on, tell more. Please, please!"

"We won't tell anybody. I swear!" I say. And to establish faith, . pinch the skin on my throat.

"I swear I won't either! You know you can trust me," says my mistrustful cousin, adequately humbled and at his most adult and charming. He too pinches the skin on his Adam's apple, and on his knees moves closer to Ayah.

Ayah turns her head this way and that and rolls her eyes about the room. Cousin quickly gets up and peers into the other uninhabited rooms of the annex to make sure there are no eaves-droppers.

When Cousin returns, Ayah says: "If your mothers get to know I told you this...Hare Krishna! They'll kill me!"

Again we take an oath of silence, and further reassure her by our solemn faces.

"Look into the godown next to my quarters sometime," she says. "It's full of gallons and gallons of petrol!"

We are stupefied. Petrol is rationed. It is an offense to store it.

"Your mother brings the cans in the car," she says, guiltily removing her eyes from mine, "and takes them out again! I help her carry them in... and I help her carry them out!"

"Doesn't anyone else know about it?" enquires my stupefied, mystified and circumspect cousin.

"Only your mothers," says Ayah. "We do the loading and the

unloading when everyone's asleep. We cover the cans with sheets and tablecloths."

I am so shocked that my jaw drops. I look at Adi and Cousin. They, too, have been struck by similar thoughts. Their eyes are crossed in dismay and their jaws, too, are unhinged.

"What are you gaping like that for? Close your mouths!" says Ayah sharply—looking bewildered—sensing that we are incriminating our mothers. "If they do something we don't understand, they have a good reason for it!"

I'm astonished she has not caught on. We clam our mouths shut.

We now know who the arsonists are. Our mothers are setting fire to Lahore!

Back and forth, back and forth, go our mothers on their secret missions, carrying their sinister freight in the dicky of our Morris Minor. And the more they absent themselves, the higher rise the flames in the walled city, and all over Lahore—and the quicker they return, the closer swirl the angry billows of sooty smoke.

And by our silence we commit ourselves to complicity. We're sure Father knows. Why else would he leave the Morris for Mother?

My heart pounds at the damnation that awaits their souls. My knees quake at the horror of their imminent arrest. In ominous dreams they parade Warris Road. In high heels; in chiffon saris; escorted by soldiers; in single file: handcuffed, legcuffed, clanking chains... Their mournful eyes seeking us as they are marched into Birdwood Barracks.

For the first time, unbidden, I cover my head with a scarf and in secluded corners join my hands to take the 101 names of God. The Bountiful. The Innocent. The Forgiver of Sin. The Fulfiller of Desire. He who can turn Air into Ashes: Fire into Water: Dust into Gems! The angle of the walls deflects the ancient words of the dead Avastan language and the prayer resounds soothingly in my ears. Often I notice Cousin with his skullcap on his head lurking in locked bathrooms and I feel my concern is shared. And at night when Adi whips the darkness with his *kusti*, as he goes through the ritual of the sacred thread, I know what evil he prays to banish from our mother and aunt's thoughts.

At the end of the month when Ayah conducts her biyearly search for nits on our heads, she discovers we have each sprung one white hair!

I'm surprised our hair hasn't all turned white.

Himat Ali holds my school satchel, and I hold his finger, as we walk down Warris Road to Mrs. Pen's.

At the Salvation Army wall I tug on Hari-alias-Himat-Ali's finger to cross the road. I have become increasingly fearful of the tall brick wall with its wire-veined eyes. Today the slit vents emanate a steely reek that sets my teeth on edge—and fills me with a superstitious dread.

Himat Ali, too, is uneasy. He pulls back saying: "Stay here. There is something on the other side."

But my fear of the wall and my congenital curiosity prevail. It is only a bulging gunnysack. We cross the road.

The swollen gunnysack lies directly in our path. Hari pushes it with his foot. The sack slowly topples over and Masseur spills out— half on the dusty sidewalk, half on the gritty tarmac—dispelling the stiletto reek of violence with the smell of fresh roses.

He was lying on one side, the upper part of his velvet body bare, a brown and white checked lungi knotted on his hips, and his feet in the sack. I never knew Masseur was so fair inside, creamy, and his arms smooth and distended with muscles and his forearms lined with pale brown hair. A wide wedge of flesh was neatly hacked to further trim his slender waist, and his spine, in a velvet trough, dipped into his lungi.

The minute I touched his shoulder, thinking he might open his eyes, I knew he was dead. But there was too much vigor about him still . . . and his knowing tapering fingers with their white crescents and trimmed nails appeared pliant and ready to assert their consummate skill.

Himat Ali, trembling, suddenly buckles and squats by Masseur as if settling to a long vigil by a sick friend. He removes his puggaree, revealing his shaven bodhi-less head, and placing it on his knee wipes a smudge of dust from Masseur's shoulder.

"Oye, *pahialwan*. Oye, my friend," he whispers. "What have they done to you?" And he strokes Masseur's arm with his trembling hand as if he is massaging Masseur.

Faces bob around us now. Some concerned, some curious. But they look at Masseur as if he is not a person.

He isn't. He has been reduced to a body. A thing. One side of his handsome face already buried in the dusty sidewalk.

Chapter 23

Beadon Road, bereft of the colorful turbans, hairy bodies, yellow shorts, tight pajamas, and glittering religious arsenal of the Sikhs, looks like any other populous street. Lahore is suddenly emptied of yet another hoary dimension: there are no Brahmins with caste-marks—or Hindus in dhoties with *bodhis*. Only hordes of Muslim refugees.

Every bit of scrap that can be used has been salvaged from the gutted shops and tenements of Shalmi and Gowalmandi. The palatial bungalows of Hindus in Model Town and the other affluent neighborhoods have been thoroughly scavenged. The first wave of looters, in mobs and processions, has carried away furniture, carpets, utensils, mattresses, clothes. Succeeding waves of marauders, riding in rickety carts, have systematically stripped the houses of doors, windows, bathroom fittings, ceiling fans and rafters. Casual passersby, urchins and dogs now stray into the houses to scavenge amidst spiders' webs and deep layers of dust, hoping to pick up old newspapers and cardboard boxes, or any other leavings that have escaped the eye and desire of the preceding wave of *goondas*.

In Rosy-Peter's compound, and in the gaunt looted houses opposite ours, untended gardenia hedges sprawl grotesquely and the lawns and flower beds are overrun with weeds. There are patches of parched cracked clay in which nothing grows. Even the mango and banyan trees look monstrous, stalking the unkempt premises with their shadows.

We still wander through the Singhs' annex but the main bungalow, the Hindu doctor's abandoned house behind theirs, and parallel to ours, shows surreptitious signs of occupation. A window boarded with newspaper, a tattered curtain, a shadow of someone passing and the murmur of strangers' voices keep us away.

Months pass before we see our new neighbors. Frightened,

dispossessed, they are coping with grief over dead kin and kidnapped womenfolk. Grateful for the roof over their heads and the
shelter of walls, our neighbors dwell in shadowed interiors, quietly
going about the business of surviving, terrified of being again
evicted.

Rosy-Peter's house and the house opposite still remain un-
occupied. These are to be allotted to refugees who can prove they
have left equally valuable properties behind.

It is astonishing how rapidly an uninhabited house decays.
There are cracks in the cement floor of the Singhs' annex and big
patches of damp on the walls. Clouds of mosquitoes rise in dark
corners and lizards cleave to the ceilings. It looks like a house
pining for its departed—haunted—like Ayah's eyes are by memories
of Masseur. She secretly cries. Often I catch her wiping tears.

The glossy chocolate bloom in her skin is losing its sheen.

Ayah has stopped receiving visitors. Her closest friends have
fled Lahore. She trusts no one. And Masseur's death has left in her
the great empty ache I know sometimes when the muscles of my
stomach retract around hungry spaces within me . . . but I know
there is an added dimension to her loss I cannot comprehend. I
know at least that my lover lives somewhere in the distant and
possible future: I have hope.

She haunts the cypresses and marble terraces of the Shalimar
Gardens. She climbs the slender minarets of Jehangir's tomb. We
wander past the zoo lion's cage and past the chattering monkeys
and stand before the peacock's feathery spread. We sit among the
rushes on the banks of the Ravi and float in the flat boats on its
muddy waters . . . And as Masseur's song, lingering in the rarefied
air around the minarets and in the fragrance of gardens, drifts to
us in the rustle of the pampas grass, Ayah shivers and whispering
croons:

"The bumble-bee came—
Strutting among the flowers, strumming love..."

And holding the end of her sari in her hands like a supplicant, she buries her unbearable ache in her hands. I stroke her hair. I kiss her ears, feeling my inadequacy.

While Masseur's voice haunts Ayah, it impels Ice-candy-man to climb the steep steps of the minarets after us. He prowls the hills behind the zoo lion's cage and lurks in the tall pampas grass. He follows us everywhere as we walk, hand in hand, two hungry wombs... Impotent mothers under the skin.

Mother's jaunts in the Morris are becoming less frequent, and fires all over Lahore are subsiding. Or having become so much a part of the smoking skyline they no longer claim our attention.

Does one get used to everything? Anything?

Processions still chant from various distances and varying directions, but they have lost their urgency: sounding more like the cries of merchants hawking wares. Closer, we hear the rumble of carts as horses canter down Queens Road to Mozang Chungi, accompanied by receding cries of *"Allah-o-Akbar!"* and *"Pakistan Zindabad!"*

We shrug. They probably have wind of some abandoned house that has not been properly ransacked. These merchant-looters have bypassed our street for some time.

And then one morning we again hear the rumble of carts and the roar of men shouting slogans on Warris Road.

From the very first instant I sense danger: we all do. Perhaps it is the speed of their approach, perhaps the aim of their intent buffeting us in threatening waves. There is a heightening in the noise and a shift in the clatter of horseshoes on the tarmac: a slowing that defines their target. It is either the house in front of ours, or ours. The house opposite, with gaping holes where once there were doors and windows, has nothing left to loot.

Mother comes out and joins Ayah, Adi and me on the veranda. The inhabitants of the servants' quarters run to the front and gather before the kitchen and in the vacant portico. Father has taken the Morris to work. Apparently unperturbed, Imam Din beats eggs in the kitchen.

Mother, voluptuous in a beige chiffon sari, is alert. In charge. A lioness with her cubs. Ayah, with her haunted, nervous eyes, is lioness number two. Our pride on the veranda swells as Moti's wife and five children join us.

There is a stamping and snorting of horses and scraping of wooden wheels on the road as the cart-cavalry comes to a disorderly halt outside our gate. We see the carts milling about in the dust they have raised, the men standing in them. We hear them asking questions; debating; shouting to be heard above the noise.

And, suddenly, the men roar again: "Allah-o-Akbar!" And ride into the house opposite ours.

Ayah is not on the veranda. She has disappeared.

"Where's Ayah?" I ask. I'm hushed by a hiss of whispers. Mother communicates a quick, secret warning that is reflected on all faces. Ayah is Hindu. The situation with all its implications is clear. She must hide. We all have a part to play. My intelligence and complicity are taken for granted.

Then they are roaring and charging up our drive, wheels creaking, hooves clattering as the whipped horses stretch their scabby necks and knotted hocks to haul the load for the short gallop. Up the drive come the charioteers, feet planted firmly in shallow carts, in singlets and clinging linen lungis, shoulders gleaming in the bright sun. Calculating men, whose ideals and passions have cooled to ice.

They pour into our drive in an endless cavalry and the looters jump off in front of the kitchen as the carts make room for more carts and the portico and drive are filled with men and horses;

some of the horses' noses already in the feed bags around their necks. The men in front are quiet—like merchants going about their business—but those stalled in the choked drive and on the road chant perfunctorily.

The men's eyes, lined with black antimony, rake us. Note the doors behind us and assess the well-tended premises with its surfeit of pots holding ferns and palm fronds. A hesitancy sparks in their brash eyes when they look at our mother. Flanked by her cubs, her hands resting on our heads, she is the noble embodiment of theatrical motherhood. Undaunted. Endearing. Her cut-crystal lips set in a defiant pucker beneath her tinted glasses and her cropped, waved hair.

Men gather round Yousaf and Hari asking questions, peering here and there. Papoo and I, holding hands, step down into the porch. Mother doesn't stop us.

Still beating eggs, aluminum bowl in hand, Imam Din suddenly fills the open kitchen doorway. He bellows: "What d'you *haramzadas* think you're up to?" There is a lull in the processionists' clamor. Even the men on the road hear him and suspend their desultory chanting. The door snaps shut and Imam Din stands on the kitchen steps looking bomb-bellied and magnificently *goondaish*—the grandfather of all the *goondas* milling about us—with his shaven head, hennaed beard and grimy lungi.

"Where are the Hindus?" a man shouts.

"There are no Hindus here! You *nimak-haram* dogs' penises... There are no Hindus here!"

"There are Hindu nameplates on the gates... Shankar and Sethi!"

"The Shankars took off long ago... They were Hindu. The Sethis are Parsee. I serve them. Sethi is a Parsee name too, you ignorant bastards!"

The men look disappointed and shedding a little of their surety and arrogance look at Imam Din as at an elder. Imam Din's manner changes. He descends among them, bowl and fork in hand, a Mussulman among Muslims. Imam Din's voice is low, conversational. He goes into the kitchen and brings out a large pan of

191

water with ice cubes floating in it. He and Yousaf hand out the water in frosted aluminum glasses.

"Where's Hari, the gardener?" someone from the back shouts.

"Hari-the-gardener has become Himat Ali!" says Imam Din, roaring genially and glancing at the gardener.

Himat Ali's resigned, dusky face begins to twitch nervously as some men move towards him.

"Let's make sure," a man says, hitching up his lungi, his swaggering gait bent on mischief. "Undo your shalwar, Himat Ali. Let's see if you're a proper Muslim." He is young and very handsome.

"He's Ramzana-the-butcher's brother," says Papoo, nudging me excitedly.

I notice the resemblance to the butcher. And then the men are no longer just fragmented parts of a procession: they become individual personalities whose faces I study, seeking friends.

Imam Din is standing in front of the gardener, his arms outstretched. "Get away! I vouch for him. Why don't you ask the barber? He circumcised him."

Someone yells in loud Punjabi: "O yay, nai! Did you circumcise the gardener here?"

From out on the road, transmitted by a chain of raucous voices, comes the reply: "I did a good job on him . . . I'll vouch for Himat Ali!"

The handsome youth, cheated out of his bit of fun, tries to lunge past Imam Din.

"Tell him to recite the *Kalma*," someone shouts.

"Oye! You! Recite the *Kalma*," says the youth.

"*La Ilaha Illallah, Mohammad ur Rasulullah.*" (There is no God but God, and Mohammad is His prophet.) Astonishingly, Himat Ali injects into the Arabic verse the cadence and intonation of Hindu chants.

The men let it pass.

"Where is the sweeper? Where's Moti?" shouts a hoarse Punjabi voice. It sounds familiar but I can't place it.

"He's here," says Yousaf, putting an arm round Moti. "He's become a believer . . . A Christian. Behold . . . Mister David Masih!"

192

The men smile and joke: "O ho! He's become a black-faced gen-tle-man! Mister *sweeper* David Masih! Next he'll be sailing off to Eng-a-land and marrying a memsahib!"

And then someone asks, "Where's the Hindu woman? The ayah!"

There is a split second's silence before Imam Din's reassuring voice calmly says: "She's gone."

"She's gone nowhere! Where is she?"

"I told you. She left Lahore."

"When?"

"Yesterday."

"He's lying," says the familiar voice again. "Oye, Imam Din, why are you lying?"

I recognize the voice. It is Butcher.

"Oye, *Baray Mian!* Don't disgrace your venerable beard!"

"For shame, old man! And you so close to meeting your Maker!"

"Lying does not become your years, you old goat."

The raucous voices are turning ugly.

"Call upon Allah to witness your oath," someone says.

"Oye! Badmash! Don't take Allah's name! You defile it with your tongue!" says Imam Din, losing his geniality.

"Ha! So you won't take an oath before Allah! You're a black-faced liar!"

"Mind your tongue, you dog!" shouts Imam Din.

Other voices join in the attack and, suddenly, very clearly, I hear him say: "*Allah-ki-kasam,* she's gone."

I study the men's faces in the silence that follows. Some of them still don't believe him. Some turn away, or look at the ground. It is an oath a Muslim will not take lightly.

Something strange happened then. The whole disorderly melee dissolved and consolidated into a single face. The face, amber-eyed, spread before me: hypnotic, reassuring, blotting out the ugly frightening crowd. Ice-candy-man's versatile face transformed into a savior's in our hour of need.

Ice-candy-man is crouched before me. "Don't be scared, Lenny baby," he says. "I'm here." And putting his arms around me he whispers, so that only I can hear: "I'll protect Ayah with my life! You know I will... I know she's here. Where is she?"

And dredging from some foul truthful depth in me a fragment of overheard conversation that I had not registered at the time, I say: "On the roof—or in one of the godowns..."

Ice-candy-man's face undergoes a subtle change before my eyes, and as he slowly uncoils his lank frame into an upright position, I know I have betrayed Ayah.

The news is swiftly transmitted. In a daze I see Mother approach, her face stricken. Adi and Papoo look at me out of stunned faces. There is no judgment in their eyes—no reproach—only stone-faced incredulity.

Imam Din and Yousaf are taking small steps back, their arms spread, as three men try to push past. "Where're you going? You can't go to the back! Our women are there, they observe purdah!" says Imam Din, again futilely lying. The men are not aggressive, their game is at hand. It is only a matter of minutes. And while the three men insouciantly confront Imam Din and Yousaf, other men, eyes averted, slip past them.

I cannot see Butcher. Ice-candy-man too has disappeared.

"No!" I scream. "She's gone to Amritsar!"

I try to run after them but Mother holds me. I butt my head into her, bouncing it off her stomach, and every time I throw my head back, I see Adi and Papoo's stunned faces.

The three men shove past Imam Din and something about their insolent and determined movements affects the proprieties that have restrained the mob so far.

They move forward from all points. They swarm into our bedrooms, search the servants' quarters, climb to the roofs, break locks and enter our godowns and the small storerooms near the bathrooms.

They drag Ayah out. They drag her by her arms stretched taut, and her bare feet—that want to move backwards—are forced forward instead. Her lips are drawn away from her teeth, and the resisting curve of her throat opens her mouth like the dead child's screamless mouth. Her violet sari slips off her shoulder, and her breasts strain at her sari-blouse stretching the cloth so that the white stitching at the seams shows. A sleeve tears under her arm.

The men drag her in grotesque strides to the cart and their harsh hands, supporting her with careless intimacy, lift her into it. Four men stand pressed against her, propping her body upright, their lips stretched in triumphant grimaces.

I am the monkey-man's performing monkey, the trained circus elephant, the snake-man's charmed cobra, an animal with conditioned reflexes that cannot lie . . .

The last thing I noticed was Ayah, her mouth slack and piteously gaping, her disheveled hair flying into her kidnappers' faces, staring at us as if she wanted to leave behind her wide-open and terrified eyes.

Chapter 24

The evenings resound to the beat of drums. Papoo is getting married. In the wake of my guilt-driven and flagellating grief and pining for Ayah the drums sound mournful, and the preparations for the wedding joyless.

For three days I stand in front of the bathroom mirror staring at my tongue. I hold the vile, truth-infected thing between my fingers and try to wrench it out: but slippery and slick as a fish it slips from my fingers and mocks me with its sharp rapier tip darting as poisonous as a snake. I punish it with rigorous scourings from my prickling toothbrush until it is sore and bleeding. I'm so conscious of its unwelcome presence at all times that it swells uncomfortably in my mouth and gags and chokes me.

I throw up. Constantly.

For three days, as I scour my tongue, families of sweepers, huddled in bunches, in gaudy satins and brocades, drift up our drive, and past the bathroom window. The women shade their dusky faces beneath diaphanous shawls with silver fringes, their glass bangles and silver anklets jingling as they shuffle their feet, the men strutting amidst them like cocks in tall, crisply crested turbans.

At the back, on the servants' verandas, two old crones with missing teeth take turns beating a sausage-shaped drum with both hands and droning ribald ditties. Papoo, cowed by all the unwonted attention, sits glowering in a corner of their quarters like a punished child, her skin glowing from mustard-oil massages and applications of turmeric and Multani mud packs. Sometimes, when I sit listlessly by her holding her hand, smiling politely at the remarks and wisecracks of the women, drawing courage from my fingers Papoo's eyes regain their roguish sparkle and she snaps and lunges at the women, and flinging herself on the dirt floor enacts tempestuous tantrums of protestation. Infuriated by her daughter's intractable behavior before her kinswomen Muccho lashes out and is withdrawn cursing, while the remaining women, wheedling, cajoling and bribing Papoo with sweets, restore her to a precarious semblance of docility.

Ayahless and sore-tongued I drift through the forlorn rooms of my house, and back and forth from the festive quarters. The kitchen has become a depressing hellhole filled with sighs as Imam Din goes about his work spiritlessly. Even Yousaf cracks his smiles less frequently. Mother is out all day. And when she is home she has such a forbidding expression on her exhausted face that Adi and I elect to keep out of her way.

With no one to awaken me I sleep late on the morning of Papoo's wedding. It is Saturday: exactly a week from the day Ayah was carried off. Adi tugs my toe so it hurts and says: "Aren't you getting up? The guests have come . . . the bridegroom's *baraat* will be here soon!"

I quickly slip into a stiffly starched and frothy frock and put on my white socks and buckled shoes and run to the back.

The caterers have already lit log fires beneath two enormous cauldrons and the sultry air is permeated by the aroma of biryani and spicy goat korma. I weave through the male guests squatting like patient sheep outside the scant lemon hedge that demarcates the servants' courtyard. The yard itself is thronged by women in bright satins edged with gold and silver *gota*. The crowd is thick outside the sweeper's quarters and I have to squeeze my way through the knot of women at the door. But even after my eyes get accustomed to the dingy light in the small, square dung-plastered room it takes me a while to realize that the crumpled heap of scarlet and gold clothes flung carelessly in a corner is really Papoo. I squat by her, smiling and awkward, and, lifting her *ghoongat*, peer into her face. She has an enviable quantity of make-up on. Shocking-pink lipstick, white powder, smudged kohl: and she is fast asleep.

There is a stir among the seated women and a sudden air of

excitement. Someone outside shouts: "Tota Ram's *baraat* has come!"

I shake Papoo: "Wake up . . . Come on!" Papoo sits up, shoving her *ghoongat* back drowsily, and looks at me with a strange cockeyed grin, as if she is drunk.

I run out with the rest of the immediate kin to receive the *baraat* just as the bridegroom's party enters our gates and the six-man band, in faded red uniforms with tarnished gold braid, bursts into brassy clamor. I glimpse the short bridegroom behind the musicians, bobbing among the men in the entourage. The women, some on foot, some crammed into tongas with their babies, follow. The groom is wearing a purple satin lungi and a long, whitely gleaming satin shirt. His chest is bristling with garlands centered with gold-beribboned cardboard hearts and strung with crisp, new one-rupee notes and flowers. His head is covered by a thick white turban with a gold *kulah* and beneath it hangs the *sehra*, veiling his face with chains of marigolds. Judging by his height, Tota Ram must be Papoo's age—about eleven or twelve. I am confused. The distraught way Muccho carried on when Papoo was off her feed led me to believe that Tota Ram was an important, frightening and grown man.

The groom is led into Hari's quarters, which have been cleared of their meager belongings to receive him. Now the curious women surge to see the *doolha*. I fight my way in with them. He is sitting straight on a high-backed chair, his legs dangling brand-new two-tone shoes.

Something about his gestures disturbs me: the way he shifts in the chair, the manner in which he inserts his hand behind the tickling flowers to scratch his nose. He sneezes—an unexpectedly violent sound—and, snorting wetly, clears his throat. For a moment I wonder if someone older is responsible for the sounds. They don't belong behind the *sehra*. Again the bridegroom sneezes: so mightily that the *sehra* swings out. Then he parts the curtain of flowers hanging from his head and I see his face!

He is no boy! He is a dark, middle-aged man with a pockmark-pitted face and small, brash, kohl-blackened eyes. He has

an insouciant air of insolence about him—as though it is all a
tedious business he has been through before. I cannot take my eyes
off him as he visualizes the women with assertive, assessing direct-
ness. There is a slight cast in the close set of his eyes, and the
smirk lurking about his thin, dry lips gives an impression of cruelty.
The women in the room become hushed. He shifts his insolent
eyes to the ceiling, as if permitting the women to gape upon his
unsavory person, and then lowers his *sehra*.

After the initial shock, two or three older women from
Papoo's family pull themselves together and move forward to greet
and bless him as is ritually required. The elderly and cynical dwarf
permits their embraces and then sits back, his spread legs swinging
carelessly, and the women, some of them tittering in a shocked way
behind the fingers screening their mouths, resume their chattering.
I remain rooted to the dirt floor, unable to remove my eyes from
him, imagining the shock, and the grotesque possibilities awaiting
Papoo.

I sit quietly beside the bride. The women from the groom's
family lift her *ghoongat* and comment indulgently on the innocence
that permits the child-bride to sleep through her marriage. Bending
frequently, stepping over the satiny spread of legs and thighs of
about twenty women jammed together on the floor, they exhibit
an impressive display of the clothes and the tawdry jewelry they
have brought for the bride and her mother.

A little after noon two enormous round copper platters,
heaped with fragrant pilaf and goat curry, are brought into the
room. The women gather around them and silently fall to eating.
The caterers provide a separate china plate for the bride. Muccho
shakes her daughter awake, urging: "Come, doll, sit up and eat,
doll." I study Muccho's face with curious eyes. There is a contented smile on her lips—smug and vindicated.

As Papoo struggles groggily to sit up, her eyes swivel weakly
under her half-open lids. Muccho shakes her roughly again, and

forming small morsels of rice with her fingers, stroking Papoo's back, feeds her. Papoo chews slowly, absently, her childish, lip-sticked mouth slack. "Oi, dopey. *Ufeemi!* Wake up!" says Muccho affectionately. And though the tone of voice calling her an opium-addict is disarmingly facetious, it suddenly strikes me that Papoo has in fact been drugged. I have seen enough opium addicts to realize this. Mr. Bankwalla's and Colonel Bharucha's cooks are both addicted.

Towards evening the *doolha* is brought into the room and made to sit by his comatose bride. He keeps his face covered by the *sehra* but by the way his head shifts I can tell he is slyly ogling me and the young women moving about the room.

Later in the afternoon the Mission padre stands in the door in his long black cassock with a high, white collar. His heavy laced-up boots appear incongruous with his flowing garments. His hair is cropped very short and he has a well-bred and timid expression on his humble face. I wonder if he is the padre whose wife absconded with the seductive tailor.

The women hug their knees and shuffle back to make room for his passage as the padre, accustoming his eyes to the dark, steps hesitantly into Moti's quarters. Holding his gilt-edged Bible and rosary deferentially he makes the sign of the cross and squats be-fore the couple. Papoo is shaken awake and surreptitiously propped up by Muccho as the padre recites the Christian marriage litany in Punjabi.

Chapter 25

There are mysterious developments afoot in the servants' quarters behind the Hindu doctor's house paralleling ours. The courtyard has been walled off and a very tall and burly Sikh with curling hair on his legs stands guard outside a high, tin-sheet gate, criss-crossed with wooden beams. There is a padlock the size of a grapefruit on the gate, and a large key hangs from the steel bangle around the Sikh's wrist. He unlocks the gate sometimes to pass the women inside sacks of grain and baskets of vegetables.

The servants evade questions as if there is something shameful going on. Cousin, Adi and I are agog. And on a Sunday afternoon —it is already October—we sneak up the stairs and, minding the holes in the roof, tiptoe to look into the enclosed courtyard. Our servants' quarters roof runs in a continuous line of clay to their roof, demarcated only by a foot-high brick wall.

We assume it's a women's jail, even though they look innocent enough—village women washing clothes, crossing the courtyard with water canisters, chaffing wheat and drying raw mangoes for pickling. There is very little chatter among the women. Just apathetic movements to and fro.

The Sikh guard squats in front of a small water tank in his white cotton drawers, scouring his teeth with a walnut twig. He must have just washed his hair because it is flung round his neck like a coarse scarf to keep it from trailing in the mud.

The guard spots us on the roof and glowers ferociously. As he stands up his hair uncoils and hangs down almost to his knees. We scamper from his view like scared spiders, careful not to fall through the holes where the mud has given way between the decaying rafters.

After a while, taking care to tread quietly and not daring to talk, we peer between the rafters into the dim, smoke-filled

201

cubicles. I feel a nervous, nauseous thrill, as I make out the dark shapes of women in shalwar-kamizes moving lethargically between their cots. In one of the cubicles a thin long face looks up unseeing through the veil of smoke and the eerie desolation of that pallid face remains stamped on my mind.

The Hindu doctor's house so unobtrusively occupied by our new refugee neighbors sprawls in an ungainly oblong block between the women's jail and Rosy-Peter's annex. Its cement plaster shows beneath scabs of peeling whitewash. I don't know how many people dwell in the abandoned bungalow, but the number of its occupants appears to be increasing. There is more movement behind the windows boarded up with cardboard and newspaper, a greater frequency and laxity in the sudden shouting and subdued chatter.

We still don't know anything about them. Who they are, where they're from. They keep to themselves, unobtrusively conducting their lives, lurking like night animals in the twilight interiors of their lairs, still afraid of being evicted from property they have somehow managed to occupy.

The woman is pulling a faded kamize that is too short for her over a wash-grayed shalwar. Her head is covered by a frayed voile *chuddar* and she is standing before Mother, awkward and uncomfortably tall. I recognize her the moment I see her. Her eyes are downcast and a nervous, apologetic smile—that is more like a twitch—jerks about her lips. I feel a surge of panic. Does Mother know she's interviewing a criminal to replace Ayah? But there is a quality so anxious and despairing about the narrow pallid face that I conceal my knowledge. I would rather trust myself to the dangerous care of the jailbird than betray her: so strong is the drag of guilt and compassion she has exerted on me. She looks at Mother out of appealing eyes. Docile. Ready to please. So in need. Servilely murmuring: "Yes, *jee*, I will do everything... Anything you want."

"These are decent folk, mind you! They're not the kind that let fly dog-and-cat abuses," interjects Imam Din gruffly, leaning against Mother's bedroom door with the proprietory air of an elderly and pampered flunky. "You'll be looked after if you work properly."

He is as transparent as me. He cannot hide his pity.

"I am not frightened of work, brother," says the woman in thickly accented, village Punjabi. "I will sweep, clean, milk the buffalo, churn the butter, wash clothes, clean out latrines, make chapatties... After all, I've been a housewife."

She stops speaking abruptly and looks unaccountably guilty and even more bashful. Suddenly, folding her knees, she hunkers down on the bedroom floor and draws her *chuddar* forward over her face.

"You won't need to do any of that!" says Mother. She indicates me with her glance. "Here's your charge. All I want you for is the care of the children... Don't let them out of your sight."

The woman swivels on her heels and gazes into my eyes so intensely that I feel it is I, and not Mother, who is empowered to employ her. The jerky smile about her lips distends fearfully. "I will guard her like the pupils in my eyes," she says. "Don't I know how careful one has to be with young girls? Especially these days!" Her tone of voice and choice of words—as of village women uttering platitudes—is grotesque in the obviously straitened and abnormal circumstances of her life.

We call her by her name, Hamida. We can't bear to call her Ayah.

Looking for Ayah. We are all looking for Ayah. Mother and Electric-aunt, heads together, go goos-goosing and whispering, contorting their faces in strange and solemn ways. And when they see us they hush and dramatically alter their fierce expressions. Their reassembled, we-were-just-talking-of-this-and-that features frighten me more than the news they are attempting to spare me.

Father once again cycles to work, leaving the Morris for Mother. Electric-aunt and Mother drive off, come back, and are off again with such frequency and urgency that I ache with expectation and shattered hope each time I anxiously look into the returning Ayah-less car.

Sharbat Khan returns from the hills and Hari, alias Himat Ali, squatting on his trembling haunches and weeping shamelessly, tells him: "He sprang at me out of a gunnysack, dead!" And wiping his tearing eyes says, "The dead bastard! Didn't he know she'd be alone?"

Wrapped in a blanket, turban wound round his mouth, Sharbat Khan cycles up for low-voiced conversations with Iman Din and Yousaf. He rattles away—sometimes accompanied by Yousaf—and the way their legs pedal, and the way they lean into the wind, I can tell they are looking for Ayah.

Sharbat Khan looks different. His tiger eyes are grim and bloodshot. He drives his foot hard on the pedal of his machine and examines the edges of the knives he sharpens as though he will use them to kill us all. Sometimes he looks at me as if he is trying to probe my soul and search out the aberrations in my personality that made me betray Ayah. Then he shakes his head and bitterly says: "Children are the Devil . . . They only know the truth."

I can no longer look into his eyes.

Hamida keeps her bowed head covered and her eyes averted from Father. She shuffles and pivots awkwardly on her long legs, hunching her narrow shoulders meekly, careful not to offend anyone by her unusual height.

Hamida has to be trained from scratch. Yousaf teaches her how to make beds the way Mother likes. Mother shows her how to stack clothes in tidy piles in cupboards, how to wash woolens and dry them on spread towels. Hamida has never used an iron. She never does. She is so terrified of electricity that she doesn't even switch on the lights—until Cousin shows her how to with a wooden clothes hanger, which, it is dinned into her head, makes her shockproof.

We tell her where our things go and Mother shows her how to bathe us and massage my legs.

I barely limp now.

Hamida has to be restrained from latching on to Mother and massaging and pummelling her limbs whenever she finds Mother sitting, sewing or reading in bed. Hamida doesn't know what to do with her hands in Mother's presence. And, when idle, in fluttering panic they reach out and massage whoever is at hand. Adi wiggles and slips away from her grasp. Or, if she is too insistent, kicks out. I let her hands have their will with me and tolerate her irksome caress. She is like a starved and grounded bird and I can't bear to hurt her.

Sometimes her eyes fill and the tears roll down her cheeks. Once, when I smoothed her hair back, she suddenly started to weep, and noticing my consternation explained, "When the eye is wounded, even a scented breeze hurts."

Hamida comes to fetch me from Mrs. Pen's. When we are close to the house, she casually says: "Imam Din has guests . . . Poor things: they have suffered a lot . . . The Sikhs attacked their village."

"Where are they from?" I ask, my pulse quickening.

"Pir Pindo . . . or some such village."

I leave her hand and as I run towards the house I hear her voice trying to restrain me. "Be careful, Lenny baby," she cries. "Wait for me!" And she runs after me. My heart beating wildly, I run into the servants' courtyard.

A small boy, so painfully thin that his knees and elbows appear swollen, is squatting a few feet away concentrating on striking a marble lying in a notch in the dust. He is wearing ragged, drawstring shorts of thin cotton and the dirty cord tying them in gathers round his waist trails in the mud. His aim scores, and he turns to look at me. His face is a patchwork of brown and black skin; a wizened blemish. He starts to get up, showing his teeth in a crooked smile; and with a shock I recognize Ranna. His limbs are black and brittle; the circular protrusion of his windpipe and ribs so skeletal that I can see the passage of air in his throat and lungs. He is covered with welts; as if his body has been chopped up, and then welded. He sees my horror and winces, turning away. "Ranna," I say, moving quickly to touch him. "Ranna! What happened to you?" I can't help it; I look at the ugly scab where his belly button used to be. He stares at me, his face crumbling. And, wheeling abruptly, he runs into Imam Din's quarters, I see the improbable wound on the back of his shaved head. It is a grisly scar like a brutally gouged and premature bald spot. In time the wound acquired the shape of a four-day-old crescent moon.

I almost live in the quarters. Hamida sits with us for short periods, and when she pulls Ranna to her lap and he presses against her, her disorderly hands grow tranquil. I only go to the house to sleep. I eat my meals in Imam Din's quarters, relishing everything Ranna's Noni *chachi* cooks. That's when they talk—using plain Punjabi words and graphic peasant gestures—Ranna, bit by bit, describing the attack on Pir Pindo, Noni *chachi* recounting her part in the story, and Iqbal *chacha* intervening with clarification, conjecture and comment. It is hard to grasp that the events they describe took place only a couple of months ago... that, like Ranna, Pir Pindo is brutally altered... that his family, as I knew it, has ceased to exist...

No one realized the speed at which the destruction and the rampage advanced. They didn't know the extent to which it surrounded them. Jagjeet Singh visited Pir Pindo under cover of darkness with furtive groups of Sikhs. A few more families who had close kin near Multan and Lahore left, disguised as Sikhs or Hindus. But most of the villagers resisted the move. The uncertainty they faced made them discredit the danger. "We cannot leave," they said, and, like a refrain, I can hear them say: "What face will we show our forefathers on the day of judgment if we abandon their graves? Allah will protect us!"

Jagjeet Singh sent word he was risking his life, and the lives of the other men in Dera Tek Singh, if he visited Pir Pindo again. The Akalis were aware of his sympathies for the Muslims. They had threatened him. They were in control of his village.

Jagjeet Singh advised them to leave as soon as they could, but it was already too late.

Ranna's Story

Late that afternoon the clamor of the monsoon downpour suddenly ceased. Chidda raised her hands from the dough she was kneading and, squatting before the brass tray, turned to her mother-in-law. Sitting by his grandmother, Ranna sensed their tension as the old woman stopped chaffing the wheat. She slowly pushed back her age-brittle hair and, holding her knobby fingers immobile, grew absolutely still.

Chidda stood in their narrow doorway, her eyes nervously scouring the courtyard. Ranna clung to her shalwar, peering out. His cousins, almost naked in their soaking rags, were shouting and splashing in the slush in their courtyard. "Shut up. Oye!" Chidda shouted in a voice that rushed so violently from her strong chest that the children quieted at once and leaned and slid uneasily against the warm black hides of the buffaloes tethered to the rough stumps. The clouds had broken and the sun shot beams that lit up the freshly bathed courtyard.

The other members of the household, Ranna's older brothers, his uncles, aunts and cousins, were quietly filing into the courtyard. When she saw Khatija and Parveen, Chidda strode to her daughters and pressed them fiercely to her body. The village was so quiet it could be the middle of the night, and from the distance, buffeting the heavy, moisture-laden air, came the wails and the hoarse voices of men shouting.

Already their neighbors' turbans skimmed the tall mud ramparts of their courtyard, their bare feet squelching on the path the rain had turned into a muddy channel.

I can imagine the old mullah, combing his faded beard with trembling fingers as he watches the villagers converge on the mosque with its uneven green dome. It is perched on an incline; and seen from there the fields, flooded with rain, are the same muddy color as the huts. The mullah drags his cot forward as the villagers, touching their foreheads and greeting him somberly, fill the prayer ground. The *chaudhry* joins the mullah on his charpoy. The villagers sit on their haunches in uneven rows lifting their confused and frightened faces. There is a murmur of voices. Conjectures. First the name of one village and then of another. The Sikhs have attacked Kot-Rahim. No, it sounds closer. . . It must be Makipura.

The *chaudhry* raises his heavy voice slightly: "Dost Mohammad and his party will be here soon. . . We'll know soon enough what's going on."

At his reassuring presence the murmuring subsides and the villagers nervously settle down to wait. Some women draw their veils across their faces and, shading their bosoms, impatiently shove their nipples into the mouths of whimpering babies. Grandmothers, mothers and aunts rock restive children on their laps and thump their foreheads to put them to sleep. The children, conditioned to the numbing jolts, grow groggy and their eyes become unfocused. They fall asleep almost at once.

Half an hour later the scouting party, drenched and muddy, the lower halves of their faces wrapped in the ends of their turbans, pick their way through the squatting villagers to the *chaudhry*.

Removing his wet puggaree and wiping his head with a cloth the mullah hands him, Dost Mohammad turns on his haunches to face the villagers. His skin is gray, as if the rain has bleached the color. Casting a shade across his eyes with a hand that trembles slightly, speaking in a matter-of-fact voice that disguises his ache and fear, he tells the villagers that the Sikhs have attacked at least five villages around Dehra Misri, to their east. Their numbers have swollen enormously. They are like swarms of locusts, moving in marauding bands of thirty and forty thousand. They are killing all Muslims. Setting fires, looting, parading the Muslim women naked through the streets—raping and mutilating them in the center of villages and in mosques. The Bias, flooded by melting snow and the monsoon, is carrying hundreds of corpses. There is an intolerable stench where the bodies, caught in the bends, have piled up.

"What are the police doing?" a man shouts. He is Dost Mohammad's cousin. One way or another the villagers are related.

"The Muslims in the force have been disarmed at the orders of a Hindu Sub-Inspector; the dog's penis!" says Dost Mohammad, speaking in the same flat monotone. "The Sikh and Hindu police have joined the mobs."

The villagers appear visibly to shrink—as if the loss of hope is a physical thing. A woman with a child on her lap slaps her forehead and begins to wail: *"Hai! Hai!"* The other women join her: *"Hai! Hai!"* Older women, beating their breasts like hollow drums, cry, "Never mind us . . . save the young girls! The children! *Hai! Hai!"*

Ranna's two-toothed old grandmother, her frail voice quavering bitterly, shrieks: "We should have gone to Pakistan!"

It was hard to believe that the decision to stay was taken only a month ago. Embedded in the heart of the Punjab, they had felt secure, inviolate. And to uproot themselves from the soil of their ancestors had seemed to them akin to tearing themselves, like ancient trees, from the earth.

And the messages filtering from the outside had been reassuring. Gandhi, Nehru, Jinnah, Tara Singh were telling the peasants to remain where they were. The minorities would be a sacred trust . . . The communal trouble was being caused by a few mischief-makers and would soon subside—and then there were their brothers, the Sikhs of Dera Tek Singh, who would protect them.

But how many Muslims can the Sikh villagers befriend? The mobs, determined to drive the Muslims out, are prepared for the carnage. Their ranks swollen by thousands of refugees recounting fresh tales of horror they roll towards Pir Pindo like the heedless swells of an ocean.

The *chaudhry* raises his voice: "How many guns do we have now?"

The women grow quiet.

"Seven or eight," a man replies from the front.

There is a disappointed silence. They had expected to procure more guns, but every village is holding on to its meager stock of weapons.

"We have our axes, knives, scythes and staves!" a man calls from the back. "Let those bastards come. We're ready!"

"Yes... we're as ready as we'll ever be," the *chaudhry* says, stroking his thick moustache. "You all know what to do..."

They have been over the plan often enough recently. The women and girls will gather at the *chaudhry*'s. Rather than face the brutality of the mob they will pour kerosene around the house and burn themselves. The canisters of kerosene are already stored in the barn at the rear of the *chaudhry*'s sprawling mud house. The young men will engage the Sikhs at the mosque, and at other strategic locations, for as long as they can and give the women a chance to start the fire.

A few men from each family were to shepherd the younger boys and lock themselves into secluded back rooms, hoping to escape detection. They were peaceable peasants, not skilled in such matters, and their plans were sketchy and optimistic. Comforted by each other's presence, reluctant to disperse, the villagers remained in the prayer yard as dusk gathered about them. The distant wailing and shouting had ceased. Later that night it rained again, and comforted by its seasonal splatter the tired villagers curled up on their mats and slept.

The attack came at dawn. The watch from the mosque's single minaret hurtled down the winding steps to spread the alarm. The panicked women ran to and fro screaming and snatching up their babies, and the men barely had time to get to their posts. In fifteen minutes the village was swamped by the Sikhs—tall men with streaming hair and thick biceps and thighs, waving full-sized swords and sten-guns, roaring, *"Bolay so Nihal! Sat Siri Akal!"*

They mowed down the villagers in the mosque with the sten-guns. Shouting *"Allah-o-Akbar!"* the peasants died of sword and spear wounds in the slushy lanes and courtyards, the screams of women from the *chaudhry's* house ringing in their ears, wondering why the house was not burning.

Ranna, abandoned by his mother and sisters halfway to the *chaudhry's* house, ran howling into the courtyard. Chidda had spanked his head and pushed him away, shrieking, "Go to your father! Stay with the men!"

Ranna ran through their house to the room the boys had been instructed to gather in. Some of his cousins and uncles were already there. More men stumbled into the dark windowless room—then his two older brothers. There must be at least thirty of them in the small room. It was stifling. He heard his father's voice and fought his way towards him. Dost Mohammad shouted harshly: "Shut up! They'll kill you if you make a noise."

The yelling in the room subsided. Dost Mohammad picked up his son, and Ranna saw his uncle slip out into the gray light and shut the door, plunging the room into darkness. Someone bolted the door from inside, and they heard the heavy thud of cotton bales stacked against the door to disguise the entrance. With luck they would remain undetected and safe.

The shouting and screaming from outside appeared to come in waves: receding and approaching. From all directions. Sometimes Ranna could make out the words and even whole sentences. He heard a woman cry, "Do anything you want with me, but don't torment me . . . For God's sake, don't torture me!" And then an intolerable screaming. "Oh God!" a man whispered on a sobbing intake of breath. "Oh God, she is the mullah's daughter!" The men covered their ears—and the boys' ears—sobbing unaffectedly like little children.

A teenager, his cracked voice resounding like the honk of geese, started wailing: "I don't want to die . . . I don't want to die!" Catching his fear, Ranna and the other children set to whimpering: "I don't want to die . . . Abba, I don't want to die!"

"Hush," said Dost Mohammad gruffly. "Stop whining like girls!" Then, with words that must have bubbled up from a deep source of strength and compassion, with infinite gentleness, he said, "What's there to be afraid of? Are you afraid to die? It won't hurt any more than the sting of a bee." His voice, unseasonably light-hearted, carried a tenderness that soothed and calmed them. Ranna fell asleep in his father's arms.

Someone was banging on the door, shouting: "Open up! Open up!"

Ranna awoke with a start. Why was he on the floor?

Why were there so many people about in the dark? He felt the stir of men getting to their feet. The air in the room was oppressive: hot and humid and stinking of sweat. Suddenly Ranna remembered where he was and the darkness became charged with terror.

"We know you're in there. Come on, open up!" The noise of the banging was deafening in the pitch-black room, drowning the other children's alarmed cries. "Allah! Allah! Allah!" an old man moaned nonstop.

"Who's there?" Dost Mohammad called; and putting Ranna down, stumbling over the small bodies, made his way to the door. Ranna, terrified, groping blindly in the dark, tried to follow.

"We're Sikhs!"

There was a pause in which Ranna's throat dried up. The old man stopped saying "Allah." And in the deathly stillness, his voice echoing from his proximity to the door Dost Mohammad said, "Kill us . . . Kill us all . . . but spare the children."

"Open at once!"

"I beg you in the name of all you hold sacred, don't kill the little ones," Ranna heard his father plead. "Make them Sikhs . . . Let them live . . . they are so little . . ."

Suddenly the noon light smote their eyes. Dost Mohammad stepped out and walked three paces. There was a sunlit sweep of curved steel. His head was shorn clear off his neck. Turning once in the air, eyes wide open, it tumbled in the dust. His hands jerked up slashing the air above the bleeding stump of his neck.

Ranna saw his uncles beheaded. His older brothers, his cousins. The Sikhs were among them like hairy vengeful demons, wielding bloodied swords, dragging them out as a sprinkling of Hindus, darting about at the fringes, their faces vaguely familiar, pointed out and identified the Mussulmans by name. He felt a blow cleave the back of his head and the warm flow of blood. Ranna fell just inside the door on a tangled pile of unrecognizable bodies. Someone fell on him, drenching him in blood.

Every time his eyes open the world appears to them to be floating in blood. From the direction of the mosque come the intolerable shrieks and wails of women. It seems to him that a woman is sobbing just outside their courtyard: great anguished sobs—and at intervals she screams: "You'll kill me! *Hai Allah* . . . Y'all will kill me!"

Ranna wants to tell her, "Don't be afraid to die . . . It will hurt less than the sting of a bee." But he is hurting so much . . . Why isn't he dead? Where are the bees? Once he thought he saw his eleven-year-old sister, Khatija, run stark naked into their courtyard: her long hair disheveled, her boyish body bruised, her lips cut and swollen and a bloody scab where her front teeth were missing.

Later in the evening he awoke to silence. At once he became fully conscious. He wiggled backwards over the bodies and slipping free of the weight on top of him felt himself sink knee-deep into a viscous fluid. The bodies blocking the entrance had turned the room into a pool of blood.

Keeping to the shadows cast by the mud walls, stepping over the mangled bodies of people he knew, Ranna made his way to the *chaudhry*'s house. It was dark inside. There was a nauseating stench of kerosene mixed with the smell of spilt curry. He let his eyes get accustomed to the dimness. Carefully he explored the rooms cluttered with smashed clay pots, broken charpoys, spilled grain and chapatties. He had not realized how hungry he was until he saw the pile of stale bread. He crammed the chapatties into his mouth.

His heart gave a lurch. A woman was sleeping on a charpoy. He reached for her and his hand grasped her clammy inert flesh. He realized with a shock she was dead. He walked round the cot to examine her face. It was the *chaudhry's* older wife. He discovered three more bodies. In the dim light he turned them over and peered into their faces searching for his mother.

When he emerged from the house it was getting dark. Moving warily, avoiding contact with the bodies he kept stumbling upon, he went to the mosque.

For the first time he heard voices. The whispers of women comforting each other—of women softly weeping. His heart pounding in his chest he crept to one side of the arching mosque entrance. He heard a man groan, then a series of animal-like grunts.

He froze near the body of the mullah. How soon he had become accustomed to thinking of people he had known all his life as bodies. He felt on such easy terms with death. The old mullah's face was serene in death, his beard pale against the brick plinth. The figures in the covered portion at the rear of the mosque were a dark blur. He was sure he had heard Chidda's voice. He began inching forward, prepared to dash across the yard to where the women were, when a man yawned and sighed, *"Wah Guru!"*

"Wah Guru! Wah Guru!" responded three or four male voices, sounding drowsy and replete. Ranna realized that the men in the mosque were Sikhs. A wave of rage and loathing swept his small body. He knew it was wrong of the Sikhs to be in the mosque with the village women. He could not explain why: except that he still slept in his parents' room.

"Stop whimpering, you bitch, or I'll bugger you again!" a man said irritably.

Other men laughed. There was much movement. Stifled exclamations and moans. A woman screamed, and swore in Punjabi.

There was a loud cracking noise and the rattle of breath from the lungs. Then a moment of horrible stillness.

Ranna fled into the moonless night. Skidding on the slick wet clay, stumbling into the irrigation ditches demarcating the fields, he ran in the direction of his Uncle Iqbal and his Noni *chachi*'s village. He didn't stop until deep inside a thicket of sugarcane he stumbled on a slightly elevated slab of drier ground. The clay felt soft and caressing against his exhausted body. It was a safe place to rest. The moment Ranna felt secure his head hurt and he fainted.

Ranna lay unconscious in the cane field all morning. Intermittent showers washed much of the blood and dust off his limbs. Around noon two men walked into the cane field, and at the first rustle of the dried leaves Ranna became fully conscious.

Sliding on his butt to the lower ground, crouching amidst the pricking tangle of stalks and dried leaves, Ranna followed the passage of the men with his ears. They trampled through the field, selecting and cutting the sugarcane with their *kirpans*, talking in Punjabi. Ranna picked up an expression that warned him that they were Sikhs. Half-buried in the slush he scarcely breathed as one of the men came so close to him that he saw the blue check on his lungi and the flash of a white singlet. There was a crackling rustle as the man squatted to defecate.

Half an hour later when the men left, Ranna moved cautiously towards the edge of the field. A cluster of about sixty Sikhs in lungis and singlets, their carelessly knotted hair snaking down their backs, stood talking in a fallow field to his right. At some distance, in another field of young green shoots, Sikhs and Hindus were gathered in a much larger bunch. Ranna sensed their presence behind him in the fields he couldn't see. There must be thousands of them, he thought. Shifting to a safe spot he searched the distance for the green dome of his village mosque. He had traveled too far to spot it. But he knew where his village lay and guessed from the coiling smoke that his village was on fire.

Much later, when it was time for the evening meal, the fields cleared. He could not make out a single human form for miles. As he ran again towards his aunt's village the red sun, as if engorged with blood, sank into the horizon.

All night he moved, scuttling along the mounds of earth protecting the waterways, running in shallow channels, burrowing like a small animal through the standing crop. When he stopped to catch his breath, he saw the glow from burning villages measuring the night distances out for him.

Ranna arrived at his aunt's village just after dawn. He watched it from afar, confused by the activity taking place around five or six huge lorries parked in the rutted lanes. Soldiers, holding guns with bayonets sticking out of them, were directing the villagers. The villagers were shouting and running to and fro, carrying on their heads charpoys heaped with their belongings. Some were herding their calves and goats towards the trucks. Others were dumping their household effects in the middle of the lanes in their scramble to climb into the lorries.

There were no Sikhs about. The village was not under attack. Perhaps the army trucks were there to evacuate the villagers and take them to Pakistan.

Ranna hurtled down the lanes, weaving through the burdened and distraught villagers and straying cattle, into his aunt's hut. He saw her right away, heaping her pots and pans on a cot. A fat roll of winter bedding tied with a string lay to one side. He screamed: "Noni *chachi!* It's me!"

"*For a minute I thought: Who is this filthy little beggar?*" Noni *chachi* says, when she relates her part in the story. "*I said: Ranna? Ranna? Is that you? What're you doing here!*"

The moment he caught the light of recognition and concern in her eyes, the pain in his head exploded and he crumpled at her feet unconscious.

"*It is funny,*" Ranna says. "*As long as I had to look out for myself I was all right. As soon as I felt safe I fainted.*"

Her hands trembling, his *chachi* washed the wound on his head with a wet rag. Clots of congealed blood came away and floated in the pan in which she rinsed the cloth. "*I did not dare remove the thick scabs that had formed over the wound,*" she says. "*I thought I'd see his*" *brain!"* The slashing blade had scalped him from the rise in the back of his head to the top, exposing a wound the size of a large bald patch on a man. She wondered how he had lived; found his way to their village. She was sure he would die in a few moments. Ranna's *chacha* Iqbal, and other members of the house gathered about him. An old woman, the village *dai*, checked his pulse and his breath and, covering him with a white cloth, said: "Let him die in peace!"

A terrifying roar, like the warning of an alarm, throbs in his ears. He sits up on the charpoy, taking in the disorder in the hastily abandoned room. The other cot, heaped with his aunt's belongings, lies where it was. He can see the bedding roll abandoned in the courtyard. Clay dishes, mugs, chipped crockery, and hand fans lie on the floor with scattered bits of clothing. Where are his aunt and uncle? Why is he alone? And in the fearsome noise drawing nearer, he recognizes the rhythm of the Sikh and Hindu chants.

Ranna leapt from the cot and ran through the lanes of the deserted village. Except for the animals lowing and bleating and wandering ownerless on the slushy paths there was no one about. Why hadn't they taken him with them?

His heart thumping, Ranna climbed to the top of the mosque minaret. He saw the mob of Sikhs and Hindus in the fields scuttling forward from the horizon like giant ants. Roaring, waving swords, partly obscured by the veil of dust raised by their trampling feet, they approached the village.

Ranna flew down the steep steps. He ran in and out of the empty houses looking for a place to hide. The mob sounded close. He could hear the thud of their feet, make out the words of their chants. Ranna slipped through the door into a barn. It was almost entirely filled with straw. He dived into it.

He heard the Sikhs' triumphant war cries as they swarmed into the village. He heard the savage banging and kicking open of doors: and the quick confused exchange of shouts as the men

217

realized that the village was empty. They searched all the houses, moving systematically, looting whatever they could lay their hands on.

Ranna held his breath as the door to the barn opened.

"Oye! D'you think the Musslas are hiding here?" a coarse voice asked.

"We'll find out," another voice said.

Ranna crouched in the hay. The men were climbing all over the straw, slashing it with long sweeps of their swords and piercing it with their spears.

Ranna almost cried out when he felt the first sharp prick. He felt steel tear into his flesh. As if recalling a dream, he heard an old woman say: He's lost too much blood. Let him die in peace.

Ranna did not lose consciousness again until the last man left the barn.

And while the old city in Lahore, crammed behind its dilapidated Mogul gates, burned, thirty miles away Amritsar also burned. No one noticed Ranna as he wandered in the burning city. No one cared. There were too many ugly and abandoned children like him scavenging in the looted houses and the rubble of burnt-out buildings.

His rags clinging to his wounds, straw sticking in his scalped skull, Ranna wandered through the lanes stealing chapatties and grain from houses strewn with dead bodies, rifling the corpses for anything he could use. He ate anything. Raw potatoes, uncooked grains, wheat flour, rotting peels and vegetables.

No one minded the semi-naked specter as he looked in doors with his knowing, wide-set peasant eyes as men copulated with wailing children—old and young women. He saw a naked woman, her light Kashmiri skin bruised with purple splotches and cuts, hanging head down from a ceiling fan. And looked on with a child's boundless acceptance and curiosity as jeering men set her long hair on fire. He saw babies, snatched from their mothers, smashed against walls and their howling mothers brutally raped and killed.

Carefully steering away from the murderous Sikh mobs he arrived at the station on the outskirts of the city. It was cordoned off by barbed wire, and beyond the wire he recognized a huddle of Muslim refugees surrounded by Sikh and Hindu police. He stood before the barbed wire screaming, "*Amma! Amma!* Noni *chachi!* Noni *chachi!*"

A Sikh sepoy, his hair tied neatly in a khaki turban, ambled up to the other side of the wire. "Oye! What're you making such a racket for? Scram!" he said, raising his hand in a threatening gesture.

Ranna stayed his ground. He could not bear to look at the Sikh. His stomach muscles felt like choked drains. But he stayed his ground: "*I was trembling from head to toe,*" he says.

"O *me-kiya!* I say!" the sepoy shouted to his cronies standing by an opening in the wire. "This little motherfucker thinks his mother and aunt are in that group of Musslas."

"Send him here," someone shouted.

Ranna ran up to the men.

"Don't you know? Your mother married me yesterday," said a fat-faced, fat-bellied Hindu, his hairy legs bulging beneath the shorts of his uniform. "And your *chachi* married Makhan Singh," he said, indicating a tall young sepoy with a shake of his head.

"Let the poor bastard be," Makhan Singh said. "Go on: run along." Taking Ranna by his shoulder he gave him a shove.

The refugees in front watched the small figure hurtle towards them across the gravelly clearing. A middle-aged woman without a veil, her hair disheveled, moved forward holding out her arms.

The moment Ranna was close enough to see the compassion in her stranger's eyes, he fainted.

With the other Muslim refugees from Amritsar, Ranna was herded into a refugee camp at Badami Baug. He stayed in the camp, which is quite close to our Fire Temple, for two months, queuing for the doled-out chapatties, befriended by improvident refugees, until chance—if the random queries of five million refugees seeking their kin in the chaos of mammoth camps all over West Punjab can be called anything but chance—reunited him with his Noni *chachi* and Iqbal *chacha*.

Chapter 26

Cousin's cook drops hints. He tells Cousin he suspects where Ayah is. Yes, he thinks she's in Lahore.

Then he clams up. And no matter how much Cousin threatens or cajoles him, doesn't add one illuminating word. I dare not question the cook. In front of me he clams up. And in private threatens Cousin he won't tell him anything if he blabs to me.

I roam the bazaars holding Himat Ali's wizened finger, Hamida's glutinous hand. I visit fairs and *melas* riding on Yousaf's shoulders, looking here and there. And when I ride on the handlebar of his bicycle, peering into tongas, buses, bullock-carts and trucks, I sometimes think I spot Ayah and exclaim! But it always turns out to be someone who only resembles Ayah.

Godmother is influential. Even Colonel Bharucha visits her. Neighbors of all faiths drop in to talk and to pay their respects. But Godmother seldom ventures out. She only visits if someone is very sick or in extreme need of her.

Or if she feels the call to donate blood.

The call nags her this stifling July morning. Godmother tucks a cologne-watered handkerchief into a little pocket in her sari-blouse, puts on her maroon velvet going-out slippers, pins her going-out beige silk sari to her hair and armed with a black umbrella sets off in a tonga to bequeath blood. I accompany her. Schools and tuitions are suspended for summer vacations and I am spending the week with her. Hamida and Adi spend most evenings with us. Mother visits occasionally and I feel distanced from her—as with a guest.

Godmother lies down on a hard hospital bench covered only

with a white sheet. A nurse bends her arm back and forth and rubs the crease in her arm with cotton wool that smells just like the muzzle did when Colonel Bharucha operated on my leg. The lady doctor approaches with a hideous injection syringe and, sick to my stomach, I turn my face away and squeeze Godmother's hand. Her answering grip remains steady.

When I look at her again, the blood-sucking needle withdrawn, she appears to have grown longer—as if the noble deed has added stature to her horizontal form. I am certain her blood will save many wounded lives.

Perspiring and half-dead from the heat, we return from the hospital. Mini Aunty hands Godmother a precious half-glass of iced water from a thermos and says she would also like to donate blood.

Godmother is firm with her middle-aged kid sister. "No," she says, "you may kindly not donate your blood! I can't afford to have you go all faint and limp on me."

Slavesister looks unutterably deprived. "All right," she says, sagging against the kitchen door jamb. "Go to heaven all by yourself, then. Deny me even good deeds!"

Godmother is truly astonished.

"Is that what you believe?" she asks, staring at Slavesister slack-jawed and openmouthed; for once at a complete loss.

At last, shaking her head, Godmother rotates her thumb against her temple: "A screw loose somewhere," she says, looking dazed. "What's to become of her, I don't know . . . In heaven or in hell!"

Over the years Godmother has established a network of espionage with a reach of which even she is not aware. It is in her nature to know things: to be aware of what's going on around her. The day-to-day commonplaces of our lives unravel to her undercurrents that are lost to less perceptive humans. No baby—not even a kitten—is delivered within the sphere of her influence without her becoming instantly aware of its existence.

And this is the source of her immense power, this reservoir of random knowledge, and her knowledge of ancient lore and wisdom and herbal remedy. You cannot be near her without feeling her uncanny strength. People bring to her their joys and woes. Show her their sores and swollen joints. Distilling the right herbs, adroitly instilling the right word in the right ear, she secures wishes, smooths relationships, cures illnesses, battles wrongs, solaces grief and prevents mistakes. She has access to many ears. No one knows how many. And, when talking incessantly about my resurrected friend I relate to her the rigors of Ranna's experience, she achieves for him a minor miracle! Ranna is suddenly siphoned into the Convent of Jesus and Mary as a boarder.

It surprises me how easily Ranna has accepted his loss; and adjusted to his new environment. So. . . one gets used to anything . . . If one must. The small bitternesses and grudges I tend to nurse make me feel ashamed of myself. Ranna's ready ability to forgive a past none of us could control keeps him whole.

The Convent is on the outskirts of Shahdara, about halfway between Imam Din's village and Lahore. Barricaded by tall brick walls the girls' school accepts boys up to a certain age. Getting a poor refugee child admitted to a Convent school is as difficult as transposing him to a prosperous continent, and as beneficial. Not only for him, it is said, but for seven succeeding generations of the Ranna progeny. Ranna visits us on the weekends he can get a cycle ride into Lahore.

Godmother can move mountains from the paths of those she befriends and erect mountainous barriers where she deems it necessary.

She is on to something. I can tell. When I catch her goosgoosing with Slavesister and they stop whispering abruptly, I know they are talking of Ayah. Slavesister behaves as if they are not hiding anything from me. But Godmother, to her credit, looks guilty as hell.

She has never let me down yet. I have more faith in her investigative capacities than I have in Mother's and Electric-aunt's sorties.

The mystery of the women in the courtyard deepens. At night we hear them wailing, their cries verging on the inhuman. Sometimes I can't tell where the cries are coming from. From the women—or from the house next door infiltrated by our invisible neighbors.

There is a great deal of activity by day: of trucks going to and from the tin gates sealing the courtyard; of women shouting; but no hint of the turmoil and suffering that erupts at night.

And closer, and as upsetting, the caged voices of our parents fighting in their bedroom. Mother crying, wheedling. Father's terse, brash, indecipherable sentences. Terrifying thumps. I know they quarrel mostly about money. But there are other things they fight about that are not clear to me. Sometimes I hear Mother say, "No, Jana; I won't let you go! I won't let you go to her!" Sounds of a scuffle. Father goes anyway. Where does he go in the middle of the night? To whom? Why . . . when Mother loves him so? Although Father has never raised his hands to us, one day I surprise Mother at her bath and see the bruises on her body.

And at dawn the insistent roar of the zoo lion tracking me to whatever point of the world I cannot hide from him in my nightmares.

It gets so that I cannot sleep. Adi is asleep within moments, but I lie with my eyes open, staring at the shadows that have begun to haunt my room. The twenty-foot-high ceiling recedes and the pale light that blurs the ventilators creeps in, assuming the angry shapes of swirling phantom babies, of gaping wounds forming deformed crescents—and of Masseur's slender, skillful fingers searching the nightroom for Ayah.

And when I do fall asleep the slogans of the mobs reverberate in my dreams, pierced by women's wails and shrieks—and I awaken screaming for Ayah.

Mother rushes to my side and bends over me. In the faint glow from the night-light I see her hand sweep my body as she symbolically catches mischievous spirits and banishes them with a loud snap of her fingers. At the same time she blows on me, making a frightening noise like moaning winds: Whooooo! whoooooo! The sound is eerie enough to banish any presence: natural or supernatural. She places a six-inch iron nail, blessed by the Parsee mystic Mobed Ibera, the disciple of Dastur Kookadaru, under my mattress to ward off fear.

Sometimes Mother lies beside me, her touch as fresh and soothing as daylight, and tells me the old story of the little mouse with seven tails. Mother has wisely changed the ending. "And then there was only one tail left," she says, "and the little mousey came home laughing: 'Ha, ha, ha, ha!' " Mother's artificial laugh bounces off the walls so heartily that it dispels fear and I, too, laugh. "And the little mousey said," says my mother, " 'Mummy, mummy, no one teased me. They said, "Little mousey with one tail. Nicey mousey with one tail!" ' "

I have outgrown the story—but the intimacy it recalls lulls the doubts and fears in my growing mind.

Mother asks Hamida to sleep on a mat in our room. Hamida squats by my bed and we talk in whispers till I fall asleep.

One cold night I am awakened by a hideous wail. My teeth chattering, I sit up. I must have just dozed off, because Hamida is still sitting by my bed.

"Shush," she says. "Go to sleep . . . It's just some woman."

I lie down and Hamida patiently strokes my arm.

"Why do they wail and scream at night?" I ask.

It is not a subject I have broached till now, mindful of Hamida's sensibilities.

"Poor fate-smitten woman," says Hamida, sighing. "What can a sorrowing woman do but wail?"

"Who are those women?" I ask.

225

"God knows," says Hamida. "Go to sleep... there is nothing we can do... She'll be all right in the morning."

My heart is wrung with pity and horror. I want to leap out of my bed and soothe the wailing woman and slay her tormentors. I've seen Ayah carried away—and it had less to do with fate than with the will of men.

"Did you cry?" I ask Hamida.

"Who doesn't? We're all fate-smitten..."

"I mean, when you were there?"

Her hand on my leg goes still.

"I saw you before you came to us, you know. I saw you in the jail next door." I speak as gently as I know how.

"What nonsense you talk..."

"I looked down at you from a hole in the roof. You couldn't see me—but I saw you. I recognized you straightaway when you were talking to Mother about the job... But I didn't tell her!"

After a pause, breathing heavily in the dark, Hamida says, "Your mother knows I was there."

The woman in the jail has stopped wailing. It is so quiet—as it must be at the beginning of time.

"Why were you in jail?" I ask at last.

"It isn't a jail, Lenny baby... It's a camp for fallen women."

"What are fallen women?"

"*Hai!* The questions you ask! Your mother won't like such talk... Now keep quiet..."

"Are you a fallen woman?"

"*Hai*, my fate!" moans Hamida, suddenly slapping her forehead. She rocks on her heels and makes a crazy keening noise, sucking and expelling the air between her teeth.

"What's the matter? Don't do that... please don't do that," I whisper, leaning over to touch her.

"If your mother finds out this is how you talk, she'll throw me out! *Hai*, my fate!"

Again she slaps her forehead and makes that strangling nasal noise.

"I won't tell her... I promise! Stop it. Please don't do that!"

226

I get out of bed and press her face into my chest. I rock her, and Hamida's tears soak right through my flannel nightgown.

I won't mention her fall ever again. I can't bear to hurt her: I'd rather bite my tongue than cause pain to her grief-wounded eye.

But this resolve, too, goes the way of all resolutions.

"What's a fallen woman?" I ask Godmother.

"A woman who falls off an airplane."

Godmother can be like that sometimes. Exasperating. She can't help it.

"Wouldn't she break her head and die?" I say patiently.

"Maybe."

"But Hamida didn't break her head . . . She says she's a fallen woman."

"Oh?" Godmother's expression changes.

As I tell her of my conversation with Hamida, Slavesister loiters about the room. She pretends to arrange papers on the desk. The letters and papers are already sorted out and neatly stacked. Although she has her back to me, I can tell her ears are switched on.

"Hamida was kidnapped by the Sikhs," says Godmother seriously. On serious matters I can always trust her to level with me. "She was taken away to Amritsar. Once that happens, sometimes, the husband—or his family—won't take her back."

"Why? It isn't her fault she was kidnapped!"

"Some folk feel that way—they can't stand their women being touched by other men."

It's monstrously unfair: but Godmother's tone is accepting. I think of what Himat-Ali-alias-Hari once told me when I reached to lift a tiny sparrow that had tumbled from its nest on our veranda.

"Let it be," he'd stopped me. "The mother will take care of it. If our hands touch it, the other sparrows will peck it to death."

"Even the mother?" I asked.

"Even the mother!" he'd said.

It doesn't make sense—but if that's how it is, it is.

"That's why your mummy tells you to stay with Hamida all

227

the time—or with us," says Slavesister unctuously. "When your mother tells you something, it's for your own good."

There she goes again: butting in and making serious matters trivial.

"Her mother's not here," says Godmother. "It won't do you any good buttering her up in her absence."

"And I'm not married either! It doesn't matter if I'm kidnapped," I speak up.

"Oh yes? And who'll marry you then? It'll be hard enough finding someone for you as it is."

"Mummy says: my husband will search the world with a candle to find me!"

"Poor fellow... He won't know you the way we do, will he? Your husband will clutch his head in his hands and weep!"

"Cousin wants to marry me!" I'm surprised how smug I feel saying it. I don't think I particularly want to marry Cousin—but though he has not actually asked me to, I think he has implied it. It's a comforting thought. If only as a last resort.

"He hasn't seen any girls besides our Lame Lenny, Three For a Penny. Wait till he sees the world!" says Mini Aunty.

What an asinine thing to say about my worldly Cousin! Even Godmother suppresses a smile.

"Kindly go about your business," she tells her sister. "And stop messing with those papers! As it is, I can't find anything when I want it."

"What is the matter with you?" Cousin asks.

"Nothing."

I'm feeling despondent. When something upsets me this much I find it impossible to talk. It used not to be so. I wonder: am I growing up? At least I've stopped babbling *all* my thoughts.

This idiocy of bottled-up emotions can't be a symptom of growing up, surely! More likely I'm reverting to infancy the way old people do. I feel so sorry for myself—and for Cousin—and for all the senile, lame and hurt people and fallen women—and the condition of the world—in which countries can be broken, people slaughtered and cities burned—that I burst into tears. I feel I will never stop crying.

"Is your stomach hurting?" Cousin asks cautiously, afraid of a rebuff.

I'm grateful that he has stayed his ground at least and not gone tearing off on some pretext to avoid my irrational outburst.

"No." I shake my head. "I'm not hurting."

And then, of its own accord, my mouth blurts, "No one will marry me. I limp!" Almost at once I feel less aggrieved.

"But I'll marry you," volunteers my gallant cousin.

I search his face through my tears. Thank God, he doesn't sound the least martyred. I couldn't bear it. He looks fond and sincere. I find it hard to recall my multitudinous anguishes of a moment before. I even feel a little foolish. And alarmed—lest I irrevocably commit myself to Cousin.

"A slight limp is attractive," says Cousin, solemn and authoritative.

"Oh yes?" I say, airing my doubt.

"I like the way it makes your bottom wiggle." He waves two fingers back and forth.

I twist strenuously and, tugging my short dress taut across my buttocks, peer down. There is very little bottom to see.

"When you grow up, you'll have a much bigger bottom," asserts my solicitous and perceptive cousin. "It will look very attractive, then . . . ," he says somewhat uncertainly.

My deepening skepticism has infected him too.

"I read a story," he continues gravely, "in which the heroine limped. Her one leg was shorter. She didn't even have a pretty face. But her limp was so sexy, everybody wanted to marry her!"

I don't care for Cousin's secondhand consolations. In any case, I don't want him harping on my limp.

"Colonel Bharucha says I'll stop limping by the time I grow up."

"A pity," says Cousin. "I find it attractive."

"I can always keep it, if you like," I say politely, and further guarding my options, I add: "Let's see how I feel about marrying you when I grow up."

"Do you find me attractive?" Cousin suddenly asks, gazing compellingly into my eyes.

"Yes," I say courteously, and avert my eyes.

"How attractive?" Cousin is insistent. "Do you think you could love me passionately? Die for me?"

I reflect a moment. Cousin certainly does not arouse in me the rapture Masseur aroused in Ayah... I recall the bewildering longings the look on Masseur's face stirred in me when he looked at Ayah... And other stirrings...

"I don't find you that attractive," I say truthfully.

"I suppose you're too young," says Cousin. "You haven't known passion."

I open my eyes wide and look demurely at Cousin, and let it pass.

But Cousin can't: "Do you find anyone more attractive than me?"

"Yes," I say, "I think I found Masseur more attractive..."

I surprise myself. Mouthing the words articulates my feelings and reveals myself to me.

"But he was old!" says Cousin, equally surprised.

I suddenly feel shy and Cousin looks unutterably defeated. I think my sudden shyness convinces him of my wayward heart more than any protestations would.

"Who else do you find attractive?" Cousin asks, managing to wipe his face and voice of all expression.

"Oh I don't know... There was a little Sikh boy..."

"Do me a favor," Cousin says. "Think about all the people you find more attractive than me—and let me know."

I have been so engaged by my reaction to the names named that I fail to notice the bitterness and sarcasm that have crept into his voice.

I look about me with new eyes. The world is athrob with men. As long as they have some pleasing attribute—height, width or beauty of face—no man is too old to attract me. Or too young. Tongawallahs, knife-sharpeners, shopkeepers, policemen, schoolboys, Father's friends, all exert their compelling pull on my runaway fantasies in which I am recurringly spirited away to remote Himalayan hideouts; there to be worshipped, fought over, died for, importuned and wooed until, aroused to a passion that tingles from my scalp into the very tips of my fingers, I finally permit my lover to lay his hands upon my chest. It is no small bestowal of favor, for my chest is no longer flat.

Two little bumps have erupted beneath my nipples. Flesh of my flesh, exclusively mine. And I am hard put to protect them. I guard them with a possessive passion beside which my passion for possessing Rosy's little glass jars pales. Only I may touch them. Not Cousin. Not Imam Din. Not Adi. Not anybody. I can't trust anyone.

Not even Mother who has taken to bathing me; and with her characteristic prim and solemn expression bunches her fingers round them and goes: "Pom-pom."

"Let me, let me . . . ," says Cousin and pokes his hand out every-which-way every chance he gets. I find it fatiguing to maintain my distance from him.

And from Adi, who resolutely materializes whenever I'm bathing and glues his eye to a crack in the bathroom door. When Hamida blocks it, Adi shifts to another crack: and when that too is plugged, he jumps up and down on a ledge outside the bathroom window with a rapt determination that is like an elemental force. Hearing Hamida's twittering remonstrances and my shrill screams, Imam Din emerges roaring: "Wait till I catch you, you shameless bugger," and carries Adi, wiggling and kicking, towards the kitchen. I peer out of the window and Adi's face, flushed with a cold rage, bodes ill for any ideas Imam Din might have of sitting him on his lap. Even Imam Din could not handle that frustrated cobra fury.

As the mounds beneath my nipples grow, my confidence grows. I tell Imam Din to hold Adi in the kitchen, push Hamida out of the bathroom and lock the door. I examine my chest in the small mirror hanging at an angle from the wall and play with them as with cuddly toys. What with my limp and my burgeoning breasts—and the projected girth and wiggle of my future bottom—I feel assured that I will be quite attractive when I'm grown up.

Cousin walks with me and Hamida to the bazaars and gardens, rides with us in tongas, and I dutifully point out to him all the men and boys I find appealing. "See the boy with the cute little buck teeth?" I ask. "I could die for him!" and "Look-look-look," I say physically turning Cousin's head. "Look at that fellow in the tonga with his feet up!"

"I'm keeping tabs," says Cousin mournfully after this has gone on for some days. "You are attracted by roughly ten percent of the male population in Lahore."

"Is that too much?" I enquire.

"Why not me?" Cousin demands, ignoring my question. "What's wrong with me?"

"You're too young, maybe."

"But some of the boys you liked are younger... I'll grow up!"

My heart sinks sadly for my cousin. Why don't I feel all suffocated and shy when I'm with him? I try to fathom my emotions.

"Maybe I don't need to attract you. You're already attracted," I say.

It is like that with Cousin. He even shows me ME!

I've admitted it before: I have a wayward heart. Weak. Susceptible and fickle. But why do I call it my heart? And blame my blameless heart? And not blame instead the incandescence of my womb?

Chapter 27

I spend hours on the servants' quarters' roof looking down on the fallen women. The turnover, as they are rescued, sorted out and restored to their families, is so rapid that I can barely keep track of the new faces that appear and so soon disappear. The camp is getting crowded. If this is where they bring kidnapped women, this is where I'll find my Ayah.

Hamida knows where to find me when Mother asks for me—or when someone is going to Godmother's on an errand and thinks of taking me along. Sometimes, furtively climbing the stairs, Hamida sits quietly with me and together we look at the dazed and dull faces. If they look up we smile, and Hamida makes little reassuring gestures; but the women only look bewildered and rarely smile back.

I wonder about the women's children. Don't they miss their mothers? I pray that their husbands and families will take them back. Hamida seldom mentions her children. All I've been able to get out of her is that she has two teenage sons and two daughters, one as old as me and one younger.

"The youngest was just beginning to walk," says Hamida one crisp afternoon as we sun ourselves on the roof. Hamida has come to fetch me for lunch, but she is willing to stay for a while.

"Don't you miss your children?" I ask.

"Of course," says Hamida.

"Then why don't you go to see them?"

"Their father won't like it."

"They must miss you. You could see them secretly, couldn't you?"

"No," says Hamida, turning her face away. "They're better off as they are. My sister-in-law will look after them. If their father gets to know I've met them, he will only get angry, and the children will suffer."

"I don't like your husband," I say.

"He's a good man," says Hamida, hiding her face bashfully in her *chuddar*. "It's my kismet that's no good. . . we are *khut-putli*, puppets, in the hands of fate."

"I don't believe that," I say. "Cousin says we can change our kismet if we want to. The lines on our palms can also change!"

Hamida gives me a queer quizzical look. "Have you heard of the prince who was eaten by a tiger?" she asks.

"No," I say, shaking my head and settling comfortably against the roof wall to listen.

It is the perfect day for a story. The sun is warm on our skins, casting a quiet, lazy spell on the afternoon. It is the first story Hamida tells me. Later I discover she has a fund of unusual and depressing little tales.

Once upon a time there was a king who had no children, says Hamida. Night and day the king and his queen prayed for a son. They traveled afar, visiting one holy-man after another, and visited all the shrines of saints in their kingdom. The queen wove temple saris for the various goddesses, stuck flowers in their images and covered the goddesses with gold.

One night the king had a dream. In his dream a ragged holy-man with wild hair said: "O, king, your dearest wish will be granted. Before the year is out you will have a son. But you have accumulated an unfavorable karma. In your past life you were disobedient to your guru and, at times, even irreverent. You will be punished for your insolence. Your son will be eaten by a tiger in his sixteenth year."

As foretold, the royal couple was blessed with a beautiful son. The king and queen rejoiced and diligently distributed food and money among their poorer subjects to improve the condition of their karmas and earn blessings.

The king decreed that all tigers be hunted and killed. He organized tiger hunts and rode at the head of the elephant cavalry to decimate the beasts rounded up by the drummers. He offered handsome rewards for the pelts brought by the hunters.

The prince grew tall and beautiful. He was compassionate and filled with laughter. The more they loved him the more his subjects feared the prophecy.

By the time the prince was ten years old they had killed all the tigers and, as an added precaution, all the domestic and alley cats: for what is a cat if not a miniature tiger? The tigers in the surrounding kingdoms were also killed.

As the prince grew older he yearned to hunt: and at last the king was satisfied that it was safe for the prince to venture into the forest. Most people had forgotten what a tiger even looked like!

The fateful year dawned. The prince turned sixteen.

Once again the wild-haired holy-man appeared in the king's dream. "The tiger who will eat the prince is already near," he said to the trembling king.

Again the hunters beat the bushes and searched the woods. There were no pug marks or droppings even—no trace to show that tigers had once inhabited the forests.

The prince was confined to the palace. He was never left unattended. Huntsmen patrolled the forests and armed guards the palace gates.

The king and queen prayed more, fasted oftener and did all manner of penance. The king gave his fine robes to the beggars and wore the coarse garments of the fakirs. He distributed large portions of his wealth among the poor and donated fortunes to shrines, mosques, temples and churches. He undertook vows and oaths that would bind him to a lifetime of penitence if his son was spared.

The year was almost past. The king, in his penitent's sackcloth, was discussing affairs of state in the *darbar* when the prince walked in. The king made room for his son on the marble *takth*, covered with silk rugs. The assembly bowed till the prince settled amidst the velvet cushions and signaled them to sit. He lay back on the bolsters and after a while he fell asleep.

The *darbar* was almost over when the prince awakened from a terrifying dream. His frightened eyes opened on a finely wrought hunting scene painted on the ceiling. Royal huntsmen, spears poised in varying attitudes of attack, surrounded a fierce tiger, bare-fanged and richly striped. Suddenly the prince screamed and cried: "Oh! The tiger! The tiger! He's got me!" He fell back and writhing in agony died.

In the pandemonium that followed, the king's eyes quickly traced the path of his son's congealed stare: and, horrified, he saw the lifelike glow on the rich pelt dim, and the tiger's shining eyes revert to yellow paint!

Hamida, who has been gawking skywards like the horrified monarch, returns halfway to earth and looks at me.

But I'm in no mood to countenance tragedy. Despite the unnatural angle of my upended hairs, despite the accelerated beat of my heart, despite the gloaming images of the screaming prince and the chill on my skin, I rend the story with savage logic. If the king's karma was so lousy how come he was king? And why should the poor prince suffer for his father's...? And how can a painted tiger...?

"Perhaps it's not so unreal as it is unfair!" I conclude.

"What does Fate care?" says Hamida with placid and omniscient certainty. "That's why it is fate!"

We become still: cocking our ears to a din and uproar coming from the kitchen.

"Imam Din's caught the *billa!*" says Hamida, her narrow face lighting up. And just as Ayah and I ran to the back at the sounds of struggle with Hari's dhoti, we now run towards the kitchen: Hamida holding me by the hand and my feet flying to match her long strides.

Neighbors and the servants already form a small crowd. Imam Din, one leg on the ground and one on the kitchen steps, has a huge black and battle-scarred cat trapped in the screen door and is pressing his whole weight on the frame to hold the slippery intruder. The cat, caught below its ribs, is suspended a foot off the floor. Frantically twisting, its teeth bared, the panicked creature is spitting wildly.

Imam Din roars: "That'll teach you to sneak into the kitchen, you one-eared monster! Make all the noise you want! I'm not letting go of you, you badmash *billa!*"

The crowd outside the kitchen grows as more people run up from the road. Someone shouts: "That tom sneaks into our kitchen too! Teach the fellow!" and someone else yells: "He sure won't poke his snout into your pans again!" And Yousaf yells, "That's enough, *yaar! Bas kar!*" and Imam Din says, "This time I'm going to teach him . . . It's the third time I've caught the thug! Poke your nose into the milk will you?"

"Let him go," I scream. "He'll die."

"He's not about to die," says Hamida. "He's a tough old alley cat!"

The Morris rolls up the drive and comes to a stop in the porch. Mother beeps the horn and shouts: "What's going on?"

Imam Din is so intent on chastising the cat that he doesn't hear her, and oblivious of her presence roars invective at the caterwauling animal.

"Let her go at once!" screams Mother, slamming shut the door of the car. She cannot see the cat's gender—it is secreted behind the door—but the rest of us seem to know it's a *him.*

Mother grabs hold of Imam Din's shirt and pulls but I don't think he even notices.

"Get the fly-swat, Lenny!" screams Mother in an absolute frenzy.

I dash in and fetch the fly-swat with a long reed handle and a wire-mesh flap. Mother snatches it from my hand and, waving her arms in an awkwardly feminine and energetic way, swats Imam Din with it. She strikes his legs, arms, shoulders and even his shaven head.

All at once Imam Din lets go the door and grips his arm. The surprised cat bounds down the steps and spitting and bouncing like a charred firecracker streaks zigzagging past the startled crowd.

Imam Din turns to face Mother. Glasses dramatically awry,

face flushed, she continues to whack him. Imam Din looks bewildered—and searches confusedly for the flies she is swatting on his person. When he realizes her fury is directed at him, his bewilderment turns to incredulity, and then to shock. He holds out his hand and like a man taking away a dangerous toy, snatches the fly-swat from Mother. He examines it as if he's never seen a fly-swat before.

Surprised at being so peremptorily disarmed Mother yells: "Get out of my sight! *Duffa ho!*"

Large tears welling from his old eyes, Imam Din turns his broad back on her, and followed by my excited mother walks zombie-like into the crowd. Absorbed and protected by the crowd Imam Din visualizes the tears in his shirt and the fine lines of blood congealing on his forearms.

"Shame on you! Tormenting a small cat! Get out of my sight!" Mother shouts once more, and whirling around in her silk sari and tinted glasses marches inside.

"Look!" says Imam Din to the sympathetic crowd. "I can't believe it...She drew blood!"

"It was only a fly-swat, *yaar*," says Yousaf taking hold of his arm. He shouts at the gawkers: "What's there to see? Go on, push off!"

Muttering and laughing among themselves the crowd breaks up. Some vault the walls to neighboring houses and some walk down the drive to the road.

Yousaf leads Imam Din into the kitchen. Hamida and I follow. Hamida saying in her conciliatory and submissive manner: "What if *Baijee* had a whip, brother? What would you've done then? Oh, ho! Look at the tears in your clothes," she exclaims. "Tch-tch-tch! Don't worry. I'll sew them so they'll look like new!"

Imam Din refuses to have his clothes mended and remains sullen all afternoon.

When Father returns late in the evening Imam Din presents himself before Father's bicycle and with a most injured countenance says: "*Baijee* struck me with a fly-swat! I bled!"

Father places his cycle on its stand and raising his brows in a clutch of surprised wrinkles looks at us out of baffled eyes.

"Imam Din caught the *billa* in the kitchen door, and wouldn't let him go. And Mummy hit him with the fly-flapper," I explain.

Father turns his astonished eyes upon Imam Din.

Turning and twisting, Imam Din displays a scattered and spidery mesh of wounds where the wire scratched him. "This . . . And this. And see this!" he says stretching the small tears in his lungi and shirt.

Father locks his cycle. Making a few clucking noises of insincere sympathy he prepares to go in, when Mother bursts out of banging springdoors shouting: "Stop sniveling in front of Sahib, you big idiot! You're lucky it was only a fly-flap! Go in, someone, and get him bangles. If he whines like a woman he must wear bangles!"

Despite her shouting Mother sounds good-humored and we release our suppressed laughter. Even Father cannot suppress his tight little smile.

Shaking his head sheepishly Imam Din ambles off towards the kitchen and Mother laughs and clings to Father and Father continues to smile, despite her clinging, and says: "The fly-flap's upset him. If you'd used a stick he wouldn't have minded so much."

Adi and I laugh and laugh and hug Father and our clinging mother. I feel deliriously lighthearted. So does Adi. Father has spoken directly to Mother: addressing her instead of the walls, furniture, ceiling—or using us as deflecting conduits to sound his messages off. It is becoming an increasingly rare occurrence—this business of his talking to our mother: out of public or party view that is.

And suddenly, the hunt for Ayah is off. I sense it. So does Adi.

They only pretend to look for her. Mother still takes off in the Morris but I know it is not to look for Ayah. I can tell by the way the car's wheels flatten on the stones and by the determined angle of Skinny-aunt's chin—that the car's dicky is loaded with petrol. They can set fire to the world for all I care! I want my Ayah.

Chapter 28

It is a bad phase in my life. Even Cousin is avoiding me. I haven't seen him for a week. I must talk to him about my concerns or I'll crack up. Adi and I go over to Electric-aunt's. Cousin is studying for his exams.

"I don't know where the sun rises these days," says Electric-aunt in awed and perplexed pleasure, holding the screen door open and ushering us in. "Your cousin doesn't wish to be disturbed even by you!" She looks at me archly and flashes all her little goat's teeth in a conceited smile.

Electric-aunt parts the navy-blue curtains and, poking only her head through, quietly whispers: "Lenny and Adi are here, dear. Won't you see them for just five minutes?"

Since I can't hear his response, and I'm determined to see him, I throw him a line: "All work and no play makes Jack a dull boy!"

I know he'll bite. Imagine getting away with calling Cousin *dull*.

Cousin drifts into the sitting room in his long shorts and short socks, looking all standoffish and preoccupied, and greets us unenthusiastically. He perches on the edge of the three-piece sofa, tilting his legs primly to one side and, as if he's a grown man masquerading in short legs, makes desultory small talk with Adi. He doesn't even look at me. Except when I force him to by addressing him insistently and then he glances my way briefly and coldly, before again bestowing his attention on Adi. To leave no doubt of his tedium at our presence he folds the newspaper into a stiff bat and, with nerve-racking springs and explosive whacks, swats flies on the sofas, tables and radio top.

Electric-aunt covers her ears. "Oh! Do stop being so jumpy, dear," she exclaims and, like an angular streak of zigzag lightning, darts from the room.

Cousin perches on the sofa again, elegantly crossing his ankles this time and hastily, before he has a chance to spring up and swat more flies, I whisper: "They've stopped looking for Ayah!"

"Have they?" says Cousin, looking down at me coolly, and turns to Adi as if I've said something as uneventful and uncomplicated as: "Godmother rapped Mini Aunty's knuckles with her punkah!"

I can't understand it. I'm furious. "Let's leave him to his dreary studies," I say witheringly. But Adi, who has not received such singular attention from Cousin since the time he was almost kidnapped and basked for two days in glory, is reluctant to leave. I have to drag him away.

It is unnerving. The more aloof Cousin becomes, the more I think about him. I find my daydreams, for the first time, occupied by his stubby person and adenoidal voice. They are pedestrian and colorless compared to my caveman and kidnapper fantasies, but they are as completely engrossing. I thrill. I feel tingles shoot from my scalp to my toe tips. And Cousin's proximity, compared to the remoteness of imagined lovers tucked away in unseen wildernesses, drives me to reckless excess.

Against all my instincts and sense of dignity, I chase Cousin. I hang around Electric-aunt's house and around Cousin—when he tolerates my presence. I fetch him glasses of water and bunches of grapes and sharpen his pencils and copy out his homework and follow him wherever he goes. If he goes into the bathroom I wait patiently outside the door—hungering for any crumbs he might throw by way of aloof comment or observation. These he restricts—like my father with Mother—to impatient and disparaging monosyllables, mute signals and irate scowls.

And while I hang about Cousin, my eyes hang on him, and I shamelessly and eloquently ogle Cousin.

"Are you in love with him or something?" Adi asks artlessly, but I catch a sly glitter at the edge of his eyes when he turns away. I don't care. Let him think what he likes.

Ranna still visits us on Sundays, if he gets a ride on a bicycle or in a cart. But this Sunday when he comes, his scars covered by crisp white cotton, his bruised face eager; though my heart goes out to him, my mind is filled with thoughts of Cousin. My time consumed in his pursuit. Ranna tags along. But after this he visits less frequently. He goes to Imam Din's village instead, to be with his uncle and Noni *chachi* and his cousins. In any case we are growing apart. It is inevitable. The social worlds we inhabit are too different; our interests divergent.

Cousin is restored to me on a great surge of excitement when he bursts into my room and bolting the door breathes into my ear, "I saw Ayah!"

My heart pounds so wildly I cannot speak. Where? Here? In our house? But then Cousin wouldn't have bolted the door. Ayah must be at the Recovered Women's Camp!

"Where is she—in the camp?" I ask, voicing my assumption. And feeling weak-kneed, I sit on the bed.

"I saw her in a taxi. At Charing Cross," says Cousin, breathing so close I'm forced to lie back. Looking annoyingly complacent and placing an arm on either side of me, Cousin, the bearer of great good news, the restorer of withheld warmth, bears down on me: and in that instant I realize that his aloofness was only a sham calculated to arouse my ardor. Bent on further pleasuring me, squashing his panting chest on my flattened bosom, Cousin gives me a soggy kiss. Poor Cousin. His sense of timing is all wrong. The news about Ayah has cooled my passion. Pushing him back and holding him at arm's length, I say, "If you don't tell me everything at once, I'll knee your balls!" (I have grown up!) "Who was she with? Where is she?"

Cousin, resuming his aloof stance, examines his nails and snottily says: "I said, I saw her in a taxi. You know . . . pass by."

"You could have followed the taxi," I howl.

"How? I have engines in my legs?"

I'm not perturbed by his sarcasm or his disdain. His coldness is a hoax anyway.

"Did she see you? How did she look? Did you wave?"

"I don't think she saw me," says Cousin, thawing before my importunate queries. "She was all made up!"

"Really? Tell me! What do you mean, made up?"

I scramble across the bed on my knees and grab Cousin by his curly hair.

"Like a film actress," he says.

Cousin turns in order to accommodate the rest of his body to his twisted neck and, focusing his eyes on my chest, carefully places his hands on my breasts. I draw back, slapping his hands till my palms sting, feeling sick and all shriveled up.

Cousin looks at me, lovesick and sheepish, his spanked fingers quivering guiltily on his thighs.

"If you ever do that again, I'll break your fingers, knuckle by knuckle," I say severely. (The previous threat appears to have had no effect—hence the changed perspective.)

"But I love you," says Cousin. As if that condones his lascivious conduct.

"Well I don't!"

"Then why did you hang around me? And make all those funny eyes and stare at me?"

"I won't anymore. You were only pretending to be stand-offish! You're a phony!"

"Ha! It worked, didn't it? I had you panting with passion!"

"You didn't!"

"Oh, yes? Look," says Cousin, conciliatory: "I love you. But I can't pretend not to all my life just so you'll run after me."

"You're supposed to chase me!" I say. "Boys are supposed to chase girls!"

"But you run away!"

"It's only when you put your hands here and there and everywhere."

"Even before you grew your breasts you didn't love me," says Cousin bitterly. "You find everybody but me attractive!"

"I can't help it. If that's the way I feel—that's how it is."

The next day, angrily hauling me by my organdy sleeve before Godmother, Cousin complains, "She loves approximately half of Lahore . . . Why can't she love me?"

Godmother, in her wisdom, says: "It's simply a case of *Ghar ki murg; dal barabar.* A neighbor's beans are tastier than household chickens."

"But she's just a household chicken, too! Still I love her!" wails Cousin, his nasal voice cracking and squeaking. Passion does make one silly . . . I should know! I feel awfully sorry for him.

"Don't worry," says the slave, waddling up and mussing his hair. "It's only puppy love. Wait'll you start noticing your neighboring chicks!"

"So?" demands Godmother. "What about the young cocks Lenny will notice?"

"Yes? What about them?" I repeat.

If Cousin wasn't trying so hard to be manful, he'd be crying.

We arrive at a compromise, a finely delineated covenant: I will keep an open mind and let bygones be bygones, and Cousin will stop wooing me and wait a couple of years before touching my breasts again. We shall see how I feel about it then.

In the meantime Cousin sensibly sets about becoming indispensable. Knowing the way to my heart, he scurries about trying to find out the whereabouts of Ayah. He brings me rumors, and acting on the misleading leads, wastes energy on futile forays into the remotest, seediest and most dangerous parts of the congested city.

Chapter 29

And then, late one evening, I, too, see Ayah. It doesn't register at
once. It is only after the taxi has driven past, slowing at the corner
of Mozang Chawk and Temple Road, that I realize that the flashy
woman with the blazing lipstick and chalky powder and a huge
pink hibiscus in her hair, and unseeing eyes enlarged like an actress's with kohl and mascaraed eyelashes, sitting squashed between
two thin poets, was Ayah.

In the evening I pester Hamida to take me to the Queen's
Garden. She has never taken us there. She says she feels shy sitting
among all those strangers.

When I finally get her to agree to take us, Mother announces
that Godmother wants Adi and me to spend the night with her.

Dr. Manek Mody is visiting again, and he wishes to see us.

"It's the third time I've told you to put the water to boil!"
scolds Godmother from her bed. "What's the matter with you? The
Demon of Laziness finally get you?"

"I'm going, I'm going." Slavesister's string-bed creaks as she
stands up in her crumpled nightie. "Rodabai, you are so impatient.
Really . . . "

"I'm impatient? Do you know what time it is? Do you know
Manek attended to the milkman while your Lazyship snored?"

Dr. Manek Mody peeps alertly from behind his rustling newspaper. Having been awake for an hour, he's ready for excitement.

Adi stirs beside me and sits up sleepily. I prop myself up on
my elbows.

"Even the children awake before you," says Godmother
sternly.

"Shame, shame," says Dr. Mody fastidiously holding the tip of his nose. "Poppy shame!"

Slavesister's rat-tail braid has come loose and untidy strands of graying hair plaster her neck and back. Although it is only the middle of April we require the ceiling fan that is groaning round and round. Slavesister wipes her moist face on her sleeve.

"I think the demon has found permanent lodging in her!" mutters Godmother.

Abandoning the newspaper, the doctor springs out of his chair, saying, "I'll exorcise the demon. I know how!"

Tilting forward and extending his index finger he says to Mini Aunty: "Here, pull it."

"Don't be silly, Manek," says Mini Aunty.

"Come on, pull," coaxes the doctor, looking like a brown-domed elf. "I swear, you'll hear the demon leave."

The flaps of Adi's ears move forward. He's that curious.

So am I.

Godmother, propped on her pillows, displays a solemn face. But curiosity and amusement quiver in the tension of her restrained muscles.

"Do as Manek says," she orders, as if instructing a child to drink Milk of Magnesia.

Ignoring her and shaking her head, Slavesister carries her drowsy, martyr's smile into the kitchen.

Dr. Mody rushes in after her and, listing forward once again, points his finger.

"Please, Mini Aunty, please pull it," Adi and I clamor, crowding into the kitchen.

Godmother lowers her feet to the floor and, sitting forward on her cot, peers at us. "Your hand won't fall off you know," she calls. "Here's someone perfectly willing to exorcise your demons and what do you do? Insult him!"

"He's a doctor, not a magician!" says Slavesister.

"I practise exorcism in my spare time—didn't you know? Try it . . . My finger won't explode."

"Stubborn as a donkey!" decrees Godmother through the door.

"Please, Mini Aunty, be a sport," I beg. Adi is so excited, and

247

so nervous that the exorcism may not materialize—or take place in his absence—that he dances from foot to foot and has tears in his eyes.

"Oh, all right!" says Slavesister, suddenly capitulating. She tugs at the doctor's finger and, acquiring an air of intense concentration, the gifted doctor farts.

He stands up straight and looks as startled as us. "Some demon! Did you hear him? He almost tore my ass!"

"Much obliged to you, Manek," calls Godmother from her bed.

"What d'you have in your stomach? Atom bombs?" enquires Mini Aunty, giving the doctor a whack on his chest.

"That's no way to treat an exorciser," the doctor says, staggering back a step and looking at her with a slighted countenance.

"It is," says Mini Aunty, giving him another whack.

"Behave yourself, Mini!" shouts Godmother from the bedroom. "The poor man risked his life for you!"

"How did you do that?" asks Adi, his legs perfectly still, his face agog.

"Prayer and practice," says Dr. Mody. "Here, pull my finger."

He tilts forward and Adi tugs at his pointing finger. With compressed lips and quivering chill the doctor lets loose a crackling battery of crisp wind. Again Adi pulls and again he farts.

"Me too," I clamor.

The doctor obligingly directs his finger at me. When I pull nothing happens. I'm disappointed.

"Too bad," says the doctor. "You have no demons today. We'll try tomorrow."

In the next three days Cousin, Adi and I are possessed by a posse of demons so numerous that the doctor is hard-pressed to exorcise them. He directs Mini Aunty to feed him huge quantities of what he calls anti-demon potions: and Godmother's rooms reek of cabbage, beans and hard-boiled eggs.

Since we all ingest the same nourishment, I fall asleep to a medley of winds: the doctor's magnificent explosions, Godmother's and Slavesister's muted put-putterings, Oldhusband's bass bubblings and Adi's and my high-pitched and protracted eeeeeeps.

Oldhusband? He's still inhabiting the pages?

Clearly, he has not, as I'd thought, passed away.

Let him stay, as we all stay, in Godmother's talcum-powdered and intrusive wake.

I cannot believe my eyes. The Queen has gone! The space between the marble canopy and the marble platform is empty. A group of children, playing knuckles, squat where the gunmetal queen sat enthroned. Bereft of her presence, the structure looks unwomaned.

The garden scene has depressingly altered. Muslim families who added color when scattered among the Hindus and Sikhs, now monopolize the garden, depriving it of color. Even the children, covered in brocades and satins, cannot alleviate the austerity of the black burkas and white *chuddars* that shroud the women. It is astonishing. The absence of the brown skin that showed through the fine veils of Hindu and Sikh women, and beneath the dhoties and shorts of the men, has changed the complexion of the queenless garden. There are fewer women. More men.

Hamida, her head and torso modestly covered by her coarse *chuddar*, holding her lank limbs close, sits self-consciously on the grass by herself. There is little comfort in laying my head on her rigid lap.

Adi and I wander from group to group, peering into faces beneath white skullcaps and above ascetic beards. The Azan must have sounded. Some women spread prayer mats on the grass and kneeling start to pray. I feel uneasy. Like Hamida, I do not fit. I know we will not find familiar faces here.

"I saw Ayah! It was her!"

It is cool outside. The sun has set—and in the protracted dusk I am straddling Godmother and clutching her face in my hands. My legs have grown so long I can touch the ground with my toes.

"It must be someone who looks like Ayah. With all that make-up on it's hard to tell."

Godmother is being intractable.

"I saw her with my own eyes," I say, pulling down the skin beneath my eyes.

"Sometimes we only see what we wish to see," says Mini Aunty, issuing the nugget of wisdom as if she's an oracle. "And don't do that," she adds, "you'll grow pouches under your eyes."

"I know the difference between what I see and what I only want to see," I shout. I wish she wouldn't intrude. As it is, it's harder to convince Godmother than I'd expected. She must believe me. She's the only one who takes me seriously—except Cousin—and he hasn't been able to unearth anything yet.

"But Cousin also saw her," I say.

"It can't be her. Ayah is with her family in Amritsar!" Godmother conveys a certainty that for an instant undermines mine. It can only mean that her network has failed her. I am dismayed.

"How can you be so sure?" I ask.

Godmother hesitates, then she says, gravely, "Ask your mother."

"What's she got to do with it?"

I'm surprised. It's not like Godmother to pass the buck. "What's happening?" I cry. "Why isn't anyone telling me anything?"

"Lenny, there's some things best left alone," says Godmother.

"You should send for the family exorcist, Rodabai," says Mini Aunty. "Manek will rid her of her stubbornness."

"If you can't keep your mouth shut, go inside," Godmother says sharply. Her nostrils are twitching. I've seldom heard her talk to Slavesister like this—totally without her tongue in her cheek.

I feel hopeless. I rub my runny nose and my tears on Godmother's blouse. I'm horribly frightened that Godmother, despite all her canny and uncanny resources, might be misled.

And Godmother, unable to bear my confusion and anguish, and guilty because of her own deviousness, says, "Lenny, have you noticed how busy your mummy's been all year? Going out all the time?"

I nod.

"I'll tell you a secret," says Godmother, "but I want to be sure you won't tell anyone. It could get your mother into real trouble."

I draw back and permit Godmother to search my solemn face and my honorable eyes. She trusts what she sees because she says:

"Mummy and your aunt rescue kidnapped women. When they find them, they send them back to their families or to the Recovered Women's Camps. She arranged for Ayah to be sent to her relatives. She didn't want you to know. She felt you had accepted her absence—you'd only start fretting again."

Don't I know they went on futile Ayah hunts? Or were they just pretending to look for Ayah, using it as a cover for more sinister activities? Doesn't Godmother know about the petrol in the dicky? Doesn't she know that Electric-aunt and Mother were dashing off armed with petrol cans and tinted glasses long before anyone had even heard of kidnapped women?

Obviously Godmother does not know. I'm dumbfounded. Godmother, who makes it her business to know everything about everybody, doesn't know about the arsonists! I still live in dread of my mother and aunt's imminent arrest. Hand-and-leg-cuffed and jangling chains! And Godmother's naivety compounds my fear. She is slipping dangerously, just when her capabilities are most needed. I am tempted to tell her the truth, but I bite my wretched truth-infected tongue just in time. One betrayal is enough. I, the budding Judas, must live with their heinous secret.

It is getting quite dark. Already the dew is settling on our clothes. I shiver on Godmother's lap. Godmother says, as if musing aloud: "Come to think of it, we haven't seen that popsicle-man in a long time."

Mini Aunty calls from within, "You'd better get in, or someone will be sneezing her head off tomorrow."

Cousin, too, binds me to secrecy. Crowding me into a corner of Rosy-Peter's still deserted room he whispers into my ear: "Want to know why Ayah was all made up?"

251

I respond with a breathless nod.

"Because she has converted her profession!"

"She's become Christian?" I enquire tentatively, not knowing what to make of the revelation.

"Not her religion, silly! Her profession. D'you think Virgin Mary'd be caught dead wearing all that makeup?"

"I don't know," I confess. What does Virgin Mary have to do with Ayah?

"She wouldn't!" declares my knowing Cousin. "Ayah has become the opposite of Virgin Mary. She's become a dancing-girl!"

"An actress!" I exclaim, enthralled. That would explain the makeup. The only dancing-girls I've seen are in Indian films.

"Well," says Cousin, a trifle uncertain. "Dancing girls do grow into actresses sometimes..."

"Oh?" I say, and wait patiently.

"Ayah is just a dancer in the Hira Mandi...The red-light district."

Hira Mandi means Diamond Market. Cousin is being deliberately obtuse. He knows how important any news of Ayah is to me. I would like to shake him. Instead, like stepping on eggshells, I ask, "Where is this Diamond Mandi with the red light?"

"Behind the Badshahi mosque. It's where dancing-girls live."

"And the diamonds? Who sells the diamonds?" I prod gingerly.

"There are no real diamonds there, silly. The girls are the diamonds! The men pay them to dance and sing...and to do things with their bodies. It's the world's oldest profession," says Cousin as if he's uttering profundities instead of drivel.

My patience is wearing thin. Still, "What things?" I ask.

Although I'm cautious with Cousin, wary of surprises, the gullibility that made me climb a stool to insert my finger into the AC current remains.

Ever ready to illuminate, teach and show me things, Cousin squeezes my breasts and lifts my dress and grabs my elasticized cotton knickers. But having only the two hands to do all this with he can't pull them down because galvanized to action I grab them up and jab him with my elbows and knees, and turning and twisting, with my toes and heels.

252

Becoming red in the face, Cousin lets me be. And standing apart, and with exasperation, says: "How do you expect me to tell you what? If you don't let me show you how?"

And Cousin starts all over again to show me, and pulling my kicking feet from under me, succeeds in de-knickering me. And putting his hand there, trembles and trembles...

Until I punch his ears and shout: "You're breaking your promise!"

"Who told you all this?" I demand, pulling my knickers up and scowling, my sharp elbows bristling like dangerous quills as I settle down warily in the corner.

"My cook told me."

"Which men do such things to her?" I demand to know.

"Oh, any man who has the money... My cook, wrestlers, Imam Din, the knife-sharpener, merchants, peddlers, the governor, coolies..."

If those grown men pay to do what my comparatively small Cousin tried to do, then Ayah is in trouble. I think of Ayah twisting Ice-candy-man's intrusive toes and keeping the butcher and wrestler at arm's length. And of those strangers' hands hoisting her chocolate body into the cart.

That night I take all I've heard and learned and been shown to bed and by morning I reel dizzily on a fleetingly glimpsed and terrible grown-up world.

I decide it's time to confront Mother.

I hound Mother with a mute and dogged sullenness. It is Friday, the day to invoke the great Trouble Easers, the angels Mushkail Assan and Behram Yazd. (In troubled times they are frequently evoked by the Parsees.) As Mother prepares for the ceremony, spreading a white sheet on the bedroom floor and placing the small fire altar and photographs of the saints on it, she casts perplexed eyes my way. The less I am able to speak out, the more turbulent grows the temper of my pent-up accusations. Mother kneels on the floor and strikes a match to light the joss-sticks. She arranges the sandalwood shavings on the fire altar and places a criss-cross of small sandalwood sticks on top of them. She holds out the box and says: "Here, Lenny, would you like to light the fire?"

I whip my hands behind my back as if she has offered me a scorpion. I shake my churlish head.

"What's the matter?" she enquires, on her knees before the unlit altar.

In a harsh, squeaky rush of words I can hardly believe are issuing from me I hear myself say: "Don't think we don't know what you're up to with the petrol cans and matches!"

Mother looks so bewildered and alarmed that I wonder for an instant if Cousin, Adi and I are not mistaken. The twinge of doubt passes.

"I know about the petrol in the car's dicky!" I accuse, once again steadfast in my righteous and indignant conviction.

"Oh?" says Mother looking, if anything, more perturbed and baffled. "I didn't think it necessary you children should know about it . . . It could be dangerous . . ."

"But we do know!" I cry. "We aren't dumb! You and Aunty should be ashamed of yourselves! Deceiving everybody! Pretending to look for Ayah and instead burning Lahore!" I can no longer hold back my tears or prevent the tragic break in my voice.

"Oh my God!" Mother exclaims. "Is that what you think?"

And as understanding slowly replaces the astonishment on her face, she pulls me to her lap. Wiping my tears with her soft hands, speaking simply and gravely, she says, "I wish I'd told you . . . We were only smuggling the rationed petrol to help our Hindu and Sikh friends to run away . . . And also for the convoys to send kidnapped women, like your ayah, to their families across the border."

"You should have trusted me!" I cry, trying to stay the threatening surge of self-loathing and embarrassment from annihilating me.

"Yes," she says, solemnly shaking her head up and down. "I should have!"

How could she have? How can anyone trust a truth-infected tongue?

On Monday I come straight to Godmother's from Mrs. Pen's. I remove my satchel, kick off my shoes and I am peeling off my damp socks when Godmother abruptly says:

"You were right. Ayah is still in Lahore."

I feel goose-bumps erupt all over. My body feels drained of strength. I totter across the cool cement to Godmother's bed. "How did you find out?" I ask, when I am able to get my breath back.

"I have my sources," she says.

I realize the question was redundant.

"What did you find out?" I ask.

"She's married."

"I heard she's converted into a dancing-girl," I say.

Godmother is taken aback. "Who told you that?"

"Cousin told me," I say. "His cook told him."

"She isn't a dancing-girl anymore: she's a wife. Her husband is coming to see me this evening."

"Is Ayah coming?" I ask at once.

"He isn't bringing her."

"Who's her husband?" I ask eagerly.

"You'll see."

I can't wait for evening. When's evening? Four? Six? Eight o'clock? It is already three. The waterman is spraying the drive from the leather pouch slung on his back, and the fine dust clings in little balls to drops of water. I can see him through the screen door and smell the steam off the parched earth.

"Let's sit out," I say impatiently.

"We'll go outside at five o'clock. Like we do every day," says Mini Aunty.

"Can't I take the chairs out at least?" I say impatiently.

"My, my! One would think someone was expecting her own

255

bridegroom! He'll come when he comes and your sitting outside will not hurry him the tiniest bit!"

"When you've finished laying your eggs of wisdom," says Godmother, "you can make me some tea."

Mini Aunty, sitting in her petticoat and blouse, fans herself harder. Her face is beaded with sweat. "Let me cool off a bit," she says: "I haven't had a moment's respite all day."

She is exaggerating of course. She has been flopped in that armchair for the past half-hour.

"If you think you have too much to cope with you can live someplace else," says Godmother.

"I didn't say that, now, did I?" says Mini Aunty placidly.

"Oh? I need to oil my ears?" says Godmother. "I thought I heard you say you were overworked."

Mini Aunty gets up with a sigh and, shifting her weight from one bulging bunion to the other, waddles into the kitchen.

By five o'clock we are seated outside, waiting. It is oppressively hot. The thin, pointed leaves of the eucalyptus droop in brittle clusters over our heads and rattle as the sparrows, twittering feverishly, settle for the evening. The table fan is ineffectual against the dust suspended in the air.

"We're bound to have a dust storm. It's too still," Mini Aunty remarks. Raising her petticoat above her spread knees she flaps a punkah before her modestly averted thighs.

"I wish you wouldn't chatter so witlessly," says Godmother, sounding unduly irascible. "Predicting dust storms in the season for dust storms is not very bright."

I stall my restless movements on Godmother's lap. I realize how tense she is. We are all tense, waiting. It is almost six o'clock . . . then behold! The bridegroom comes. Lean, lank and loping, in flowing white muslin, raising dust with his sandaled feet, the poet approacheth.

Only now do I realize that one of the lean and languid poets flanking Ayah was Ice-candy-man.

❀

Ice-candy-man acknowledges our presence through dreamy kohl-rimmed eyes and removing his lamb's wool Jinnah cap, touching his forehead in a mute and protracted salaam, squats bowed before Godmother. He has grown his hair and long oily strands curve on his cheeks. He smells of Jasmine attar.

"Live long," says Godmother, leaning forward to stroke his shoulder—and crushing me in the process.

Ice-candy-man shuffles back and, pushing his hair behind his ears, draws us into the orbit of his poetic vision. He waits quietly while we absorb his incredible transformation. He has changed from a chest-thrusting *paan*-spitting and strutting *goonda* into a spitless poet. His narrow hawkish face, as if recast in a different mold, has softened into a sensuous oval. He is thinner, softer, droopier: his stream of brash talk replaced by a canny silence. No wonder I didn't recognize him in the taxi.

"Where have you been all these months?" exclaims Godmother pleasantly. "It was impossible to trace you. I was worried. God forbid, I thought you died in the riots!"

For a startled instant Ice-candy-man's eyes lose their poetic mist and focus as clearly as an eagle's on Godmother. But quickly retrieving his composure he says: "I'm truly sorry. Had I known you wished to see me I would have presented myself earlier." He recites Faiz:

> "*Tum aye ho na shab-e-intezar guzri hai—*
> *Talash main hai seher baar baar guzri hai!*
> You never came . . . The waitful night never passed—
> Though many dawns have passed in the waiting."

Astonishingly, we are not amazed at the surge of words pouring from him: so well do they suit the poetic mold of his metamorphosed character.

"*Shabash!* Well said!" says Godmother.

With a start, I scrutinize her face. Except for a thin smile it is clear of all expression. Yet, in some indefinable way, ominous.

"You have become a gifted poet! And not, as rumored, a Mandi pimp!" The thrust of her words is still smooth. "But tell me," she says, "why do you live in the Hira Mandi? It's the red-light district, isn't it? No wonder tongues wag. It is not a suitable place for a family man."

The lines on the poet's face trace his hurt feelings. "Not a suitable place? No place could be more suitable," he says, settling lower on his heels. "Why do you think the Mandi lies in the shadow of the Old Mogul Fort?"

"How should I know? I don't frequent brothels," says God-mother.

An uncertain smile flickers on Ice-candy-man's face. But then he casts his eyes down: he doesn't know what to make of God-mother's remark.

"*Baijee*, I don't want you to misjudge me," he says circum-spectly. "You know how deeply I respect you... I want to explain something almost no one remembers anymore... I want very much that you understand... Then judge me!"

Godmother nods slightly, gravely, her face deadpan.

"The Mogul princes built Hira Mandi—to house their il-legitimate offspring and favorite concubines," says Ice-candy-man, speaking with less assurance than before. "But you know our world... Who cares for orphans? Each emperor provided only for his own children, and neglected the sons of his father. The girls, left to fend for themselves, danced, and themselves became royal concubines. And the boys became musicians, singers and poets. Royal indulgences—in those days at least."

Had I not been looking at Ice-candy-man as he spoke, I would not have believed it was him. Not only has his voice changed, but his entire speech. His delivery is flawless, formal, like an educated and cultured man's. And, continuing in that same confiding man-ner, he murmurs, "You are my mother and father... I've told no one this—they wouldn't understand... You see, I belong to the *Kotha* myself... It is the cradle of royal bastards."

Ice-candy-man's eyes shine with a curious, prickly mixture of shame and pride as he glances at Godmother.

Godmother's eyes on his face remain impassive.

"My mother was from the *Kotha*," he says. "She moved to

Bhatti Gate when she married my father. He died when I was very young... He was a well-known puppeteer.

"My mother belonged to the old stock—she came from the House of Bahadur Shah. There's a strict distinction—the old families from distinguished houses don't mix with the new girls and their setup. They are nothing but prostitutes—young girls kidnapped by pimps! Anything goes where they're concerned. Poor girls... Their lot is pitiful and hideous, I admit. They are forced into all kinds of depravities on pain of death... and often die. But we protect our women. We marry our girls ourselves. No one dare lay a finger on them! They are artists and performers... beautiful princesses who command fancy prices for their singing and dancing skills!

"Because of my family connection my wife and I live in the old quarter of the Mandi. They have accepted her. For my sake... and for the sake of her divine gifts! She has the voice of an angel and the grace and rhythm of a goddess. You should see her dance. How she moves!" And then in another poetic outburst Ice-candy-man declaims:

"She lives to dance! And I to toast her dancer's grace!
Princes pledge their lives to celebrate her celebrated face!"

I am hypnotized by the play of emotion on Ice-candy-man's elastic face: by the music in his voice conjuring voluptuous images of smitten Mogul princes and of Ayah dancing as statues of Hindu goddesses come to life. Considering his revealed lineage it is little wonder he sounds like a cultured courtier. His face, too, has acquired the almond-eyed, thin-lipped profile of the handsome Moguls portrayed in miniatures.

So carried away am I by the virtuosity of his performance that I don't notice Godmother's reaction until she speaks.

"Have you said all you wish to say?" she asks, and I turn on her lap to look at her again. Knowing her as I do I can tell by the hooded droop of her wrinkled lids, by the somber shape of her tongueless cheeks, that she is in a cold rage: and God help Ice-candy-man.

259

But Ice-candy-man doesn't know her as well. Quoting Wali, misjudging her fury, and as if presenting credentials, he declares:

> "Kiya mujh ishq ne zalim ko aab ahista ahista
> Ke aatish gul ko karti hai gulab ahista ahista.
> Slowly, my love has compelled her, slowly—
> The way the sun touches open the rosebud, slowly."

Affected at last by Godmother's stony silence, Ice-candy-man lowers his eyes. His voice divested of oratory, he says, "I am her slave, *Baijee*. I worship her. She can come to no harm with me."

"No harm?" Godmother asks in a deceptively cool voice—and arching her back like a scorpion its tail, she closes in for the kill. "You permit her to be raped by butchers, drunks, and *goondas* and say she has come to no harm?"

Ice-candy-man's head jolts back as if it's been struck.

"Is that why you had her lifted off—let hundreds of eyes probe her—so that you could marry her? You would have your own mother carried off if it suited you! You are a shameless bad-mash! *Nimakharam!* Faithless!"

"Yes, I'm faithless!" Stung intolerably, and taken by surprise, Ice-candy-man permits his insolence to confront Godmother. "I'm a man! Only dogs are faithful! If you want faith, let her marry a dog!"

"Oh? What kind of man? A royal pimp? What kind of man would allow his wife to dance like a performing monkey before other men? You're not a man, you're a low-born, two-bit evil little mouse!"

Ice-candy-man is visibly shaken. His hazel eyes dart frantically—like the sparrows he once trapped for the mems—as he glances at Mini Aunty, the road, me, for sympathy or a means of succor. And then, his yellow eyes narrowed, he stares at God-mother with naked malevolence.

I see him now as Godmother sees him. Treacherous, danger-ous, contemptible. A destructive force that must be annihilated.

"You have permitted your wife to be disgraced! Destroyed her modesty! Lived off her womanhood!" says Godmother as if driven to recount the charges before an invisible judge. "And you talk of princes and poets? You're the son of pigs and pimps! You're not worth the two-cowries one throws at lepers!"

Struck by the naked power and fury of her attack, Ice-candy-man's body twitches. His head jerks forward and his long fingers gouge the earth between his sandals. And, as if committed against his will to witness the litany of his transgressions, his gaze clings to Godmother's. "I s-saved her," he stammers. "They would've... killed her...I married her!"

"I can have you lashed, you know? I can have you hung upside down in the Old Fort until you rot!"

Ice-candy-man shifts his eyes to the ground. And in the pause that follows, tears, and a long strand of mucus from his nose, drip into the fissures at his feet.

"It's no good crying now. You'll be shown as little mercy as you showed her."

"I don't seek mercy," he says, his voice so muffled and blocked that it registers like an afterthought. "If I deserve to be hung, then hang me!"

It is frightening to watch the silent tumult of Ice-candy-man's capitulation. The back of his neck is stretched in a long, shallow arch and his head hangs between his knees. His arms move helplessly, not knowing where to rest.

"Get out of my sight, you whining *haramzada!*" says Godmother.

Ice-candy-man just squats there, excreting his pain and tears, and as I look at him, I realize there is more to his turmoil than the rage and terror generated by Godmother's attack.

"It's too late to repent," says Godmother with a magnitude of grief that makes my eyes smart with sudden tears. "You have trapped her in the poisonous atmosphere of the *Kotha.*"

"Allah is my witness, I'm married to her," he says in a horrible, gruff voice.

"There is no God for the likes of you *shaitans!*" Godmother says remorselessly. "You are no more married to her than I am."

"What do you want me to do? Slit my throat? Stab my

261

heart?" His cap lies on the ground. His dusty hands, the nails dark with dirt, tremble on his knees.

"Restore her to her family in Amritsar."

"What if she refuses to leave me?" says Ice-candy-man, as if dredging from a deep doubt in his chest a scrap of hope. "I have been a good husband... Ask her. I've covered her with gold and silks. I'd do anything to undo the wrong done her. If it were to help to cut my head off, I'd cut my head and lay it at her feet! No one has touched her since our *nikah*."

"When did the marriage take place?" asks Godmother, unmoved.

"In May."

"She was lifted in February and you married her in May? What were you doing all that time?"

Ice-candy-man remains silent.

"Why don't you speak? Can't you bring yourself to say you played the drums when she danced? Counted money while drunks, peddlers, sahibs, and cutthroats used her like a sewer?" Godmother's face is slippery with sweat. Her thighs beneath me are trembling. I have a potent sense of her presence now. And when I inhale I can smell the formidable power of her attack.

"Did you marry her, then, when you realized that Lenny's mother had arranged to have her sent to Amritsar?"

Ice-candy-man, his muddied hair falling forward from his bowed head, remains still.

"Why don't you speak? A little while back you couldn't stop talking!"

Suddenly Ice-candy-man clenches his hair in his fists. His eyes are bloodshot. His face is a puffy patchwork of tears and mud. He tugs his hair back in such a way that his throat swells and bulges like a goat's before a knife, and in a raw and scratchy voice he says: "I can't exist without her." Then, rocking on his heels in his strange, boneless way, he pounds his chest and pours fistfuls of dirt on his penitent's head. "I'm less than the dust beneath her feet! I don't seek forgiveness..."

There is a suffocating explosion within my eyes and head. A

blinding blast of pity and disillusion and a savage rage. My sight is disoriented. I see Ice-candy-man float away in a bubble and dwindle to a gray speck in the aftermath of the blast and then come so close that I can see every pore and muddy crease in his skin magnified in dazzling luminosity. The popsicle man, Slavesister and we and our chairs and the table with the fan skid at a tremendous angle to dash against the compound wall and the walls bulge and fly apart. Godmother's house and Mrs. Pen's house sway crazily, the bricks tumbling.

The images blur and I try desperately to suck the air into my deflated lungs and Godmother holds my violently shivering body tight and I hear her say as if from far away, "Look how you have upset the child! You've turned us all insane!" And she pats my breathless face and sharply says, "Stop it! Stop it! Take a deep breath! Come on, inhale. Everything is going to be all right!"

She must have signaled to Slavesister because the slave heaves herself off her stool and, anxiety quickening her movements, stoops to lift me. Her face, too, is streaked with tears and her eyes red and she is muttering: "Finish it now, Rodabai, that's enough. Pack him off." And I cling to Godmother. And stretch like bubble gum when Slavesister tries to pull me away. And at a signal from Godmother she lets me be. And I, rubbing my face in Godmother's tightly bound bosom, grind the cloth between my teeth and shake my head till the khaddar tears and I smell blood and taste it.

"Ouch! Stop it! You've turned into a puppy have you?" says Godmother pushing my face away.

And when my teeth are pried away from her bloodied blouse and I at last look into her shrewd, ancient eyes, I can tell her tongue is once again in her cheek.

Everything's going to be all right!

Jinnah cap in hand, Ice-candy-man stands before us. His ravaged face, caked with mud, has turned into a tragedian's mask. Repentance, grief and shock are compressed into the mold of his features . . . And his inflamed eyes are raw with despair.

The storm that has been gathering all day rushes up the drive, slamming open the doors and windows. The three-pronged eucalyptus dips threateningly above our heads. As we scurry to shut the windows and carry the chairs inside, waves of mud obscure the drive and swallow the poet's fluttering white clothes.

The innocence that my parents' vigilance, the servants' care and Godmother's love sheltered in me, that neither Cousin's carnal cravings, nor the stories of the violence of the mobs, could quite destroy, was laid waste that evening by the emotional storm that raged round me. The confrontation between Ice-candy-man and Godmother opened my eyes to the wisdom of righteous indignation over compassion. To the demands of gratification—and the unscrupulous nature of desire.

To the pitiless face of love.

Chapter 30

Just as Godmother feels the urge to donate blood, she is impelled by an urge to pop up at the right place in the hour of a person's need. Yet I am surprised when, fingering her gray silk sari and matching blouse laid out on the stack of trunks, I ask, "Where are you going?" and she, after an unintended and dramatic pause, replies, "I'm going to see Ayah."

My heart stops. I feel as if I've run all the way from Warris Road instead of walking here, holding Hamida's finger. If I don't hold her finger Hamida turns hysterical and babbles, "*Hai!* We'll be run over by the cars and tongas."

It is Saturday morning. Adi and Cousin have gone to the grassless Warris Road park to play cricket. That is, Cousin will play and Adi will probably be forced to spectate. Mother is out.

I cannot speak. Godmother holds my twiggy arm beneath my starched and puffed-out sleeve and pulls me to the cot. Oldhusband, sitting before his desk on the bentwood chair, is reading his prayer book. Sibilant hisses flutter between his lips and every short while he clears his phlegmy throat. And, in a voice that sounds inaudible, and quivers with anxiety, I finally ask, "Can I come with you?"

Godmother stares somberly before her and remains quiet.

"Please." I swallow a lump in my throat.

"I can't take you," Godmother says. "It's no place for children."

"I want to see Ayah," I say, my longing making me sigh between the words.

"I really wish I could take you."

"Why don't you ask her to come here? Won't her husband bring her?"

"He is willing to. But she refuses to come."

I cannot believe Ayah wouldn't want to see me. See us.

"Her husband is lying," I say fiercely. "He's making excuses."

"No, she is ashamed to face us," says Godmother.

"Ashamed?" I say surprised. And even as Godmother says: "She has nothing to be ashamed of," I know Ayah is deeply, irrevocably ashamed. They have shamed her. Not those men in the carts—they were strangers—but Sharbat Khan and Ice-candy-man and Imam Din and Cousin's cook and the butcher and the other men she counted among her friends and admirers. I'm not very clear how—despite Cousin's illuminating tutorials—but I'm certain of her humiliation. Sensing this, I more than ever want to see Ayah: to comfort and kiss her ugly experiences away.

"I want to tell her I am her friend," I say sobbing defenselessly before Godmother. And remembering Hamida's remarks, I cry, "I don't want her to think she's bad just because she's been kidnapped."

I have never cried this way before. It is how grown-ups cry when their hearts are breaking.

Mini Aunty returns, silently bearing grocery bags and ice, looking like a fat and elderly sari-clad wax doll melting.

Godmother greets her. "I thought the tongaman had run off with you! What took you so long?"

It is a purely rhetorical salutation and Mini Aunty need not reply if she doesn't want to. Ignoring Godmother, looking neither guilty nor annoyed, Slavesister is preoccupied with stashing the groceries and splintering and stuffing the ice into a thermos.

We hear a horse snort, and the creak of tonga wheels outside the door. Then a steady liquid noise, as of water gushing from a hose under pressure.

Oldhusband raises his praying voice in forbidding censure.

"Ummm, umM, uMM, UMM!" hums Godmother in a rising

crescendo of disapproval, and breaking into speech she says, "My God! How do you expect us to sit outside this evening?"

"It will evaporate . . . You can't imagine how hot it is!" says Slavesister, unperturbed.

"Can't I? Where do you think I live? In the North Pole?" and then, reverting to the matter in hand: "What if the horse decides to perform on a grander scale? Will that evaporate too? How often must I tell you not to let the tonga come in?"

"I've told the tongawallah to take care of that."

"Oh? What will he do? Diaper the horse?"

Mini Aunty continues placidly to unwrap her sari, and turning mildly pleading eyes to Godmother says, "The tongawallah said the poor horse really had to get some water or he'd collapse."

We hear the tongaman cluck his tongue and lead his horse and tonga to the trough at the back.

"You'd better remember to sprinkle the evaporated puddle with rose water before we sit out," says Godmother sarcastically, but in a softer tone, thereby conceding Mini Aunty a reprieve on compassionate grounds.

"I've arranged for the tonga to take you to—" In deference to my youthful presence Mini Aunty abruptly checks herself. She ends by enigmatically saying, "You-know-where, at two o'clock."

"Then you'd better set about getting lunch ready," says Godmother.

Godmother's fingers are slightly trembling. Not with the tremor of age but with nervous concentration as she drapes her sari, with its finely embroidered floral border, before a slender half-mirror embedded in the cupboard. Her concentration is a tribute to the six yards of heavy gray silk, and to the occasion for which it is being worn. Normally, not bothered with their appearance, both she and Slavesister wrap their saris without the aid of mirrors. Unlike Mother, who pivots fastidiously in high heels in front of a full-length mirror to adjust the hem of her sari and precisely arrange the dainty fall of her pleats. It wouldn't be fitting if Mother dressed with less circumspection. In her case I feel adorning and embellishing her person is an obligatory rite and not a vanity.

Godmother moves closer to the mirror. As she carefully begins to pin the border to her hair, Mini Aunty, looking as if she has arrived at a decision, suddenly and gravely declares: "I think I'd better come with you. You'll need my support!"

Her teeth clamped on a tangle of U-shaped hairpins Godmother turns abruptly. Facing Slavesister she says: "Since when have I started needing your support in such matters?"

"You can't go there alone, Roda. You must have someone with you."

Notice the unembellished Roda? Mini Aunty uses this form of address to sidle into a more dominant role. This has been occurring with alarming frequency of late: and the slave gets away with it—and the meager Roda—with alarming frequency.

"Oh, all right! If it makes you feel any better, I'll take Lenny along," says Godmother, attempting to appear reasonable but only managing to sound devious.

"You can't be serious!" exclaims Mini Aunty.

"Why not? She won't be contaminated—if that's what you're afraid of."

"How can you even dream of taking the child there!" says Mini Aunty, her eyes brimming with reproach, the chubby disk of her cheeks lengthening in solemn consternation.

"I'm not taking her *there*," says Godmother. "We are only visiting a simple housewife in her simple house. The house merely happens to be *there*."

"But what will her mother say?"

"That's between me and her mother. You know perfectly well she trusts my judgment. . . Not like some ungrateful brats I could name!"

"I know you. . . ," says Slavesister, pale and hangdog. "The more I say the more stubborn you become. One can't tell you anything. Have your way . . ."

268

"Have I ever done otherwise?"

"Oh, I know! You always have your way . . . "

"Then why are you wasting my time?"

"But have you given a thought to what people might say?"

"That I've become a dancing-girl? With bells on my ankles? Or worse?"

It is too much for Slavesister. Blinking tears she goes into the kitchen and commences mumbling.

Come to think of it, I'm hearing her mumbles after a long time.

At two o'clock the tongaman taps on the door with the bamboo end of his whip and shouts: "I've arrived, *jee*. I'm parked by the gate."

Godmother quickly compresses her lips and daubs her face with talcum powder. She peers at me through the chalk storm and, almost shyly, winks into my awed and smitten countenance. She looks grand. Her noble ghost-white face and generous mouth set off to advantage by the slate-gray sari and its pretty border. She is my very own whale—and her great love for me is plain in her shining eyes.

"We are going. Lock the door," Godmother calls, and hand in hand we step into the abrasive heat.

The increasing congestion and uproar in the streets as we pass Data Sahib's tomb and approach the Badshahi mosque barely registers as leaning against Godmother I fall into a stupor induced by the heat and glare and the jolting rhythm of the tonga.

When Godmother gently shakes me awake we are already parked beneath a straggling *sheesham*, its small leaves brittle with the heat and dust, in front of a narrow alley. The tongaman has placed the feed sack in front of his horse and is tying the reins to the shaft. The sweat-darkened animal just stands there, its neck hanging, too exhausted to feed. Preceded by the tongaman we walk into the blessed shade of the constricted gullies of the old city.

Godmother is nervous. I can tell from the pressure of her grip.

After the clamor of the streets the silence in the alleys is vaguely discomforting. There are few people about and too few children. The naked babies tottering about the drains and doorsteps whimper listlessly and are scolded by irritable mothers from inside who sound as if it's dawn instead of three in the afternoon.

We emerge on a broader lane which has the appearance of a bazaar with rows of shops at the ground level and living quarters with frail arched windows and decaying wooden balconies teetering above. Still half asleep and drugged by the oppressive humidity and heat, I look for a tin can, or anything else to kick as I walk, but there is hardly any litter.

We walk past two young women, yawning and stretching in front of a stall overflowing with garlands of scarlet roses, jasmine and mounds of marigolds. The owner, wearing only a lungi, is perched like a contented and contemptuous deity amidst his wares.

Coming suddenly upon the fragrance of sprinkled flowers and the blaze of colors freshens my senses. The women chatting with the flower-man look tousled, as if they have just awakened and are still loitering in the shalwar-kamizes they have slept in. Except for the betel-leaf and cigarette stalls and a few eating places where meat and *pakoras* are being fried, there is very little sign of commerce. The ancient, roughly carved doors are shut for the most part. And the few that are open reveal steep flights of narrow steps or twilit interiors I cannot see into.

My previous excursions inside the old city had been enlivened by the cries of shopkeepers and hawkers and the bawling and shrieking of urchins; the lanes teeming with men and burka-veiled women and littered with the discarded newspaper bags used by vendors. I miss the mounds of rotting fruit and vegetables and the bones picked clean by the kites, their enormous wings stirring in the garbage: and the sudden yelp of kicked mongrels and raucous flights of crows and scraps of cardboard and rusted iron and the other debris even the poor have no use for.

Godmother pinches her sari austerely beneath her chin and maintaining her eyes straight in front of her marches regally behind

the tongaman. Her sari, catching the breeze the cunningly struc-
tured alleys miraculously generate in an otherwise windless city, billows grayly about her shoulders and back. None of the women
here is veiled. The bold girls, with short, permed hair, showing
traces of stale makeup, stare at us as if we are freaks. They whisper
and burst into giggles when we pass and bury their faces in each
other's shoulders and necks. Their crumpled kamizes are too short
and the *pencha*-bottoms of their shalwars too wide. Even I can tell
they are not well brought up. I have never seen women of this
class with cropped and frizzed hair: nor using the broad and comfortable gestures of men. The few men, in singlets and faded lungis,
scratch their carelessly bared stomachs as they loiter in the lane, or
pause to joke with the girls. Some have their hands inside their
lungis and are cleaning themselves after urinating as prescribed, un-
consciously indulging in what I've heard snidely described as "the
national pastime."

Our tongaman halts before a weathered door with deep
grooves. I glimpse the chain holding the panels closed from inside.
"This is the address, *Baijee*," he says, and at a nod from Godmother, batters the door with his hand.

There is an instant shout: "Coming!" followed by the
lightfooted patter of a lightweight poet hastening down the steps.
The door opens and the poet blinks his kohl-rimmed eyes in the
glare. Ice-candy-man looks subdued, flustered, honored. Displaying
the exquisite courtesy of Mogul courtiers, spouting snatches of
felicitous verse, picking me up with one hand and supporting Godmother with the other as we slowly mount the steps—Godmother
pausing to catch her breath—Ice-candy-man ushers us into the sitting room. Guiding Godmother to a sofa covered in glossy green
velvet, he adjusts the cushions behind her and draws a peg table
conveniently close. Then he breathlessly says: "I'll fetch Mumtaz,"
and disappears behind the pink and white checked curtains.

"So!" whispers Godmother, blinking and nodding impishly.
"He has christened our ayah Mumtaz!"

"I like the name," I say.

271

I think it fitting that a courtier's wife be named after a Mogul queen. And the room, too, is befitting: long and narrow, filled with ornate chairs covered in velvet, sporting little tables with crocheted doilies and thick glass and brass vases crammed with red paper poppies. The arched windows are shaded by reed screens and the walls are a gleaming pink. The room has the gratifying appeal of a cool and delicious tutti-frutti ice cream.

And then Ayah comes: teetering on high heels, tripping on the massive divided skirt of her *garara*, jangling gold bangles. Her eyes are lowered and her head draped in a gold-fringed and gauzy red *ghoongat*. A jeweled tika nestles on her forehead and bunches of pearls and gold dangle from her ears. Ice-candy-man guides his rouged and lipsticked bride to sit beside Godmother. Godmother lightly strokes Mumtaz's covered head and says: "Bless you my daughter. . . Live long."

I feel frightfully shy. I had expected to leap on Ayah and hug her to bits. But now that she is here, in the awesome shape of a bride, I can do no more than shift uneasily in my chair and stare at her. I notice the tiny pieces of tinsel glitter stuck on her chin and cheeks.

"Lenny baby, aren't you going to embrace my bride?" Ice-candy-man asks.

And Ayah raises her eyes to me.

Where have the radiance and the animation gone? Can the soul be extracted from its living body? Her vacant eyes are bigger than ever: wide-opened with what they've seen and felt: wider even than the frightening saucers and dinner plates that describe the watchful orbs of the three dogs who guard the wicked Tinder Box witches' treasures in underground chambers. Colder than the ice that lurks behind the hazel in Ice-candy-man's beguiling eyes.

At last Ayah casts her lids down: and bowing her head, extends her hennaed hands to me. I move awkwardly into the voluminous skirt of her brocade *garara*. And through the prickling brocade and silver lamé of her kamize at last feel the soft and rounded contours of her diminished flesh. She buries her head in me and buries me in all her finery; and in the dark and musky attar of her perfume.

Leaving Mumtaz to sit awkwardly with us Ice-candy-man goes inside to make the tea.

Godmother moves to the edge of the sofa and tenderly raises Mumtaz's chin, saying, "Let me have a good look at our bride."

Ayah's face, with its demurely lowered lids and tinsel dust, blooms like a dusky rose in Godmother's hands. The rouge and glitter highlight the sweet contours of her features. She looks achingly lovely: as when she gazed at Masseur and inwardly glowed. But the illusion is dispelled the moment she opens her eyes—not timorously like a bride, but frenziedly, starkly—and says: "I want to go to my family." Her voice is harsh, gruff: as if someone has mutilated her vocal cords.

Even Godmother can't bear the look in her eyes. She gently removes her hand, and Ayah's unsupported face collapses and is again half hidden in the *ghoongat*. Godmother composes herself with a visible effort. And the look of shock and pity fading, sitting taut on the edge of the sofa, she at last says: "Isn't he looking after you?"

Mumtaz nods her head slightly.

"What's happened has happened," says Godmother. "But you are married to him now. You must make the best of things. He truly cares for you."

"I will not live with him." Again that coarse, rasping whisper.

I have moved to my chair across the room but I hear Ayah's discordant murmurs clearly. (It is not without reason Mini Aunty has designated my talented ears "cricket ears.")

"Does he mistreat you . . . in any way?" Godmother asks with uncharacteristic hesitancy.

"Not now," says Mumtaz. "But I cannot forget what happened."

"That was fated, daughter. It can't be undone. But it can be forgiven . . . Worse things are forgiven. Life goes on and the business of living buries the debris of our pasts. Hurt, happiness . . . all fade impartially . . . to make way for fresh joy and new sorrow. That's the way of life."

"I am past that," says Mumtaz. "I'm not alive."

Godmother leans back and withdraws the large cambric handkerchief tucked into her blouse. She wipes her forehead.

"What if your family won't take you back?" she asks.

"Whether they want me or not, I will go."

We hear the clatter of ill-fitted cups and saucers. The curtain bulges and Ice-candy-man comes through, carefully bearing a tray. He pauses in front of the curtain and manifesting an awed and felicitous aspect, sweeping his dramatic eyes from Godmother to the pink walls of his house, recites Ghalib's famous couplet:

> "Tis a miracle wondrous that you have come:
> Marveling, I look from you to the walls of my house . . . "

He places the tray on a small table near Godmother and, interminably stirring the tea with a spoon to dissolve the sugar, deferentially hands her the cup. "Is it strong enough?" he enquires. "More milk? Sugar?"

Godmother takes a sip. "It's all right," she says tersely.

Turning to me, flourishing an autumnal forest of popsicles, Ice-candy-man says, "Look what I have for my Lenny baby."

I take two sticks. One for each hand.

Ayah refuses her tea with a shake of her lowered head. Ice-candy-man stoops and, holding the cup close to Ayah's fingers, coaxes, "Have some, *meri kasam*. Drink it for *Baijee*'s sake at least . . . "

"I don't want any," she says harshly. While he passes the pastry with the little dabs of jam, his anxious courtier's eyes keep alighting on Mumtaz. Assuming the role of the misused lover so dear to Urdu poets, he quotes Mir:

> *"Hai ashiqi ke beech sitam dekhna hi lutf*
> *Mar jana ankhe moond ke kuch hunar nahin.*
> 'Tis nothing . . . to roll up one's eyes and die.
> I endure my lover's tyranny wide-eyed."

274

Ice-candy-man appears to have sensed the content of the exchange between Godmother and his bride. Maintaining a nervous stream of chatter, quoting snatches of poetry, pressing us to eat and drink, he attempts to conceal his misgiving.

"I'll get the kebabs," he says after a while, looking at our faces hesitantly, seeking our approval. "They should be done by now."

Godmother nods briefly.

Ice-candy-man leaves the room and, slipping to the floor like a floating bundle of crumpled silk, Ayah grasps Godmother's legs. "Please—I fall at your feet, *Baijee*—please get me away from him."

"Are you sure that's what you want?" says Godmother, bending to look into her face. "You might regret your decision. . . You should think it over."

"I have thought it over. . . I want to go to my folk."

"Let's see what I can do," Godmother says gently. "I'll try my best."

Ayah is sniffing and rubbing her face on Godmother's legs.

"Get up, my daughter. . . Have faith. . . Have patience," says Godmother, holding her and trying to pull her to the sofa.

Stepping on and getting entangled in her enormous skirts, Mumtaz scrambles to rise just as the poet enters with a fragrant dish of kebabs. He quickly reaches for Ayah and helps her to sit on the sofa.

The poet's manner is subdued, his face drawn, apprehensive: and his eyes, red with the strain of containing his tears, hover caressingly on Ayah. They flit to Godmother in mute appeal.

Godmother strokes Ayah's back. Ayah is huddled over, silently weeping, her body trembling. "Have patience, daughter, have faith. Go. Go and wash your face," says Godmother, helping Ayah to stand up. Gathering her skirt with both hands, Ayah clumsily staggers out of the room on her unnatural heels.

Godmother's mouth is set. She turns her austere eyes on Ice-candy-man.

"How long has she been like this?"

"Like how?"

"Emptied of life? Despairing?"

In a slow, coiling movement Ice-candy-man squats directly in front of Godmother. "The past is behind her," he says. Taking the kitchen rag from his shoulder he wipes his face. It is as if he has wiped off all artifice, all pride: his humility and despair are manifest. "I cannot help the past," he says. "But now she has everything to live for."

Godmother's eyes on the poet's exposed face are dispassionate. Cold. And gliding forward on his haunches Ice-candy-man clasps her hands in both his and places them on his bowed, penitent's head.

"Please. Please persuade her . . . explain to her . . . I will keep her like a queen . . . like a flower . . . I'll make her happy," he says, and succumbing to the pressure of his pent-up misery starts weeping.

"We shall see," says Godmother, and in a coldly significant gesture withdraws her hands from Ice-candy-man's head. He remains like that, stranded, crouched forward, his face hidden by long black strands of falling hair. After what seems like hours he turns to me, swiveling on his haunches, and his beguiling eyes, weighed with insupportable uncertainties, plead his cause.

The longer I look at him the more willing I am to be beguiled by those tearing, forlorn eyes. How long have they been like that? When I think of Ayah I think she must get away from the monster who has killed her spirit and mutilated her "angel's" voice. And when I look at Ice-candy-man's naked humility and grief I see him as undeserving of his beloved's heartless disdain.

He is a deflated poet, a collapsed peddler—and while Ayah is haunted by her past, Ice-candy-man is haunted by his future: and his macabre future already appears to be stamped on his face.

I am feverish to see Cousin. I haven't told anyone about our visit with Ayah. Not even Adi. I sit on Electric-aunt's veranda waiting for the school bus to deliver my cousin. Hamida is in the kitchen talking to the cook. Electric-aunt is inside, whirling herself into her sari, issuing a battery of instructions to her sweepress and at the same time listening to the four o'clock news.

The minute I see the bus I run to the gate to receive my cousin. The school bus, windows crammed with boys' faces, lurches away spewing exhaust smoke and Cousin scowls at me. He doesn't like me seeing all those boys—or all those boys looking at me. Besides, he's embarrassed to be seen associating with such a skinny girl.

Cousin is flushed and sweaty and weighed down by his school-bag. I relieve him of the precariously bulging geometry box in his hand and say, "I went to see Ayah and Ice-candy-man yesterday!"

Cousin comes to a dead stop just inside the gate.

"Where?"

"At their house."

Cousin looks amazed. Then pale, and very serious, he leads me into the shade of the gardenia hedge in front of the garden wall. We sit on the warm and dusty grass and Cousin enquires, grimly: "Who took you there?"

"Godmother."

"Godmother?" Cousin is incredulous. He is also disconcerted.

"She didn't want to take me. But I cried . . . and she took me along."

"She shouldn't have," says Cousin, in a tone of voice that suggests he is Godmother's age, and Godmother a naughty little girl.

"Okay," he continues, in the same censorious tone. "Tell me what you saw in the Hira Mandi. Tell me what happened. Tell me everything."

I tell him everything. I tell him the details of Ayah's despair and the spurned courtier-poet's anguish.

"Is that all?" Cousin appears disappointed, and at the same time mollified. "You would have seen a lot more if you'd gone there after dark."

"Like what?" I say, feeling that either he is deliberately aggravating me, or we are at cross-purposes.

"Girls dancing and singing—and amorous poets. And you would have been raped."

"What's that?"

(I never learn, do I?)

"I'll show you someday," says Cousin giving me a queer look.

I don't press the point. "What do you think will happen now?" I enquire instead.

"If Godmother says she'll help Ayah get away, she'll get her away."

You see? Everyone has confidence in Godmother.

"What did you say Ayah's new name was?" Cousin asks.

"Mumtaz."

"That's a nice name for a dancing-girl," says Cousin, rolling the words and rolling his eyes and leering horribly.

"Can't you talk straight?" I say, ready to hit him.

"You've been to the *Kotha*! You visit the dancing-girls! and you want *me* to talk straight?"

"I think the heat has scrambled your brains," I declare, standing up in disgust.

Cousin yanks the hem of my skirt and I thud back on the scratchy grass.

"If you want me to stay," I say, "you'd better mind how you talk!"

"Okay," says Cousin changing his tone and composing his features. "You want me to tell you what goes on there?"

He knows he has me hooked.

"As long as you tell me and don't start demonstrating," I say, warning him with my voice and also a wagging finger.

I wait for my message to sink in, and then I ask, "What's *Kotha*?" Godmother had used the word when talking to Ice-candy-man: and now Cousin.

"The Hira Mandi," explains Cousin, "is also known as the *Kotha*. Roof. Because the dancing-girls carry on their main business upstairs."

As Cousin talks a fascinating picture emerges.

The *Kotha* is the cultural pulse of the city. It is where poets are inspired, where their songs are sung and made famous by the girls, and singing-boys. It is also a stepping-stone to film stardom for the nautch-girls. The girls are taught to sing and dance and talk elegantly and look pretty and be attractive to men. It sounds very much like a cross between a Swiss finishing school a female cousin of mine in Bombay was sent to and a School for the Fine and Performing Arts.

After mulling over the complexities of the discourse on the cultured *Kotha*—which I know is also the cradle of royalty, I enquire, "But what are pimps?" Another word that arouses peculiar reactions in people.

"They look after the dancing-girls," says Cousin.

"A kind of male ayah?"

"No," says Cousin, sounding condescending and painfully adenoidal. "They protect the girls from drunks and look after money the girls get. They bring men and introduce them to the dancing-girls."

I'm beginning to understand. The pimps are a kind of adult and mercantile cupid.

I also have an insight into the potent creative force generated within the *Kotha* that has metamorphosed Ice-candy-man not only into a Mogul courtier, but into a Mandi poet. No wonder he founts poetry as if he popped out of his mother's womb spouting rhyming sentences.

But all this still doesn't explain the twittering flap and the hush-hush any mention of the Hira Mandi evokes. Or the contempt in which everybody appears to hold this Institute of Culture.

. . . Or the girls who looked too at ease loitering in the Mandi gullies and lacked the docile modesty of properly brought up Muslim women.

I have many questions, but Cousin appears to have had his fill of enlightening me. He is hungry and thirsty and we go inside.

Chapter 31

"Dr. Selzer! Come here. Come here," Mother yells cheerfully from the veranda: summoning him also with a snappy wave of her hand. She is pouring tea for Mr. Phailbus, his daughter Maggie, and his son Theo. Since they are Indian Christians they are among the few remaining neighbors we still know.

The Shankars' rooms at the back have been let to Dr. Selzer. The German doctor does not inhabit the rooms as much as possess them. He lives alone and he padlocks the rooms when he goes out. He has only one servant.

The doctor's steps, deflected from their course by my mother's voice, falter. And turning round politely he approaches us from the drive.

"I was just this minute talking about you!" warbles Mother enthusiastically, flashing all her beautiful teeth in a magical smile.

Dr. Selzer is taller than Colonel Bharucha. Taller even than the murdered Inspector General of Police, Mr. Rogers. But he is much less intimidating. He lacks Colonel Bharucha's charge of thunder and the departed policeman's I'm-in-charge-here air of haughtiness. He is polite and assured in a subdued, understated way. And though he doesn't talk much I can tell from the expression on his face that he is a gentle gentleman. He keeps so much to himself I think because he's shy.

Dr. Selzer practices his calling in two rooms he has rented on Birdwood Road, behind Warris Road. One room is occupied by a self-trained and indigenous chemist who deciphers and dispenses the prescriptions.

The doctor walks to and from his office. He says he needs the exercise. He says he will buy a car when his wife comes from Germany. Even Father likes him. Mother is so impressed by his doctoring that she has transferred my diminishing limp—and sundry colds, coughs and attacks of diarrhea—to his care and taken it upon herself to promote his practice. Between his permanent presidency of the Parsee Anjuman and his thronging patients Colonel Bharucha has become too busy in any case.

Mr. Phailbus, who is a retired magistrate—and a budding homeopath besides—stands up to shake hands. Mr. Phailbus's kindness and congeniality twinkle in his dark eyes. His sere shock of cropped white hair barely clears the German doctor's shoulders. Theo, lean, reserved and dark as a thundercloud, also shakes Dr. Selzer's hand.

"Mrs. Sethi was just telling us all about you," says Maggie affably. She is comfortably ensconced in the chair, one slipperless foot resting jauntily on her red-satin-shalwared thigh. She wiggles her dusty toes invitingly and Dr. Selzer, with quiet resignation, settles down beside her.

"Look at Lenny!" Mother exclaims, yanking me closer to the Phailbuses for better observation. "Isn't she looking better already?"

"Much better. Much better," murmur the three Phailbuses, nodding their heads.

"Eat and run! Eat and run! That's all she's done all year!" says Mother, lovingly and graphically squeezing both my bottoms. "It's a wonder she has any bottom left."

"Tch, tch, tch," says Maggie Phailbus sympathetically.

"Look," says Mother. Jacking up the skirt of my starched pink frock and the rim of my knickers she points out a small incision and bump in my groin. "He inserted the pill here: right under the skin: and overnight her dysentery was finished! Have you ever heard of amoebic dysentery being cured just like that?" She snaps her fingers.

Heads nod again and eyes widen in wonder as the spell of my mother's voice conjures the Jewish doctor into a savage wizard and my cure into a feat of unparalleled sorcery.

"He's excellent! I tell you, he's excellent!" asserts Mother exuberantly. "Lenny, walk!" commands Mother, and like a performing poodle I parade up and down before the Phailbuses, taking care to place my awkward heel on the floor.

"See?" says Mother triumphantly. "He's cured her limp!"

Dr. Selzer stretches his lips in a mild smile and his eyes, assured yet shy, search her face for a clue to his release.

But Mother has no mind to let him go yet. In her zeal as promoter and town crier of Dr. Selzer's genius she has neglected Mr. Phailbus's accomplishments: and being scrupulously fair she informs Dr. Selzer—in an awed whisper that portends revelations—that Mr. Phailbus is a homeopath: another miracle worker! Holding her shapely lips and chiseled chin in the refined and mannered way she assumes when talking to Englishmen and others of the white species, she says: "God bless our Mr. Phailbus. Do you know I had a cyst that big inside here?" She gathers her fingers into a fist and waves the fist discreetly and vaguely in the direction of her lower abdomen. "Even the date for the operation was fixed. It was just by chance that I told Mr. Phailbus about it. He said: 'Let me have a try. If my powders work you may spare yourself an operation.' I know homeopathy is harmless. So I had one of those sweet powders of his before going to bed. The next morning the cyst had melted! I couldn't feel it: just a little bit of discharge. Colonel Bharucha was amazed! He said he had never seen a cyst vanish like that!"

Mr. Phailbus's gentle eyes beam and twinkle above his half-moon glasses and Dr. Selzer looks mildly and suitably impressed.

At this point I become aware of a sudden commotion in Rosy-Peter's compound. Mingled with the thud of hooves and the creaking of wooden wheels are the raised voices of men squabbling and cursing and the sounds of running feet and of combat. We cock our ears and exchange alert glances. And taking advantage of our momentary inattention Dr. Selzer, discreetly murmuring his good-byes, slips away.

Mother and I, followed by the Phailbuses, run down the veranda steps. Imam Din is already standing on the handy kitchen stool looking over the wall and Hari and Yousaf are scrambling on to it for a ringside view.

"What happened?" Mother shouts.

Hamida, her head covered, is hovering excitedly near the men. She directs a squeaky stream of sentences at us that we cannot make anything out of.

"Oye, Sardarjee, stop it! You'll kill him!" shouts Imam Din.

Moti-alias-David-Masih is running up from the back, followed by his wife and progeny and parents and sisters and the other inhabitants of the servants' quarters. The sounds of combat increase. A man bellows in pain and then belts out a breathless string of vintage Punjabi curses in a hoarse, wailing voice. Hari-alias-Himat-Ali and Yousaf jump the wall and disappear on the other side.

"Will someone tell me what's going on?" Mother shouts in an imperious frenzy.

I climb aboard the kitchen stool and clamor to be picked up by Imam Din and he lifts me up and sits me on the wall.

Three horse-drawn carts are crowded any-old-how to the far side of our neighbors' compound and in front of them, quite close to the wall, is the scene of battle: an entwined jumble of arms and legs and torn clothing tumbling through a mesh of snarled hair. Yousaf, Himat Ali and the other men in the forefront are trying to restrain and lift the hefty Sikh guard. The Sikh is entwined with someone on the floor and is viciously attacking and bellowing: "Dog! Motherfucker! Son of an owl!"

Just then the men succeed in pulling the fighters apart and slowly, assisted by several pairs of hands and dusting his clothes, a man arises from the dust. His face and arms are grimed with blood and dirt and his hand is twisted at an unnatural angle. Someone wipes his face with a wet rag and as the man, in obvious pain, pushes the rag away, I see frantic amber eyes.

"It's the Ice-candy-man," I scream to Mother. "They've beaten him up!"

A group of men hastily bundle him into a cart and three scruffy-looking *goondas* in singlets and lungis jump in after him. One of them, standing up in the carriage, whips the horse savagely and the cart, followed by the other carts, groans and creaks down the rutted drive.

The remaining men group around the outraged Sikh who is hollering: "I'll break the bastard's neck next time! I've never had trouble before! Let anyone touch the women . . . See what I'll do to their cocks and balls! They are my sisters and mothers!" He thumps his massive chest. His knee-length hair, mauled by Ice-candy-man, is in dramatic, spiky disarray. The men stare at him in wonderment and nod their heads.

Imam Din plucks me off the wall and deposits me near Hamida. Mother is yelling at the gate. Trailed by Hamida I run to her as Mother screams after the departing cart, "*Duffa ho!* Show your blackened faces at someone else's door! That scoundrel! He can't deceive me again! If he dares show his face I'll call the police and have him hung upside down!"

She is flushed and fuming and panting in a fierce way.

Her penetrating voice I am sure can be heard by the men in the disappearing carts.

Maggie and Mr. Phailbus try to soothe Mother. Mr. Phailbus, who has the power to heal and calm in his hands, strokes Mother's head and shoulders and Mother's rage subsides somewhat. The Phailbuses say goodbye at the gate and saunter away, talking in subdued voices, and Mother marches up our drive with a preoccupied expression that betrays the battle she is still engaged in with the object of her recriminations.

Hamida and I run to the back and rush up the stairs to the servants' roof. The women and children from the quarters are already looking over the short parapet wall into the courtyard. Since it would be improper for Moti and Hari to look at the women, they are squatting at a polite distance, anxious for whatever news of Ayah they can acquire secondhand. The women in the courtyard appear agitated. They flutter in and out of the rooms and answer our insistent queries with more animation than they have ever displayed before. Their voices rise up to us from upturned faces: Ayah is exhausted. She's all right. She doesn't wish to see you . . . best leave her alone. She's being registered.

"Let her be. It'll take hours if she's being registered," says Hamida, slapping her forehead in a gesture of sympathy, and talking from experience. "They'll be asking her a hundred-and-one questions, and filling out a hundred-and-one forms." She is referring to the clerks from the Ministry for the Rehabilitation of Recovered Women. "Yes, sister, let her do as she wishes . . . ," say the women on the roof.

And I chant: "Ayah! Ayah! Ayah! Ayah!" until my heart pounds with the chant and the children on the roof picking it up shout with all their heart: "Ayah! Ayah! Ayah! Ayah!" and our chant flows into the pulse of the women below, and the women on the roof, and they beat their breasts and cry: *"Hai! Hai! Hai! Hai!"* reflecting the history of their cumulative sorrows and the sorrows of their Muslim, Hindu, Sikh and Rajput great-grandmothers who burnt themselves alive rather than surrender their honor to the invading hordes besieging their ancestral fortresses.

The Sikh guard, noisily splashing himself at the tap outside the gate, stands up to look at us—and when he beholds only the women and children on the roof, he holds his peace—and once again settles to wash the blood and mud from his clothes and hair.

"Ayah! Ayah! Ayah!" we chant and *"Hai! Hai! Hai!"* the weeping women: and supported by two old women Ayah appears in the courtyard. She looks up at us out of glazed and unfeeling eyes for a moment, as if we are strangers, and goes in again.

I institute a vehement and importunate enquiry. After a great deal of painstaking probing and prying, I ferret out a fairly accurate account of the events that led to Ayah's extradition from the Hira Mandi.

The long and diverse reach of Godmother's tentacular arm is clearly evident. She set an entire conglomerate in motion immediately after our visit with Ayah and singlehandedly engendered the social and moral climate of retribution and justice required to rehabilitate our fallen Ayah.

Everything came to a head within a fortnight. Which in the normal course of events, unstructured by Godmother's stratagems, could have been consigned to the ingenious bureaucratic eternity of a toddler nation greenly fluttering its flag—with a white strip to represent its minorities—and a crescent and star—from the National Assembly building behind the unqueened garden and its eviscerated marble marquee.

Brand-new flags flutter, too, from the filigreed turrets of the pink High Court and the General Post Office and other government offices and the new fronts of bazaar shops in the Shalmi and Gowalmandi and the oil and engineering companies—those ubiquitous visitants from foreign lands and the domes and minarets of new mosques erupting all over Lahore . . . some beautiful as poems and some bedraggled.

And armed with the might of a small and fluttering green flag, a posse of policemen in a jeep—and a wired black van—squeezed their way right into the constricted, drain-divided heart of the Hira Mandi and stopped before the popsicle-man's splintered door. The police, waving signed papers and batons, swarmed through the rooms of Ice-candy-man's *Kotha* and finding Ayah there took her away, a willing accompanist, to the black van. And all the Mandi pimps and poets and musicians . . . and all the flower-sellers, prostitutes, butchers, cigarette and *paan* vendors, wrestlers and toughs of the cultured *Kotha* could do nothing about it. Nor do Ice-candy-man's threats, pleading, remonstrance, bellows, declamations, courtly manners, resourcefulness or wailing impede the progression of the van in its determination to deposit Ayah, with her scant belongings wrapped in cloth bundles and a small tin trunk, at the Recovered Women's Camp on Warris Road. To be followed there in three galloping carts by Ice-candy-man and his cronies—all their outrage and broken bones and pimpy influence to no avail.

Chapter 32

Give me the (mystic) wine that burns all veils,
The wine by which life's secret is revealed,
The wine whose essence is eternity,
The wine which opens mysteries concealed.
Lift up the curtain, give me power to talk.
And make the sparrow struggle with the hawk.

—Iqbal

Ice-candy-man has taken to patrolling Warris Road, his broken left arm supported in a sling and pressed to his chest as if affirming a truth.

Sometimes he squats across the road from our wall and sometimes inside Rosy-Peter's compound—patiently, and from a distance, watching the tin-sheet gates. Occasionally he recites Zauq:

"Why did you make a home in my heart?
Inhabit it. Both the house and I are desolate.
Am I a thief that your watchman stops me?
Tell him, I know this man. He is my fate."

The guard is getting used to his presence; and to his poetic outbursts. When he first spied him, the Sikh advanced threatening to tear him limb from limb and stuff his genitals every-which-where. Our household, attracted to the wall by the shouting, saw Ice-candy-man's splintered arm raised to defend himself from the blows, and his tearing eyes, and Imam Din and Yousaf shouted: "Let him be, *yaar,* he's harmless."

The Sikh merely pulled the popsicle-man to his feet by his unbroken and frail arm and Ice-candy-man meekly walked away.

Even the Sikh has given way to his indefatigable persistence and now eyes him with a certain awe. For Ice-candy-man is acquiring a new aspect—that of a moonstruck fakir who has renounced the world for his beloved: be it woman or God. Repeating a couplet by Faiz as if it is a prayer, he murmurs:

> "There are other wounds besides the wounds of love—
> Other nights besides passionate nights of love—"

Driven more, I suspect, by private demons than by fear of Mother's threats, Ice-candy-man has not stepped inside our gates. Sometimes he brings with him his thermos of popsicles and does business in a desultory fashion, giving away more ices than he sells. And sometimes, when the Sikh guard accompanies our unseeing and unfeeling Ayah to Mr. Phailbus for homeopathic treatment, Ice-candy-man squats patiently outside the Phailbuses' wall.

Often I accompany Ayah to Mr. Phailbus's; and when we walk past the candy-man, he greets us courteously and does not stare at Ayah, but casts his eyes down. Ayah behaves as if he is invisible. And, his overgrown hair shading his eyes, he sometimes murmurs a couplet by another romantic poet, Ghalib:

> "My passion has brought me to your street—
> Where can I now find the strength to take me back?"

Ayah behaves as if he is inaudible too.

He has become a truly harmless fellow. My heart not only melts—it evaporates when I breathe out, leaving me faint with pity. Even the guard lets down his guard and at times, when in the mood for company, squats by Ice-candy-man, gleaning wisdom from his comments on life and its ways and the wayward ways of God and men and women, until it's time to accompany Ayah back. Then, Zauq's poems and Ice-candy-man's voice humming in our minds, we murmur:

> "Don't berate me, beloved, I'm God-intoxicated!
> I'll wrap myself about you; I'm mystically mad."

Each morning I awaken now to the fragrance of flowers flung over our garden wall at dawn by Ice-candy-man. The courtyard of the Recovered Women's Camp too is strewn with petals; and sometimes with the added glitter of cheap candy wrapped in cellophane. And after Himat Ali sweeps up the red roses crushed by the sun, and the camp women the petals scattered near the tin gates in their courtyard as if they were no more than goat droppings, Ice-candy-man's voice rises in sweet and clear song to shower Ayah with poems.

> "Bewitching faces don't remain buried
> They reappear in the shapes of flowers."

Until, one morning, when I sniff the air and miss the fragrance, and run in consternation to the kitchen, I am told that Ayah, at last, has gone to her family in Amritsar.

. . . And Ice-candy-man, too, disappears across the Wagah border into India.

Acknowledgments

I thank Rana Khan for sharing with me his childhood experiences at the time of Partition. He still bears the deep crescent-shaped scar on the back of his head and innumerable other scars.

I would also like to acknowledge my friend Nergis Sobani for typing my manuscripts; Phillip Lopate and Rosellen Brown for their good cheer and support; Ali Asani and Noman Haq for assisting me with the selection of the Urdu poems; the late Venketash Kulkarni whose literary enthusiasm I miss, and Reetika Vazirini, my flatmate, who so tragically passed away. I thank the Bunting Institute and the National Endowment for the Arts for providing me with the time and means to complete this novel and Inprint, in Houston, for the encouragement it gives all writers.

Grateful acknowledgement is made for permission to reprint excerpts from Urdu Literature edited by D. J. Matthews, C. Shackle, and Shahrukh Husain.

I thank Deepa Mehta for transforming *Cracking India* into the warm and poetic film *Earth*, and my friend Nasreen Rehman for her superb translation of the script into Urdu.

As always I thank my husband, Noshir, my brothers Minnoo and Feroze, and my children Mohur, Koko, Baku, and Parizad for their support and encouragement.

And finally I thank Emilie Buchwald, Hilary Reeves and all at Milkweed, and the friends of Milkweed, for their dedication to the cause of literature and quality publishing.

About the Author

Born in Karachi and raised in Lahore, Bapsi Sidhwa has been widely acclaimed as Pakistan's finest contemporary novelist. She is the author of four novels: *An American Brat, Cracking India, The Bride,* and *The Crow Eaters.* Her work has been published in translation all over the world.

Sidhwa served on the advisory committee to Prime Minister Benazir Bhutto on issues of women's development, and her novel *Cracking India* has been made into the film *Earth* by Indian director Deepa Mehta.

Sidhwa has taught at Columbia University, the University of Houston, Mount Holyoke College, Brandeis University, and Southampton University in the United Kingdom. She has also been the recipient of numerous honors and awards, among them a NEA Fellowship, a Lila Wallace-Reader's Digest Writers' Award, and the *Sitara-I-Imtiaz,* Pakistan's highest honor in the arts. She lives in Houston.

More Fiction from Milkweed Editions

To order books or for more information,
contact Milkweed at (800) 520-6455
or visit our Web site (www.milkweed.org).

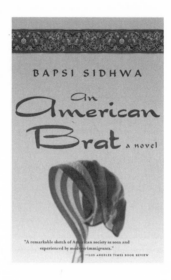

Growing up in Pakistan in the 1970s, Feroza Ginwalla is precocious, impetu-
ous, and deeply affected by a rising tide of religious fundamentalism. When
her family decides to send her to America for an extended holiday, a chain of
amusing events and encounters ensues. She enrolls at a conservative Mormon
college in Idaho, falls in love with a young man who is clearly not Parsee, and
experiences her new country as only an immigrant can, even while her family
worries that she is straying too far.

"Sidwha's writing is brisk and funny, her characters painted so vividly you can
almost hear them bickering."—*New York Times Book Review*

"Affecting, amusing, and profoundly enjoyable."—*Washington Post Book World*

"An exceptional novel."—*Los Angeles Times*

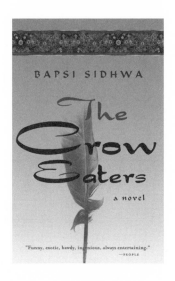

BAPSI SIDHWA

The Crow Eaters

a novel

"Funny, exotic, bawdy, ingenious, always entertaining."
—PEOPLE

Loading his pregnant wife, infant daughter, and widowed mother-in-law into a bullock cart, Faredoon Junglewalla—Freddy for short--leaves his ancestral village in the forests of central India, bound for the bustling city of Lahore. Despite the nagging of his unbearable mother-in-law, Freddy's business and family flourish, and he soon becomes a patriarchal figure in the thriving Parsee community. Through a series of comical yet illuminating events, this enduring family saga provides a vibrant window onto life in India under British colonial rule. And as the novel comes to a close, it is clear that this world stands on the threshold of historic transformation.

"A rollicking comic tale."—*New York Times Book Review*

"A delightful and perceptive view of a Parsee family's rise from rags to riches. . . . A most intelligent and enjoyable novel."—*Seattle Times*

"[Bapsi Sidhwa's] roguish hero is a genuine charmer, and her book is as warm and vital as it is funny."—*Miami Herald*

Milkweed Editions

Founded in 1979, Milkweed Editions is the largest independent, nonprofit literary publisher in the United States. Milkweed publishes with the intention of making a humane impact on society, in the belief that good writing can transform the human heart and spirit. Within this mission, Milkweed publishes in five areas: fiction, nonfiction, poetry, children's literature for middle-grade readers, and the World As Home—books about our relationship with the natural world.

Join Us

Milkweed depends on the generosity of foundations and individuals like you, in addition to the sales of its books. In an increasingly consolidated and bottom-line-driven publishing world, your support allows us to select and publish books on the basis of their literary quality and the depth of their message. Please visit our Web site (www.milkweed.org) or contact us at (800) 520-6455 to learn more about our donor program.

Interior design by R. W. Scholes.
Typeset in Trajanus Roman
by The Typeworks.
Printed on acid-free EB Natural recycled paper
by Edwards Brothers.